D0672220

the FALL of the KINGS

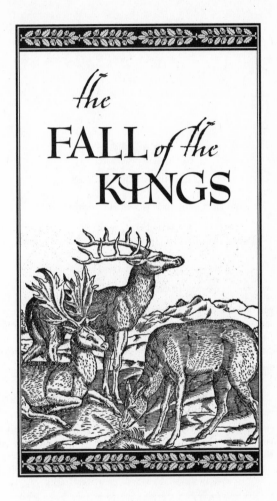

the FALL of the KINGS

Ellen Kushner & Delia Sherman

BANTAM BOOKS

THE FALL OF THE KINGS

Bantam Spectra trade paperback / November 2002

All rights reserved.
Copyright © 2002 by Ellen Kushner and Delia Sherman

Cover art copyright © 2002 by Thomas Canty

BOOK DESIGN BY LAURIE JEWELL

No part of this book may be reproduced or transmitted in any form or by any means, electronic or mechanical, including photocopying, recording, or by any information storage and retrieval system, without permission in writing from the publisher. For information address: Bantam Books.

ISBN 0-7394-3193-5

Published simultaneously in the United States and Canada

Bantam Books are published by Bantam Books, a division of Random House, Inc. Its trademark, consisting of the words "Bantam Books" and the portrayal of a rooster, is Registered in U.S. Patent and Trademark Office and in other countries. Marca Registrada. Bantam Books, 1540 Broadway, New York, New York 10036.

PRINTED IN THE UNITED STATES OF AMERICA

For in art there is no such thing as a universal truth.
A Truth in art is that whose contradictory is also true.

— OSCAR WILDE, *The Truth of Masks*

What thou lovest well remains,
the rest is dross
What thou lov'st well shall not be reft from thee
What thou lov'st well is thy true heritage

— EZRA POUND, *Pisan Cantos*, LXXXI

the FALL of the KINGS

PROLOGUE

A SPLATTER OF RED ON A DISCARDED BOOT. MILKY blue glass lying shattered in a pool of water. Garlands of greenery swirling everywhere, with little eddies of leaves torn loose from them. And everywhere the sheets, torrents of white fabric lying in fantastic patterns, twisted and ruched, almost spinning, creating lines dipped in and out of shadow, now black, now white, following the logic of the candles placed above them, interrupted here and there by the crosshatching of random streaks of harsh, dull red.

The sheets spilled over the edge of a platform; in front of it, a naked man, streaked in the same red, his long hair matted with it, but clotted also with bits of ochre and vermilion, burnt sienna and indigo.

The woman watching him from across the room was silent. She was dressed from neck to ankle in a plain white smock, smeared in places with the same colors. Her hair was bound up with a twisted scarf, leaving her face a clear and perfect oval.

"Theron," she said. "You moved. I have particularly asked you not to do that."

With one hand he tore a sheet from the platform, sending spatters of paint flying in every direction. "What will you paint, then," he shouted, "the aftermath, the destruction you have wrought?"

"*I* have wrought? I'm not the one who's just torn the studio apart. Now, would you please take up the pose again?"

He froze, staring at her. "You have no heart."

"I told you that, ages ago." She dipped her finger in the paint of her canvas and sketched his lines into it. "You should listen to me. I said this would be the last painting I wanted you for. Stand still, I'm not done with you yet. I'm using you for the murderer as well as for the king. It makes a nice effect."

Incredulous, he almost laughed. "You want me to pose killing myself."

"I *want* you to put your body in some interesting positions—"

The laugh burst out. "Oh—haven't I been satisfying you that way, either?"

"Theron." Still sketching with naked fingers, she talked. "You have satisfied me entirely. I've got maybe twenty-five finished canvases, and dozens of studies. You have been satisfying in every sense. But I've run out of things for you to do. I've told you all along, no one can hold me forever. I can't find any more ways to enjoy you."

A year ago he would have shown her one or two on the spot. Now he said, "Ysaud. Please." She shook her head as though the noise were a distraction. "Paint what you like, who you like—I don't care. But don't send me away."

"I don't want you if I'm not painting you."

"You're mad."

"You've just wasted a lot of my materials, Theron." She crossed the floor to take a dab of ochre from his chest with one finger.

"Don't do this to me. I love you."

"Please hold still."

He lifted a hand to his chest. Where her finger had run over his collarbone, there lay exposed a pattern of vines and leaves. It had been etched into his skin with ink.

"You can't take this back," he said, "nor what it means. It marks me forever yours."

"No," she said. "It's the paintings that mark you forever mine." She returned to her canvas. "My vision of you will be alive when your pretty skin is turned to dust. That should make you happy."

"Stop," he said. "Stop painting and look at me."

Now it was she who laughed. "All I've done is look at you. If you can't stop talking, then put on your clothes and go." He followed her, breaking an unspoken law of the studio, treading on forbidden ground, a space he entered only with her permission. The artist glared at him. Then, with a hiss of exasperation, she stepped back and let him go around the easel to see what stood there.

Coming alive in the candlelight was an image of death: a pale man splayed out on the bed, one hand lying open as if in invitation, the other still clutching a deerskin across his chest. Theron recognized himself, his own body in the languor after sex. The deerskin and bedsheets were speckled with blood. Next to them, she had begun another figure. His dark hair was a waterfall of grief spilling between the hands he pressed to his face with bloody fingers. A shadow of horns rose on the wall behind them, as if a phantom stag had lifted its head.

"This is different," Theron said, "from the others."

"Yes." She observed the canvas and the man together. "This is the last of them; it has to be, you see, because it's heading off in a new direction. That's how I know the series is over."

"I could be a new direction for you."

"No, you can't." Ysaud pressed his chest gently with the brush's tip. "Not you. Not for me. Go be a new direction for someone else, will you?"

He went out into the night, caked with her colors. He was very sure that he would never love again.

book I

HARVEST TERM

chapter I

FIVE HUNDRED YEARS AGO AND MORE, A KING RODE
out of the North at the head of an army. He rode with a
company of splendid men, all armed to the teeth. They
rode not to war, but to a wedding. After centuries of conflict, the
rocky North and the fertile South were at last to be joined into
one kingdom in the persons of their King and Queen and their
heirs perpetual, united against their common enemies and increasing in mutual prosperity.

The Southern Queen's Chronicler, Valerian Hollis, had described the King's army in horrified detail. Their armor was
leather and hammered bronze. Under their helms, their long hair
was braided with leather and bones and beads and even nuggets
of gold. Every one of them was blood kin to his king, and as they
came through the streets of the capital city, they sang.

In the eyes of the Southern nobles, the King's Companions
were strange enough, with their barbaric mien and their uncouth
songs of war and the hunt. But they brought with them men that
they called wizards, and the wizards were worse.

The wizards did not sing. Indeed, they barely spoke, except

to one another. There were (according to Hollis) fifteen of them, riding horseback just behind the king. The King's Wizards were robed in black or brown, russet or ochre: peasants' colors, colors of the land. Some were cloaked in the skins of animals. Their faces were bearded, their hair unbound and crowned with leaves. From the hands of certain of them, tendrils of ivy grew.

Thus wrote Hollis in the final chapter of his *Chronicle History of the Northern Kings*, a work written at the behest of Queen Diane and her new consort, Alcuin, later called the Diplomat. It was a book every historian should own; Basil St Cloud had bought his when he was still a student, and lived on bread and cheese for the rest of the month to pay for the used, leather-bound volume. Now he was a Doctor of History, and the margins of its pages were lined with notes, the leather cover buttery with handling. But it had failed to enlighten him on the subject he was currently researching.

With a sigh, he set the volume aside. If only Hollis had not insisted on cluttering up his account with so much about the wonder of these so-called wizards. Wizards, indeed! The very word evoked nameless rituals and dark mysteries, when everyone knew that their "magic" had been nothing more than sleight-of-hand coupled with diplomacy. But they certainly had made an impressive show. As many times as Basil had read the description, it still gave him a chill: ". . . their hair so twined about with leaves of Ivie and of Oak, as to make them seem in themselves to be Trees and Creatures of the Wood come riding into our Citie to take it through the Greening of the verrie Stones. . . ."

Basil shook his head. Very pretty. Very fanciful. Charged with collecting facts from his new compatriots, but unable to understand most of what they said, Hollis had simply conflated history and legend. Still, the book was pretty much all modern scholars had to go by. The pre-Union North was known for the strength of its warriors, not its record-keeping. And Hollis really had witnessed the events of the Union. Now, if only he'd been more interested in laws of inheritance than in trees on horseback. . . .

A knock on his door interrupted his fulminations. "St Cloud!" He recognized the voice of his friend Thomas Elton,

Doctor of Astronomy. "St Cloud, I know you're in there, now open up!"

Without regret, the historian opened the door to his rooms. "How now, my fair one!" It was an old joke. Elton had the face and figure of a bull-dog, but his hair, which he wore long by University tradition, was an incongruously beautiful honey-colored mane that his friends loved to tease him about. "Have you come all this way to invite me to dinner, or do you just want to stick your ridiculous astral spyglass out my window again?"

Elton grinned. "I'll accept your kind offer, if it ever clears up. You live so much closer to the heavens than the rest of us, and I want to get another good look at that comet. Stars with fiery hair, they don't come around that often. And this one's such a beauty, Basil."

"Yes, you've said. But that's not what you're here for."

"Right. If I thought you had any wine to offer me I'd make you produce it—but instead, I come to tell you that there's been a sighting of Leonard Rugg in the fiery precincts of the Blackbird's Nest, ordering the ingredients for a brandy-punch!"

Basil said archly, "I don't suppose it was Cassius who spotted him?"

"*And* is saving us a couple of seats."

"Blessed Cassius." Basil finally found his cap and jammed it on his head. "A mathematician can always be relied upon to count the right number of guests. Onward, let us onward, like the invading Ophidian army on the Plains of Garrawan. Look out for the broken step."

The streets of the University were the streets of the city, and some of the oldest. They lay on the east bank of the river, where, it was said, King Alcuin's wizards had first taken up residence after the Union. Certainly the streets were close and twisty and notoriously difficult to navigate, particularly late at night. The school had been tiny at first, not much more than a few class-rooms nestled in a warren of government edifices. But time and history had wrought their changes. Buildings that once had been halls of state were now lecture halls, and the dens of civil servants and kings' companions had been turned to students' quarters, rented out to as many aspiring young scholars as could fit in a room. The taverns that dotted every corner were probably the oldest structures that retained their purpose. Across the troubled maelstrom of time, people always need a beer.

The tavern known as the Blackbird's Nest was awash in the dark-robed scholars who gave it its name. Its ceiling was low and black-beamed, its ancient walls as deep as a man's arm from hand to elbow, its windows sunk in alcoves. The feet of untold generations of drinkers and debaters had worn troughs into the stone of its floor; their shoulders had polished the stone walls black and smooth. Basil had been coming there since he was a young student, fresh off the farm—not as many years ago as he liked to think. He'd met Elton and Cassius there, accomplished scholars of two years' standing. They had advised him on University ways, from simple matters like letting your hair grow long to avoid looking like a country bumpkin and always giving way to a magister on the street to the intricacies of getting credit in a tavern and the maximum number of lectures he might attend without paying the magister a fee. And they'd invited him along with them to meet the brilliant young Doctor of Metaphysics, Leonard Rugg, known for his generosity with the punchbowl and his stimulating debates on everything from women to the meaning of the stars.

For all four men, the meeting had been a momentous one. The three young scholars had found a shrewd mentor; Rugg had found three kindred spirits. He was not surprised when each of them had resisted the world's call for educated men to stock its law courts and schoolrooms, its nobles' secretarial staffs and charitable institutions. Elton, Cassius, and finally St Cloud remained at University, become Fellows and then Doctors of their chosen subjects, and had been licensed to lecture by the Governors. The four of them had become a familiar sight: Basil St Cloud of History, sturdy and pale, with perennially stubbled cheeks and black, unruly hair; Thomas Elton of Astronomy, stocky and cheerful; Lucas Cassius of Mathematics, lean and saturnine; and Leonard Rugg of Metaphysics, not nearly as old as he pretended to be, his skin pink, his forehead high, his thinning reddish hair standing out from his scalp like new-shorn fleece.

"Time marches on," Rugg was saying testily to Cassius, "but

the boy with the brandy is slower than a tart with a noble client. And didn't you say young St Cloud and Elton were coming?"

"On their way," the mathematician answered. "Remember, patience is the virtue of the truly wise."

Rugg snorted. "Nonsense. Patience gets you nothing but a cold bed. Who's been filling your head with platitudes, eh? Your old mother?"

"Placid," Cassius said smugly, "in his *Of Manners and Morals*. I remember you lecturing on it, Leonard. You were, of course, much more eloquent at the time."

"Don't you quote Placid to me, you damned cabbage-counter. Always thought Placid was a damned fool," Rugg said, "when he wasn't being a genius. Ah, here's the brandy!"

Easing a laden tray onto the table, the potboy unloaded two steaming jugs, four heavy pottery mugs, and several little dishes containing sugar and spices. Rugg pushed back his bench, stood ponderously, cracked his knuckles and began to assemble the punch. A savor of cinnamon and cloves rose above the table in an alcoholic cloud.

"Is that brandy-punch I smell?" Elton said brightly, looming over them.

"It will be," Rugg answered, "if you don't jog my arm. Sit down, Elton—no, over there, with St Cloud. Basil, dear boy, where have you been hiding?"

"Nowhere I can't be found," Basil answered mildly, "as Elton has just happily proved."

Cassius sighed with an exaggerated melancholy, and laced his skinny fingers in his lanky hair. "Would that all proofs were so easily made! Basil, I hear you're writing another book, and good for you. In fact," he caught Elton's eye across the table, "very good for you, indeed."

"Which means what, exactly?"

Basil's question went unanswered as Rugg lifted the ladle high and made a brief speech about friendship and taverns and wine. Rugg favored the rhetorical style of the Gerardine metaphysicians, his current academic preoccupation. Basil cupped his hands around his steaming mug. Autumn was coming on chill this year.

The four friends toasted each other and the beginning of the Harvest Term, wishing each other plenty of paying students for all and a new, more faithful mistress for Rugg. They ordered up a dinner of roast chicken, greens, and buttered squash, and tucked into it as if they'd not eaten for days.

"The Horn Chair lecture's back on, had you heard?" Elton asked through a mouthful of chicken.

"Impossible," said Rugg. "The Horn Professor's at death's door. Has been since Midsummer."

Cassius sipped his punch. "It's not like you to be so far behind the gossip, Rugg. Doctor Tortua *was* at death's door, but he's better now. Not enough better, I'd have thought, to go about giving public lectures, but I'm no physician. You were Tortua's man, St Cloud. What do you know about it?"

St Cloud shrugged. "Not much. We haven't been friendly since my monograph on the Treaty of Arkenvelt."

"I remember," said Rugg. "You took his chapter in *The Fall of the Kings* and made mincemeat of it, didn't you, against all advice and common sense."

"But he got it wrong, and all because he didn't go back to the treaty itself and relied instead on Delgardie's report in *A Mirror of History*, which was already second-hand at best. As I said at the time." He glared at Rugg, who looked ready to argue the whole point again. "It's done, Rugg, and can't be undone. Doctor Crabbe's his heir apparent now, and much joy may he have of him."

"You're hopeless, Basil." Elton looked over his shoulder into the Blackbird's noisy, candlelit room. "Doesn't Roger Crabbe drink here too?"

"I haven't seen him," St Cloud said. "Not since Spring Term, not here."

"Well, his friends, then. You don't need to like Crabbe, but there's nothing to be gained by making an enemy of him."

"And what would his friends tell him?" St Cloud demanded. "He already knows I don't like him; I've told him as much to his face. And he's welcome to hear that I'm sorry I quarreled with Doctor Tortua—well, not sorry, exactly, since I'd do the same again. But sad. I'd like to make it up with him."

The eminent doctor had recognized in the young St Cloud a love of ancient things that matched his own. In Basil's second year, he'd wooed him away from the law he'd come to the city to study and shepherded him up through University ranks. It was Tortua's influence, as well as his own industry, that had made Basil the youngest man ever to achieve the rank of Doctor. He had loved the old man like a father, and had been proportionately wounded when Tortua had taken Basil's monograph on the Treaty of Arkenvelt as a personal attack rather than a simple scholarly correction.

"Make it up with him!" scoffed Elton. "I doubt Tortua would even see you, especially as Crabbe's his doorkeeper these days, they say."

"I thought Crabbe was avoiding me," St Cloud said.

"You flatter yourself," said Cassius. "He was nursing Tortua."

"Lobbying to be the next Horn Chair of Ancient History, if you ask me," Elton said, and Rugg nodded.

"That's disgusting," exclaimed St Cloud. "Not even Crabbe would do a thing like that."

His three companions exchanged the superior smiles of men who, knowing a friend's weakness, love him in spite of it.

"So," said Rugg after a pause, "are you still going to the lecture?"

St Cloud, with little else to stand on, stood on his dignity. "Of course I'm going. I'm in ancient history. I'd go whoever was giving the lecture, even if it were Crabbe himself."

"We'll see you there, then," said Elton cheerfully.

"Yes," said Cassius. "Sit with us. You can tell us when he's getting it wrong."

"You'll just have to figure it out for yourselves," Basil St Cloud told them. "I shall be sitting with my students."

chapter **II**

THE KINGS RULED THE UNITED KINGDOM FOR BET-
ter than three hundred years before they were deposed
by the nobles, who established rule by the Council of
Lords. The later kings had been a byword for decadence and corruption, with special emphasis on assassination, rape, and exces-
sive taxation. Of their special councilors, the wizards, the less
said the better; progress and the Council of Lords swept even
their memory aside. The country prospered. Technology ad-
vanced. Carriages were invented, and the nobles left their townhouses in the Riverside district behind, seduced by the broad
avenues and terraced banks of the Hill that lay across the river-
bank northwest of the Old City. There they built magnificent
houses set in exquisite gardens sweeping down to the river.

The lords of the city did have a tendency to quarrel amongst
themselves, though, especially in the Council's early days. There
were high walls around their gardens and guards at the gates. But
even these were not enough to protect a man from the fury of his
peers and their relations when blood feuds heated up. To keep the
important people from killing each other off, a class of profes-

sional swordsmen evolved to take on the nobles' challenges, and elaborate rules were constructed to keep them within the bounds of law. Some of the houses still boasted the traditional liveried swordsman, but not all. Times had changed, as times will. Like the swordsmen, the walls around the Hill's great houses were chiefly decorative. But not all. The gates of Arlen House, in particular, were not easily breached. Behind them lived and worked the Serpent Chancellor of the Council of Lords, Geoffrey, Lord Arlen. Like the serpent, he was cunning and elusive and well-defended. No one entered Arlen House except by invitation. And even then, the Serpent Chancellor was not so easily seen.

LORD NICHOLAS GALING LEANED HIS FOREHEAD against the window of Arlen House and watched the clouds rolling away over the river. It had rained all afternoon, and even now the occasional drop pocked the wet stone of the promenade outside. The room Galing was waiting in was warm and dry and furnished with a set of books on natural history. Still, he had been waiting there for three hours.

He turned from the window and examined the tray his absent host had sent in some minutes earlier. Old cheese, new bread, a decanter of deep red wine, a silver pitcher of water. An apple and autumn pears, along with a pearl-handled knife to peel them with: enough food to acknowledge that he'd been kept waiting longer than expected; not enough to indicate that he would be kept waiting all the afternoon.

He took the knife and an apple and peeled it in a thin, continuous spiral, which he arranged jauntily on the edge of the tray. Then he sat down with the cheese and the decanter by the excellent fire to refresh himself. When the summons came, it wouldn't do to appear before Arlen hungry or—he replaced the decanter on the tray and filled his glass with water—inattentive in any way. This meeting could make or break him with the enigmatic Serpent Chancellor. Nicholas had spent the past year maneuvering his way into Lord Arlen's sphere, and had obliged his mysterious lordship in one or two small matters of interest to the

Council, matters in which discretion and the ability to ask innocent-sounding questions had proved useful.

Nicholas smiled into the fire. He'd had no idea, going in, how exciting it was simply to have a secret. His new profession transmuted balls, picnics, card parties, even morning calls on ladies whose lowered lids and low-cut gowns held no allure for him into backdrops for a drama understood by only a select few. Everyone knew that Lady Talbot was enjoying a liaison with the Montrose heir, but only Nicholas—and Emil Montrose, and now the Council—knew that Emil was also enjoying the revenues of Lady Talbot's farm in Stover, which he was plowing into his own exhausted estates. What Arlen and the Council would do with this information, Nicholas neither knew nor cared. The thing at the moment was to know it.

The door opened, and the soft-footed servant who had brought the tray slipped inside and cleared his throat.

"Lord Nicholas. Lord Arlen will see you now, if you would be so good as to follow me."

The servant showed Nicholas into a largish room lined with old books and panels of painted wood—portraits, Nicholas supposed, of Arlens dead and gone. He was about to take a closer look at one when a small noise froze him where he stood, breathing slowly to still the sudden pelting of his heart. When he was sure he had himself under control, he turned to face the shadowy corner of the room and bowed deeply.

"Lord Arlen," he said. "How delightful."

A deep chuckle came from the shadows, followed by the scrape and flare of a lucifer, which revealed a tall, white-haired man sitting behind a great carved desk. He put the flame to the wick of an ornate brass lamp and replaced the glass.

"Do you mean my making you kick your heels for hours, or do you mean my trying to startle you out of your skin?"

Nicholas reflected that it was more pleasant to play with tigers when you weren't in the cage with them and said, "I mean, delightful to see you, sir, and your beautiful house."

"I already know you are a plausible rogue, Galing," said Lord Arlen. "You needn't keep trying to impress me. Sit down, do. And take a glass of wine. I'm going to ask you a favor."

Nicholas carefully poured himself two fingers of crimson liquid from a gold-chased decanter.

"Very good," said Arlen when Nicholas was settled. "Your hand didn't shake and your face showed no more than polite interest. You handled the Montrose affair very well, did I tell you?"

Nicholas made a gesture expressive of modesty and pleasure. "I am your lordship's to command," he said.

"Yes," Lord Arlen said. "I believe you are just the kind of man who will betray any confidence as long as he's sure that it's in the service of some greater good, preferably his own."

Nicholas was able to school his expression, but felt an angry flush rising up his cheeks. "I believe I serve your lordship," he said stiffly.

"Fifty years ago," remarked Lord Arlen, "you could have cried challenge on me for that statement, hired a swordsman to do the deed for you, and the Court of Honor would have held you justified even as I wallowed in my gore. Times change. I have a swordsman in my employ for the look of the thing, and he's very good. But I don't expect I'll ever need his services, not in the same way my father did."

"No," said Nicholas evenly. "I don't expect you will. I can't afford a first-class swordsman, as you very well know, and I'm not really inclined to cry challenge on you for speaking the truth, particularly as there's no one else present."

Lord Arlen smiled, his dark eyes bright in the lamplight. He was a handsome man, with the kind of long, lean face that ages well and beautifully curved lips, oddly sensual in his ascetic countenance. "It's a pleasure to talk to a man who understands what he's being told. It's the only kind of fencing that custom allows us, eh?" He leaned forward, laid something on the desk in front of Nicholas, and sat back again. "Tell me what you make of that."

It looked like an oak leaf, leathery and dry, curled at one end. When Nicholas picked it up, it proved to be carved out of wood. The workmanship was competent but not fine. There was a pin affixed to the back so that the leaf might be worn as a brooch. Nicholas turned it over in his hand. "Not your usual taste, Lord Arlen," he said.

"Not my taste at all," said Arlen shortly. "It belonged to a man from the North, from Hartsholt. I believe he carved it himself."

Nicholas set the trinket on the desk, where it lay as if blown in through the window, incongruous and faintly disturbing. "It means a great deal to him, then."

"He won't be missing it," Arlen said. "He bled himself to death by chafing in his chains. I wouldn't have thought it possible myself, but the guards are sure no one entered his cell. The brooch was taken from him when he was arrested. What do you think of it?"

Nicholas picked up the brooch again and examined it closely. If it had any secrets, they weren't to be read in the tiny marks left by the dead man's knife. It was the brooch itself that was important. "A badge," said Nicholas thoughtfully. "You said the man was from Hartsholt. I seem to remember the Duke of Hartsholt at Lord Halliday's, complaining about troublemakers over dinner. Now that I think about it, I do recall something about oak branches."

"Yes," purred Lord Arlen. "Now, cast your mind even further back than Halliday's dinner, to your schoolroom lessons. What was the most significant event in our history?"

Nicholas thought for a moment. "The fall of the monarchy."

"Before that."

"I never cared much for history," Galing said. "I don't know. Unless"—he groped at a distant memory—"you mean the union of the kingdoms."

Arien smiled benignly. "Precisely," he said. "And would you happen to remember where the old capital of the North Kingdom was?"

"Ah— Aldersyde? No, it's Hartsholt, isn't it—that's why Hartsholt's a duchy."

"Very good, Galing. The capital was indeed in Hartsholt, or somewhere near it—there's nothing left of it now. So tell me, Lord Nicholas, what do you deduce from available evidence?"

It was like pacing through honey, trying to figure out why Arlen was leading him this dance.

"I'm being most unkind, making you go through all this," Arlen remarked sympathetically. "But really, it would be a shame for all that expensive tutoring your father gave you to go to waste. As I recall, you even flirted with the University for a year or two."

"I went to a few lectures, to keep my friend Edward Tielman company."

"Ah, yes. Edward Tielman. Secretary to the Crescent Chancellor. Very sound man. Discreet. His father was your family's steward, wasn't he?"

"He still is," said Nicholas shortly. Did Arlen know he and Edward had been lovers? Was he asking whether they still were? Why should he care? Because Edward was somehow connected to the favor Arlen wanted from him, Nicholas answered himself— Edward and the old capital at (or near) Hartsholt and the oak leaf brooch and the dead man from the North. There was one thing missing, one fact connected to his schooldays, when his tutor had taught spelling and rhetoric and mathematics and history to him, to his older brother the heir, and to Edward, the steward's son.

"The kings," Nicholas said slowly. "Before the Union, the kings lived in the old capital city. There was a sacred grove, wasn't there? An oak grove." Lord Arlen nodded, very much as the tutor had nodded, glad to see his student performing well. "The man from Hartsholt must have been a royalist, and you think this oak leaf is a royalist badge. And you want me to use Tielman's connections at the University to find out if there are royalists there, too."

Arlen laughed. "That's the bones of it. Very good." Nicholas felt himself flushing again, this time with pleasure and something else, something he knew Lord Arlen was unlikely to return.

"Quite," said the older man, disconcertingly. "Now. You are no doubt asking yourself why I am concerned about a handful of unlettered hobbledehoys whose ancestors have been diverting themselves with rebellions for five hundred years."

Nicholas made a gesture designed to convey his complete confidence in the Serpent Chancellor's political acuity.

"Nevertheless. The situation is this. The current Duke of Hartsholt's a wastrel and a bad landlord. His steward is a thief, and his heir is as great a spendthrift as his sire. And it's not only Hartsholt's private estates that are suffering. There is famine all through the North, and great poverty. Young men are pouring down to the South, looking to better themselves. There's nothing wrong with that—it's what the ancient kings did, after all. But there are more of them every year, and all of them are angry. They wear their Northernness like a flag, flaunt their braided hair and their barbaric customs, shout out incomprehensible Northern slogans in City Sessions. This fellow"—Arlen touched the oak leaf—"was all too comprehensible. He got up in open Sessions before the Mayor and offered a formal petition for the king to be restored to the land."

Nicholas felt as amused as shocked—it seemed like such a stupid, pointless thing to do. But Arlen was studying him gravely, no hint of amusement lighting his face. "What did he imagine it would gain him?" he offered diplomatically.

"I don't know," said Arlen. "All he would say under questioning was that the land needed its king again, and the time was at hand."

"Is it a general uprising, then?"

"No. I don't think so. It's more like creeping sedition, with mystic complications. Call it an illness. We need to study it, to discover whether it's a plague or a mild fever. I've sent men North. I need someone here, to determine the extent of the contagion and its severity." He leaned forward slightly. The effect was of a dark lantern suddenly unshuttered. "I need to know if these royalists have a specific king in mind, and whether it's one of them or one of us." He lounged back in his chair again. "There's what they would consider to be royal blood in all the noble houses, you know."

A light tap heralded Lord Arlen's servant, carrying a tray of cold beef. They sat in silence while he pulled the heavy blue curtains over the rainy darkness and lit the lamps. When he'd bowed himself out again, Nicholas helped himself to a slice of beef. "I didn't know," he continued, as if they'd not been interrupted. "As I said, I don't know much about history."

"You'd best learn, then." Arlen yawned suddenly and rubbed his face. "Your friend Tielman may be able to help you. I understand he keeps up his University friendships."

Nicholas smiled, glad to catch his patron out. "Tielman goes down to University twice a year to get drunk with his old friends and impress them with his being the Crescent Chancellor's secretary—it's his pet vice. If he suddenly started asking questions, it would occasion remark."

"Do what you think best, then. If I didn't trust your judgment, I wouldn't have asked your help. This affair of the oak leaf may be nothing, but it may equally be very important. It would be a pity if you guessed wrong." He fixed Nicholas with his hooded eyes.

"Of course, sir," said Nicholas quietly. "I won't fail you."

"Quite." Lord Arlen nodded, and rang for the servant to show Galing to the door.

⌒

ACROSS THE RIVER, IN AN OLD, OLD HOUSE OF STONE, a young man slept, and as he slept, he dreamed. In his dream he stood in an oak wood, very old, with dusty sunlight pouring down in bars around him. He moved forward carefully, not sure of what he might find. There was a clearing ahead, a grove. As he entered it, his body was bathed in golden light. He heard a voice: "Welcome, Little King." A man was standing in the shadows, by a pool of still water, amongst bushes of dark green holly. He was afraid of the man; but all the man said was, "Welcome. I have been waiting. You come on your time, and now we can begin."

The man held up a deer's skin, and a stone knife, sharp as glass. "Do not be afraid," he said, but the dreamer was afraid. He shuddered, and the oak leaves fell around him.

chapter **III**

THE HARVEST TERM HAD BEGUN. ON THE STREETS
of University, students were suddenly everywhere, a
constant tide of long black robes, rushing from tavern to
lecture and back again. Window-stalls along the winding streets
did a brisk trade in steamed buns and pens and penknives and
tomato pies and other scholarly necessities. Excited male voices
bounced off the stone of buildings and cobbles, arguing, bargaining, greeting friends.

To Basil St Cloud, the noise of the University streets was
pure music: a concert of learning, of ambition and community.
And the sight of the black-robed students, punctuated by the colored sleeves of the University Doctors (green for Humane
Sciences, red for Physic, yellow for Natural Sciences, white for
Law), was all he needed to gladden his eye. He moved through
the lively streets on his way to the Great Hall and Doctor
Tortua's lecture like a fish swimming the ocean, answering greetings and ducking out of the way of the occasional heedless student with a smile.

The Great Hall was where the kings had once held their audiences; now, it was the place for public lectures—particularly appropriate, Basil thought, for a lecture on ancient history. Anyone
could come to a public lecture, and this one was drawing quite a
crowd. Under the frieze of watchful stone kings, the Hall's broad
steps were as crowded as the plaza outside a theatre. From stalls at
the bronze feet of the Anselmian statues of Reason and Imagination flanking the steps, people hawked nuts and drinks and
even green ribbons in honor of the Humanities. Basil pushed his
way through a swarm of scholars, the bright sleeves of his doctor's
gown allowing him precedence, until he finally reached the floor
of the Great Hall itself.

"Hey! Doctor St Cloud! Over here!"

It was one of Basil's students, Benedict Vandeleur, waving his
sleeve like a black flag.

"We've kept you a seat, sir!" Vandeleur's confident baritone
carried easily over the buzz and chatter of conversation. "Fremont,"
Vandeleur ordered the man next to him. "Go fetch Doctor St
Cloud."

The seats in the Great Hall were built up in a horseshoe
around three sides of the high, vaulted room, bench rising on
hard wooden bench. The benches were full; even the steps were
packed solid. Henry Fremont was adroit enough, St Cloud noticed, to step only on students; he followed him nimbly back up
the same route.

Vandeleur must have been there for hours to get such good
seats. St Cloud had a clear view not only of the dais and the
high-arched painted glass window above it, but of one leg of the
horseshoe and the men sitting there. He saw Tom Elton, Cassius,
and Rugg, as promised, and below them a clutch of brightly-clad
nobles. Gone were the days when the city's young nobility would
rather admit to drinking bad wine than to attending a serious
lecture. Now there was a certain prestige in spending a year or
two just learning something useless like mathematics or astronomy. When they became men of power and wealth, some still
came to University to revisit the intellectual stimulation of their
youth, or to attend public lectures by the distinguished doctors

who held Chairs in their disciplines. Basil didn't mind them; they were colorful, and when they attended his own lectures, they paid up.

In the front row, hard by the dais, was the narrow, dark face of Roger Crabbe, Doctor of History. He was chatting with a University Governor, but he stopped quickly when an old man began shakily mounting the stage.

"Is that Tortua?" Fremont asked. "He looks a hundred years old. Two hundred. He looks like he knew Gerard the Last King personally."

St Cloud stared at Doctor Tortua with horrified pity. The old magister moved as if he were walking over smooth ice, and even from the other side of the great room St Cloud could see him trembling and nodding. Tortua arranged his notes on the podium, perched a pair of round spectacles on his nose, and began to speak.

In a few minutes it became painfully clear that rumor had only exaggerated a sad truth. Gone was the mellifluous voice Basil remembered and the great analytical mind that had driven it.

"Welcome to you all." His voice was a barely audible mumble, but the lofty vault of the Great Hall caught it up and magnified it. "I wrote a book, you know, and I doubt I shall write another one. So I wish to share with you today . . . with you today. . . ." He fumbled with his notes. "Oh, yes. Now, this is very interesting. The court wizards were curious sorts. They made rituals out of everything—like women, eh?—only worse. Even the act of love. Especially the act of love. Vespas writes of goings-on between the first kings and their court wizards that would bring blushes to a dockman's cheek. There was a reason for it all, he said, but the annoying bastard did not say what it was. Apart from the obvious, of course."

Basil winced. It was all too clear that his illness had robbed Doctor Tortua of his discretion as well as everything else.

"Of course the kings were very naughty. And as we know, the wizards were worse. They encouraged them. How else could they do it? They didn't fight—the king and his Companions did that. This was in the North, of course. I'm speaking of the Northern kings. Who were ruled by the wizards. A king who doesn't rule . . . what, then, does he do, eh? Answer me that! He is ruled by powerful men who—who—well, I don't like to say, but scholarship demands—who *dominate* him. . . ."

This was intolerable. The nobles left, not very quietly. A clutch of scarlet-robed Governors conferred in shocked whispers. Basil shifted uncomfortably in his seat. Pity and grief for his old magister's public decline warred in him with acute embarrassment. He took refuge in studying the ancient stained glass window, brought, it was said, by Alcuin from Hartsholt in the North. It was very beautiful, a window onto a bright, sharp world. A hart knelt to a man robed in a bear's pelt, who held a collar of gold suspended above the hart's antlered head. A pool of blue water sparkled at their feet and a flat, golden sky arced over their heads.

The sun burned down through the colored glass of the window, flooding one bank of benches in green and brown and gold and blue. Basil's eye was caught by a young man sitting there, a young man of remarkable beauty. He was slouched forward in his seat with his ankle on one knee, his elbow on the other, and his chin in his hand, looking very interested and somewhat puzzled. The light burnished his long fall of dark hair and gilded his pale skin, making him look as bright and sharp as the stained glass. As St Cloud stared, he looked up, and their eyes met across the horseshoe.

The young man smiled deeply at him and St Cloud hastily turned his gaze back to Doctor Tortua.

"So you see—you see—"

Between one word and the next, Doctor Tortua dropped all his notes and began painfully, terrifyingly to bend down to gather them up again. Then Roger Crabbe was standing beside him, holding him upright with one strong hand, gesturing angrily to a servant, who brought forward a chair. Doctor Crabbe eased the old man into the seat and at last, at long last, Doctor Tortua fell silent.

For a horrible moment, St Cloud thought no one was going to do anything. Then a furious clapping broke out on the lower benches. Soon the hall was ringing with somewhat hysterical cheering. Some men began to push toward the dais. Out of pity and ancient affection, St Cloud joined them. Flanked by his students, he made his way to the front of the crowd, and greeted the old man respectfully, braced against a rebuff.

"Welcome back, Doctor Tortua. It's good to see you so well."

Doctor Tortua peered shortsightedly at him, lifted his silver-rimmed glasses from his lap, and hooked them over his ears. "Thank you, young man. I don't think . . ."

Roger Crabbe leaned over his shoulder. A short man, he didn't have to lean very far. His features were large for his narrow face: a heavy nose, lips made for sneering, and shallow-set, heavy-lidded eyes of a curious pale brown that was almost gold. "It's Basil St Cloud," he informed Tortua. "He was a student of yours. He lectures now in Ancient History."

Ignoring Crabbe, Basil said, "You took on a difficult topic, Doctor."

The old man drew up all his wrinkles like a pleased tortoise. "Why, thank you, young man," he said. "Thank you. Yes. The court wizards. Fascinating. I have been rethinking Vespas's *The Book of Kings*. We've been misreading him all these years." He munched his jaws as if chewing upon Vespas.

"Misreading?" prompted Basil.

"Misreading. Though Crabbe here doesn't want me to talk about it." The old man shot a sharp look at his colleague. "Read a lot over again, you know, when I was ill—Delgardie's *Mirror of History*, Vespas; I even went back and read Hollis's chronicles. And do you know, they all mention the same things: the intimacy between wizard and king, the mysterious ritual of coronation, the killing of a deer. What do you think of that, eh? All of them. Do you know what I think? I think it's because it's true!"

"What's true, sir?"

"Why, that the wizards of the North really did work magic, you foolish boy!"

By now, all that was left of the lecture audience was crowded around them, listening to the discussion with breathless attention. Nobody denied that the kings had had their wizards, sinister and mysterious counselors with roots in ancient barbaric ritual that could be mistaken for magic. When they were children, their mothers had threatened them: "Be good or the nasty wizards will come and eat you up!" From their first teachers, they'd learned that the wizards had been cynical charlatans who coupled the skills of fairground magicians with an insatiable lust for power, who inspired the mad kings to greater and greater acts of tyranny and depravity.

Nobody believed that their magic had been real. Except, apparently, now, the greatest historian of the age. Who was probably gaga, but still . . . The Horn Lecture had suddenly become a lot more interesting.

"Doctor Tortua," Crabbe interrupted. "I really don't think . . ."

"A fascinating theory," said Basil helplessly. "But there's no way to prove it. The Council of Lords burned all the wizards' books and papers, and declared all mention of them outlaw."

"Aha!" Doctor Tortua's wizened face became almost frighteningly animated. "Aren't you forgetting something?" For a moment, Basil felt as if he were back in old Tortua's lecture hall, and the moment of truth was upon him. "The Book of the King's Wizard," the old man hissed. "A complete book of spells, brought down from the North with Alcuin's wizard, Mezentian. Hollis mentions it, and so does Vespas."

Crabbe cleared his throat. "Trevor states categorically that it did not exist."

"Trevor," Basil St Cloud asserted crisply, "would have stated categorically that his mother did not exist if the Council told him to."

Crabbe smiled thinly. "There again, Doctor St Cloud, we disagree. Trevor's *Of Decadence and Deceit* is well-recognized as the most authoritative text on the subject of our country's sublime history."

"It hardly matters," Basil said irritably. "What is indisputable is that the nobles burned the wizards' books along with the wizards."

"But even with this fabled Book of the King's Wizard," Crabbe went on aggressively for the benefit of the crowd; "even if we had right here before us a page of ancient text instructing us in just how to turn straw into gold—" He paused for the laugh he knew he would get. "Even then, there is no proof of actual magic. The wizards may have been charlatans, but they were also clever politicians. By itself, a Book of the King's Wizard would prove only that they took care to persuade their royal masters of the reality of their charade."

St Cloud smiled coldly and said, "Very true, Crabbe. Another possibility is that the wizards believed themselves capable of true magic."

"Absurd!" bleated one of Crabbe's students.

"Pay attention," said Doctor Crabbe. "He's not saying they *were* magic; he's saying they *thought* they were magic. An original viewpoint, but not wholly unreasonable. Most of us believe that the magic they convinced others they performed was in fact mere trickery and legerdemain. But if, like our friend St Cloud here, you want to entertain the thought that the wizards themselves were victims of their own delusions . . ." He let a thin, pitying smile finish his sentence for him.

A young voice chimed in, "But if someone did find the Book of the King's Wizard and cast one of the spells from it and it really worked, wouldn't that clinch it?"

Basil recognized the voice of Peter Godwin, one of his own students, and wished, not for the first time, that youth were endowed with common sense as well as enthusiasm. Doctor Crabbe had a zealot's light in his shallow golden eye, and his students were studying the hapless Godwin with predatory intent, like wolves studying a wounded hound.

"Godwin," said Basil. "Please consider what you have said. If an old book of wizards' spells were to turn up in someone's attic, say, or in a job-lot of mildewed rejects from some nobleman's library, there's no guarantee that it would be recognizable or even readable. Hollis speaks of a secret language, for instance, and Vespas writes of all public rituals being conducted in a kind of gibberish."

Godwin flushed to the roots of his curly brown hair.

"Even if you could read such a spell, it would prove nothing," Crabbe added. "If the spell had no effect, it could be argued that it was too subtle to be immediately apparent, or that only a wizard would have the training necessary to cast it successfully."

Doctor Tortua, who had to all appearances nodded off during this exchange, roused himself. "They were a disgrace, those wizards, no matter what else they were. All the same, it's a pity we'll never know."

"We certainly know that there is no such thing as magic," Crabbe said firmly.

"Oh, really?" Doctor Tortua looked at him keenly, a quick flash of the man Basil had loved. "And always have known, I suppose. And that would be why the Council of Lords outlawed all magic, eh? Because they didn't believe in it? One of those little conundrums of history: why pass a law against something that never existed? It's still on the books, you know: even saying that magic once existed is a civil offense. Forgot that, did you, Roger? I thought you were a scholar of modern history." He chuckled wickedly to himself. "Well, never mind. Good thing nobody ever pays any attention to what happens at University, or we'd all be in trouble, eh?"

NICHOLAS GALING HAD STUCK OUT THE LECTURE AS long as he could. Really, he thought, someone should have taken pity on the old fool and stopped him before he got started. Wizards and kings, indeed. It was mildly titillating to hear they'd been lovers back in the mists of time, but it shed no light on the Northern man who'd so upset the City Sessions. Ancient gossip wasn't modern politics. Wizards were bugabears to frighten naughty children. If the University sheltered a royalist plot, poor, miserable, doddering Doctor Tortua certainly wasn't at the center of it.

WHEN THE MONARCHY FELL, THE NOBLES ABOLished nearly all of their particular titles. Everyone became a Lord, for to be styled a Lord of that free realm was felt to be honor and dignity enough. An exception was made for the three Ducal Houses: Hartsholt, Karleigh, and Tremontaine. For the great good they had done the country and the ancient lineage they bore, these dukes retained their titles, even though they no longer wore their coronets or took precedence in Council. The duchies did inherit seats on the Court of Honor and they retained the right to choose their own heirs from amongst their relations. The title usually passed conventionally to the eldest male; but there were exceptions. The present Duchess Tremontaine had inherited from her uncle, her mother's older brother, still remembered as the Mad Duke. He had no legitimate children, nor was he dead when he fled the city under a severe cloud, leaving his sixteen-year-old niece in charge of considerable estates with even more considerable income, as well as fistsful of manor houses, hunting lodges, and city property that included one of the nicest estates on the Hill.

Katherine was a practical girl, but she never could have done it if he had not also left her his manservant, a boy named Marcus, who had been in charge of keeping track of everything the Mad Duke could not, from estate revenues to his lovers' names. Very little unsettled Marcus, and he was happy to show the new Duchess Tremontaine the ropes.

Now, some forty years later, he was still her partner in the Tremontaine fortunes, and she still relied on him for friendship and advice. As the Duchess Katherine sat in her sunny study in Tremontaine House, reading a letter newly arrived from her cousin Jessica, she wondered what Marcus would make of it.

The letter had been written the previous spring. It was stained and crusted with sea salt. *Dear Katherine,* she read. *The funniest thing happened and I thought you would like to know about it. I picked up a man who said he was your first swordsmaster. He remembered both you and the old Duke very clearly. He was in a bad way, being surrounded by bandits in Fulati Pass and also down on his luck. We took care of it. I brought him on board with me and was able to drop him in Chartil, where the sword is still honored. He told some very amusing stories. I had no idea you had almost killed Lord whosis in your youth. Too bad.*

"Katherine? You look like you've just bitten into a green plum."

It was Marcus, his hands full of papers.

"Jessica." The duchess waved the letter. "She says she met Venturus—my old teacher, remember?—out over the sea somewhere, rescued him from bandits. I wonder if she's telling the truth?"

He settled himself down on the windowseat. Middle age had thickened him, but his solidity was very much in keeping with his temperament, as though the outside man had finally caught up with the inside and was very comfortable there. "I don't see why not. It's not as though she goes to the trouble of writing very often. Is she trying to hit you up for anything?"

"Let me see." The duchess scanned the letter. "No. I don't think so. Just international gossip. Oh, wait—here's a bit about wool prices in Chartil . . . I knew that. When did she write this, last year? Hold on—oh, this is too silly, Marcus. It's wizards. Yes, indeed, a whole tribe of renegade wizards from hundreds of years ago who made their way east outremar, and established a school on a mountaintop . . . she ran into one in a marketplace somewhere in the Kyrillian Archipelago. She said he hailed her as— oh, this is too silly."

"Sounds like her." He grinned.

"He spoke our language with a fearsome accent, and asked for news of home. You will think this is even sillier than I did— Well, she's right there. I told him we were all very well, thank you. He asked how the land prospered, without a king. I told him that we have a lovely duchess instead, who manages everything beautifully— A compliment! There's a change! —plus a few lords and chancellors to make up the balance. —And does not the land hunger for a king? I said it was years since I'd seen it.

"What do you think, madam duchess? Does it? And, if so, do you have a candidate? Let me know at once if a coronation is toward, for I would certainly drop everything to celebrate a king of your choosing." She folded the letter with an exasperated sigh. "Oh, Jessica."

"You'd think she'd have gotten over baiting you by now."

"I suppose I should be glad she writes at all. She can't be expecting an answer. But poor Venturus! Imagine him still being alive after all these years! If it really is him, I should track him down and send him a pension. Ask Angela to step in here, will you? I'll draft the instructions."

chapter IV

THE DAY AFTER THE TORTUA LECTURE, LEONARD
Rugg sat in the Blackbird's Nest, debating Placid's clas-
sic text *Of Manners and Morals* with Roger Crabbe.
Placid had touched on both metaphysics and history, so it was an
even playing field. Their students, who were standing by, ready to
pick up the rhetorical ball as needed, understood that what was
really being debated was Doctor Tortua's sanity and that Rugg
was deliberately being provoking.

"Now, I'm no historian," Rugg was saying, "and correct me if
I'm wrong, but Placid wrote *Of Manners* during the reign of
Anselm the Wise, some two hundred years after the Union, isn't
that so?" The historians nodded; the metaphysicians sniggered.
"So when he says that wizards are, let me see, 'perfidious, perni-
cious and given to unholy appetites,' he's talking about the ones
he knows, the ones in Anselm's court." Everyone nodded. "These
wizards are men he knows, men he's observed, men he's probably
eaten with. Maybe one stepped on his toe, or spilled soup on
him! How, then, can we take his opinion of them seriously? He's
biased. It's not history, it's not manners, and it's certainly not

morals. I think we should simply delete the chapter and be done with it."

This sally was greeted by hissing and expostulations, but Crabbe's students fell silent when the little magister raised his hand. "Say what you like about morality, Magister Rugg—and we all know that you are the expert there—" Sniggers, this time from Crabbe's historians. "But whose opinion can we trust, if not that of a man who was present at the time and wrote so eloquently about the decadent world he witnessed?"

"The world he witnessed was in essence the same world we live in today. 'Worlds do not change over time, nor the people in them,' " Rugg quoted sententiously.

Crabbe closed his eyes in weary disdain. "And it therefore follows that the study of history is a pointless exercise, I suppose?" He folded his arms across his chest and jerked his chin at the massive youth perched precariously on the end of the bench. "Blake, you answer him. You know my arguments, or you should."

The student he addressed nervously raked his sandy hair behind his ears, which were prominent and, just now, rather red. Justis Blake was a large, slow young man, with large, slow thoughts. He did not like to be hurried, nor did he have the smallest idea how Doctor Crabbe would answer such a statement. He had only been attending his classes for two weeks. But he licked his lips and tried anyway. "History teaches us that worlds do change. We don't have wizards now. That's a change."

The metaphysicians hooted at this statement of the obvious. Rugg said, "Yes, the nobles took care of that. They burned the old charlatans like so much cordwood, and there's an end to it. We still have nobles, though, don't we? Nothing really changes."

But Justis went on, "People don't change their basic natures, perhaps, but their surroundings can change the way they see things. For instance, a year ago I was still myself, but I lived on a farm—" Somebody mooed; it might even have been a historian.

"Honestly, Blake," Doctor Crabbe said. "If you can't reason logically, at least you could remember my lectures. Or quote Trevor's glorious words on the subject. You have read Trevor, haven't you?"

Blake's cheeks and ears burned. This was Doctor Crabbe's way, he reminded himself. He'd endured it in class and he'd survived it. The history magister's habit of leaping on you and shaking your ignorance out of you reminded him of his mother's terrier, hunting rats. Justis Blake had chosen to attend Crabbe's lectures because he thought it would be good for him to be shaken up a bit. Now he wasn't so sure.

Doctor Rugg turned a comradely smile on him. "Take heart, boy. Scholarly debates draw no real blood. Try again."

Blake took a deep breath. "Thank you, sir. All right. If the question is, what was the wizards' real function, and Placid can help elucidate it, then his opinion is as good as anyone's, isn't that so? Placid knew the kings, he knew the wizards. He didn't think much of their magic."

"What Placid thought about magic was very much what we still think," Rugg pointed out mildly. " 'Magic is like strong drinke,' " he quoted; " 'for the man who trusteth therein trusteth to the shadow and the image of power, that in itself is naught.' *Of Manners and Morals*. Book IV."

"Well, yes, but—" Justis swallowed. The whole room was looking at them. His mother had been so proud when he left to study in the city. He wondered what she would say when he appeared at her garden gate, cast out and utterly humiliated. He took a deep breath. "But we ought to look at other things besides Placid. It's like a stool, you see, that can't stand on one leg alone. Placid is one leg of the stool. He doesn't like wizards and he doesn't think much of their magic. Why isn't he afraid of them, though? Because he isn't, you can tell."

Crabbe's honey-colored eyes narrowed to little sharp points. "I had no idea what an original mind you had, Blake. Go on; I'm fascinated."

As well be hung for a wolf as for a lamb, Justis thought, and forged on. "He's more afraid of the king than of the wizards. Anselm curtailed their power. It's one reason he's called 'the Wise.' I think. Anyway, another leg of the stool is: Anselm enacted laws."

"Laws?" Crabbe sneered. "What do you know about laws,

after two whole weeks studying history? Yesterday, you didn't know the names of the first Inner Council of Lords, and now you're an expert on Anselm's laws!"

"It was a monograph I found," Justis went on doggedly. "About some documents to do with laws enacted to limit the wizards' political role when Anselm came to the throne—"

"'Some documents'!" Crabbe threw up his hands. "There you have it! You turn your back on the great ones, on Fleming and the immortal Trevor, and go picking through moldy papers, and what happens?"

"You get some remarkable insights." The new voice came from over the heads of the ring of onlookers. Like rushes in the wind, everyone turned to face the speaker. He was a large, solid-looking man, with broad shoulders and springy dark hair escaping from its ribbon. To Blake's country-bred eyes, there was something of the peasant about the way he stood, as if the Nest's uneven floor were a ploughed field. But his green sleeves proclaimed him a Doctor of Humane Sciences. "You learn what lies behind the formal statements approved by the court censors for publication, for one."

"Ah!" said Leonard Rugg happily, as though finding Basil St Cloud at his usual table at the Blackbird's Nest was the most unexpected of chances. "St Cloud! Going to set us all straight, are you?"

"If you like," Basil said mildly. "You, Rugg, of all people should admit that two-hundred-year-old gossip can still be valuable in evaluating historical data. Take the story about Placid dedicating *On Thought* to King Anselm. When Placid read the dedication out before the court, the king rewarded him with a purse of money and a writ of banishment."

Leonard Rugg blew what in a less distinguished personage would have been a raspberry of disgust. "Yes, yes, we all know that story—if it's true."

Crabbe chopped at the air impatiently. "Of course it's true, Rugg. Vespas reported it, and Trevor saw no reason to doubt the account."

While Crabbe and Rugg bickered, Justis Blake studied his rescuer. At a table by the window, Basil St Cloud stood surrounded by his students, the usual band of black-robed men of various shapes and sizes. But there was something about them all that reminded him of a team of kickball players from another village: they had the ball and they knew it. And right now their ball looked a lot more attractive than Rat-Catcher Crabbe's. On that impulse, Justis Blake did something very simple that would change the course of the rest of his life: he got up from the bench and made for the table by the window.

"Good idea," Crabbe called after him, unwilling not to fire a parting shot. "Maybe St Cloud can knock some basic history into your thick skull. When you've learned what atrocities the kings committed when they came South, then you may be able to understand why they had to be deposed, and their performing wizards along with them."

But Justis wasn't listening. St Cloud's black-robed throng closed ranks around him, shutting him off from Crabbe's table— and St Cloud invited him to explain himself. Smarting from Crabbe's needling, Justis was inclined to stammer at first, but Basil St Cloud's clear, intelligent eyes never left his face, and soon he was constructing the kind of argument that had inspired his teacher in the village school to lend him book after book, and finally the means to make his way to the city and its university, where he'd been feeling like a prize fool ever since.

"So you see," Justis concluded, "our society grows out of his. We cannot understand what we are if we do not understand where we came from."

Basil St Cloud smiled, and Justis felt as if he'd just scored a difficult goal.

"I agree with you, Blake—it is Blake, isn't it?" Justis nodded. "What do you make of that story about Placid and Anselm, by the way?"

"Do you really want to know?" Justis was incredulous; Doctor Crabbe was seldom interested in what his students thought of the material he taught them.

"Yes," said Doctor St Cloud simply. "I do."

"Trevor says . . ."

"I know what Trevor says," St Cloud interrupted. "I want to hear what you think."

"It seems pretty obvious, sir. Anselm must have taken Placid's indictment of luxury and vice in *Of Manners and Morals* as a personal attack."

"Pretty obvious indeed. What if I were to tell you that Anselm banished the man because he found him a sententious bore?"

"I'd say that you were just guessing," Justis answered promptly. "There's nothing like that in any of the histories."

A man like a fence-post draped in black leaned over his shoulder and said truculently, "Careful. Someone might think you were calling Doctor St Cloud a liar."

"Let him be, Fremont. It's a fair point." St Cloud turned to Justis. "But consider: you yourself have noted that Anselm was instrumental in limiting the power of the wizards, so he certainly wasn't going to banish Placid for disliking them. Furthermore, papers do indeed turn up from time to time—in attics, in old chests, even in the University Archives." A slight young man whose long, fine hair was the color of copper laughed appreciatively and was rewarded with a smile. "In this case, it's a notation on the writ of banishment itself. I don't think it's been looked at since the Fall, but it's in the Archives. You can see it for yourself, if you're interested. In the margin, above the king's signature, there's a single word. *Ass!* It's the same hand as the signature."

"And he was, too," said the fence-post. " 'A man who would live well must live wisely.' " He minced out the words savagely. "What does that *mean*, anyway?"

"That you should think before you speak, Fremont," said Doctor St Cloud repressively.

Justis shook his head. "If you don't mind my saying so, sir, that doesn't contradict what I said. *On Morals and Manners* was pretty hard on Anselm's whole court, after all, not just the wizards."

St Cloud looked at him so blankly that Justis began to wonder just how stupid he'd been, and then smiled slowly, like the sun rising over the Hill. "No more it does, Blake." He slapped the astonished young man on the shoulder. "Overlooking the obvious can be as dangerous as not looking beyond it. And you're not afraid to speak your mind. Good for you."

Justis grinned. It was good to feel intelligent again.

"Someone else's monograph doesn't constitute evidence," Fremont pointed out.

"Shut up, Henry." The speaker's voice was high and clear, like a girl's, but full of authority. A boy, no more than fourteen, with a fine suit of clothes under his black robe.

"It does if the author went to the original documents," St Cloud said. "Which he did. I know. He was one of my students."

Justis was inspired with a sudden and overwhelming desire to have the young magister say the same of him someday. "Doctor St Cloud," he said. "I . . . I'd like to attend your lectures formally, if you'll accept me."

St Cloud put his hand on Justis's shoulder. "I'm flattered, Master Blake, but I need to be sure you've thought this through. You've already begun with Doctor Crabbe, who is interested in the Fall of the Kings; I am interested in their rise. And our methods of study are as different as our fields."

"Yes, sir. I realize that. That's why I want—"

"I wasn't finished. I presume you are already studying some rhetoric, geography, and metaphysics?"

"Of course," Justis said.

"Good man. Then you will come to my lectures. You will think about history and why you wish to study it, and how. You will read Hollis's *Chronicle History of the Northern Kings*. It may read like a collection of fables, but is the closest thing we have to a standard text on the pre-Union North. You will read Vespas, if you haven't already, and my own humble offering on the altar of scholarship, *The Origins of Peace*. You will attend lectures by Doctors Ferrule and Wilson, and weigh their ideas against mine. And at the end of—shall we say three weeks?—if you still find yourself yearning after kings and their doings, come to me and we'll see if something can be arranged."

Dazzled, Justis nodded. "Good man," said St Cloud, and squeezed his shoulder. "I'll see you tomorrow morning."

He rose, threw some coppers on the table to pay the tally, smiled at the clustered students, and picked his way out through the tables and benches. He liked young Blake; a country boy with more imagination than discipline, but discipline could be learned.

By the fire, Basil's path was blocked. A student with a long tail of sleek, burnished hair occupied a chair, his legs sprawled luxuriously out toward the hearth, taking up more than his share of room in the crowded tavern. His arms were folded over his chest and his eyes were closed, giving him the look of some beautiful young warrior of old, struck down in his prime and carved on a tombstone. As Basil's shadow came between him and the fire, he looked up and smiled an indolent smile.

He looked familiar, but Basil could not place him. The magister continued to stare until the young man sat up and pulled in his legs to clear the path. He did not apologize, and Basil did not thank him.

Basil's students watched their magister go, almost reverently silent; then someone shouted to the barman for more beer, and the redhead Lindley turned to Justis.

"Well," he said acidly, "*you* certainly made an impression."

It took Justis a moment to frame a response. The country was different from the city, with different rules of conduct. At home, he'd have fought anyone who'd baited him, and bought him a beer after. But he didn't want to fight Lindley, who was half his size, and all too obviously hopelessly in love with the young magister. "My mother always told me I should be seen and not heard," Justis said peaceably. "I wish I'd listened to her. I felt like a prize calf on market day."

The redhead hesitated, then smiled more naturally. His eyes were a dense pastel blue, like dyed velvet. "I was thinking you looked rather like a prize calf myself, but I won't say so now," he said. "I'm Anthony Lindley, of History. That rudesby with the needle nose is Henry Fremont. The infant in the gaudy coat is Peter Godwin, and the stalwart gentleman to your left is Benedict Vandeleur. We've been studying with St Cloud for two years now, and consider ourselves his chief disciples."

Justis shook Lindley's hand and acknowledged his introductions with a nod. "Justis Blake, of heaven knows what, unless Doctor St Cloud takes me on. Some days, I think I'm getting the hang of it. Some days, I've got cowflops between my ears. Like today."

Everyone looked at Benedict Vandeleur, who fixed the newcomer with a measuring eye. If every dog-pack has its leader, Vandeleur was clearly top dog here. A city man's son, perhaps, twenty or a bit over, well-muscled, with a stubbly jaw, deep-set eyes, and coarse, dark hair bound back in a thin strip of linen. Him, Justis could have fought, but he smiled at him instead, frank and unthreatening.

There was a charged pause, and then Vandeleur nodded. "Crabbe's a thug," he said.

Taking this as a provisional acceptance, Justis recklessly ordered a round of beer for his prospective colleagues. The gesture no less than the beer loosened their tongues, and soon Justis knew that Peter Godwin was a nobleman's son but nobody cared; that Henry Fremont liked insulting people but nobody cared; and that Anthony Lindley could be perfectly sensible when he wanted. He also knew that, as far as this particular group of historians was concerned, Roger Crabbe was a lick-boot toady who had insinuated himself into old Tortua's good graces, and Ferrule and Wilson were idiots who hadn't had a new idea since they'd traded their mothers' breasts for tankards.

"Yes, yes, I believe you," said Justis, "but Doctor St Cloud said to go hear them, so I will. One can learn something even from the barking of dogs, as my mother used to say."

Vandeleur laughed. "You'll do," he said. "Tell you what. Come by my rooms later, and I'll show you my notes."

"Done," said Justis. "I'll bring a pie, shall I?"

"Oh, a rich man," sneered Fremont. "Bring a bottle, too, and I'll lend you my copy of Hollis."

"Oh, a rich man," said Justis, in perfect imitation, earning himself a rap over the head from Fremont. He hadn't been so happy since he first came to University. To the Seven Hells with the rigors of Crabbe. Doctor St Cloud's disciples knew how to enjoy themselves.

I F THERE WAS ONE THING BASIL ST CLOUD LOVED
more than digging out long-forgotten knowledge, it was pre-
senting that knowledge to his students. Years of rooting
around in the University Archives had turned up treasures: royal
proclamations, letters from decades of Councils to decades of
kings, paymasters' rolls for royal households, lists of King's
Companions, drafts of laws and treaties, signed and unsigned.
These documents revealed a world that was far more interesting,
more brightly colored, more real than the stately abstractions of
the historians Trevor and Fleming, White and even Tortua. Basil
remembered the almost sexual thrill he'd felt on first handling
Anselm's letters to the Dragon Chancellor and seeing the sweeping, confident signature above the royal seal. It was that more than
anything else which had ignited his fascination with the mysteries
surrounding the kings of the North and their descendants.

Of course Basil was perfectly acquainted with all the standard
texts, or he never would have been made a Doctor of History. But
where his fellow historians were content to rehash the writings of

their revered predecessors, turning argument and analysis on increasingly tiny points of interpretation and shading, Basil was quietly reaching into whole new sources—some of them very old indeed. He mined ballads and ancient legends for the grains of truth they might hold; and where most historians relied on, say, Vespas's summary of the Ophidian Treaty in *The Book of Kings*, Basil had been known to appear at a lecture brandishing the actual document like a banner, its red seal dark with the blood of ages, captured like a prize from the University Archives.

The small, drafty hall known as LeClerc where Basil St Cloud delivered his lectures was tucked away behind a stone wall and a small, cobbled courtyard, not easy to find. After the Tortua debacle, though, the early kings and their wizards were a hot topic, and this morning LeClerc was as full as a tavern at festival-time. Basil looked out over a floor packed with black gowns and eager young faces. More students perched along the gallery like untidy crows, elbowing one another and whispering and eating steamed buns.

It was an audience Basil could not resist. They'd come to hear scandal; well, he'd give them scandal. As it happened, he'd come across a particularly juicy morsel just yesterday.

"A treat for you today," Basil said. "I'm going to skip over some three hundred years of councils and treaties and legislative acts, and talk about the reign of the last king but one, Mad Hilary, also called Hilary the Stag."

He began dryly enough, with material drawn from Doctor Tortua's *Hubris*, for the benefit, he said kindly, of any visitors who might not be familiar with the basic texts. But soon he was filling out the long-agreed-upon events of Hilary's reign with the details he'd found in the hitherto lost memoirs of Hieronymus, Duke Karleigh, who had represented the Council of Nobles in Hilary's court.

"Shortly after his coronation, Hilary began to show signs of the peculiar delusion that earned him his name. He spent more and more time in the compound where the royal deer were raised, and interested himself in their care and nurture to the length of feeding a young fawn pap and milk with his own hands, and bringing it into the palace to sleep in his own bedchamber. When Queen Amelia objected, he had her moved into another part of the palace."

Laughter in the gallery, quickly shushed. Rows of dark and light heads bent over tablets with a small scratching of pencils, like hens after worms.

"It came as a considerable surprise to his court, therefore, when Hilary chose to revive the ritual, abandoned back in his great-grandfather's time, of hunting a yearling buck and sacrificing it to the land. Hilary insisted upon hunting the deer himself and bringing it to the wizards and participating in the sacrifice, even though the ritual so disturbed him that he kept to his chamber for days after. The court wizards adored Hilary, even though almost no one else did."

A movement caught his eye: a head shaking, as if in amused wonder. He focused on it to see slanting cheekbones, a long, fine jaw—faintly familiar, but unplaceable. Distracted, St Cloud paused to gather his thoughts.

Ah. He had it now. The young man from Doctor Tortua's lecture, and from the tavern yesterday. The young man who had smiled at him then, who was smiling at him now. Basil hurriedly returned his full attention to King Hilary and his peculiarities. Which, in his later years, centered increasingly on beautiful young lovers of no birth and little common sense, who seldom had a choice in the matter. One of them had cut his throat for him. Hilary had been naked at the time, save for a fine deerskin. The young murderer had been discovered weeping over the corpse, his monarch's blood smeared over his face and chest.

"The court wizards questioned him, of course," Basil said, "but they could get nothing out of him save the babblings of madness: first he accused the king, and then the wizards themselves, of commanding him to do the deed. He died under the questioning, much irritating Hilary's heir Gerard, who had been looking forward to executing the traitor. Not to be cheated of his revenge, King Gerard commanded that the murderer's corpse be drawn, quartered, and burned just as if it had been alive. Gerard was a great believer in following ritual. The problem was that many of the rituals of the North were remnants of a harsher, more barbaric time, when the wizards had been a great deal more involved in government. Tomorrow, I will explain just what all this has to do with the kings of the early Union. Unless, of course, you can work it out for yourselves."

The University bell tolled heavily over his last words, and there was a general rustle and scuffle as the students gathered up their effects. They'd always known the last kings were corrupt and mad: it was the foundation of every lecture on the monarchy they'd ever heard. But even Crabbe, who was accounted a good lecturer, never really made *corrupt* and *mad* as real as St Cloud's account of Hilary's death.

"Thank you." It was the strange young man, standing below the lectern. "That was interesting, about King Hilary and his lover. All those details, about the slit throat and the deerskin on the bed, they aren't in Tortua or Trevor, or even Vespas. But I know I've seen something like it, something very like it, and I'm trying to remember where. . . ."

Something about him—his voice, perhaps, or his arrogance, or his suggestion that St Cloud's discovery was not as astonishing as he'd thought—put Basil's back up. "Indeed?" he said. "When you remember where, you must certainly let me know. Independent corroboration is always important."

"In case someone thinks you made it all up," the young man agreed.

St Cloud considered ignoring this, but could not. "Will you hear some advice, Master . . . ?"

"Campion." The young man swept a courtly bow. "Theron Campion."

"Master Campion. A scholar's facts are a scholar's honor. I was not made a Doctor of this University for inventing colorful details."

"Of course not, Doctor St Cloud." Campion's glance flicked up mischievously. "But . . . how charming of you if you had!"

His eyes were greenish. Basil found that he was looking into them. Theron Campion smiled engagingly, and Basil felt his heart begin to hammer with what, under the circumstances, could only be outrage. "Truth is hardly a jesting matter," he said coldly.

A moment later, the young man and his disturbing eyes were pushed aside by a group of students wanting to carry Doctor St Cloud off to the Blackbird's Nest for a drink and more stories. They were disappointed, but not entirely surprised, when he laughingly informed them that being a magister did not absolve him from the exercise of scholarship.

"If I'm to be as immortal as Trevor and Fleming are, as Doctor Tortua will be, I need to write a text as great as theirs. Such texts are not written in taverns, my friends, not even taverns as stimulating as the Blackbird's Nest."

ALL THE GREAT HISTORIANS HAD MADE THEIR REPU-tations on a single defining work. Tortua, for instance, had written a study of the Inner Council and endless monographs on various pre-Fall laws and treaties, but *Hubris and the Fall of the Kings* was the thing he would be remembered for, just as Trevor was remembered for *Of Decadence and Deceit* and Fleming for *The Tragedy of Kingship*.

Basil St Cloud doubted that he would be remembered for *The Origins of Peace*. He considered it a journeyman work, competent but not inspired. The book focused entirely on the nobles' activities around the Union. It was little more than a paean to the Council of Nobles for forging an alliance that would bring peace and prosperity to both kingdoms and put an end to the interminable border wars that harvested too many lives and not enough food. What finally brought them together was an invasion that threatened both kingdoms; what had kept them together was the marriage of the monarchs. He'd used only established sources, and had come to the unexceptionable conclusion that the barbaric North had gained more from the Union than the civilized South.

Basil had written *Origins* to suit the Doctors and Governors, before he'd discovered the heady joys of true scholarship. And before he'd realized the truth about the ancient kings.

For too many years, that truth had been buried; buried not only by courtiers and scholars eager to please their noble masters,

but by the genuinely despicable behavior of the kings immediately preceding Gerard, who had quite rightly been deposed by
the Council of Lords. It had been nearly two hundred years since
the last king was slain; now, Basil thought, might be time to un-
cover the truths about the first ones, who ruled the land for hundreds of years: strong and beautiful warriors who had united the
two kingdoms against foreign invaders despite the bickering of
Northern and Southern partisans; men of daring and imagination
who had left their mark on treaties and laws still in place, on stable borders and prosperous farms.

It was a truth that would be hard for anyone now living to
accept. The assumption was that all the kings had been more or
less as mad as Hilary, as wicked as Gerard. But Basil had read
their very words, had touched the paper that they had touched,
breathed the dust of their official documents and private corre-
spondence, and Basil knew better. There was nothing of madness
in Anselm's letters to his councilors, no wickedness in the love
poetry Roland the Stout wrote to his wife, Queen Isabelle, or in
the clever sketches Orlando the Fair had scribbled in the margins
of the draft of the Arkenvelt Treaty. For generations after the
Union, the kings had ruled fairly and well, presiding over courts
in which scholars and statesmen practiced their crafts, and young
men danced, fenced, debated, jousted, dallied with the daughters
of nobles and with each other. And before that, the Northern
kings had kept their rocky little kingdom independent and prosperous against the twin threats of foreign invasion and famine.
Basil loved the ancient kings. He loved them for their mystery,
for their bright courage, for the love and poetry and art that they
had inspired. He loved them because nobody else did, and because loving them seemed to be the same as loving buried truth.
He loved them, and wanted justice for them.

The problem, of course, was evidence. Charming as he found
Hollis's *Chronicle History of the Northern Kingdom*, Basil understood it to be a piece of political puffery, commissioned by Alcuin
the Diplomat and his queen to introduce the history of the king's
ancient land to their new subjects. Their descendants were better
documented; but in his heart Basil knew that the key to it all lay
in Alcuin's predecessors in the North, in what they had brought

to the Union and how it had worked its way into this land's liv-ing heritage. The ancient North kingdom had yielded precious few written texts, and those that survived were so fragmentary as to be almost incomprehensible. Basil believed the history of the North lay encoded in ballads and poetic fragments, in legends of skin-changers and wizards and tales of glorious battles and hope-less loves—but that was not the kind of evidence even the most liberal-minded of historians would accept as authoritative.

The Treaty of Union, however, was a document whose his-torical authority even Roger Crabbe could not question. And an astute scholar could deduce a great deal about the laws and cus-toms of the mysterious northlands from the provisions of that treaty. Inheritance, for example. Why should a whole section of the treaty be devoted to ensuring that the throne never pass to a woman? It set the queen's nobles against the king from the begin-ning, flying in the face of their own traditions. What did the kings and their wizards have against women, and in whose inter-est was such a law? What tradition did it spring from?

In pursuit of answers, Basil devoted himself to sifting through the stacks of books and papers he found in the Archives, or bought from the rag-and-bone men who made their living comb-ing through the city's trash. Among the useless bills and tallies and notes, occasionally he discovered historical gold: letters from an ancient Lord Davenant to his son, or a half-filled book of pri-vate musings by a Lord Montague in the reign of King Alcuin's great-great-grandson Rufus. He'd found that one in a box of old romances and household accounts belonging to an impoverished Karleigh cousin, which had also contained the diary of old Hieronymus where he'd read the remarkable story of Hilary's death.

Basil was annoyed, but not surprised, to find the wizards mentioned everywhere. Davenant urged his son to seek their help with his wife's infertility. Montague cursed them for interfer-ing in a drainage scheme before he'd told anyone about it. Montague also quoted a certain Pretorius, who "performed a rit-ual of Sweet Water over the well at Hemmynge House. No more sickness there, the Land be thanked. But like the shepherd in the tale, now the King desires the river purified, and P. doubts the whole College of Wizards would have sufficient power for that monstrous task, and is much given to crying, 'Alas for the days of Guidry!' "

At least, it looked like *Guidry*. There was a Guidry's Well up north. But Basil supposed it could have been *Cully*. Or even *Godfrey*. Montague's handwriting was scratchy and faded, but he was close to the king, and every sentence was precious.

Basil kept at the notebook until his ink ran low and the fading light reminded him that he was out of candles. Whereupon he noticed that his head also ached, his mouth was as dry as the Twelve-Months' Drought, and his belly was as empty as his inkwell. Beer was what he needed, and some food, and more ink, and probably firewood and candles as well. Which meant that he was going to have to go out.

He swore, and put on his hat. If he had a servant, he wouldn't have to interrupt his work for trifles. But a servant's yearly hire was a half-dozen new books, a winter's worth of wood. He simply could not afford it.

Basil blew out his candle and locked his door behind him. The Horn Chair of History paid a good stipend, he thought as he felt his way down the stairs. It would cover not only a manservant, but new rooms and bookshelves and wax candles and all the books he needed. His chances of capturing that prize were small, though; when Tortua stepped down, the Chair would inevitably go to an established historian, not a jumped-up country boy with a minor book and a couple of mildly controversial monographs to his credit. It was foolish to think otherwise, wasn't it?

In the dank front hall, the scruffy boy who kept the door let him out. The evening was clear but cold. Shivering, Basil made for the nearest tavern, the Ink Pot, traditional gathering-place of poets and rhetoricians. Disinclined to company, he found an empty table by the wall and ordered burned ale and a fowl pie. The ale appeared almost immediately; Basil watched over the edge of his tankard as a hilarious group of students by the fire argued some fine point of rhetoric. One boy had his foot up on a bench, lunging like a swordsman with an accusing finger to his laughing opponent's nose. Only eight years ago, he'd still been one of them. He sipped the fragrant brew and smiled to himself. And now he was dreaming of the Horn Chair. Still, why shouldn't he dream? Because, he answered himself, he was not even thirty yet; an infant among magisters. Yet who were his rivals, after all? Ancient history was not a popular subject, and Doctors of History were few. Only Crabbe posed any real competition—but Crabbe had many enemies. As far as Basil knew, his only enemy was Crabbe himself.

The fowl pie came; he ate it and was contemplating more ale when a black-gowned student detached himself from the group by the fire and headed toward Basil's corner.

"Doctor St Cloud," said the young man brightly. "Good evening."

This time, Basil recognized him immediately. "Campion, isn't it?"

"May I sit down?" The green eyes were a little glassy with drink, the white hand heavy on the table's edge.

Basil saw no reason why he should mince words with a man who was, after all, both drunk and rude. "No," he said flatly.

Theron Campion staggered, catching himself against Basil's shoulder. "Oops," he said. "Sorry. Just sit here quietly. You won't know I'm here." He eased himself onto the bench next to Basil, thigh to thigh. Basil recoiled as though the touch had burned him.

"Sorry," said Campion again, and moved away.

"Don't you think you should go home while you can still walk?" Basil asked coldly.

"I'm not so drunk as all that," said Campion. "I can still say 'Seven seditious swordsmen sailed in exile to Sardinopolis.' Shall I buy you a drink? The wine's not so bad here, if you know what to ask for." He smiled like a cat who knows where the cream is kept. "I know what to ask for."

Basil laughed. "I'm sure you do. No, you shall not buy me wine."

"Brandy, what about brandy? Or beer. Men who drink beer are seldom beautiful, but it's the exception proves the rule, or so 'Long John' Tipton would have us believe."

" 'Long John'?" Basil said, ignoring the reference to beauty.

"Is that how you refer to Doctor Tipton? What do you call *me*, then?"

The boy smiled a very creamy smile. "Now, that would be telling. I would call you Basil, if you would permit it."

Basil eyed Campion with the fascinated curiosity of someone watching a man walking blindly into a brick wall. The boy was clearly too drunk to know what he was doing. "I can't stop you," he said shortly.

"Oh, yes, you can. One hard look from your eyes could turn my tongue to stone. Everyone is afraid of you."

"You exaggerate."

"I do not, sir. I always pay ver-ry particular attention when you speak." An aristocratic drawl was beginning to bleed through the University sharpness. "Though, mostly, I watch your mouth. It is austere, yet sensuous. It bears watching."

Basil repressed an urge to cover his mouth with his hand. "I wasn't aware that you had had much opportunity to watch it before today. You are hardly a regular attendee of my lectures."

"It's a morning lecture," Campion explained apologetically. "I have come before, though. I heard you speak on the rise of the Inner Council and the court wizards. You're wrong about the wizards, you know." He leaned closer. "I understand about them, you see, because I have studied the *rhetoric* of the situation. Being a student of Rhetoric. Which I am—this year. Last year I did Geography . . . but never mind. I like History, too. What I'm trying to say is," he sat up straight and drew a deep breath: "What were the court wizards? What was their function, after all? They were counselors to the kings. They gave advice. All this business we read in Hollis about their seeing into men's hearts, binding the kings with chains of gold . . . it's figurative language. A rhetorical device. Any poet can tell you that. What they really were . . . they were like you, Basil: they sifted the evidence, looking for truth. They were scholars of the heart." Pleased, he repeated it: "Scholars of the heart. And because they were good scholars, they got it right often enough to be credible and thus gain a reputation for real magic."

The boy spoke earnestly, leaning close enough for Basil to smell the brandy on his breath. In the candlelight, his eyes seemed huge, and green as forest leaves. He waited for a response, and when none was forthcoming, sat back on the bench with a complacent smile. "I knew you'd agree, once I'd demonstrated it to you," he said.

Basil recoiled. "Agree? Master Campion, the only thing you've demonstrated is your ability to spin theories out of thin air. There's not a single fact in that whole farrago of nonsense—not one."

Unrepentant, Campion said, "But we know so few facts about those days, and those few we know are so unreliable. Are you suggesting—*you*, Doctor St Cloud—that I . . . let me see now . . . *set about inventing colorful details?*"

Basil gritted his teeth. "I am suggesting that you trouble to inform yourself before you start formulating theories."

"I know as much as most of your students do. I've read Tortua and Hollis, and one of the others—Delgardie, that's the one. What else is there?"

A student reeled past them, or nearly—at the last moment he did a drunken bounce off the table and into Campion's lap. "Bugger off, Hemmynge." Campion dumped him on the ground. Hemmynge wandered off in the other direction, with people shouting after him.

"What else?" Campion persisted. "If I want facts."

"I provide those at my lectures, young man. For a fee."

Campion groaned. "There are a lot of things I'm better at than getting up in the morning. And you won't let me buy you a drink. Tell me now."

"We can't talk here," Basil said. "It's too noisy."

"Out on the street, then?"

"Too cold."

"I don't suppose your rooms are nearby . . . ?"

B ASIL ST CLOUD'S ROOMS WERE UP FOUR FLIGHTS OF stairs in an old stone building that had originally been part of the royal dependencies. Some time after the fall of the kings, it had been cut up into a warren of more or less cramped apartments. Basil's was a largish room, furnished with a wooden bedstead, a table and a chair, and scores of books and papers piled and drifted on the floor, against the walls, in the corners, and spread out on the mattress like an eager lover.

"The scholar's mistress," observed Campion, folding his body down onto the bed. He laid his hand on one closely written sheet. "Is this your new book?"

On the way from the Ink Pot, Basil had had time to regret his impulsiveness. "No," he said coldly.

"*Do* you have a mistress?"

Basil, who was poking up the fire, jerked upright, his lips compressed. The young man returned his look gravely, like a curious child. He'd loosed his shirt at the neck, laying open the fine linen to bare the hollow of his throat, which was also fine, and very pale. Firelight polished the fold of hair over his shoulder and touched the high curves of his brow and his aquiline nose with a warm light, lending them the look of alabaster or carved ivory. His eyes, shadowed, were blank.

Basil's world spun once and realigned itself around a figure descended from the marble frieze above the Great Hall, now sitting on his bed: the living image of an ancient king.

Theron Campion moved two books onto the floor, clearing a larger space on the bed. The movement broke the illusion, but not the enchantment. Basil took one step toward the bed, and then another, his hand held out in unconscious supplication. Theron grasped it and pulled him down into a long kiss that ended with his lying back on the bed amid the papers.

"Watch out," Theron murmured against Basil's mouth. "She has nails!"

"*What?*"

"Your mistress. She's scratching my back. And this can't be doing her any good. Let's get rid of her."

Basil propped himself up on his elbow and leaned over Theron to scoop papers and books off the end of the bed, lifting him to get at the papers he was lying on, pressing against his belly, working his hands under the gown, the jacket, the tight waistcoat, the shirt, to the strong, smooth back beneath. The young man's flesh was warm and supple under Basil's hands; his mouth was sweet and firm under Basil's lips. Theron rolled him away, laughing, and helped him disentangle himself from his scholar's robe and the suit of clothes beneath it.

Then Theron pulled his own shirt over his head. His skin was a little flushed, and winding up his chest to his throat was a tracery of leaves so beautifully etched that it might almost have grown there of itself, like ivy on a stone wall. The ivy leaves were intertwined with oak. Basil lifted his hand to touch the decoration and hesitated, overcome.

Theron glanced down at himself, his expression closed. "It won't smudge," he said.

"I'd like to see the rest of it," said Basil unsteadily.

The leaves coiled around Theron's waist to end under one high, round buttock. Basil stroked it, half-expecting to feel leaves rustling under his fingers. Theron gasped and burrowed his hand into the dark hair of Basil's chest. His fingers were cold. "I've always wanted a fur coverlet," he said. "Come and warm me."

And Basil did warm him, until they threw the blankets on the floor, until they flared and leapt and burned themselves out to lie at last in a smoldering glow of satisfaction.

"I'm curious about something," Basil said sleepily. "Have you been following me? Lately, I seem to see you everywhere."

The young man settled himself more comfortably against his shoulder. "I thought you'd never notice."

"I noticed you at once!"

Basil felt the smile against his skin. "No, you didn't. I attended lectures; I saw you in the Nest surrounded by your students, your particular followers—"

Basil chuckled.

"What?"

"The way you say that. Par-*tic*-u-lar. You sound as though you're picking up something tiny with silver tweezers. Never mind. Go on."

The student shifted. "Well . . . I studied you until I knew you, or at least the public parts of you: your learning, your passion, the way your voice slows when you answer a question. I studied your hands, and wondered how they'd touch me; your hair, and how it would smell. I wondered about all that, and about the rest of you

I could not see. I wanted to know you. And I wanted you to know me. I wanted you to see me."

"Have you gotten what you wanted?"

Theron trailed his hand down Basil's breastbone to his belly. "Yes," he said. "I have."

A FTER THERON HAD LEFT HIM, BASIL BANKED THE fire, threw his gown over the bed, and crawled between icy sheets that had so recently been more than warm enough. He had no idea how late it was—he wouldn't have heard the University Clock bell tonight if it had rung directly in his ear. But as they lay together, half-dozing, Theron had suddenly said, "I have to go home tonight, you know. Sophia worries when I don't come home at all."

A small serpent of jealousy stirred in Basil's breast. "Sophia?"

"Lady Sophia Campion. My mother."

Campion, Campion . . . An old family, but fairly minor in the great scheme of things. Basil knew plenty of dead ones. There was a Bertram Campion who had seen King Tybald slain at Pommerey; a Raymond Campion who had written a monograph on ancient campaign maps. But what the Campions had done lately, he had no idea. He'd have to ask someone, discreetly.

The serpent stilled, Basil had helped the young man disentangle his shirt and breeches from the bedclothes, watched him dress, and kissed him in parting. "Tomorrow," Theron murmured against his mouth. "I'll see you tomorrow."

Basil blew out his candle and smiled into the darkness. They hadn't talked about history after all, or much else, for that matter. Tomorrow, Theron had said. There would be time to talk about many things tomorrow. And perhaps for day upon day after that.

chapter VI

L ONG BEFORE THE KINGS RODE SOUTH, EVEN BE-
fore the Southern lords had claimed their noble titles—
before, in fact, the city was anything but a collection of
huts and fishing boats, its inhabitants were concentrated on a
tiny island in the midst of the river. When they expanded to the
eastern bank, they built a cathedral, and a fort to defend the
river, and a school that would grow into a University, and a Hall
of Princes and a palace and all the outbuildings that government
demands.

The Hall of Princes became the nobles' Council Chamber,
the Fort a prison for important people, and the University burst
its walls to take over the government buildings; but people went
on living on the little island, known as Riverside. Of course, as
the rest of the city grew, Riverside came down in the world.
Steep-roofed old townhouses still lined its narrow streets, but bits
of their elaborate stonework had given way to the elements and
bits had been stolen to replace other bits. When Theron's father
first lived there, Riverside was the haunt of thieves and swordsmen and worse. In these latter days they had not altogether aban-

doned the district, but now the pimps and pickpockets shared the crumbling buildings with poets and musicians and artists waiting to be discovered where the rent was cheap.

Lying between two banks of the river, Riverside was still an in-between sort of place, too full of poor people to be grand, but too well-loved by its various inhabitants to be truly degraded. It boasted a sort of ramshackle palace built (by Theron's father) of old houses strung together, which sheltered a number of dependents and an infirmary run by Theron's mother. Things had a habit of changing quickly in Riverside: people's fortunes, their lives, their expectations. And the buildings witnessed it all, unmoved. In Riverside the past slept, but it slept lightly.

B ETWEEN WAKING AND SLEEPING, A YOUNG MAN LAY dreaming in his high, curtained bed. He dreamed that his hands and feet were bound, and that a dark figure was standing over him. He smelt wood smoke and musk, and thought, "I have dreamed all this many times. But this time, it is not a dream, and I will have to—" But he could not remember what was to happen next.

The dark figure came closer, choking him with its animal smell. "Think, Little King," it said, and Theron drew a deep breath and choked and cried out and woke up.

He lay in the darkness of his curtained bed, soaked with sweat, his heart pounding. It was the King Dream again, returned to plague him. It had been years: not since he was a child, and had run crying to his mother night after night, wailing, "The King Man! The King Man, Mama!" Sophia had tucked him in, and sung him songs from her native land, about a goat and a little boy on a bright hillside. . . . Well, he could hardly run to her now. But he could untangle himself from the knot of sheets, and pull back the curtains and see if it were day yet, or still night. And if it were day, he could ring for his valet to bring him something for the headache he realized he had, something to take away the metallic ghost of brandy haunting the back of his throat. There was no help for dreams, but Terence knew all about curing hangovers.

Theron struggled upright and tugged the curtains aside, letting in a cheerful glow from a newly made-up fire. His conscience clear, he rang the bell.

Theron's bedchamber was in the oldest of the ancient mansions his father had cobbled together to make Riverside House. None of the doors fit properly, the floors slanted, and the windows filtered the light through thick, green glass that transformed the brightest sunshine into an underwater murk. Theron loved it. His room boasted such charms as carved paneling and little steps up to the deep, shuttered windows. Best of all, the room was at the top of a stair that led to an outside door, so that no one need be bothered by late-night comings and goings.

A soft knock at the door heralded Terence, carrying a covered cup on a tray. He shook his head when he saw his master, but said nothing except, "We're nearly out of this particular tisane, sir. And you asked me to remind you that you're to dine on the Hill tonight. The blue velvet is clean and brushed, but if you'd prefer the russet, tell me now so I can sponge the stain."

Theron sipped the tisane, fragrant with licorice and chamomile, and sighed as its warmth soothed away his headache and the last of the dream. "The blue will do just fine, Terence, thank you. Is my mother in?"

"As to that, sir, I cannot say for certain." Terence picked Theron's breeches from the floor and smoothed them over his arm. "Cook was making an omelet when I went for the tisane, sir," he admitted; "I'd venture to say that Lady Sophia is at breakfast."

Theron flung back the rumpled bedclothes and slid from the bed, shrugging himself into his dressing-gown. "Never mind my hair, Terence, just give me a ribbon. I don't want to find the breakfast-room occupied only by dirty plates."

A few minutes later, Theron was striding down an uncarpeted flight of stairs and into a long, white-plastered hall that led to the breakfast-room, where his mother sat frowning over a folio volume propped against a porridge-bowl.

Lady Sophia Campion would have laughed to hear herself described as a formidable woman, but it was true nevertheless. She'd been born on the distant island of Kyros, and her dark eyes and olive skin marked her out as a foreigner no less than her slight accent and her habit of saying precisely what she thought. She always wore black—in mourning for Theron's father, she said, the love of her life, who had died twenty years ago, two months before the birth of his only son. Privately, Theron thought she continued to wear black because it was a practical color for a woman who never knew when she might be called upon to stitch a wound or deliver a baby.

"You're up early, my dear," she said without looking up from her book. "The toast is burnt, but the porridge is warm and the milk quite fresh."

He came around the table to kiss her cheek, caught sight of an illustration of a human belly cut open, with all the guts colored a garish pink, and averted his eyes.

"Good morning, Mama."

She looked at him narrowly. Conscious of his unshaven cheeks and heavy eyes, Theron sat with his back to the window and busied himself with chocolate and grater, sugar and milk and whisk and cup. "What are you reading?" he asked.

"Tanner on surgery," she answered. "You'd better go back to bed when you've breakfasted if you intend to dine at Katherine's tonight."

"Nothing I'd like better. But Doctor Tipton's lecturing on Divisions and Definitions this morning. And there's a friend I've promised to see in the afternoon."

Lady Sophia sighed. Attending a two days' labor did not make her feel her age as much as dealing with her only son these days. He'd always been susceptible, going at love as if it were a parlor game to be played with as many different partners as possible. Well, he was young, and it was only right that a young man be allowed his freedom. She had certainly taught him everything he needed to know about preventing unhappy accidents of the flesh. So his love affairs had never caused her much anxiety until he'd fallen into the web of that spider disguised as a woman, that Ysaud.

Lady Sophia turned the page with a vicious snap. In the months since Ysaud had tired of him, Theron was much improved. At first he had sulked in Riverside House, hiding from the inevitable gossip that swirled outside. Slowly he had ventured out to his classes, to Riverside's musical taverns and to family parties, and finally back to the Hill's society balls, where his absence had been noticed. But he still seemed perpetually tired, as though the effort of being around other people was draining him. And as far as she knew, he always came home at night, alone. She was annoyed with him and worried in equal measure; but he wasn't a child anymore, to be scolded or coaxed or lectured into reasonable behavior. All she could do was to love him, and wait for experience to teach him a little sense.

"You don't get enough rest," she said mildly.

"Now you sound like a mother." He lifted the chocolate to his lips and blew upon it to make little creamy ripples chase one another across the dark surface.

"I sound like a physician," Sophia corrected. "A mother would worry about your heart as well as your health."

Theron smiled into his chocolate. "My heart is very well, Mama."

Her eye still on Tanner, Sophia missed the smile. "It would be worse even than breaking your heart, if Ysaud should have frozen it." She glanced up at her son, who looked peeved. "Yes, I know you will not speak of it. Your father was the same. I do not understand it. Every physician knows that a wound must be searched if it's to heal cleanly."

She paused hopefully. Theron, avoiding her gaze, picked a piece of leathery toast from the rack and buttered it. Sophia sighed and changed the subject. "I've a demonstration this afternoon—a simple goiter for the first-year surgeons. Would you like to attend?"

Theron said, "I fear that watching you cut into some poor old man's goiter no longer counts as a high treat for me." She stiffened slightly, and he looked contrite. "I'm sorry, Mama. That was badly put."

"It was. But if you behave as a child, it is that I treat you as one." As always when she was upset, Sophia's grammar strayed toward the forms of her native tongue. "Well, it is no matter. I will demonstrate the excision of a goiter and you will see your

friend, and we shall meet at Tremontaine House in the evening."
She looked him sternly in the eye. "Shall we not?"

"We shall, Mama. And I further promise to be there in good
time, so that Cousin Katherine may have ample opportunity to
tell me what a fribble I am before the other guests come and family loyalty forces her to hold her tongue."

Sophia shut Tanner. "As you wish," she said gently, and rising, gathered up the book and went to the door. She was so obviously trying not to scold him that Theron got up to open the door
for her, put his arms around her, book and all, and murmured into
her ear, "I *am* sorry, Sophia. I shall spend the day in pursuit of my
manners, and I promise to find them before I set foot in
Tremontaine House, which I further promise to do at a decent interval before dinner."

Against his cheek, he felt his mother smiling. "If you do that,
Katherine will think you a changeling. It is sufficient if you come
in time for the soup. It's only a family party after all, with Marcus
and Susan."

Theron stood away from her. She was a tall woman: their
eyes were almost at a level.

She kissed his brow. "Until tonight," she said, and strode
away from him down the corridor to the grand staircase that led
to the front door. Theron returned to the breakfast-room, poured
his cold chocolate into the slop bowl, made himself a fresh cup,
and drank it before ringing for more toast and a steak.

⌒

THERON WAS NOT PRESENT AT DOCTOR ST CLOUD'S
lecture on the reign of Gerard the Last King. Basil was not
really surprised, but he was disappointed. He'd hoped young
Campion would be interested in his ideas as well as his body. I'm
as much of a fool as poor King Hilary, he thought bitterly as he
described Gerard's bloody additions to the rites of the Festival of
Sowing. And Hilary had had the excuse of being mad.

Reluctant to return to his cold rooms and his love-tossed
bed, Basil sought food and warmth at the Blackbird's Nest. The

first thing that met his eye was Doctor Leonard Rugg sitting with his back to the room, staring morosely into a bowl of snapdragon gone cold. Basil went up to him. "You're looking glum, Rugg. What's the matter?"

"Nothing important," said the metaphysician. "I don't want to talk about it. The bitch." He gestured at an empty bench. "Sit down, St Cloud; have a drink. Have you heard the latest?"

"Probably not."

"You should get out more." Rugg peered at him over the rim of the bowl. "You look pale. You need to stir up your blood. I'll pass along my mistress if you like—the bitch. She'll stir anyone's blood."

Basil snagged the potboy, ordered brandy, and settled back. "Is that the latest?"

"Oh, no, no. It's Tremontaine again. Trouble all 'round. Lady Sophia's trying to endow a chair for *women*, if you please—"

"Lady Sophia?" Basil sat up. He had heard the same name from Theron's lips not twelve hours ago. "Lady Sophia *Campion?*"

"That's the one."

Basil was aware that there was a certain danger in pumping the greatest gossip in the University for information about his new lover. But he thought he might manage the trick, with a little care. "I suppose young Campion's trouble, too," he said wisely.

"I wouldn't say that." Rugg started to look more cheerful. "Never saw anything wrong with him myself; harmless enough puppy—though I hear that last mistress of his did him some damage. Still, no harm in him. Been coming to lectures since he was a lad. Can't stick to a subject, loves 'em all: an academic flirt, eh? Still, he probably knows more about history than I do . . . and more about metaphysics than you do. What kind of trouble do they say he's in?"

Basil racked his brains for an unrevealing answer, aware that he was better at analyzing intrigue than engaging in it, even at this mild level. "Ah, disappointment to the family?" he hazarded at last.

"Ha!" Leonard Rugg roared. "It would take a lot of work for Campion to give his family a sleepless night, after what the father put them through!"

Basil tried to look knowing. "Yes, but . . ."

Rugg said expansively, "Oh, you're thinking of the Tremontaine Chair of Astronomy—certainly the old fellow did all that for us, and a great deal more besides. No one can say he wasn't generous to the University, although the women's mathematics scholarship created a considerable stir. But one can't imagine him as a *husband,* if you catch my drift."

Basil gave up trying to be subtle. "Leonard," he said as lightly as he could. "Who is Theron Campion's father?"

"Oh, don't you know? He's dead; be well over eighty now. Something in your line, I'd think, St Cloud, being history and all: he was Tremontaine, the Mad Duke. That one."

Basil said absently, "I don't do modern history," while his mind raced, trying to place the late Duke Tremontaine.

"No more do you," said Rugg, amused. "Listen carefully, then; there'll be a test when I'm done." He began ticking points off on his fingers: "Scandal number one: young noble went to University to study instead of to drink. Not done back then—not sure about now, either, but at least there's a pretense. Scandal number two: got kicked out, went to live with a swordsman in Riverside. Not done then either—living there, I mean. Not like now. Watch wouldn't even go there then. Scandal number three: inherits Tremontaine and fills the house with scholars, reprobates, and lovers of all, ah, shapes and sizes. Men, women, even historians." He dug his elbow into Basil's side. "If you know what I mean. The list goes on and on. Bestowed a rather colorful bastard on the city, too, though I hear she left town long ago. Scandal number . . . What was I up to?"

"Four," said Basil, fascinated.

"Scandal number four: he was driven into exile, passing the duchy to his niece, the Lady Katherine Talbert. Then back he comes, years later, with a beautiful foreigner in tow, who claims to be his lawful wife, and conveniently produces a legitimate heir two months after the Mad Duke's death."

"And the beautiful foreigner is the Lady Sophia."

"Damned queer woman. But odds are the boy will still inherit on his cousin's death."

"Inherit the duchy?"

"So it really doesn't matter what he studies, does it?"

"On the contrary," said Basil shortly. "I think it matters a great deal. If there's one thing history has to teach us, it's the importance of educating the ruling class in the realities of life."

Rugg laughed. "They'll hardly learn that in University, dear boy."

"Oh, I don't know," a voice above them drawled. "Unheated lecture rooms, watered beer, incomprehensible feuds, indiscriminate sex, casual violence, and a general shortage of sleep seems uncommonly like real life to me."

Basil started as if he'd been shot. He wondered how much of the conversation Theron had overheard. He wondered whether the pounding of his heart were visible through his robe. He feared it might be.

Theron was speaking. "Doctor St Cloud, I wonder if I might trouble you for a word in private?" His light voice sounded annoyed, but that just might have been his aristocrat's drawl. Basil turned to look at him. The long mouth was hard and still.

Leonard Rugg punched him on the arm. "New student, eh? I wondered. . . . Well, congratulations, St Cloud. Don't take a copper less than twenty for the term. He can afford it, can't you, Campion?"

Theron smiled tightly. "Yes," he said. "I can."

"Thank you, Rugg," said Basil. "I'm not exactly new at this, you know." He rose and looked around the tavern. "There," he indicated an empty table with his chin.

Basil stalked across the room. The boy should have told him who he was; he should never have approached him in public; he might at least have smiled at him. Basil sat down stiffly, determined to preserve his dignity, and saw that Theron was convulsed with silent laughter.

"Was I perfect?" he chortled. Basil stared at him suspiciously. "Well, *Doctor* St Cloud?"

"Campion, are you mad?" Basil growled. "Or am I supposed to say, *Lord Theron?*"

"I'm sorry." The student wiped tears from his eyes. "I'm ruining the effect, aren't I?" He reached across the table, touched

Basil's hand lightly. The scholar's insides lit up like fireworks. "Let us discuss fees, then, so as not to disappoint Doctor Rugg. Tell me—" He leaned forward. Basil smelled his mouth, sweet with mint and the tang of his breath. "How much must I pay for another lesson like last night's?"

The green eyes were flecked with gold. Basil smiled. "I wonder," he murmured, "if you remember your lesson?"

"Perfectly," the boy smiled back. "I paid particular attention. And now I would know more."

"Would you, indeed?"

"You are the subject of my study, Doctor St—Basil. My desire is to understand you thoroughly, to uncover your mysteries, to pass examinations in your history and your tastes."

Basil laughed. "My history is not so interesting as yours, Master Campion."

"Oh?" said Theron, then, in a very different voice: "What has old Firenose been telling you? That I have a boundless appetite for men, women, and ponies? Or merely that I change lovers as often as I change suits of clothes? Not quite true. I deny the ponies. Are you going to bar me from your lectures?"

He looked at once haughty and so wounded that Basil reached out to him. Theron glanced down at Basil's hand, square and dark against his own fair skin, and smiled. "A tutorial," he murmured. "I've an hour free before Tipton's lecture."

TWO HOURS LATER, THEY LAY TOGETHER IN A WELTER of discarded garments and blankets. Theron's hair was spread over them both like a damp scarf.

"You're like one of the Forest Men in the old stories," Basil said dreamily, "the ones who could drive mortals mad with desire. But if you could get one to love you, they said you'd be young for a hundred years."

"And then what happened?"

Basil stroked a lock of shining hair around his finger. "You died of galloping old age."

"Ech." Theron shivered and pulled a random piece of fabric up over his leafy chest. "I've never heard that one before. Who told it to you?"

"Oh, my mother, probably. She knew a lot of stories."

"Really?" Theron was amazed at the things he and his erudite lover had in common. "So did mine! But they're all from Kyros."

"I'd like to hear them someday."

"Mmm." The end of Theron's hair had somehow found its way to the soft skin inside Basil's elbow, and was making quiet havoc there. "But mostly she told me about my father. You know, the famous Mad Duke. Who wasn't a duke by the time she married him on Kyros—and not mad, either, at least by her account."

"A flexible fellow."

"You have no idea. My father," Theron went on, warming to his theme, "was a colorful character. I thought, when I was younger, that I would try to be more colorful still. Finding that to be impossible, I settle for pleasing myself. A variety of lovers is a family tradition, really."

"It's an older tradition than that," Basil informed him. "Hollis tells us the most ancient kings were encouraged to take many lovers of both sexes. The wizards—"

"Wizards and kings," interrupted Theron, "are not of any great interest to me right now. They're dead, after all."

"And so are Aria and Palaemon and Redding, and all the other great poets and playwrights you rhetoricians swear by." Basil pulled himself upright against the pillows. "The past is never dead, Theron. It lives on in the present, in our laws and our customs, even in the way we think and speak. Stop that, Theron, I'm making a speech."

Theron lifted his head and smiled. "It's a very good speech," he said, "and I don't disagree with you. I'm hoping to find immortality through my poems, when I finally write some worth saving. At the moment, though, I'm far more interested in you and your body and my body and the pleasure we can give each other."

Since he'd been busy with his fingers as he spoke, Basil was in no state to argue with him, and Theron's moment spread to encompass Basil's past, present, and future in one brief eternity of perfect sensation. They were just sinking into sleep when Theron sat up suddenly. "There's the bell striking five, and if I don't hurry, I'll be late to dinner again and I promised Sophia faithfully that I would be on time. Shall I see you tomorrow?"

He was out of bed now, picking up his clothes from the floor and the bed. Basil pulled the quilts around himself and watched his lover dress, stopping him once to kiss the oak leaf drawn along his collarbone before it disappeared under his linen shirt.

"You haven't told me about that tattoo yet," Basil said as Theron shrugged into his braided jacket.

"No," said Theron shortly. "I haven't. It's a long and silly story, and I don't want to waste our time on it."

He put on his cloak, then half-knelt on the bed to kiss Basil's mouth. Basil caught his face in his hand and held it firm. "I'll hear it tomorrow," he said. "Dine with me—I'll have Bet send up a pie. We'll have the whole evening."

The greenish eyes looked into his. "It may take all night," Theron said.

"Good," said Basil, his heart racing. "I like long stories."

chapter VII

To please his mother, Theron was not late
for dinner at Tremontaine House. He was, in fact, early,
which gave him time to wander about the wet gardens
of its impressive grounds. He was drawn to some of his favorite
childhood spots: the rose bower, where a few autumn blossoms
doggedly bloomed, and the boxwood walk, dotted with classical
sculpture. From old habit he touched the nose of the piping Goat
God for luck, and even walked past the Transformation of Laurel
with his eyes closed. He always used to hate the sight of the
young man being engulfed in bark. He was far too old for such
fancies, but he felt it again this time, a frisson of fear such as a
child feels, who dreamed and cannot remember what frightened
him.

There was nothing to fear. Life was good. He had a new
lover, the young magister, so brilliant, so eager; it was just what
he'd wanted, exactly what he'd dreamed of happening between
them all these weeks. But Ysaud, too, had filled him with this
crystal joy at first.

Theron broke a twig off and crushed it. Ysaud had chosen

him, seduced him, really, with her artist's eye and her craftsman's hand. Her master's hand. And he had been her masterpiece for a while. He smelled the crushed yew rich on his fingers and something else as well, and sighed with sensual pleasure. Basil, he had chosen for himself. Just when Theron had thought his heart was frozen forever he'd seen the magister in a tavern and been drawn to him, and wondered. And so he'd gone where Basil St Cloud had gone, watching him cast off those bright sparks of wit and insight, passion and faithfulness to learning that bespoke an honest man, a sincere man, a man to be pursued. For a while, Theron had wondered whether Basil's eye would ever fall on him at all, and if it did, whether it would regard him with favor. Now he knew.

Theron found himself looking straight up at the dangerous Laurel sculpture. Rain had washed some dirt down it, and lichen was growing there, making the sculptor's highly textured tree seem even more lifelike in the twilight. A young man with marble skin reached out beseechingly from the bark encasing his legs, his thighs . . .

> *As one who, human, offered not his fruit*
> *To one bright god*
> *Must live condemned to offer it to all.*
> *Ah! Bitter immortality! Majestic—something—*

He'd forgotten the rest of the verse. There probably was a copy in the duchess's library. Lord Theron strode through the gathering shadows into the bright-lit halls of Tremontaine House.

By the time he emerged from the library with the book he wanted, he was indeed late for supper.

THE DUCHESS KATHERINE'S GUESTS WERE NOT UNAWARE of Theron's absence, but for a variety of reasons were trying to pretend it didn't matter. They were assembled in a sitting room overlooking the river, furnished with comfortable peacock blue chairs, tables covered with curios, a card table with a game board, and a little escritoire in case anyone was suddenly struck with the urgent need to write a note. The duchess was deep in conversation with Marcus. Marcus's wife Susan was playing tric-trac with their youngest son, Andrew, who was simultaneously trying to explain the rules to Lady Sophia. Sophia, out of courtesy and the sense that she was never really going to understand the ways of her adopted country if she didn't keep making an effort, was trying gamely to be interested, but her attention kept straying to the two very pregnant young women seated side by side on the divan, their feet propped up on stools.

Diana and Isabel Ffoliot were identical twins. Both had married last year, but Diana was a bit farther along than Isabel, and Sophia was dying to ask her about false contractions. But Andrew was saying, "Now it looks like Mother's got me beaten. But if I can throw Doublets here. . . ." He picked up the dice. Sophia nodded absently.

"I'm starving," Diana growled to her sister. "Where's Theron?"

Their mother flashed them a warning look. Susan Ffoliot was looking forward to as pleasant an evening as could be hoped for considering the family's various colorful personalities. "Pass your sisters the biscuits," she instructed her son.

The twins were Theron's age, and as close to sisters as he could get; he had grown up tumbling about with Susan's brood in their cozy house as much as he had in the imposing mansion of the Duchess Katherine, or his mother's rambling Riverside home. He had always prayed that neither twin show any interest in scholarship; either one of them at the University, choosing to open her mouth, and he would be ruined. They knew far too much about him.

Diana took two biscuits, frowned, and put them down again. "I'll bet you anything our Theron is still in bed somewhere. Maybe we should send out the dogs."

Isabel snickered. "Oh, hush, Di. Mother says he's a reformed character."

"Mother," said her twin, "doesn't know him as well as we do. I would say it's just taking him a while to creep his way back up from the slimy bottom of whatever well that artist was keeping him in."

Lord Alexander Theron Tielman Campion chose that moment to enter, bright-eyed, in a swirl of long hair and a blue suit that didn't really go with the room. "Sorry," he said to everyone; "I was here, didn't Farraday tell you? I just ducked into the library to look something up. I thought you'd start without me."

"Hello, Alexander," said his cousin Katherine, Duchess Tremontaine. She'd used his actual first name. Not good. "What were you reading—nothing modern, I imagine?"

Oh, wonderful. He'd just walked in the door and managed to put her back up already. He darted an eye at the gravid twins on the sofa; they returned the look blandly. No help there. He dealt the duchess the most charming smile he could muster. "How well you know me. Poetry, actually. Did you know you have a hand-scribed copy of Aria's *Transformations?*" He really didn't feel up to Katherine before soup. She'd be a lot more agreeable when she'd eaten.

Fortunately, Marcus stepped in. "Katie," he said to the duchess, "consider the source." There he stood, graying and bland, the perfect factotum: Marcus Ffoliot, marshal of the Tremontaine fortunes for the past forty years. He'd taught Theron to spin a top. Right now, Theron wanted to kill him. "Allow me to observe," Marcus went on with mock severity, "that, as a point of law, being *in the house* does constitute being *here;* although the status of the library as a separate branch limits . . ."

". . . limits all our access to dinner." Laughing, Katherine finished the sentence for him. No one else knew what the two of them were talking about, but they were all used to it.

"I think dinner is an excellent idea," said Susan Ffoliot. Marcus's wife had long suspected that she was the only person of the whole menage who understood how families were actually supposed to operate. But she enjoyed watching the rest of them playing at it, and so she interfered only when things threatened to get out of hand. "With your permission, Duchess?"

After the soup, matters improved. The twins unbent enough to answer Theron's inquiries about their absent husbands, and even to tease him about his hair. Mostly they discussed childbirth with Theron's mother.

Lady Sophia did, however, ask about Aria's *Transformations*, which got everyone onto the subject of the statues in the garden. Interest in things Tremontaine was always acceptable at the dinner table.

Susan Ffoliot gave Theron a grin. "I am so glad those statues are there. The girls learned such a lot about human anatomy without my ever having to explain it to them. Andrew, sit up straight or you'll grow up hunchbacked."

Andrew shrugged his shoulders and hunkered down in his seat.

The conversation at the duchess's end of the table had shifted back to current affairs. Katherine was leaning across the table, making a point to her old friend and confederate. Theron heard her tell Marcus, "And now the Serpent wants the Crescent's man to look into it, though I can't imagine what for. I refuse to get dragged in, that's all; it's nothing to do with Tremontaine. Let Hartsholt worry about it; it's his land."

Theron wondered what Basil would make of the group gathered at the family table. He made a note never to try and explain to Basil that Marcus and Susan *were* family. It would probably serve as further proof that the ruling classes were somehow decadent—not that Theron would call Katherine decadent, himself. A woman near sixty who rose at five, did paperwork for two hours, and practiced the sword before breakfast was not his idea of the thing at all.

He took a bite of fish just as Katherine turned her attention to him: "What about you, Theron? Do you hear anything about the ancient kings there at University?" He nearly choked. "Or are you studying geography these days?"

"Rhetoric, actually." Theron coughed, and waved away the helping hands. "Language. Are you talking about Tortua's lecture?"

"Poor Doctor Tortua," mused Sophia. "He was so lively when he was young; I remember him at one Sowing Festival being very silly with a painted pole. I suspect a seizure of the brain, though Treadwell thinks it's an excess of bile in his liver."

Katherine tried not to look annoyed. "I was talking about the

City Sessions, not University gossip. Honestly, doesn't anything penetrate those streets from outside? And they say that the Council of Lords is out of touch with the City! I bet you didn't even hear."

"Didn't hear what?" Diana asked. "Do you mean that lunatic standing up in open Sessions and petitioning the Mayor for the kings to be reestablished? My husband told me. Everyone in the banks was talking about it."

"Kings." Isabel shuddered. "Just what we need. Power-mad tyrants pushing us all around. Who on earth thinks that's a good idea?"

"The kings weren't all bad." Theron hated ignorance. "If you go back far enough, you find—"

"Death to tyranny!" shouted Andrew. It hadn't been that long since he and his friends had played Wizards Against Nobles up and down the stairs, and he knew his lines. His sisters shushed him.

"It's the North," his father said. "They're having terrible times up there, with the weather and rotten harvests. Either too much rain or too little. How they hope a king will help is beyond me, but it seems to be the way people think: that radical troubles call for radical change. What did the Duke of Hartsholt say about this kings business?" he asked Katherine. "Was he there?"

"Hartsholt miss a meeting of the Inner Council? He loves getting the chance to dress up almost as much as I do."

It was true. If the formidable duchess had a weakness, it was clothing. And she had a wide range to draw on. From her earliest days in the city, when her uncle, Theron's father the Mad Duke, had had her trained as a swordsman, she had worn men's clothing more often than not. But she also possessed a notable collection of ball dresses. Tonight the duchess was wearing a gaudy, shapeless over-gown, the sort she favored at home, where she fondly believed what she looked like didn't matter. She had quite a collection of these, in various jewel-toned velvets and silk brocades. She tended to throw them on over just about anything and consider herself dressed. Once Theron was sure he'd seen her dine in one over a nightshift.

"What's amazing," she continued, "is that Arlen himself was there, all got up in his Serpent Chancellor robes. I was surprised; he doesn't usually so honor us. But with Lord Horn beginning another term as Crescent, and Edmond Godwin stepping down as Raven although we specifically asked him not to—well, Arlen must have wanted to show where he stood, with the Crescent and Dragon."

Marcus leaned over the table to his young son. "You have not, of course," he said, "heard any of this."

It used to work with Theron when he was that age: the implication that all political discussions were very secret and important, that he was not to understand them—and therefore would try as hard as he could to decode them. He'd even followed Katherine and her staff into the Council Hall—where he'd discovered that the sessions of the Council of Lords did not consist of men garbed as mythic beings fighting for great causes. The chancellors had colorful names and colorful robes, but it was only symbols. (He'd actually dreamed of being Dragon Chancellor someday, until he found out all it was was Chancellor of the Exchequer.) Half the Council of Lords behaved like a theatre audience, and the other half like boring lecturers droning on and on about taxes and rights of property and procedure. Even the exclusive meetings of the Inner Council, comprised only of the ducal houses and the elected Chancellors, which he'd been permitted once to attend as Katherine's heir apparent, was far too much like just another grown-up party, without any drinks. Finally, it all boiled down to a lot of bad-tempered people trying to disagree without appearing to be rude to each other.

Still, it kept things running, and he'd be doing it himself some day—a thought that gave him no pleasure at all. Now he had the idea that the duchess would be very pleased if he contributed something to the discussion she'd begun. "The University," Theron said, "looks at the kings from another angle. Not political, but historical."

Katherine gave him a long look that was meant to be benign, but failed. "And I'm sure that's very interesting. But when you're ready to come and join us here in the present, I hope you'll let me know."

Theron stood his ground. "But history is what has created the present!"

"Theron," Marcus said indulgently, "it's theory versus application. You can't win."

"You need a theory to apply!" Theron protested.

"But a theory based on what? On present fact."

"On precedent."

"Precedent says that monarchy is a useless form of government," Katherine put in. "That's all the history we need to know." She wrinkled her nose. "How can you stand to study that stuff? Dates and treaties; I never could abide it."

"Our very own rights and privileges come from precedent," Theron persisted. "If we want to maintain and perpetuate them into the future, don't you think we need to understand why?"

"Here's a future for you," Marcus grinned. "Right now, Hartsholt's lands are in disarray, and his son is running him into debt. He has two daughters. Marry one of them, and you can add huge Northern holdings to Tremontaine."

"I wouldn't allow it," Katherine intervened cheerfully. "The North has never been anything but trouble. Theron's going to have to look elsewhere for his bride. Have you considered anyone new lately, cousin?"

Andrew sniggered. Oh, to be thirteen again, Theron thought enviously, and just shrug his shoulders and glower.

"Stop tormenting the boy," Susan told her husband and his employer. "This is a dinner, not a Council meeting . . . honestly. More peas, Theron?"

His mother said to Susan, "I never know if you're just being kind, or if this is something I still don't understand, of what is all right to talk about with food, and what is not?"

Susan opened her mouth, but her youngest son spoke up unexpectedly. "It isn't the food, Lady Sophia, it's the meal. Dinner together," he quoted piously, "is supposed to be a pleasant occasion."

"So," Sophia reiterated: "nothing to do with human bodies, dead or alive or in transition . . . this I understand for many years, now. But—no business? Or"—she glanced at Theron—"just no business my son doesn't want to hear?"

The duchess applauded. "I do love hearing you figure things out, Sophia, it makes it all so much clearer. But honestly, Susan, all any of us is interested in is business of one kind or another. Can't the family get some kind of exemption? Or is it all to be Andy's latest kickball match, and whatever Theron is studying?"

"I study, too," Andrew objected.

"Of course you do," said his father warmly. Marcus persisted in adoring all his brood, no matter what sort of difficult stage they were passing through. "Your schoolmaster tells us you're a wizard at spelling."

Theron said, "You've still got him in school, Marcus? Let me know when you're ready to get him a tutor. I know plenty of good men at University who could use the employment."

Andrew kicked his chair leg. "I like school. We play ball at the breaks. And anyway, my master says that University men know all too much about all too little—whatever that means," he added, hoping to save himself from a scolding.

Lord Theron laughed. "I'll bet he does. But you see, Andy, learning can be a joy in itself, when you find something that interests you."

Andrew gave him the age-old look the young reserve for the idiocies of their elders.

His very well-mannered father said, "Thank you, Theron. When he is ready for a tutor, I'll ask you for advice."

"It's not that we haven't thought about it," Susan added. "If Andy takes to a subject when he's a little older, we thought he might go straight to University." Andrew made a face. His mother gave him a look.

"In any case," Marcus went on, "while we'd be glad to help out any of your friends, Theron, I hardly think teaching a city man's son is the prize they're aiming for."

"Well, of course most of them would love to devote themselves to pure scholarship, but that being a starving sort of proposition, I expect they could be induced to teach this brat the astrolabe," Theron said fondly.

Katherine dangled a golden ring over her wineglass; she had a habit of taking her rings off and on during a meal. "What Marcus meant, Theron, is that I'm sure the post they'd all be aiming for would be something on your own staff, when you have one."

Susan and Lady Sophia exchanged a look across the table.

Theron said haughtily, "My friends are not aiming for any sort of position."

"Oh, come, my dear." Katherine was doing her best not to provoke him, but her best wasn't very effective, since she was not one to back down on a point. "I'm sure they're very fond of you, but they know that when you take your place in Council there will be important positions to be filled. University men are ideal to fill them, and you seem to know them all."

"I know them well enough to know a friend from a toady."

The Duchess Katherine took a long drink of wine. Her face emerged from the goblet a reasonable shade. She said mildly, "I should like to meet these admirable friends of yours."

Concerned for her feelings, Sophia said, "Theron does not have his friends to the house, not even in Riverside with us."

But the duchess was just warming up. "I wonder," she asked the air, "what is so particularly unappealing about Tremontaine House? Jessica never wanted to bring anyone here either."

"You can't compare Theron to poor Jessica," Susan Ffoliot put in unwisely.

Katherine ignored her. "I have entertained a great many people in this house, at this very table, in fact. Few, if any, have ever complained of the comfort, the food, or the conversation."

A glacial stillness descended on the room. Marcus was looking at Katherine with puzzled concern. He never understood what made her pick at her heir, and privately she admitted that she didn't really either. "It's the way he just closes us off," she essayed once. "It makes me want to break him open—to see what's in there, maybe. If anything is at all."

Theron was priding himself on not losing his temper. He might be a great disappointment, but at least he maintained his self-control and dignity.

Sophia grieved, not for the first time, over the trouble between her son and his cousin. Sophia loved Katherine with the fierce loyalty of a stray who had been taken in out of the storm, given a safe place to raise her son and support in her chosen career. She loved the duchess for being a woman who commanded and did not care what people might think. At the same time, Sophia felt protective of her; she knew how hard it was.

None of these feelings was useful when Theron and Katherine butted heads. But Tremontaines, she had discovered, could almost always be distracted by asking them a question with a complicated answer. She was sifting her brain for one, when Diana, who had been oddly silent, let out a shout.

The girl looked sheepishly around at the startled faces. "Sorry. This has been going on for days. That one just surprised me, is all."

Sophia glanced from her sweating face to her untouched dinner and said, "You'd better walk about for a bit. I will attend you."

"I'm sure it's nothing." Diana waved her away, then yelped and clutched her belly. "Oh, dear. Is this it? It is, isn't it? What happens next?"

"I will tell you as we walk," Sophia said. "It is not proper dinner table conversation." She helped Diana to her feet. "Marcus, take the boy home and send word to Martin. Theron, ask Farraday to send to Riverside for my bag. Oh, there's no need to hurry. First babies are never anxious to come into the world. Sit down, all of you, and eat your fruit."

Whatever people might say about the Tremontaines and their habits—and they said a lot—Sophia was still one of the best midwives in the city. Sure enough, Diana's son was born the next day, having already done much to improve the atmosphere of the family circle.

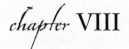 *chapter* VIII

THE AIR GREW CRISP, THE LEAVES IN THE HILL GAR-
dens colored, and ripe nuts fell from the chestnut trees.
Basil St Cloud found that regular physical satisfaction
sharpened his mind. He was getting more work done in less time,
the patterns of fact and opinion lurking in the documents he read
leaping to his eye as they'd never done before. Chastity was bad
for you—he'd always suspected it. He was contemplating writing
up a paper about it for the natural scientists.

He was walking home from the University Archives, his
head full of Theron and the problem of Article Twenty-four in
the Treaty of Union. His feet were pretty much looking out for
themselves, and he'd surely have come to grief if the students
weren't so accustomed to avoiding the erratic path of a man lost
in thought. He was just considering the significance of the
Wizard Mezentian's stipulation that King Alcuin could take as
many mistresses as he pleased, provided that none of his bastards
could inherit the throne, when he became aware that someone
was tugging on his sleeve. Basil swore and turned around to face

something like a tall pile of rags crowned with a shock of iron-gray hair.

"Foster Rag-and-Bone," he said, stifling his irritation. "It's been a long time. Do you have anything for me?"

The shock of hair split to reveal three brown teeth. "Something," Foster Rag-and-Bone said. "Looky here and see."

"Here" was the wooden handcart that served as Foster's shop. Just now, it contained a bundle of rags that looked to be someone's worn-out bed curtains, some tarnished brass lamps, and a small and battered wooden chest, bound and clasped in pitted metal. Not iron, it wasn't rusty—bronze, maybe. Old, at any rate. Very old.

"What's in it?" Basil asked.

"That's the question, isn't it?" Foster sneezed juicily and wiped his nose with the heel of his hand. "Don't have the key, do I? Might be valuable, might be shit. It'll cost you twenty silver to find out."

"Twenty silver?" Basil laughed. "For a moldy chest full of someone's ancient linen? Do you think I'm soft in the head?"

" 'S not linen," Foster insisted. "Heavy; shifty. Like papers or books or boxes. I know."

"Linen." Basil was enjoying himself. "Ancient handkerchiefs and stockings, all packed up neatly for storage."

"Too heavy. Books. Papers. Letters. I should know the sound by now, I've been looking that long for you."

"Old bills, then. Shopping lists. The odd love letter, if I'm lucky, from someone history has forgotten to someone history remembers. A book on cheese making. I'll give you one hundred coppers."

"Fifteen silver. History remembers these papers. There's a crest on the lock, see?"

Basil peered at the lock. The metal was severely corroded, but there was definitely something there: A deer? A tree? Nothing he recognized in either case, but interesting, definitely interesting. The chest itself reminded Basil of some of the older document boxes he'd seen in the Archives. His heart began to race. This could hold something very important indeed. How much money did he have? Not fifteen silver, at any rate. And Foster Rag-and-Bone did not believe in extending credit.

"It does look a little like a crest," he said to Foster at last. "But it's not one of the great families, or I'd recognize it. Five silver, and if you think you can get more for it from someone else, you're welcome to try. Remember, though, that someone else might actually care how you came by such an ancient and valuable item."

Foster Rag-and-Bone grumbled and Foster Rag-and-Bone whined, but in the end he nodded his verminous head and spat on the pavement to seal the bargain. He followed Basil to Minchin Street with his handcart and waited in the entrance, exchanging amiable insults with the scruffy boy while Basil ransacked his rooms for the strongbox in which he kept his students' fees. It contained precisely fourteen silver coins and a handful of coppers.

"There's another copper in it for you if you carry it up to the landing," he told Foster when he'd counted out the silver coins into his hand.

The scruffy boy interfered. "Not a step further—it'll take me all day to get the smell out as it is. I'll carry the box for you, Doctor St Cloud."

It was indeed heavy, too heavy for the boy alone, and the contents did indeed slide and thunk against the sides as books would slide. And it was locked fast. After some thought, Basil sent the boy down to his nest for some oil and a feather and a wooden wedge and a hammer, with which he forced the lock as gently as he could manage. When he was done, it would never lock again, but the crest wasn't much more damaged than it had been. The hasps were all but frozen shut, but he released them at last and the trunk opened reluctantly, with a screech of hinges. Inside were bundles of yellowed paper tied with tape: letters, folded and sealed with colored wax. Swan, Tower, Phoenix, Raven—that might be interesting. Basil smoothed the brittle page on his desk and peered at the spidery writing. *Wheraas . . . Nort Countree . . . Wizards their exemption . . .* that next word had to be *taxes,* or maybe the one after. Not very interesting after all.

He'd found their like before. Still, he'd have to comb through them carefully, later, just in case. A good job for one of his students, that.

Next was a pair of finely bound notebooks that announced themselves as the daybooks of the Wizard Arioso. It seemed to contain notes on the daily life of a court wizard of some three hundred years back, judging by the language. Interesting indeed, possibly exciting in a slightly distasteful way, and likely to shed some light on whether or not the wizards believed in their own lies. At least Arioso wrote a fairly clear hand and used expensive ink that had not faded. Basil scanned a page eagerly for the name of the ruling king. Oh, there it was: "A plague of rattes in Treymontayne—King Rufus, hys eye being to the Duke his datter, did commaund of mee thatt I ridde the playce of them." Too bad. Rufus was one of the boring ones.

Another packet of papers crumbled when Basil touched it—a pity, but such things had happened before, and there was no use mourning over them. That left a square package wrapped in yellowed linen.

Basil picked it out of the box—it was remarkably heavy for its size—and laying it on his lap, eased aside the folds of cloth like petals. A book, quarto size, its brown leather binding sueded with age and damp. Stamped on the cover was an oak leaf, its gilding all worn away save for a few bright flakes. Basil stroked the spine with one finger. The leather suddenly reminded him of Theron's skin, cool and a little sticky with drying sweat. He sat for a moment, lost in erotic reverie, his hands idly caressing the book. When he came to, he wasn't so much shocked at what was going through his mind—it had often enough, since he'd met Theron—as at the strange vividness of it, as if he had the boy there and naked before him.

Hurriedly, he wrapped up the book without looking at it, packed it in the document box with the rest of the papers, and slid the whole under his bed. Wizards' journals, indeed! He might as well have bought a box of pornographic sketches. The contents of the document box were intensely interesting, even historically useful in a perverse sort of way, but not at all respectable. Worth five silvers, though, no doubt about it. Basil smiled. It

wasn't often he got the better of one of Foster Rag-and-Bone's
bargains.

S OME WEEKS AFTER HIS INTERVIEW WITH LORD ARLEN,
Nicholas Galing found himself on his way to the Middle
City. His attempts to penetrate University society had yielded
very little save frustration. All that his frequenting of taverns had
taught him was that Northerners drink cider, not ale, and, like
nicely-brought-up children, refuse to speak to strangers. Even the
Southern scholars had not been welcoming. University people,
he thought, were like virgins at a ball: there was no getting near
them without an introduction. Nicholas didn't want to get near
them. They bored him glassy-eyed, with their long hair and their
long words and their impractical ideals. Yet his instincts told him
that Arlen was right. Something was going on—he could feel it
running under the most innocuous conversations like a hidden
current. What he needed was help, and the only man he trusted
to ask for it was his old playmate and lover, Edward Tielman.

Somewhat to Nicholas's surprise, Edward Tielman had done
very well for himself after University. He had impressed Julian,
Lord Horn, with his Fellowship in Metaphysics and his calm
common sense, rising from general dogsbody to private secretary
in an indecently short span of time for a man who was neither
well-born nor beautiful to look at. And Lord Horn had risen at
the same time; Edward's employer had recently been elected
Crescent Chancellor of the Council of Lords. On his patron's ele-
vation, Edward had bought a little house off Tilney Market between the Council buildings and the Hill. It was a part of the city
Nicholas seldom frequented, so he hired a linkboy to lead him.

It was raining like arrows in a siege, a vile night for walking.
The linkboy squinted at the fine gentleman in his dandified
caped coat and his fancy boots and asked hopefully, "D'ye want
me to fetch you a chaise, sir? It's cruel mucky underfoot."

"No," said Nicholas. "I prefer to walk."

The linkboy shrugged his opinion of men who ruined their
boots and gave themselves chills slogging through the wet when

they could perfectly well afford to ride, thus robbing poor boys of their cut from the chaise-drivers. "Where to, sir?" he asked.

"Fulsom Street," said Nicholas.

The linkboy hoisted his torch and trudged off stoically. The follies of the rich were no business of his and he was already wet through. Nicholas, on the other hand, was soon uncomfortably chilled and damp. Pride kept him walking, however, and before long his guide had led him from the wide streets of the Hill to the Middle City, where houses and shops stood side by side and the linkboys gathered on street corners, ready to carry bundles for housewives out shopping or light their husbands home for dinner.

As they passed Dupree's chocolate-house the door opened, releasing two gentlemen in earnest conversation and a blast of cinnamon-flavored air. Nicholas hesitated. He'd been there once with Edward, and it did smell so warm and enticing. Alerted by the sixth sense common to his profession, the linkboy appeared at Nicholas's side. "That'll be three coppers," he said, "if you ain't going no further."

Nicholas made his decision, gave the boy his coppers, and pushed into the noisy, fragrant room. He was immediately rewarded by a familiar voice hailing him: "Lord Nicholas! What good wind blew you here? Come and sit down."

It was Edward Tielman, in the midst of a convivial group of clerkly men. Nicholas nodded courteously, but made no move to join them. "I was just on my way to your house," he told Tielman. "Got a craving for a quiet evening by another man's fire, watching his wife darn socks. Came in here to warm my feet." He stamped to demonstrate how cold they were. "Lucky thing, eh? I'd have had to walk home again if I hadn't."

"Can't imagine why you walked in the first place." Tielman slipped his cloak around his shoulders, threw some coins on the table, and held out his bowl of chocolate. "Take this for the road, Galing—it's still quite hot—and we'll be off. Felicity *will* be pleased."

"To see you, you dog," said Nicholas, and drank off the chocolate. It was typical chocolate-house stuff—too sweet and not strong enough—but it was hot. He realized just how wet and cold he really was.

Tielman's house wasn't far from Dupree's, and soon enough Nicholas found himself seated by the fire in Tielman's bright parlor, a pair of borrowed slippers on his cold feet, a borrowed dressing-gown around his shoulders. Everything in the room was very cozy and comfortable, even the pretty brown-haired young woman in a loose gown, who was adjusting Galing's coat over a chair back and making sure his boots were the proper distance from the fire.

"We don't want them to scorch, do we?" she asked rhetorically. "Really, we should just let them dry by themselves—any degree of heat whatsoever is *fatal* to good leather, but it takes forever!"

Nicholas liked Felicity Tielman. She was the daughter of the richest wool-merchant in the city, a man who kept a house in the country that he was too busy to visit. She was as well brought up as any daughter of the nobility, and much better educated than most. He bore her no ill-will for taking Edward from him—she hadn't. When Nicholas had come to the city and the noble who was then Raven Chancellor had taken a fancy to him, he had discovered that he preferred a man of power in his bed. These being somewhat hard to come by, he'd made do since with men from the docks and the services offered by discreet establishments catering to specialized tastes. Edward was welcome to his Felicity. She was the perfect wife for a rising politician.

"There," she said, resuming her chair and picking up her tapestry-work. "Soon Fedders will be here with the soup, and then you will be perfectly comfortable."

"I am already perfectly comfortable," said Nicholas, sipping at a tumbler of hot rum punch.

"Wonderful!" said Tielman. "Then you can tell me all the gossip. Horn keeps my nose so tight to that infernal Corn Bill, I've no chance to think of anything else."

Felicity set a stitch with an impatient little jerk. "Men! All they talk is scandal, which *they* call politics, and then they have the effrontery to call women gossips!"

"I'm sure I never called you a gossip, my dear," Tielman protested. "I've always maintained that you were as disinterested as the Court of Honor and at least twice as discreet."

"I'm not impressed," said Felicity, unmollified. "As far as I know, twice nothing is still and always nothing."

"You must confess she has you there," said Nicholas.

Tielman shrugged. "I never went in for mathematics. Very well, my love. You may never gossip, but I am starved for it. What news on the Hill, Galing? I want to hear everything."

Nicholas launched into a lively description of Lady Nevilleson's last ball, with all changes of partner, both apparent and speculative, fully noted. Felicity exclaimed in pretended shock and rang for cold meat and wine. The conversation wandered inevitably onto politics. The Corn Bill came in for a particularly thorough examination, in which Felicity bore an enthusiastic part until she chanced to catch sight of the pretty gilt clock on the mantelpiece.

"It's past midnight," she announced. "It's no wonder you're making no sense—you're tired. I'm going to bed. You may stay up and talk nonsense as long as you like. I'll have Fedders make up a bed for Lord Nicholas."

"No," said that gentleman, rising politely. "I've a word of business to drop in Ned's ear, and then I'm off to my own bed."

Tielman laughed. "Why is it," he inquired, "that one may easily stay up until dawn in company, but is yawning at midnight in the bosom of one's family? We'll finish the bottle, Galing, and then, if you don't care to sleep here, Fedders will find you a chaise."

"Do," said Felicity cordially. "I have a novel to finish; it's due at the library tomorrow. You'll be doing me a favor by keeping Edward for at least an hour longer."

Nicholas thanked her, kissed her cheek in a brotherly manner, and settled down into his chair again. Despite the rum punch and wine, he felt his mind to be as clear and sharp as a winter's night. It was time to broach Arlen's matter to Edward. He took breath to speak.

"Dear girl," said Tielman, resuming his chair. "She's in the family way, you know."

"Is she, by Heaven! Congratulations, Tielman. You must be very pleased."

"Yes."

A silence fell between them.

"Strange business last Sessions," said Tielman thoughtfully. "No telling whether there's anything in it beyond a madman and moonshine. Still, it never hurts to be sure. I'm entirely at your disposal."

Nicholas stared at him, a prey to complicated feelings. At last he said, as temperately as he could, "I understood it was a se‑cret."

"Oh, it is," Tielman assured him. "Not even the Crescent knows that Arlen is putting his oar in. Officially, it's a tempest in a teapot, something for the old farts to shake their heads over af‑ter dinner. He doesn't want a fuss made. That's why he's put it in the hands of such politically small fish as the two of us."

"Small fish," murmured Nicholas. "I see."

"Small," said Tielman, "but daily growing. And we could be very big fish indeed if we scotch the plot in, er, the bud."

"If there is one," said Nicholas dryly. "You were never any good at rhetoric, you know."

"Nor was I. I am, however, pretty good at organizing things, which is a lot more useful."

"And I, it seems, am good at being told what to do."

Tielman looked at him sharply; the unsteady firelight cast a stranger's mask over his plump, good-natured face. "Nose out of joint?" he asked sympathetically. "It needn't be. You know he hates telling anyone anything straight out. There always has to be something held back."

"Everything's a test," said Nicholas bitterly. "I just wish I knew what he thinks he's testing."

"Don't think about it, Nick—don't think about him, or what he's testing, or you'll come to grief."

As he leaned forward earnestly, Nicholas found himself re‑sponding to Tielman's presence as he hadn't since they'd first been lovers. Being the Crescent's secretary had changed the stew‑ard's son in ways Nicholas hadn't seen until now. The Crescent's secretary was at the center of power, with access to the Crescent's ear and, through him, to the whole Inner Council. Edward—kind Edward, simple, hard-working Edward—was getting to be a pow‑erful man.

Nicholas blinked and sat back. "Of course," he said. "Silly of me. Now. About those royalists."

There was a lot to talk about. Edward was an excellent inter-locutor, asking pointed questions, offering theories, analyzing data. He was of the opinion that the Middle City would collec-tively drown itself in the river before it would countenance the least hint of royalist sentiment.

"Romantics don't become bankers and shopkeepers," he said. "What my colleagues know about the kings is that they were much more interested in the country than the city and favored farmers and woodsmen over merchants and manufacturers. You won't find any royalists in the Middle City. The University, though. That's another kettle of stew."

"Stew indeed." Nicholas sighed. "I wish I knew how to tell what was gristle and what was meat."

"You need a scholar." Tielman drank off the last of his wine. "University folk don't like strangers asking questions. A pa-rochial bunch. Still, I think I can drum up a scholar to spy for you. I won't even have to tell him why, if I make it mysterious enough. Students, unlike bankers, are romantics to a man. And these days, with all the fuss over the Horn Chair, it's easy to tell where everyone stands on the subject of the ancient kings."

"Ah," said Nicholas. "The Horn Chair. I've heard bits and pieces here and there, but I confess the importance of the whole escapes me."

"Felicity will have finished her book twice by now. I'll tell you tomorrow."

"Felicity is probably fast asleep." Nicholas smiled a slow, cat-like smile he'd been told was irresistibly charming. "Tell me about the Horn Chair."

Tielman yawned. "The old Horn Chair of Ancient History will probably be asked to step down: ill-health, age—incompe-tence, really. At his last lecture, I hear he came this close to an-nouncing that the wizards' magic was genuine, if you can believe that." He yawned again, painfully. "Damn it, Nick. This can wait."

"But I can't." Nicholas leaned forward to touch the back of Edward's hand and left his own hand lightly covering it.

Tielman lifted their linked hands and kissed his friend's fingers before removing his own from their grasp. "This is going to be complicated enough, Nick," he said gently.

Nicholas shrugged, reached for the poker, and stirred the dying fire into a brief blaze. Edward collected the boots from the edge of the hearth and felt the leather.

"Still damp, I'm afraid. But drier than they were, if you insist upon leaving. It's not too late to change your mind about the bed, you know."

Suddenly Nicholas was very tired and rather grateful that Tielman hadn't accepted his offer. "No, Ned. It's kind of you, but no. I'll take a chaise, if Fedders can roust one out at this hour."

While Nicholas pulled on his boots—which were, indeed, damp and somewhat stiff—and exchanged the borrowed dressing-gown for his dry jacket, Tielman rang for Fedders and instructed him to summon a chaise.

"He won't be long," he told Nicholas when the man had gone. "As for the University problem, I'll see to it myself. There's not much I can do before Harvest—the Corn Bill, you know—and it's important to find the right man. I'll let you know. In the meantime, you need to arrange a drop-off for his reports. You won't want him to send them to Lord Nicholas Galing, of course."

"Of course," echoed Nicholas, who hadn't given it a thought until that very moment. "He can direct them to, let's see, Green's chocolate-house on Lower Hill Street, to the attention of Mr. Black."

"Very colorful," said Tielman doubtfully. "Very memorable."

Nicholas controlled his temper with an effort. "Tell him to address them to Nicholas, then—it's a common enough name. I'll have someone collect them every few days."

Fedders appeared at the door, red-nosed and damp, announcing his lordship's chaise. Tielman accompanied Galing to the door and insisted upon helping him into his cloak. "It's been like old times, staying up too late with you, Nick," he said. "We must do this again, soon."

"Soon. Yes," said Nicholas, and stepped outside. His breath plumed out of his mouth—it had grown much colder. He'd been a fool to let desire overcome his judgment like that—he blamed the hot rum punch. No more rum punch and no more desire, he resolved, not unless it furthered his purposes. But he had the chaise-driver take him to Glinley's establishment in Riverside, and spent the remainder of the night in the embrace of a beautiful and expensive man with white hair and pale, amused eyes.

chapter IX

EVERY NIGHT, BASIL DREAMED: YOUNG MEN WITH lithe bodies and long, braided hair raced and wrestled on a great field while he looked on, weighing them against each other in his mind. When Theron lay under him twisting in his passion like a fish hooked on a line, Basil sometimes seemed to enter the dreams in a waking state. The bright flashes of his pleasure seemed to be the flashes of sun on the young men's shields, his cries the ringing of the tiny bronze bells braided into their hair. And his arms holding Theron became the strong arms of an animal.

One night Basil woke alone with his heart shaking his chest, his lungs laboring, his mind muzzily certain that his dream sprang from something in the box under his bed. He found a lucifer and a candle, pulled on his shirt and gown, stirred up the fire, and unearthed the document box.

Not the packet of edicts and proclamations: they were as dry as week-old bread. Not Arioso's notebooks—he hadn't read them through, but what he had read suggested nothing like young men wrestling in green fields. That left the book with the leaf stamped on its cover.

Basil unwrapped it briskly, ignoring his reluctance. It was just a book, after all. An old book. He'd read old books before. It was his profession to read old books, the older the better.

The brown-black leather lay between his hands, swallowing the light from fire and candle, save for the sparks of gilding that lingered in the lobes of the oak leaf.

He knew it, then. Even before he opened it, he knew what it was. In it lay his dreams, and the dreams of many before him. Ancient as the Northern mountains, heavy as death, shrouded in linen, what else could it be? He opened it with fear, with awe, with trembling hands carefully wiped dry on his gown.

The pages were supple—some kind of skin, scraped fine as glove leather. They were covered from edge to edge with writing: a central block of text with notes swarming around its margins like gnats.

The text was no language he knew or had heard of: a lost language, a secret language marching across the fragile parchment pages in a square, bold hand. Some later hand had written headings in a comprehensible if archaic script: *For the Forcynge of the Trutthe, when Suspected of Treason; To Lend Glamore and Hony-tonge; For Callying upp the Wilde Beaste in a Man, Eche According to Hys Nature. For the Calmyng of Maydens at Progresse-tyme.*

Basil scanned the blocks of text, first eagerly, then with a sickening frustration. The letters were recognizable, but they seemed to have been strung together at random into nonsense syllables. Hollis and Vespas had been right. The book was unreadable. The wizards had been charlatans. Or else they hadn't. It was impossible to tell.

Tears of pure frustration blurred Basil's sight. The words danced mockingly in the firelight. One of them winked from the margin: "Guidry." Basil wiped his eyes and squinted: "To uncover such a coverynge," he read aloud, "would take the wit of Ca . . . no, Cephalus and the cunning of Guidry."

Guidry. He'd seen the name before. In Hollis? There was a place to start, anyway. And Cephalus—another wizard name, it had that slightly exotic flavor. He could send his students into the Archives, have them look up the lists of wizards, research some of the other names he now saw, scattered like candles around the darkly impenetrable central text. The hands were various, and their arguments obscure. "I did walk with it seven times, but waked only the seventh," one ran. And another, tantalizing, "This displeased His Maj., but when he has killed the deer he will think differently."

When he finally raised his eyes from the book, the window over his bed glowed with the pale blue-gray of dawn. Basil stood up and stretched. He was stiff and cold, and in a state of mental exaltation that surpassed delivering his first lecture, accepting his Doctorate, discovering the original Treaty of Union in the Archives. He had found the one book that would make it possible to revise not only the history of the City, but how it should be studied. In his two hands, Basil St Cloud held the lost Book of the King's Wizard.

A S THE TERM WORE ON, DOCTOR ROGER CRABBE began to give small dinners for select magisters of the Faculty of Humane Sciences. Wine flowed freely at these dinners, and the main topic of discussion was radical styles of scholarship.

It was a pity, Crabbe said, that some scholars should seek out the crass and sensational just to swell their coffers with the coin of the idly curious. This matter of St Cloud and his lectures on kings and wizards, for example. Anyone who said his lectures flirted with treason was simply ignorant: certainly kings had existed in the ancient North, and had their wizards, too, and they must have done *something* besides do coin tricks and oppress the innocent. (Pause for the inevitable laughter.) No, it was St Cloud's methodology that was at fault. Sending his students digging in the University Archives, teasing them with unanswerable questions, encouraging them to trot out antique and unprovable stories, and then treating whatever they found him as useful lessons from the past when in fact they were nothing but fairy tales.

It was clear St Cloud was only going outside the traditional historical sources and approved regimen of study for the notoriety it gave him. You had to remember that he was young. There wasn't an ounce of harm in the boy, really.

And the older magisters, who had always taught as they themselves had been taught, shook their heads grimly at what the world was coming to.

The malicious whispers seeped like marsh gas out of Doctor Crabbe's rooms and through the streets and taverns of University. The younger, more forward-thinking scholars waited anxiously for Doctor St Cloud's countermove. But St Cloud seemed to have lost what little interest he'd had in public life, giving his controversial lectures and vanishing again without so much as buying his colleagues a beer or pointing out to them that there were many documents of unimpeachable authority, some of them in the University Archives, which, although they may not have found their way into the holy scriptures of the accepted authorities, were available for anyone to pick up and read. And that these documents supported not only his theses, but his teaching methods. Instead, he neglected even his most intimate friends to such an extent that Cassius was ready to wash his hands of him, and even Rugg and Elton were annoyed.

Still, they tried to be sympathetic, even jocular, when he made a rare appearance at the Blackbird's Nest. "Ancient kings keeping you busy, Basil, eh? Wizards casting spells of solitude on you?"

Basil blinked. "Did I miss our dinner, Cassius? I'm so sorry. I was working on my book."

"And very diligent you are, too." Rugg cleared his throat. "But a book alone won't get you the Horn Chair. Now is not the best time for you to disappear into your study."

Basil eyed the metaphysician with annoyance. "How else am I to get my work done? Shall I make speeches on street corners, like Crabbe? It's much more useful for the ancient kings to keep me busy." His mouth twitched in secret amusement.

Had any of them cared to question the scruffy boy who kept the door at Minchin Street, he could have explained a lot. His fourth-floor tenant came in these days at odd hours, in the company of a long-haired student who tipped like a god. Sometimes they stayed in the magister's rooms together for hours at a time, and the boy made extra tips by running out on errands for wine and bread and meat pies—though seldom for candles, as before, and never paper or ink.

But no one asked him, and speculation ran unchecked.

I T WASN'T JUST BASIL'S RIVALS WHO WERE INTERESTED in the fate of the Horn Chair. The mathematicians at Bet's Good Eats were figuring the odds, and Basil's students were passionately monitoring their teacher's progress. They may not have known about his frequent visitor, but they certainly knew he always looked tired and he never wanted to come out for a drink. They were annoyed, they were worried, and they were as curious as cats.

Near the massive hearth of the Blackbird's Nest, up against one of the small-paned windows, was a table that was known as Historian's Corner. Blake and Vandeleur had staked it out when the weather began to turn cold, judging their money better spent on ale and tips to the potboy to save the corner for them than on wood to heat the little room they now shared. There they met and, in the magister's absence, subjected their observations on his recent curious behavior to the same kind of analysis he'd taught them to apply to historical texts.

"It's money trouble, count on it. He's spent it all on books and can't pay the rent."

"That's you, Lindley, not St Cloud," Benedict Vandeleur said. "No, it's his own book he's writing that's eating him alive. What I think is that he's out to win the Horn Chair. What do you think, Blake?"

In the weeks since he'd paid Basil St Cloud his student's fee, Justis Blake's life had changed utterly. He'd gone from being "of heaven knows what," the butt of Doctor Crabbe's humor, a country bumpkin hanging at the fringes of University life, to being Blake of Ancient History, St Cloud's follower. He was at ease among these men as he had not been among Crabbe's Modernists or the men he'd met in the Mathematics and Natural Science lectures he'd attended the year before. His friendship with Benedict Vandeleur had grown over evenings spent listening to a new fiddler or spinning laughing shop-girls through the energetic steps of a country dance at the Spotted Cow. Some spirited arguments had shown him that Lindley was not as much of a drooping violet as he seemed; Lord Peter Godwin, four years his junior, reminded him of his little brother back on the farm. Even Henry Fremont wasn't so bad if you sat on him from time to time. And Doctor St Cloud. Well, Doctor St Cloud may have been well able to argue his way through a brick wall, but he hadn't the common sense of a day-old puppy. Justis felt quite fatherly toward him sometimes.

Justis thought for a moment. "You think he's writing about the North?" he asked Vandeleur, who nodded.

"Of course!" Lindley exclaimed. "It's coming clearer and clearer in the lectures that you can't understand the Union without knowing the old ways. The magister's writing a book that will change the world."

Justis Blake had gotten used to ignoring Lindley's romantic outbursts. He said to Vandeleur, "And you think that'll get him the Horn Chair?" It didn't seem likely to Justis that a book in which kings and wizards, however ancient, figured as heroes and statesmen was likely to find favor with the Governors. But it was not his place, as the newest of St Cloud's followers, to say so.

"Who else is eligible?" Godwin asked.

Vandeleur frowned thoughtfully. "Well, Doctor Wilson, for one."

"Don't make me laugh."

"He has more students than the Ferret—Doctor Ferrule, I mean," young Peter Godwin observed.

"Have you ever heard him lecture?" said Henry Fremont. "Well, neither have I, even though I sat for an interminable three hours last winter watching puffs of steam rise from his mouth."

Justis smiled. It was a fair description of Doctor Ferrule's lectures, one of which he had obediently attended because Doctor St Cloud had told him to. "How does he manage to make a living?" he wondered aloud.

"He doesn't," said Godwin. Everyone stared at him. "He has money of his own," he explained. "He's a relation of ours, on his mother's side. He's not stupid, he writes books," he went on defensively. "He's the one who wrote the history of the University. And what he doesn't know about the House of Godwin isn't worth knowing."

"Oh," sneered Henry. "Is there anything worth knowing about the House of Godwin?"

Young Peter rose to the bait like a trout, and for a moment it looked as if there might be a scrap. But as Vandeleur prevented Godwin from crawling across the table, Justis came to the end of his train of thought and said, "Then it seems that Doctor St Cloud's only plausible rival is Doctor Crabbe. Whose scholarship is widely known to be more orthodox, and therefore more acceptable to the Governors. He has seniority, as well—almost ten years, isn't that right?"

Everyone nodded.

"However," Vandeleur said, "Crabbe's students are mostly loungers who contribute nothing new to their field. Many of them are nobles, who will not (shut up, Peter, you know they won't) continue in the University. On the other hand, St Cloud has revived interest in an obscure branch of history. There are more of us each month, as the word of his lectures gets out and men from other disciplines come to see what the fuss is about. That has to count for something with the Governors."

They silently tallied up the score so far. Lindley said, "What about those Northern boys who sit up in the gallery at LeClerc? Do they count for or against the Doctor?"

"Oh, them," said Henry Fremont, clearly feeling it was high time he got some attention. "Well, it depends on whether they're University scholars or stray actors from some theatre troupe. Those braids and beads in their hair make them look like they'll start declaiming the king's speech from *Fair Rosamund* or *The Wizard's Revenge* at any moment. Do you think they're taking notes, or are they just up there waiting for Doctor St Cloud to give them their cue?"

Justis remarked, rather wistfully, that he had never seen a play on a real stage; and the talk moved on to theatres and

actresses and whether lust for a boy dressed as a girl or a girl playing a boy really counted, and other similar questions that engage
the inquiring mind of youth.

T HE MAN WHO KILLED THE LAST KING WAS HIS BROTHER-
in-law, David, Duke Tremontaine. It was done perfectly
legally, through the Rules of Challenge. Thirty-three nobles from
the Council of Lords came together and one after another called
challenge on King Gerard. As was their right (and, indeed, their
duty), the King's Companions accepted each challenge on the
king's behalf. But they were a roistering bunch, chosen by the
king more for their ability to drink, gamble, and invent clever ways
to torture his enemies than for their fighting or diplomatic skills.
Some were old men, inherited from his father, mad Hilary the Stag.
Their swords were no match for the nobles, who had all been
training for some time. One by one they cut down the king's de-
fenders, until the monarch stood alone, facing Tremontaine.

The wizards might have tried to put a stop to this, but they
were nowhere to be seen. As soon as the king was dead, they were
condemned as well, rounded up and burned along with their
books. Their pupils were disbanded, killed, or sent into exile.

What the dead king's sister, the Duke Tremontaine's wife,
thought about it all is not recorded. Her husband was the hero of
his country, and surely that pleased her.

H OW DID THE DUKE KEEP THE WIZARDS OUT OF THE
way?" Peter Godwin brought up the question with his
friends at the Blackbird's Nest after the morning's lecture. It was
not a question he would have thought of asking a year ago: everyone knew that Tremontaine had invited all the wizards to a great
banquet and locked them in. But according to what they'd been
studying with St Cloud lately, the wizards were notorious for
knowing everyone's business before they did—"hearing thoughts

on the wind," Delgardie poetically put it, which everyone took to mean the wizards had a fabulous network of spies. But did they? If so, who were they? How were they paid? And how had they failed so spectacularly in the end, when it really mattered?

"He was rich," said Henry Fremont in disgust. "Trevor says he bound them in chains of silver and gold—that means money, obviously. The duke bribed people to keep them out of the way, or give them false information or something."

"Maybe the Council made promises with them to share power, which they never had any intention of keeping."

"Or Tremontaine did it himself, and turned coat at the last minute."

"Oh, it's hopeless!" Vandeleur groaned. "We're just inventing stories, like village wives. How are we ever going to *know* anything?"

"Dig, dig, dig," said Theron Campion cheerfully. "And keep on digging." He'd just come in out of the cold, and his face was flushed and cheerful. "Hello, Vandeleur, sorry you're suffering— you should have stuck to Geography, with me. At least there are maps to consult."

Benedict grinned. "Hello, Campion. I hear you're in Rhetoric now, so don't tell me about maps." He indicated the table. "Do you know these gentlemen?"

Theron nodded politely. "Godwin, Lindley . . . I'm sure I'd enjoy knowing all of you, but I was just wondering whether anyone had seen Doctor St Cloud?"

"He's never in here anymore," Godwin piped up. "Don't tell me you're thinking of switching to History now!"

"No, I'm enjoying Rhetoric, thanks. Poetry, parts of speech, no dates and no dust."

"Campion *is* History," said Henry Fremont snarkily. He knew perfectly well they'd met at least twice, and that Theron did not remember him. "He's a direct descendant of David, Duke Tremontaine. So tell us, Campion, what's the family secret? You're all so wildly successful. Is it brains? Beauty? Connections? How does a man become a hero to his country by knocking off a close relation?"

Basil would have recognized the way Theron's face went perfectly still when he was asked about his family. In response, Theron simply quoted Redding: " 'Inquire of the Dead, O inquire of them; but as they died, their answer will be blood, and blood, and blood again.' "

"Is that conduplicatio?" Vandeleur tried to lighten the mood.

Theron relaxed a little. "Diacope, actually: repetition to express deep feeling. But close, Vandeleur; very close."

A sallow young man at the other end of the table snorted: "Blood is right, Tremontaine. There's enough of it spilt, and enough on your hands. King Gerard trusted the duke. He'd given him his sister's hand in marriage. He loved him. And what did Tremontaine do? Killed him, that's what. Where I come from, we call that treachery."

A shocked silence ensued, broken by a few uncomfortable chuckles. Even Henry Fremont was speechless, staring with everyone else at the sallow young man. He returned their gaze truculently. Under his scholar's robe, he wore a threadbare doublet that looked old enough to have been his grandfather's. His dun-colored hair hung in a dozen tiny braids around his bony face.

Godwin said, "If that was a joke, Finn, it wasn't a funny one."

It was at that moment that Basil St Cloud entered the Blackbird's Nest.

"Doctor St Cloud!" Peter Godwin called out imperiously. "An interesting question has arisen." His voice broke halfway through the sentence, which, combined with his pomposity, was irresistibly funny to the men at the table. In the lull, St Cloud approached the group. When he saw Theron Campion there, he looked surprised. Campion nodded to him politely, and said, "We're just having a scholarly debate. I expect it will be over soon."

"Well then," St Cloud said formally, "pray do not let me interrupt." And he sat down to listen.

Henry Fremont took this as an opportunity to regain the upper hand and show off. "The question is this: was David, Duke Tremontaine, called the King Killer, a hero to the country and a liberator of his people, or was he a traitor to his king?"

"Rhetorically," Theron answered carefully, "he could be both, since they are two different things. Unless, that is, you consider king and country to be one and the same." The historians nodded. St Cloud had made the same point in a recent lecture. "If I read Hollis correctly, the wizards considered them so, and the kings did, too: for them, the king was the land, and the land was the king. But the nobles did not, and so it follows that the duke could at once be savior to the one and traitor to the other, without a speck of a stain on his noble character."

The Northern boy, Finn, burst in impatiently, "Very pretty, Master Rhetorician." Basil remembered Finn; he'd started coming to lectures three weeks into the term, and paid his student's fee in tarnished old silver coins. "But what would you call a man who murdered his own kin?"

"Well, it depends on why he did it," Theron said coolly. "If his relatives were irritating bores, I'd call him perfectly justified."

People laughed. But Alaric Finn was not to be put off. His sallow, bony face with its small narrowed eyes was like an old boot next to Theron Campion's animal beauty; yet he radiated a fierce passion that compelled attention. "I see," he said. "So much for scholarship, eh, my lord?"

The debate was drawing people across the tavern, including a few other boys who, like Finn, were decorated with those outlandish braids. Basil thought they looked self-consciously antique, like the old tapestries of King Alcuin's Companions.

"It's only what I'd expect," Finn added, "from a man claiming such kin."

One quick retort, and Theron would have the rest of them back on his side. But Finn's words made him catch his breath in anger, and he missed his moment. The other students pulled away, leaving Theron at bay in the middle of an angry pack.

Theron felt it. He slung off his black scholar's robe with showy gallantry. "Hold this for me, Godwin, will you?" Rolling up the white linen of his shirt sleeves, he addressed Finn: "So. You don't like my answers, and you don't like my ancestors. To whom do I have the pleasure of defending their honor?"

The Northern boy shook back his braids. "My name is Alaric

Finn. My father is Master Finn of Finnhaven. And I don't take gaff from a Southron whelp who claims kin to the False Duke who did old Gerard down."

Drawn by the smell of a fight, more men were drifting in. A clutch of young nobles, some in scholars' gowns, came up behind Theron. "Calling good old David false, is he? At him, Campion!" It was Lord Sebastian Hemmynge, a student of Geography by day, a haunter of ballrooms by night.

Young Lord Peter Godwin, who'd been drinking more than was good for him in the company of his elders, remembered an old grievance: "Watch it, Hemmynge! Your family got rich enough off Godwin lands after the Fall—"

"A loyalist?" sneered Lord Sebastian. "Isn't it a bit late for that, Godwin?"

Henry Fremont had wisely retreated to the edge of the circle. "Who says history is dead?" he remarked to Anthony Lindley. But Lindley had turned his dense blue eyes on Doctor St Cloud, who was watching the scene with silent abstraction, as though it were all happening off in a foreign country.

The tavernkeeper made his way through the crowd, his knuckles bristling with empty tankards. "Gentlemen, scholars, if you please—" He saw who else was there— "and my lords. None of that in here, if you please. Outside, the lot of you. Yes, you! And you, too . . . No, no, Doctor St Cloud, you stay put, sir— young men will have their studies, every way they can . . ."

The young men struggled out of doors, cursing and shoving at each other, retreading grievances two hundred years old and more. They formed a circle around Theron Campion and Alaric Finn, while Benedict Vandeleur tried to interpose himself between them.

"Come off it, men!" he reasoned. "Debate if you want to, but don't drag it down to the level of ruffians!"

A noble seized his elbow. "Who are you calling a ruffian?"

Theron, who had learned to fight on the streets of Riverside with boys much tougher than these, threw a punch at Finn's pointed nose, producing a dramatic jet of blood. Finn howled and swung at Theron; but before it could escalate to a free-for-all, Benedict Vandeleur took a happy inspiration from the rules of swordfighting, and shouted "Blood!" at the top of his lungs. "First blood!"

Everyone fell back a step as ancient order moved into place. Although dueling with swords was not a privilege of scholars, they knew what the rules of challenge were.

Vandeleur grabbed the arm of the foremost Northerner, a tall blond youth named Greenleaf, and announced, "We witness first blood to Theron Campion. Campion, are you satisfied?"

Theron looked at Finn, who was trying and failing to stop the bleeding with the back of his hand. One of Basil's students, the delicate redhead Lindley, was kneeling beside him with a handkerchief. "More than satisfied," Theron answered.

"Alaric Finn," Greenleaf asked in turn. "Is the quarrel resolved?"

Finn looked up, his bony face half-masked in blood, pure rage glittering in his deep-set eyes. Vandeleur felt Greenleaf tense, ready to intervene if Finn urged the quarrel on.

But Alaric Finn believed deeply in ritual. "Resolved," he snuffled.

"Resolved," echoed Vandeleur and Greenleaf.

The tension went out of the crowd as if a string had been cut. The Northerners bore Finn off with Anthony Lindley's handkerchief pressed to his nose. Shaking his head in disgust, Benedict Vandeleur drifted back into the tavern. Henry Fremont caught up with him. "Quick thinking," he said. "You probably want a beer." Which was as close to a compliment as he was likely to come.

Lord Sebastian and his mates had their arms around Theron: "Good on you, Campion—can't let that dirt-boy speak ill of our folk. We're with you—horsewhip the Northern bastard if he shows his face again in the Nest."

"It's nothing," said Theron. His temper had cooled to the point where he couldn't imagine what had gotten into him. He wondered whether Basil, whom he'd been hoping to impress, thought him a quarrelsome fool instead. "He'd probably had too much to drink."

"That's no excuse," said Hemmynge. "Why be a student if you don't know how to drink?"

"It's what *I* came to learn!" added a young scion of the Perrys.

"I'm sure it is," Theron muttered.

"So we'll see you tonight, will we?"

Over their heads, Theron could see the tavern door, and Basil coming out of it, studiously avoiding them all. "Tonight? Where?"

"The Harvest Feast at the Perrys', you rogue!"

"Oh, of course," he said; "wouldn't miss it!" Just that morning, he'd been telling Lady Sophia that he'd rather be hung by his heels down a well than have to face another annual rite of privileged debauch. But he'd known even then he'd have to go. He grinned bleakly as his peers slapped him on the back, then he hurried off to make a roundabout way to Minchin Street, where he prayed that Basil would be waiting.

B ASIL WAS WAITING, AND HE DID NOT SEEM TO THINK Theron a quarrelsome fool. He held him tightly, and loosed his hair from its clasp, and tangled his fingers deep in its folds.

"You are remarkable," the historian said. "Did you know that the oldest kings, the Northern kings, were war leaders?"

"Did you know," Theron mocked, "that the tip of your ear is beginning to resemble a delicious ruby? Those damnable Northerners, there's more of them every year."

Basil held him back at arm's length. "Don't speak that way, Theron. The land is united. It was united almost five hundred years ago, and many good men, and a great queen, as well, worked hard to create a union indissoluble. The kings fell, but the Union did not. Do not you make that division now. If Finn offended you, I'll speak with him."

"Heavens, no! I'll fight my own battles, thank you. Finn—is that his name?—is new here. I'm not. I've been coming to University since I was old enough to hold Sophia's hand and cross the street. I've heard just about everything that anyone can say about the Mad Duke or any other Tremontaine, not to mention women in the lecture hall, women in the surgery, and the getting of foreign whelps. I know how to fight. Now Finn knows that."

Basil said, "Yes. I understand. But perhaps it would be best if we two should meet here. And not at the Nest."

"Yes," Theron breathed in his ear. "I agree. It nearly undid me to see you standing there surrounded by your worshipers."

Basil grinned. "Why don't you come to my lectures, then? Come early enough, and you can watch me from the front row—"

"Right!" Theron launched himself forward enthusiastically. "And we can enact for your students some Living History—pantomimes, like a village ball: King Sebastian and the Wizard Guidry! The Seduction of Mezentian! King Anselm the Wise in the bushes with his favorite groom—ouch!"

"Oh, my lord," said Basil, rising above him. "These are not games for anyone but us. Understand that."

"I do," Theron gasped, knowing the play required an answer. "I was joking."

"Joke with the others," his lover said, "but not with me."

He took Theron with brutal efficiency, and then strung out the boy's pleasure till his lover mewed with frustrated desire. Theron's skin was as rich and dense as the covers of the book, the secret book, the book that he possessed as surely as he possessed this son of the ancient kings. There was nothing he could not do, owning them both. Behind the magister's eyes, wild boys twined ivy in their long, long hair, and words in a lost language danced on the edge of sense.

When they were both done, Basil wasted no time. "Off you get." He swatted Theron's rump. "I've a lecture to prepare for tomorrow, and the Governors' Harvest Supper is tonight."

Theron groaned. "I, too, have obligations."

"I weep for you." Basil was already up and dressing. He felt invigorated, ready to write his whole book in one night.

Theron reached out his naked arms. "Let me stay here. I'll be very quiet."

Basil chuckled. "I know you." He felt the power of sex tingle throughout his whole body. He loved the fastidiousness of his dry clothing against his still-damp skin, while he gazed on his naked, impossibly beautiful lover, stretched out yearning for him on the bed. "Come back," Basil said a little huskily, "tomorrow, after my class. I'll have plenty of time for you then."

＊

AFTER THE FIGHT, THE NORTHERNERS BORE FINN OFF to The Green Man. Situated in the cellar of a lecture hall, the tavern was small, damp, and even darker than the Blackbird's Nest. But its cider was decent, its owner was Northern-born, and a man could air his opinions there without worrying about some Southron noble taking offense at hearing the truth.

Greenleaf dropped onto a wooden settle by the fire. "Bring us cider, Wat, and a key to put down young Finn's back. Harvest's not the time for blood."

His friends heard this pronouncement with solemn deference. Roland Greenleaf was First Companion, Master of the Hunt and Keeper of the Mysteries in the Southlands. He knew things about the rituals of the seasons that none of the rest of them knew, except maybe Smith, who was Second Companion. Greenleaf was the son of an ancient family descended from the seed of kings, as all the oldest Northern families were, and as proud of his lineage as any duke. The white bars on his gown-sleeves proclaimed him a Fellow of the College of Law.

"That's the last time I ever set foot in the Blackbird's Nest," Smith said. "Historians! Fancy themselves, don't they, pissing on the kings and the wizards. They'd give a lot to know what we know, eh, boys?"

"They would," Finn snuffled through the clotted mess of Lindley's handkerchief. "Don't be so hard on them, Smith; you should come hear St Cloud lecture one of these days. He gets aw-fully close sometimes."

"That's as may be," Greenleaf said solemnly. "He's welcome to all that any man knows, North or South. But hearken, Finn: you know as well as I do that the Inner Mysteries are for none but our brotherhood. If ever I discover that you've breathed a word of them outside, whether it be in season or out of season, the Land will drink of your blood."

Wat brought a pitcher of cider and a large iron key, which Greenleaf picked up and dropped without ceremony down the neck of Finn's shirt. Finn gasped and twitched. Miraculously, the flow of blood stopped.

"Cheer up," said Smith. "It's Harvest Night, and a full moon at dusk. Time to encourage the rabbits and deer, eh? Is your Horn ready? I know mine is!" He was a large, bluff youth, thick as a northland oak, and even coarser grained.

Finn managed a smile. "Had I the power of the Horn in me, I'd have beaten that Campion."

"Don't be a fool," Greenleaf said wearily. "For all his titles and his land, Campion was raised in Riverside. He could have killed you. You serve Northern honor better by keeping your tongue between your teeth just now. We all do."

The Companions nodded. Ever since that lunatic Bloodwood had come down from Harden and set the city by the ears with his public demand for the restoration of the monarchy, they'd been treading carefully. You saw things differently, living down South. The kings were gone, and the wizards with them. What they'd left behind was mighty, though, mightier than these soft Southerners understood, or needed to. Tonight, the Companions would call up the shadows of the ones who had gone before. Crowned with horn, they would dance them into being, and take their pleasure with one another, as the Companions had done from time immemorial.

chapter X

THERON CONSIDERED THE EVENING BEFORE HIM
with an eye to whether he should start drinking now or
when he got there. The Perry Harvest Feast wasn't the
only one in town, but it was the biggest and best and most prestigious, so of course Theron had been invited. He was, after all,
heir presumptive to the Duchy of Tremontaine. His mother and
the duchess had received invitations, too, but Sophia said that
Harvest was one of the liveliest nights in Riverside and she
needed to be on hand for the burn cases and the knife wounds.
Katherine had taken a fancy to go down to her estates at Fernway
and celebrate there in country style—or so she said. She had
taken Diana and the new baby with her.

So Theron was left to face the Perry crowd alone. Lord
Perry's was the largest and most traditional of the private Harvest
feasts. There would be a bonfire, and dolls made of straw from the
harvest's end, shuttled down from the Perry country estates, to be
thrown into it. It all seemed ridiculous, to keep such country customs in the city, but since the autumn Season had begun, no noble family with any pretension to style would be caught dead in

the country, so they observed the practice here in town. The Perrys had a very large courtyard where a fire could safely be lit without danger to the shrubbery.

And because the Perrys were an old Northern family, there would be the Stag Dance, usually performed by homesick farm boys who'd come to find work in the city, re-creating the customs of home: holding up branches of horn as they leapt in rhythm to the eerie notes of a pipe and tabor, clashing the stags' horns together and leaping apart.

After the mock fight of the Stag Dance came a real fight, performed by professionals with sharpened steel. The Perrys always hired the best-known swordsmen for their feast, and guests who usually saved their money for the card tables had been known to lose it all in one bet on the outcome of the Harvest duel.

Interspersed with all this, there would be dancing, and enough food to feed a village for a week, and red wine sweetened with honey and cloves, which made it go down so smooth that even generally abstemious people inevitably drank too much.

And of course, it being the opening weeks of the Season, there would be bevies of fresh young ladies being presented to adult society as potential mates for its sons and heirs.

Theron decided that the earlier he arrived, the earlier he could leave. That way, he'd get the food and the bonfire, and miss the dancing and the debauchery. He had nothing against debauchery in the abstract, but he was particular about the details. In addition to its other splendors, the Perry Harvest Feast was an evening renowned for the pleasures it afforded unmarried young men. Once they had done their polite duty by the daughters of their mothers' friends, dancing country dances and fetching them honeyed wine, they moved on to stronger stuff. Their blood heated by drink and flame and the spectacle of men fighting with ritual horns and actual steel, their subsequent pursuits were heated as well.

Mothers knew that the Perry feast was the one to be seen at, but they also knew to hustle their daughters home after the swordfight. A girl who stayed too long at the Perrys' on Harvest Night got a reputation for being fast.

Theron hastened home to Riverside before sunset, had

Terence shave him, and put on a nice clean shirt and a very good suit of dark green wool shot with silk, which, Terence pointed out, hadn't seen action since the Lassiter girl's Birthday Ball. That must be why he hadn't been wearing it, Theron reflected; it was a very nice suit, but it had been a very trying ball. He had been besieged by marriageable daughters whose mothers had told them that the Tremontaine heir liked poetry. He'd escaped to the card room, where he ended up losing a great deal of money because he did not play cards very well. He always drank too much at these affairs, and he tended to lose the ability to add and subtract when he'd been drinking.

And so he set out, wearing a fur-collared coat, heavy boots, gloves, and a broad-brimmed hat in case of rain. The sun was setting out over the river in a glorious scarlet display and the evening breeze was sharp and chill. At a brazier by the bridge, he fired up the torch he'd brought from home, and lit himself up the well-known streets.

An hour later he arrived at the Perrys with the rest of the early guests. He was divested of his outer things and escorted to a dressing room where he could change into indoor shoes and have a man brush out his hair. Terence had fastened it with a gold ribbon. Terence knew about these things.

He shared the dressing room with one of his cousins, Charlie Talbert. They had gone to children's parties together at Tremontaine House, because the duchess believed in doing right by her brothers' families and making sure for Sophia's sake that Theron was always included in normal activities despite their unorthodox life. Theron and Charlie had little in common; but both had been well brought up, and Charlie knew that Theron was likely to be the head of the family some day. So he greeted him affably, "Theron! Good to see you! Happy Harvest and all that. Don't worry about being bored—thing is, there's to be a real fight, a decent fight, out in the garden after the Stag Dance. Rupert and Filisand are finally going at it."

"What's the quarrel?" Theron asked.

It was Charlie's turn to be caught short: clearly it was unthinkable to him that anyone in their circle should be without this piece of intelligence. But he was polite enough not to say so. "It's like this," he explained. "Rupert kicked Filisand's horse before the first go at Penning—or at least, that's what Rowland says—if you can believe him. I mean, everyone knows Rupe's sister gave him the one-up at Karleigh with a vengeance, so he had a bee in his roses, if you catch my drift. Not that it matters. The horse thing stands—it's a done thing, what with Penning clearly having gone to Rowland anyway. So what else could Filisand do? He sent challenge right after the White Rose Ball—you were there, weren't you? Well, the fight would have to wait 'til summer's end, when everybody's back, you know—and didn't that give Rupert time to sweat! See, the thing is, he has no idea who Fili's hired to fight! And none of Fili's friends are talking, either. Good man to trust with a secret. Not like some—anyway. Thing is, here's poor Rupers stuck with no idea what to spend on a sword: does he waste his allowance on the best man in town, just to blood some poor hack of Fili's? Or does he go for a hack himself—a stylish hack, mind you—nobody ever faulted Rupe for style—but a wedding-and-flowers sort of fellow—and risk seeing his nose cut off by a fancy blade of Fili's?"

The amazing thing, Theron thought, was that he understood almost everything his cousin was saying. Except about the horses, which didn't really matter. He just couldn't bring himself to take an interest in riding or racing. Swordsmanship he knew: the duchess had seen to it that he had several years of lessons, as she had herself—but unlike her, he hadn't kept it up. And he did not particularly enjoy watching other people's fights.

"Wonderful!" he said, bright as new silver. "I'll try and make it."

Charlie gave him the *I can't believe I just heard that* look that he knew so well.

Theron beamed even more brightly at him. "Where are the drinks?"

An hour later, his smile was beginning to slip. "I wish this were a masked ball," he told a nice girl whom he had offered to fetch flower water for.

She looked as if she were going to cry.

"Oh!" he said, realizing what he'd done in time, he hoped, to catch it. "Not because of you. Because of me. All this smiling. Don't you find it tiring? I do!"

"Aren't you having a good time?" she asked in a small voice.

"Oh, splendid," he was forced to say; "with you."

He fetched her drink and danced with her twice, and then it was time for the Harvest Fire and the Stag Dance. Baskets of little woven dolls passed amongst the guests. "Close your eyes!" his partner squeaked; "close your eyes and pick one!" Theron reached into the basket, and pulled out a figure with a crown. "Oh, look," she said; "you've drawn the King!"

He held it up to the light. "A Little King. I wonder which one he is? A good one or a bad one?"

"Weren't they all bad?"

"No, lady; not all."

She looked at him as if he'd farted, and then waved to a friend: "Look, Amalie, Lord Theron's drawn the King!"

The other girl came up with her escort. "That's so lucky. All I've got is a Companion."

"Me, too. Too bad."

"In the ancient times, the King's Companions were all possible kings," Theron explained kindly, remembering something he'd read in Hollis. "It wasn't until the Trial that the king was chosen from amongst them. So maybe yours will yet be a king, Lady Amalie."

She was giving him that look now, but only for a moment—then she changed it to an expression of wide-eyed interest. (He could imagine her practicing in front of a mirror until she got it right in time for her first ball.) "I never knew that. About Companions. Where could I learn more about it?"

"I read it in Hollis's history of the North. But there's a better book being worked on by a man I'm studying with, a Doctor of Ancient History at University."

The young lord escorting her broke in: "Ancient history— ancient *heresy* if you ask me! Kings and wizards." He made a face. "Best forgotten."

"Ooh," squealed Lady Amalie, "history—all those dates. I never could keep them all straight. That's something you men are so much better at."

After this exchange, Theron had little stomach for the bonfire and less for the Rupert/Filisand swordfight. He gave his straw king to his partner to throw into the fire, earning a smile and a melting look he didn't in the least deserve, and bowed himself away. Feeling hunted, he slipped from the ballroom to the refreshment table, where he procured a glass of wine and a cheese tart, and went in search of an empty room.

He thought he'd found it in the library; but when he peeked around the door, he saw a girl sitting at the library table, her braids brushing the surface of a large book as she read. She looked up before he could retreat and said, "Oh. Hello. Did you want somewhere to hide, too? You can come in if you like; nobody ever comes here."

She was still a child, really, podgy and uncomfortable-looking in a little girl's stiff party dress with too many ruffles. Theron hesitated, then shut the door and sat down opposite her.

"What's that?" she asked, eyeing his provender with interest.

Theron broke the tart in half and held it out invitingly. "It's cheese. Do you want some?"

She reached for it, retreated, blushed, shook her head unhappily. "Mama wouldn't like it," she said.

"Whyever not?" Theron asked, amused.

"It's not manners to take people's food," she informed him. "Besides, I'm too fat."

Theron laughed. "Half a cheese tart won't make any difference. And your mama need never know. Take it." They sat for a little in companionable silence, chewing, and then Theron said, "I didn't know the Perrys had a daughter your age."

"I am not a Perry," the girl said, rather indignantly. "But my mother is—on her mother's side. One of my sisters is actually named Perry. We're visiting. That's why I'm at the party. Really, I'm too young."

"What's your name?" Theron asked.

"Frannie—Francesca, really. What's yours?"

"Theron—Alexander, really. But it was my father's name, so I don't use it."

She thought this over. "May I have it, then?"

"What, Alexander?"

"Yes, I like it. I think it is an excellent name, and if you really don't want it, I'd like to have it."

"You'd look a bit funny as an Alexander."

Frannie blushed and fidgeted with her braid. "It's not for me. It's for a . . . friend. Well, not an actual person. Something I'm writing."

"So you're a writer," Theron said. She looked at him defiantly. He recognized that look—he wore it himself, still, when cornered into admitting he wrote poetry. The worst thing to do would be to smile; the second worst to tell her he was a writer, too. "Good," he said. "What are you writing about?"

The defiant look slipped through astonishment into eagerness. "An adventure," she confided. "There's going to be a swordsman in. I had planned to sneak out and watch, although Mama has expressly forbidden it. But now I think it is just as nice in here. Anyhow, my grandfather says that swordsmen aren't what they were. Did you ever see any of the good ones?"

Theron was about to object that he wasn't anywhere near as old as her grandfather, who might well have seen the likes of Harding, or even St Vier—but then he stopped. Richard St Vier had been his father's first and most famous lover. The house that Theron lived in had originally been his father's idea of a joke: an urban palace in Riverside, built outward from the crumbling old house he had inhabited with Richard.

Because of this, people sometimes expected Theron to be more than a little interested in swordsmen. Because of this, he had scrupulously avoided them. But, in fact, Theron had seen Richard St Vier.

"Yes," he told Francesca. "When I was a little boy. I used to wake up at night, when the moon was bright, because I could hear thudding on the wall. Like one very heavy drop of rain, paced and regular; it would keep up for a while, and then stop, and then start up again, sometimes fast, sometimes slow. One night, I got up to see where it was coming from. I followed the sound to a room down the hall. The windows were open. It was full of moonlight. And I saw a man practicing the sword against the wall, striking it over and over. That's what the thumping was. I didn't recognize him. My mother doesn't keep swordsmen—not active ones, anyway. I didn't say anything, and he didn't notice me; he just kept on practicing."

"It might have been a visitor."

"It might. We often have people staying with us. But here's the strange thing. When I went back to the room the next day, there were all sorts of chairs and tables and things that hadn't been there the night before—in fact, it was a room I knew perfectly well."

Frannie tightened her arms around herself. "Who was it?" she breathed.

"I finally asked my mother. At first she didn't answer. Then she told me that it was someone who'd lived in the house long ago, and who liked to come back sometimes; and that it was all right with her, so I was not to bother him."

The girl snorted. "Well, at least she told you that much. I hope you asked the servants."

He grinned. "I did. I asked my nurse. She knew right away. St Vier, she said. The greatest swordsman who ever lived. That's who it had to be."

"Oh my gosh! Did you go back?"

"I think so. I must have."

"How can you not remember?" she asked scornfully.

"Because it was like a dream. The moonlight, and the man, and me standing in the doorway . . . I can remember watching him, but it all seems like one long dream. I didn't hear him every night. Sometimes I thought I'd made it up, but then it would start again. I wanted to go find him one time because I wanted to ask him to come round in the day for once and take care of some boys outside who always made me play skellies with them but they made me put in two for their one." She made a sympathetic noise. "But either I didn't go, or I didn't speak to him when I did. Maybe I got better at skellies and forgot."

"Do you still hear him?"

"No. I haven't heard him in years."

She shivered deliciously. "I'd give anything to see a ghost. In the day, anyway. I will put one in my book. Not a swordsman, though, or people will think I stole it from you."

"Actually, not. I've never told anyone but you."

"After your mother and your nurse."

"Just so."

A smile lit on her face like a moth, dusty and fragile and not very beautiful, but alluring in its fragility.

"Are you sure you're really a man?" she blurted out unexpectedly.

Theron laughed, unoffended. "I'm sure. But you're not?"

"You don't talk like my brothers or my father," she explained. "And there's your hair. Men don't have long hair."

"University men do. It's a badge of honor."

"Mama says University is a very wicked place that encourages young men in bad habits." She propped her elbows on the open book. "Do you have bad habits?"

"Of course not—well, yes, I suppose your mama would think so. They're not very bad, or very interesting, and I won't tell you about them, so don't bother asking."

"I didn't think you would," said Frannie resignedly. "Are you married?"

"No," said Theron, surprised. "I'm not."

"Would you like to be?"

"I don't—no. Not just now."

"Why not?"

Why not? He thought for a moment, and another moment. Patiently, she waited, because she really wanted to know. He thought of all the things that were possibly true. But to tell them to the little girl, he would have to talk about very tedious adult things like duty and responsibility. While she might sympathize, she probably got enough of that at home already.

Trying to be helpful, Frannie suggested, "Maybe you just haven't met the right one yet."

Theron thought, But I have. And then he knew what to tell her: "I'm in love with someone else. Someone I can't marry."

She sighed with a romantic's innocent relish. "Oh my *gosh*— that is just *tragic!*" Shyly: "Would you like to tell me about it?"

"So you can write about it? No." Her face registered her disappointment. To keep himself from laughing aloud, Theron asked, "What about you?"

"I don't think I actually will get married. I am not clever or pretty, or good at sums or sewing. All I can do is make up stories, and that won't get you a husband." She spoke with absolute certainty.

"It would if he liked stories," Theron pointed out.

"Stories are for babies," she intoned fiercely, a lesson she had been forced to memorize. "Children like stories. Men don't like stories."

"Some do. And there's history—that's all stories, and men study them for years at University."

"Yes, but they're *true!* That's so utterly, utterly different." She hid her face in her hands, and he realized that he had in some way managed to betray her after all. He wished that he had not.

She mastered herself, and straightened, holding out her hand across the book. "It's been delightful to meet you, Theron—Lord Theron, I mean. I hope you pass a pleasant evening."

He bowed and said, "And you, Lady Francesca. I wish you all success with your work." He won a smile from her, and said impulsively, "In a few years, when your hair is up and you are presented to society, I hope that you will send me an invitation to your first dance. My name is Alexander Theron Tielman Campion, at your ladyship's service."

THE THOUGHT OF THIS GIRL BEING LACED INTO COR-sets and put on the market in three years or four depressed Theron utterly. He wondered if her mother and sisters would have drummed all the "nonsense" about stories out of her head before then, or if she would continue to perplex her dinner partners by talking about it. He didn't know which fate was kinder to wish on her. He had the impulse to call on Sophia to rescue this girl, as she so often rescued street orphans and kitchen drudges from poverty. But poverty of spirit was not the same, was it? He himself had fought it successfully, making a life for himself that satisfied the needs of his mind and his spirit, despite opposition from his cousin and his peers. But the odds faced by Sophia's son were not the same as those facing a nobleman's daughter.

He stood outside the door and considered fetching some

sweet cakes and sugared almonds to bring Frannie as an offering. But she had closed the door with such gentle finality, like a queen indicating that the interview was at an end.

So Theron reentered the ballroom and passed beyond it to where the young men were sharing whiskey in a corner of the conservatory, and entered the community of bad boys drinking, which required very little conversation, polite or otherwise. There was the Randall heir, young Clarence, and Sebastian Hemmynge, who attended geography lectures when he was sober, Ralph Perry, the son of the house, and Tom Deverin, down for his first Season in the city. Theron shoved Deverin aside on the stone bench, accepted the bottle of whiskey, and took a numbing mouthful.

Clarence Randall rose, knocking over a potted fern. " 'D better get back in there," he said. "M'mother'll want to know where I am."

"Oh, hell, Randall, don't be such a pussy boy," said Hemmynge. "Stop looking for your mama; let's go out and look for some *real* women."

"You insulting my mother, Hemmynge?" Randall was a handsome boy, with powerful shoulders and muscular legs. This was his first city Season, and it showed.

"Lord, no. I am spefic—speci*fi*cally not insulting her by not lumping her with the sort of woman one goes out and finds in—in our condition."

"I'm not drunk," said Randall inaccurately. "*You* may be drunk, but I'm not drunk."

"Nobody said you were drunk," soothed Deverin.

"Not drunk. Randy!" chortled Hemmynge. "Look here—I am a Scholar of the University." He smoothed his fair hair, which fell loose below his shoulders.

"What's that got to do with the state of your dick?" Perry razzed.

"Shut up, Perry. I'm *explaining* it to you. Because last year, St Cloud explained it all to us. About the Harvest time. It's when they killed the king."

"By god, you're right!" said Randall. "My great-great-something—yours, too, Campion, and probably Perry's as well—

did kill the king in the fall. I may not be a *Scholar of the University*, but I do know that!"

"You don't know jack," said Hemmynge. "Duke David killed him in the spring. That's why we have Spring Festival, idiot!"

Theron took another drink to stop himself from giggling. They were not so bad, these fellows. Really, they were not.

"Anyway, it symbolized something," Hemmynge went on. "Sex, that's what it was. We must go out and prove the rods of our potent manhood—give our seed to the land, for the good of the harvest!"

Deverin put his rose satin arm around Theron. "You go ahead. I'm going to stay here and prove my rod with Campion, eh, Theron?"

"No." Theron slid away. "I'm going to go, too."

"I thought you didn't—"

"Oh, get the hayseed out of your ears, Tom!" Hemmynge howled. "The lady artist, remember?"

Theron shoved the bottle at him to shut him up. It worked.

"All right, then." Randall drew himself up. "If we're going, let's go."

"Let's go," echoed Deverin, a little doubtfully. "Who's going?"

They pulled together into a ragged group. "So where to? Fat Madge's?"

"I can't go to Madge's," Perry objected. "I've got a girl there who thinks she owns me."

"Hey, Theron," said Hemmynge. "Take us down to Riverside, I hear there are great girls cheap in Riverside."

There were. And some of the ones who came to Sophia for abortions or cups of tea even used to demand when he was going to bring them some of his rich friends for trade. But Theron said, "It's too far. And it's raining."

"What about the girls in the kitchen, then?" Hemmynge persisted. "Maybe they'd like a little tickle."

"Maybe my mother would kill me," said Perry indignantly. "What kind of a house do you think we keep?"

"Well, then, it's Madge's," Randall concluded. "Don't worry, Ralph, I'll keep your girl occupied!"

They poured out into the rainy street, their cloaks pulled tight against the wet. They passed other revelers, their torches sputtering. Theron was enjoying himself—there was something to be said for just going out drinking and having a good time with people.

At Fat Madge's, the tables were laden with harvest fruit and quaint earthenware jugs of wine and little figures woven of straw into shapes that left no question of the purpose of the festivities. The room was crowded; plenty of people were out for a good time tonight. Theron switched from whiskey to wine and ate grapes and watched his friends pick out girls. "What about you?" a big woman kept asking him, but he waved her away like a fly. Like a fly she kept coming back, and finally she said, "You like a boy, then? I got a nice boy, he'll be down in a minute. Or two." She guffawed.

Theron said politely, "Thank you, I've already got one."

Madge laughed. "I'll just bet you do, sweeting. You sit here and give me a cuddle, and we'll come to what you like."

She engulfed his lap with her huge presence and layers of skirts. The woman smelt like rising dough. Her breasts were huge and soft, and he nibbled them experimentally.

"She loves you, Theron!" Hemmynge roared.

At the next table, a man with his long hair in a dozen thin braids laughed and said, "She always treats the new boys thus. Wait 'til she gets to know you!"

Madge wiggled into Theron's lap. "Now don't say you don't like me," she cooed, "when I can *feel* you do!"

"I'd never contradict a lady," Theron said breathlessly.

"Aren't you the polite one?" she said. "Seeing as how you're new here, and pretty besides, I'm going to give you a little sample for hospitality." Under the huge volume of her skirts, she felt expertly for his breeches, and unfastened them, and arranged very neatly for him to sample her wares.

When he sat back, spent, she played with his hair, which had somehow come out of its gold ribbon. "A learned gentleman, for sure. Do you have any money in your purse to buy me a cup of wine or a harvest token?"

Theron felt for his purse and found—nothing. It was gone,

and he didn't know how it had happened, or when. He felt a rising flush of shame and fury. He was a Riverside boy: brought up amongst sharps and former pickpockets, he knew all the tricks, and where to keep his money safe. No one ever, ever had slipped his purse before, not in Riverside, nowhere. And here in this "respectable establishment" he'd been had.

"It's you!" he roared, ignoring the fact that Madge would hardly have drawn attention to his purse if she'd lifted it. "You whoring thief—thieving whore—"

He was shouting, and a couple of big men were hustling him out the door. He struggled, and cursed, but they did not seem to care. He skidded on the wet street, soaking his knees in a slimy puddle. A linkboy came rushing forward with a smoky torch. "I don't have any money," Theron said—but as the boy turned away, he remembered: "No, wait, I've got money at home."

"Yeah, you and your sister."

"I haven't got a sister, you punk. Light me home to Riverside, and I'll pay you when we get there."

The boy spat. "You nuts? I don't go there."

"Just give me the damn torch, then."

"For no money? Right, asshole."

Theron stood stupidly while the boy disappeared down an alley. It was black as the inside of a pig's intestines, and cold and wet.

But if he started off downhill, eventually he would come to the river, and then he could find the bridge to Riverside. Which he did, staggering rubber-legged to his private door as the sky was beginning to lighten. He found his key in another pocket, and so saved himself the indignity of having to rouse the house to let him in. There was nothing he could do about the ruined breeches—he just left them on the floor for Terence to find, and hoped that Terence would have mercy and not comment in the morning.

chapter **XI**

THE NEXT WEEK IT SNOWED, THE FIRST SNOW OF
the season. Dirty gray roofs and carvings collected fluffy
white trimmings, like fur on an old robe. Basil lay in his
low bed under the eaves holding Theron in his arms. Theron was
mildly feverish from a cold. The fire was built up and every piece
of clothing Basil owned was piled on the bed.

"This is so nice," Theron murmured. "No one's ever held me
when I was sick—not since I was a child, I mean." He coughed
and sniffled. "Are you sure you don't mind?"

Basil tightened his arm around Theron's chest. "In Anselm's
day, physicians believed that the bodily humors must be balanced, cold against hot, dry against moist. It's all nonsense, of
course. We know better now."

"The greatest School of Physic in the civilized world—believe me, I know exactly what we know now. Or at least, I'm
closely related to one who does. You have no idea, Basil, what it's
like to have famous parents."

Basil nodded ruefully. "I do know. My father was famous
throughout four villages for his rages."

"You come from the country?"

"You know that."

"No," said Theron. "I thought you'd sprung full-grown from the University clock tower."

Basil touched the thin, sensitive lips. "Hush, if you want to hear. I grew up on a farm outside of Highcombe." He felt a flash of irritable pride. "My father's the cock."

Theron heaved himself up on one elbow. "The *what?*"

"The cock of the village, the man everyone comes to for advice. He's got a fair amount of power, my father, in his way."

Theron flopped down again, laughing. "The mayor's son. I'm sleeping with the mayor's son."

"You could say that, yes. My father would like that, to be called mayor of Highcombe."

"I've been there," said Theron. "Highcombe is mine—I hold it in my own right. There's not much of the Tremontaine lands that are actually mine, not yet, but that is. My father deeded it to me." He rolled to face Basil and gripped his shoulder, grinning from ear to ear. "How would it be, if we rode to Highcombe together, visiting my property side by side with you as my companion?"

Basil shook his head vehemently. "No. Under no circumstances. Never."

"Why not?" Theron cajoled. "Your father would be proud of you."

"My father would have apoplexy. Theron, my father wanted me to be a lawyer. That's why he sent me to University. I was to return to our farm with a thorough knowledge of the law, at the service of the St Cloud family fortunes—so we could weasel our way around the duchess's rules and tariffs, I expect"—he smiled wryly—"and add to our holdings and my sisters' husbands' holdings and in general to increase and prosper. I fell in love with the dead kings instead."

"No profit in that," said Theron wisely.

Basil sighed. "That's right. No profit in that. My father would kill me if he knew we were lovers. He hates Tremontaine almost as much as he hates the University."

Theron collected him into his arms. "Your father doesn't

want you to love me. But my father wanted me to love you. And mine outranks yours."

The light, precise voice sounded unbearably smug. Basil shook off his lover and swung himself out of the bed.

"What?" came Theron's plaintive voice behind him. "What did I say?"

"Your father—your dead father—lived off the fees my father paid him for the privilege of plowing and sowing and harvesting his land. As *you* live off those fees, if I understand you correctly." He snatched up a shirt—Theron's, he realized as it strained across his shoulders.

"I suppose I do," said Theron helplessly. "I'm sorry."

"It amuses you, doesn't it?" Basil went on, flinging the shirt back on the bed. "Having a base-born lover, someone who can adore you and be flattered by your attentions, like the poor fools Hilary commanded into his bed?"

Theron was sitting up now, naked among the bed-clothes, his skin flushed and damp, his long hair clinging to his body like a second vine. "Oh, Basil, I never thought . . . I'm sorry. Look, I never knew until this moment who your father was, and I don't care. You're a magister, a full Doctor of the University: here, you outrank me." He held out a white hand. "I admire you. I've said so. Don't you know I mean it?"

Basil stared down at him. He could see it all so clearly. This boy did not know him. He did not even know himself.

Theron started coughing again. He pulled the blankets up around himself, shaken with his hacking. Silently, Basil came in with him, and held him and warmed him. He handed him a cup of water, and held him while he drank it. "Lie down," Basil said. "I was wrong. You are not Hilary: not mad, not cruel, none of those things. You are Roland, the poet; you are Orlando the Fair; you are Tybald who died on the field of Pommery; and Alexander, your namesake, who died for love, died as a stag in spring."

Theron whimpered in his arms, "No. Stop it. You're making this up. I am none of those men."

"You are of their line, you carry their seed in you."

Theron tried to stop his mouth with kisses, but Basil pulled away. "Listen to me." He pinned Theron flat with his weight, gripping his wrists hard enough to feel the long bones under the flesh. "Now you will listen," Basil hissed, the words sharp between his teeth. "Do not deny me. I smell it in you, the blood of kings; I taste it on your skin, pounding in your veins; I hear it roaring through your heart."

Half-angry, half-laughing, Theron struggled under him. "If you keep talking treason," he panted, "I'll tell the Council on you."

"Be silent!"

Theron opened his mouth, his breath coming hard, but he made no answer. His eyes were closed like a dreamer's, moving under the thin eyelids. Basil kissed them, and kissed him where the bronze-dark hair sprang back from his temples. "Ah," Theron gasped. "It's so strange! It's all green leaves now—"

"Yes," Basil breathed. "Go on."

"And I'm running—I'm running—"

"Run to me," urged Basil.

"I'm trying—I see—but I can't find—"

But Basil knew what he could see; he saw it, too, and felt it through him: the leaves on the trees, clear as coursing water, clear as the leaves that flashed on Theron's chest. The men with the banners, the bark on the trees, the moss underfoot, and the almost unbearable pleasure of the course to be run, the transformation turned back on itself through terrible knowledge . . . "Run to me, Little King," Basil whispered, and Theron said, "Not now, not yet, I'm not ready—"

"Now!" Basil said, and it was finished, in a high, clear cry like a wounded animal's.

Basil laid Theron's head on his breast.

For a time, the only sound in the room was the hushed crackle of the fire and the lovers' slowing breaths. "Was that you?" Theron said dreamily. "You seemed like someone else. Frightening. Exciting."

Basil thought of his body burning with infinite power, shot through with white lightning. "It wasn't me," he said; "it didn't feel like me."

"It was you." Theron snuggled into his arms. "Wonderful. Pure sensation. You make me forget everything: who I am, who I'm supposed to be. Like magic."

⌒

DEEP IN THE NIGHT, BASIL TURNED HIS HEAD REST-lessly on his pillow. In his dream, he was thirsty for the water he heard as a bright thread through the dark. As he lifted his hands, he felt leathery leaves against them, flat and smooth and armed with spines. Holly leaves, he thought, and a space opened around him, filled with dim green light and the scent of water.

He was in a whispering, shadowy cave of oak and holly. There was no water in it, only a flat gray stone and a sword of antique design, a wooden cup, and a long, triangular blade that was sharp all along its length, with no handle to protect the wielder from its edges.

Basil took up the cup and walked to the far wall, which opened as he approached into a leafy tunnel. His cloak dragged behind him, catching on the spiny walls, rustling the dead leaves under his sandalled feet.

The Little King was holding vigil as he'd been instructed, squatting patiently by the sacred pool. Hearing footsteps, he dropped to his knees and bowed his head so that his many braids brushed his clean-shaven cheeks. He looked smaller than he ought, slighter, younger. But then he was kneeling and afraid— they all looked younger, kneeling. Basil held out his hand. His hand was broad and ruddy and heavy with gold rings. Basil wondered at this, and opened his mouth to voice his wonder. But the words came out quite differently than he intended, and the voice in which he uttered them was not his at all.

"Will you drink, Little King?"

"If you offer me the cup, I must drink, must I not?"

"If you wish to rule, you must."

The boy lifted his eyes, green as new leaves. "Will I rule, then?"

"You will rule."

The boy accepted the cup, dipped it into the pool, and lifted it dripping to his lips. When he'd drained it, he wiped his mouth on his wrist. "They say all kings are mad," he remarked.

Basil took the cup from him and dipped water for himself. "They are right," he said. "But you must remember that madness is a gift of the land. You will never come to harm as long as I am here to guide you." He touched his lips to the edge of the cup, smelled a thick, sharp tang, as of metal or blood, and woke to cold darkness, the smell of sex, and Theron's gentle snoring beside him. The next time he woke, it was midmorning, and Theron was sitting up in bed beside him, drinking from a wooden cup.

"I feel better," Theron said. "The fever's broken."

Basil seized the cup from him, drained it, then wrestled him down, entering his mouth with kisses until he felt his body's yielding. When Theron lay warm and satisfied across him, he breathed in their mingled scent and felt perfectly happy. Basil could hear the smile in Theron's voice as he said, "I wish I spoke a hundred languages, to tell you how much I love you."

The pleasure of the moment snapped. "Don't say that. Don't say you love me."

"Why not?"

"Because that is something that should not be said between your father's son and mine."

"God!" Theron swore, and flopped back on the pillows. "Enough about my father! Not from you, too; I can't bear it. My mother thinks he was a saint; my duchess cousin thinks he was a satyr. I am what I am—no more, no less—and I would very much appreciate it if you could all stop measuring me against dead dukes I've never even met!"

Basil thought about trying to explain to Theron how much what he was—noble, bright, thoughtlessly endowed with all the riches man and nature could rain on him—made the idea of love between them as impossible as roses at MidWinter. It would be as useless as it was cruel, he decided. Theron did not understand who he truly was.

"I've offended you," Basil said gently. "I'm sorry."

Theron was silent long enough for Basil to wonder whether Theron's love had not survived the declaration. Then Theron said, "When you ask a girl to dance three times at a single ball, it means you're serious about her. It's the same with this: you can't make love with someone three times and not fall in love."

Basil shifted uncomfortably. "You make it sound like a magic spell: three times and you're caught."

"It would depend on the timing, I suppose." His lover gave the question his full attention. "Three times in one year would be safe, but three times in a week, or even a month, and you can't help falling in love."

Basil said, "You're confusing the body with the heart."

"People do, you know." Theron raised himself on one elbow. "But I'm willing to entertain the notion that you have them neatly divided. Maybe for you it takes something more direct." His fingers made an elaborate pass over Basil's face.

Before he could complete it, Basil caught his wrist and pulled him down into his arms. "Don't, Theron. It's not something to joke about."

"Are you going to cry me to the Council for practicing magic? Even though my spells don't work?"

"You have no need of spells."

"It's you who are magic, Basil, you who are the wizard. Who could resist the enchantment of your curling hair, your neck, your broad chest and narrow hips, your—"

"Stop!" Basil was laughing as Theron descended on each admired feature, while he struggled to get away. Then the University bell struck three times.

Theron yelped, jumped out of bed, and began diving for his scattered clothes. "My mother! I promised to escort her to an exceedingly dreary salon held by a woman she thinks might give her some money toward the women's mathematics chair."

Basil found Theron's stockings and his belt. "Will you come back tonight?"

"Without fail. It may be latish—I'll probably dine with her. But I'll come to you afterward, and I'll stay, Basil, I'll stay. I want to sleep with you and wake with you, night after night and day after day."

"Yes," said Basil, although he knew it was not the right answer. He knew it, and he didn't very much care. And that, too, was pleasure.

⌒

AFTER THERON HAD LEFT, BASIL SLEPT AGAIN, AND when he woke, the last rays of the sun were catching the warm stone of the building opposite, crowning it with gold. It was getting cold in Basil's room, or rather, colder. The fire was out again.

Basil groaned and heaved himself out of bed, pulling the coverlet with him. Gathering his clothes was unexpectedly difficult. His gown was puddled just inside the door, his breeches were under the bed, along with a single stocking. The other was in the far corner, behind a pile of books. He could not find his shoes, and after discovering that his last candle had been knocked from the desk and broken into three all-but-useless stubs, he sat down on the bed and sighed.

" 'The love of kings is as the sun,' " he quoted aloud, " 'that now blesses the earth, now scourges it with scorching ray.' Placid, somewhere or other. Middle of the page." His foot brushed against a shoe hiding under a drift of papers, which must have fallen from the bed. Unearthing its fellow, Basil reflected that his indifferent housewifery was hardly Theron's fault, and that he should spend his evening in setting the place to rights. But first he must buy some candles and some wood, if he could only find his purse.

It took several hours, but at last Basil's bed was made, his books were neatly stacked, his papers were sorted and tied with tape, his clothes hung up on hooks. His mug and tin bowl were washed and drying on the chimney-piece. He'd mended his pens and cleaned and filled his ink-pot. He'd sent the scruffy boy in search of candles and firewood and tipped him handsomely for hauling them up the stairs. He'd dusted his candlesticks and the engraving of Hilary he'd torn from a worm-eaten copy of Vespas and nailed to the wall. Sweeping the floor—a homely task he hated—he left for last.

When he came to the bed, he pulled out everything under it: stray papers, a copy of the history of the University he thought he'd lost, a pair of shoes, a black hat furred gray with dust. The document box. He dusted it in a housewifely fashion before opening it.

"There's no time for this," he said aloud. "Theron's coming."

Theron would be late. Basil had been avoiding the Book of the King's Wizard for too long, now. It was time.

He unfolded the linen from it as if he were undressing a lover. And he opened the cover like a man opening the door to a room where someone waited. The words were waiting for him to discover them, he knew, to unfold their secret meanings and make them live.

The letters lay dark and heavy on the page. Basil stared at the secret tongue. It teased him, dared him . . . He picked out the letters, and spoke two syllables aloud. He felt like a fool. It made no sense, and never would. They felt strange in his mouth, as if he were picking up pebbles or nuts and trying them on his tongue. He spoke them again, and despite himself, he slowly smiled. If he was right about the book, and he must be right, no one had uttered these same sounds for nearly two hundred years. He glanced up at the page heading: *To Lende a Man Greate Potencie*. Blushing, he slammed the pages shut. But the tip of his finger remained between them. Carefully, he opened the book again. *To Inspyre Love in One Unwilling: an Illusion*, read another page. Basil snorted. Certainly an illusion; weren't they all, these so-called spells? Well, weren't they?

The University Clock struck midnight. Where was the boy? Basil cast an impatient look at the door. Theron had told Basil he loved him, a declaration that begged to be answered in kind. But could he? That he was fascinated by Theron he would readily admit, drawn to his strong and slender body and his spirit that was brighter and quicker than any man's he'd ever known. Was that love?

Or was love in fact the true name of that uncomfortable feeling which kept coming over him lately, the fierce, almost cruel thrill of possession that sometimes seized him with Theron in his arms? It was not unlike the sensation he got from touching the wizards' spell-book, which was equally mysterious, in its way, as his kingly lover, and as desirable, too. Perhaps, indeed, he loved them both. Perhaps he only needed to study love.

Basil shrouded the book again and restored it to its box, and just in time: a tapping at the door announced Theron, glittering with melting snow and carrying a large basket.

"I've brought us provisions: cold beef and bread and a dried-apple pie and some potatoes to roast. And a fresh shirt, my scholar's gown, and a suit of clothes in case we want to go out. And I've told Sophia not to expect to see me for two or three days." He looked about him. "This is very cozy."

Basil took the basket from his hand, set it on the floor, and gathered the boy into his arms.

"Your wizard awaits, my king," he murmured into Theron's wet hair.

chapter **XII**

THE SUN ROSE ON A CITY ALL HUNG WITH DIA-
monds, carpeted with white, and damply cold. As the
University Clock struck nine, the scruffy boy ran out of
the door on Minchin Street and slithered through the snow, now
rapidly turning to slush, to the lecture hall at LeClerc, where he
informed the waiting students that Doctor St Cloud was indisposed. Since the magister had been looking odd for some time
now, no one was surprised. They were, however, worried. A magister with only student fees to live on cannot afford to be ill. As
one, twenty black-robed agents of mercy started toward Minchin
Street, so bent on bringing their magister succor that they might
have appeared at Basil's door empty-handed had Benedict
Vandeleur not stopped them.

"We'll need chicken soup and meat jelly, a bottle of dark
porter and a loaf of good white bread—a blanket, too."

"We'd better wait on the porter and the meat jelly." Peter
Godwin held out a meager handful of copper and brass. "This is
all I can spare. We're poor students, Vandeleur. That's poor, as in
without funds."

"You're a fine one to talk, Godwin," said Fremont. "You can go back up the Hill any time you want, eat until you're full and sleep in a room with a fire and enough blankets to keep half of us warm all winter. For you, poverty is an affectation; for us, it's reality."

"Shut up, Henry," said Vandeleur. "Godwin can't help being born noble. And his allowance has bought us all plenty of dinners, too. I'll take everything in your purse, though, Godwin, if you don't mind."

Peter Godwin laughed and emptied his purse, which encouraged two other sons of wealthy fathers to empty theirs. A discussion ensued about the best way to spend the bounty. Several students, cold and bored by the ordinary domesticity of their errand, decided to repair to the Nest for a warming drink. "Doctor St Cloud won't need us all," said one, apologetically. "Tell him to hurry back. Then come join us at the Nest. We'll keep Historians' Corner warm for you."

Vandeleur's initial enthusiasm had been cooling as fast as his toes. He weighed the purse in his hand, hesitated, and said, "Blake, you're a sensible man. Here"—he pressed the purse into his friend's hand—"send to the Nest if you need help."

"Aren't you coming?" said Lindley reproachfully. "Doctor St Cloud may be dangerously ill."

Justis tucked the purse away in the bosom of his shirt and wondered, not for the first time, how it came to be that men who could track the complexities of the Arkenveldt Treaty could be so utterly lacking in common sense.

"Think, Lindley," he said. "If the magister is dangerously ill, do you really think he'll want the whole boiling of us crowded into his room?"

Lindley would have argued, but Vandeleur said, "My very thought. If Doctor St Cloud is ill, Blake here is perfectly capable of seeing to him."

"While you're seeing to the new barmaid," sneered Fremont.

Vandeleur cuffed Fremont none too gently, and went off after Godwin and the rest, leaving Lindley, Fremont, and Blake in the cold, wet street.

Fremont glared at Blake. "This is what you wanted all along, isn't it? It's funny, it is, how you've managed to insinuate yourself into the inner circle after only three months. Why, I wouldn't take it on myself to order people around as you do, and I've been following Doctor St Cloud for two years."

"No one's stopping you from following him now," said Justis reasonably. "You can go ahead of us, if you want, and tell him we're on our way with food."

"And let you get all the glory?" asked Fremont. "Not likely."

An hour or so later, Blake and Fremont and Lindley were knocking at the street door of Basil's lodgings and telling the scruffy boy that they'd come to visit Doctor St Cloud. The boy surveyed them and their bundles with a suspicious eye, told them to wait, slammed the door, and disappeared. After a few frozen minutes of juggling increasingly damp and disintegrating parcels, Fremont rattled the latch, found it locked, swore sulfurously, and attacked the knocker.

"He'll come when he comes, Fremont," said Lindley, inspiring a scathing analysis of his opinions, his intelligence, and his character that served to while away the time until the door opened once more on the scruffy boy and his suspicious eye.

"Doctor St Cloud sends his thanks," he said, "but begs that you leave your food with me." He grinned, showing a large gap in his discolored teeth. "He's mortal indisposed to see company right now."

"We're not company," explained Lindley, elaborately patient. "We're students. If he's sick, we want to take care of him."

"So you just step aside, son," said Justis.

"He's mortal indisposed," said the boy rather desperately.

"It's all right," said Blake, kindly. "We'll tell him you delivered his message just as he told you. He won't be angry, I promise." And, gently but inexorably, he pushed past the boy and led the little procession up the carved stairs to their magister's door.

On the landing, Blake suffered a crisis of confidence and had to remind himself that when a sick sheep hides, it's a shepherd's duty to seek him out. He knocked briskly on the door. "Doctor St Cloud?"

"He's sick," snapped a male voice within. "Go away."

"It's Justis Blake, sir, and Lindley and Fremont. We've brought you a chicken."

A murmur of voices within, a sharp creak of ancient floor-boards, and the door opened a crack.

"Chicken," said Theron Campion unsteadily. "How kind of you. It's precisely what he needs. He's very run-down, I'm afraid. I had a terrible time with him, up half the night." His lips trembled and puckered. "He's better this morning," he went on, "but very tired. This should set him up nicely. Thank you."

Justis stared at Theron's hand, outstretched for the basket, at the wrinkled scholar's gown he was holding closed around himself, at his dark hair tangled over his shoulders, at his heavy eyes and bare feet and legs. It seemed that Doctor St Cloud wasn't a sick sheep after all, just a randy ram.

"We were worried," said Justis flatly. A faint color rose to Theron's throat and stubbled cheeks.

"There's soup, too. And a bottle of porter," said Lindley, choking on the words.

"I gather he doesn't need the blanket?" Fremont inquired nastily. "Or a soothing syrup? Or a physician?"

Theron's fingers tightened on the gown and his chin came up. "I'm taking care of him," he said. "If he needs a physician, I'll send for one." He held out his free hand. "Thank you for the food. He'll be very grateful."

"Here." Lindley thrust his bundles at Theron, who received them reflexively, allowing his gown to swing open on his nakedness. Lindley turned and fled down the stairs.

"Not bad," said Fremont, leering appreciatively. "Will you nurse me next time I get sick?"

Theron and Justis said, "Shut up, Henry," in disgusted chorus. Theron's mouth trembled again, clearly on the edge of laughter, and Justis lost his temper.

"Tell Doctor St Cloud," he bellowed in the voice he'd used to call his mother's pigs, "that his students eagerly await his return to full health. Tell him that we are worried about him."

Theron was biting his lips, struggling with rage and laughter and parcels. The door opened fully, revealing Basil St Cloud in shirt and breeches.

"Thank you, Fremont, Blake," he said. "I accept your good wishes and your offerings. Please inform your fellows that I will take up my lectures in two days' time—two days, Blake, neither more nor less." He took Theron's arm, pulled him back into the room, pushed the door half shut. "Go away, Justis," he said wearily. "Two days. I promise." Then the door closed, not entirely cutting off the sound of Theron's bright, helpless laughter.

THEY FOUND LINDLEY WAITING FOR THEM JUST INSIDE the street door. The skin around his eyes was taut; his lips were pressed into invisibility.

"It's not worth crying over," said Fremont. "You're clearly not to his taste."

"One of these days," said Justis, "someone is going to kill you, Henry."

Fremont bridled. "Come now. We live in enlightened times. Swordsmen are just for show, these days. Besides, what student could afford a death challenge on me?"

"Theron Campion could," said Lindley tightly.

"Thinking of calling one on him?" Fremont's voice was taunting. "I didn't know your father was a noble, Lindley. Unless there's something you've been keeping from us. Something other than lusting after Doctor St Cloud, I mean."

In the common run of things, Anthony Lindley was a gentle soul, but even the gentlest soul will turn violent when pricked in its most vulnerable part. With a howl of fury, Lindley leapt on Fremont, fists flailing. They tumbled out the door into the mud and trampled snow. Neither of them was any sort of fighter, but they made enough noise about it to attract an interested crowd of shopkeepers and idlers.

"What's it about?" the potboy of the Ink Pot inquired aloud.

A chorus of voices answered him: "A woman, of course. —A whore at Mother Betty's. —Ginger, probably: all the students are in love with her. —Idiot! It's a matter of honor. —It's money, I tell you. —Gambling. —Drink . . ."

"Students don't need a reason to fight." A large, ruddy man in a red shawl and white apron shook his head angrily. "They fall to as naturally as stags in autumn. Not a week ago now, I had a

fight break out over god-knows-what, two long tables cracked before I knew it, a bench splintered into matchsticks, and half my
tankards bent into scrap." He tweaked the potboy's ear. "Run find
the Watch, boy, tell them there's a riot brewing in Minchin
Street."

Justis, who'd been inclined to let his friends fight it out,
seized Lindley, who was temporarily uppermost, by the slack of
his robe.

"Watch, Tony!" he shouted. "They're calling the Watch. Kill
Henry later, if you like. I'll help."

Lindley scrambled to his feet, pulling Fremont up with him.
Fremont, under the impression that the fight had reached some
sort of climax, windmilled at him until Justis shook him from behind, shouting "Watch!" in his ear. By now, whistling could be
heard at the bottom of the street, and cries of "Ho, there! Halt!"

The three young men took to their heels, bolting between
two buildings into the web of alleys that netted the University
together. Fremont slipped on some ice and fell heavily. Justis
pulled him up, thrust his shoulder under his arm, and hauled him
along. A mangy dog tied up behind a shed began to bark hysteri-
cally. Sounds of pursuit grew louder; the three swarmed over a
wall into a snow-drifted garden.

As soon as he was safely on the ground, Fremont shook
Lindley's supporting hands away. "Don't touch me," he hissed.
"You tried to kill me."

Justis put a large and gritty hand over Fremont's mouth, jerk-
ing his chin significantly toward the wall they'd just scaled, on
the other side of which the dog yammered and the Watch cast
about for the scent. They shouted to one another and to the
heads that popped out back windows, banged on a few doors with
their brass-headed truncheons, and finally went away again.

Justis surveyed the damage. Fremont's gown was torn and
filthy, and his bony cheek was beginning to swell and darken.
Lindley's lip was split, and he'd gotten dung in his red hair. They
were all three muddy and soaked and cold as fresh-caught fish.

"They'll never let you into the Nest looking like that,"
said Justis. "We'd better find a pump you can stick your heads under."

S IT TURNED OUT, NO ONE EVEN NOTICED THEIR AR-rival at the Nest. Vandeleur and Godwin had relieved their anxiety over Doctor St Cloud's perilous state by knocking back a pitcher of beer, and from there had quite naturally fallen into a violent argument about magic. Quotes from Hollis and Delgardie flashed like swords, drawing the amused attention of several on-lookers.

"Are you calling the author of *The Fall of the Kings* a fool?" Godwin was demanding. "I don't care how ill he is, Doctor Tortua's read more books than you've had hangnails, Vandeleur, and if he says the kings and the wizards got together and made magic, then there's something in it."

"What's 'in it,' as you so elegantly put it, is not for children."

"Oh, shut up, you newts." It was a quiet voice, a muttered comment, but it happened to fall into a moment when both de-baters were simply glaring at each other, so everyone heard it. The students turned as one to see the man who had spoken. It was the Northerner, Alaric Finn, sitting up on a nearby table with his feet on the bench.

"I beg your pardon?" Peter Godwin said.

"Ever the gentleman, eh?" Finn sneered. "Well, my little lord, how would you like me to settle this argument for you right now? I'm about up to here with your endless babbling about things you know nothing about."

"And you do, I suppose?" Vandeleur demanded truculently.

"In fact, yes. And not from books, either. We know, up in the North, we've always known; about the Sacred Grove and the Deer Hunt and the Royal Sacrifice."

"The Royal Sacrifice, or the King's Night Out," drawled Fremont into the silence. "It sounds like a bad play."

"Shut up, Henry." The chorus was general.

"Go on, Finn," said Justis Blake. He was just as glad they'd found something to distract them from the question of what might be ailing Doctor St Cloud. "You've been hinting about this since term began. Now it's time to tell us about it."

Finn eyed the group suspiciously. "You'll laugh. Or tell me it's treason."

"Not a bit of it," said Vandeleur expansively. "Speak all the treason you like. We won't say a word."

"Of course we'll say a word," said Justis. "But we won't run to tell the Council. And we won't laugh."

"I will," said Fremont. "I'll laugh all I like. Magic! I'm not surprised Lindley and Godwin here are panting to hear Finn's fairy tales—they're barely out of the nursery, after all—but I'd credited Vandeleur and Blake with more sense. I've got better things to do." And he limped away.

"Well," said Vandeleur. "That's him gone."

"Can't say I'm sorry," muttered Lindley.

"Peevy bastard," agreed Finn. "Now, are you going to hear me out or not?"

"Have at it, Finn," Vandeleur said graciously. "We're all ears."

Finn gaped. Blake's mother would have said he looked like he'd asked for a drink of milk and been given a cow. The boy looked to be seventeen or so, of old Northern stock, proud as a peacock and poor as a charcoal-burner in summer, sent South to the City to mend the family fortunes. Blake wondered what his parents thought he was studying. Law, probably, or Natural Science.

Finn collected himself and began. "The kings came down from the North, to mingle their seed with the Southern stock, and their sons became kings in their turn."

"My little sister knows that," one of the young nobles jeered.

"You know it," Finn countered. "But you haven't thought about it. It also means that their children and their brothers married with the Southern noble families. So you've royal Northern blood in your veins, all you Southron nobles—you, Godwin, and you, too, Hemmynge. There's not a one of you doesn't carry the old magic in his blood."

"You've no call to be insulting," said Hemmynge, aggrieved. "Damned if I don't ask you to step outside."

Vandeleur put his hand on the young noble's shoulder and kept it there. "What's your point, Finn?"

"My point," said Finn impatiently, "is that you're all part of the magic of the land whether you believe in it or not."

Everyone was getting restless and annoyed, a fatal combination. Finn had no more idea how to lay out an argument than a frog had how to fly. Blake, prey to the uncomfortable feeling that he was responsible for the Northern boy's predicament, said, "Begin at the beginning, man. You need to persuade us first that the kings were magic."

Finn nodded, pulled himself together, and began. "It all starts with the Land." Justis could hear the capital letter in his voice: Land. The title of a personage, like Green God. "This is the Northern Land I'm talking about, not your soft South. It was a hungry land and dry and unfriendly to man."

"Cow dung, man." It was Hemmynge again. "That'll fix it, and clover plowed under in the fall. Or so m'father's steward says."

Finn's jaw bunched at the corners and his narrow eyes sank beneath his brows. "There were no cows," he said through his teeth. "And even the clover withered among the rocks. If you don't hold your tongue, Hemmynge, I swear I'll hold it for you."

"I'd like to see you try," sneered Hemmynge inaccurately.

This was too much. Blake exchanged a speaking look with Vandeleur, who shrugged helplessly. Vandeleur was only Middle City; Godwin was too young; everyone else would be perfectly happy if a fight broke out. It was up to him. He touched the young noble's sleeve and said, "Come on, Hemmynge. You're bored, and who would blame you; ancient history's not even your subject. Let the poor boy tell his old wives' tales in peace. I'll buy you ale."

Looking from the interested faces around him to Blake's wide, muscular hand on his gown sleeve, Hemmynge shrugged ungraciously, muttered, "Don't mind if I do," and slouched off unresisting. By the time Justis had delivered him and his tankard to a sympathetic group of nobles and returned to the historians, Finn had overcome his initial awkwardness and hit his stride. He spoke fluently, his nasal Northern accent oddly suited to the formal cadences of his story, his bitten hands underscoring, emphasizing, guiding, his narrow features animated, his deep-set eyes glittering. Blake shoved onto the end of a bench next to Lindley, who was listening with rapture.

"So the wizards chose their candidates from among all the Companions, called the Little Kings, each wizard a candidate, and taught them and loved them and filled their bodies with magic."

"I'll just bet," muttered someone, but everyone ignored him.

"And when the old king gave his body and blood to the Land, the candidates went into the grove, and suffered the Trial, which is a Mystery and not to be spoken of. He who walked alive from the forest became king, and his wizard became master over the other wizards. In times of war, the young king led the army of Companions in battle and in times of peace he went on royal progress to spread his seed throughout the land. The crop was sons of the royal blood, little kings who would grow to provide new Companions and a fresh, young king when the time was right. And the kings' blood watered the land and the kings' flesh fed it, so that it grew fat and pleasant and friendly to man, and sent sheep down from the mountain passes and the wild horses from the high meadows to serve man and clothe him, and deer from the deep forest to give him meat in winter, when no thing grows that is green."

There was a little silence when he'd done. Looking at the faces of his friends, Justis thought they were more than half convinced by Finn's tale. He certainly was. To his farm-bred soul, the whole thing made an odd kind of sense. You feed the Land; it feeds you. And University had taught him that there are many kinds of feeding, many kinds of food.

Then Vandeleur smiled and said, "You've missed your calling, Finn. You ought to be a story-teller or a writer of romances."

Finn glared at him, beetle-browed and sullen once more. "I didn't make that up," he said. "It's all true."

"Where's your proof?" Vandeleur asked pleasantly. "Where are your documents and references? And what did these wizards actually *do*? Other than make hay with the kings, I mean?"

The spell was broken. Men elbowed each other, snickering.

Above their laughter, Finn said, "Don't mock me, Vandeleur. It's in Hollis, too. The wizards chose the kings and bound them to the Land with a chain of gold."

Lindley exclaimed, "The window in the Great Hall! There's proof, Vandeleur. It's got a wizard and a grove and a deer in it. It even has the golden chain."

"Has it?" said a student behind Justis. "That's interesting."

"But it doesn't prove anything," objected Godwin, "except that whoever made the window knew the same old stories Finn's people tell."

"The window was brought down from the North," Lindley pointed out. "Alcuin brought it as a bride-gift to Queen Diane—it says so in the Official History of the University."

"You actually read that?" someone asked.

"Still," said Vandeleur. "Godwin's right. It proves nothing. I don't deny the window's antiquity or its symbolism—it illustrates Finn's fairy tales very neatly. I do, however, deny its literal truth. My grandmother has a lovely statue of the Green God in her garden, blessing the roses. That doesn't mean there's actually a god sitting in a heavenly garden combing his leafy hair with fingers made of twigs. It's just something an artist made up to illustrate the idea of growth and plenty."

Godwin laughed suddenly. "Don't let the priests hear you say that, Vandeleur, or your grandmother either."

Vandeleur turned to Finn. "You've persuaded me that the wizards effectively ruled the ancient North because they figured out how to make barren soil fertile. I'll even accept that you Northerners believed, back in the mists of time, that blood sacrifice and ritual sex gave good husbandry a helping hand. What I will never accept is that there was any more to it than that. In any case, by the time Alcuin came South, the wizards were nothing but advisors and diplomats who lost a lot of their power in the Union and were unhappy about it. And unless you can come up with something more solid than folk tales, Finn, you'll never make me change my mind."

"Or," Godwin added, "convince Doctor St Cloud that you're any kind of scholar. He'd never let you get away without at least checking . . . Oh!" His face fell. "The magister! How is he?"

Justis, momentarily at a loss, looked down at his hands. Beside him, Lindley went taut and silent.

"Oh, no," Vandeleur exclaimed, blanching. "He's not . . . You should have *said*! What shall we do?"

"He's fine," Lindley ground out between gritted teeth. "Or he will be, when he's got it out of his system."

Everyone looked at him curiously, and Justis hastily added, "A mild fever—you know the kind of thing—you just have to sweat it out. He expects to be back in two days' time."

"And the chicken?" someone wanted to know. "The wine?"

"I imagine he's enjoying them right now," said Justis rather desperately as he felt Lindley tense against his arm. "Lindley," he said, taking the goat by the horns, "I wouldn't be surprised if you were sickening for it, too." He stood and put his hand on the red-head's shoulder. "Off we go, Tony. I'll see you in bed with a hot brick to your feet, or know the reason why."

But Lindley shook him off. "There's nothing wrong with *me*," he said pointedly. "I'm going to stay here and have a drink. And discuss history with those who know something about it. You may go tuck yourself in if you choose."

Justis shrugged. As he climbed the steps to the tavern door, he glanced over his shoulder to see Anthony Lindley and four or five others sitting on the bench where Alaric Finn was resting his feet, looking up at the Northerner and talking animatedly.

chapter XIII

D URING THEIR MAGISTER'S ABSENCE, THE HEART'S
core of St Cloud's students continued to meet, though
not at LeClerc. Max, who owned the Blackbird's Nest,
sighed when he saw them appear for the second day in a row at ten
o'clock in the morning, hungry for food and drink and talk, with
not enough coin among them to pay for a cup of gruel. He was
willing to extend credit—he'd have no custom if he did not, and
he knew someone would pay up eventually. So he served St
Cloud's ancient historians and refilled their tankards as often as
they emptied them, even when one of them grew so drunk that he
could hardly lift the drink to his mouth.

The drunk was Henry Fremont, drowning the loss of an innocence he loudly denied ever having possessed. Fremont prided
himself on having been a hardened cynic from birth. No one believed this except himself, and he was alone in being shocked at
the depth of his fury at what he considered the magister's betrayal. He'd gone to tell Vandeleur the truth about St Cloud's absence that same night, seeking Benedict out in the room he
shared with Justis Blake.

Vandeleur's response had been disappointing. "You're a bit behind the fair, Fremont; Blake's already spilled the beans. So the wondrous Doctor St Cloud is human after all. With Theron Campion, too. That boy does get around. I don't see it myself, but then I prefer the girls at Mother Betty's. There's a neat little blonde there, Henry, could console you for the end of the world. My treat. What do you say?"

Fremont had said no, and a lot of other things Vandeleur would only forgive a man in pain, and left in search of a more sympathetic ear. Which he did not find. With the exception of Lindley, who wasn't speaking to him, all Basil's students were inclined to look upon their magister's fall from perfection with an indulgent tolerance.

"And why shouldn't he spend two days in bed with his new lover?" Peter Godwin wanted to know. "It'll do him good, and give us time to work on some of those questions he's having us research. You wouldn't believe the mess the Godwin archives are in."

"That's not the point," Henry said. "We thought he was writing, and instead he was rutting! He's supposed to be teaching, not scratching his itch with Theron Campion. Theron Campion. I ask you. Why, the man isn't even a historian!"

"Jealous, Fremont?" inquired Alaric Finn, which inspired Henry to try and rip Finn's nose from his face. Luckily, he was too drunk to do anything but fall sideways off the bench, which hardly even created a disturbance.

A couple of Henry's fellows picked him up and dusted him off and propped him up next to the wall. Sullenly, he accepted a fresh tankard and brooded into it while the conversation swirled around him. And then he said, loudly and suddenly, "Tha's it. I quit. No more fucking dead kings. No more fucking ancient historians or metaphysicians or eth—ethicists. I'm taking up astronomy."

"Give it a rest," said Vandeleur. "We all know you're no more interested in the motions of the stars than you are in drinking well-water. If Doctor St Cloud isn't pure enough for you, go pay your silver to Doctor Crabbe, or Wilson or Ferrule."

Henry surveyed him with a bloodshot eye. "Doctor Crabbe?

I'd rather suck a billy goat. It's all politics and ambition with him. He doesn't give two straws for the truth. All he cares about is kissing the right asses so he can settle his own ass in the Horn Chair."

Blake looked up from the corner where he'd been reading. "That's not fair, Fremont," he said. "I can't stand Crabbe either, but he's a good scholar in his way."

"That," sneered Henry, "is like saying a man who steals his bread is as good a baker, in his way, as the man who rises at dawn to knead dough."

"At least he only steals from the best bakeries," Godwin piped up, and was rewarded by general laughter.

Henry, predictably, was not amused. This was his life they were talking about, his future, his integrity. "That's it, then," he said gloomily. "I'm left with astronomy. Or the priesthood. Or suicide."

Vandeleur sighed. "You're getting boring, Fremont. Leave the University, go be a clerk or haul freight at the docks. I'm sick of your self-righteous anguish." He glanced around the small group. "There's a fiddler at the Spotted Cow could make a dead frog leap again. And plenty of sewing-girls to dance with. What do you say?"

Fremont's response was predictably foul. Vandeleur batted him gently on the head, which caused him to make a small, complaining noise and fall forward on the table, where they left him, snorting into a pool of beer.

⁓

THE NEXT MORNING FOUND BASIL ST CLOUD BACK IN LeClerc as promised, probing the finer points of Alcuin's marriage negotiations with Queen Diane. He was gloved, capped, and muffled against the cold, heavy-eyed and hectically cheerful. Had Vandeleur and Godwin been able to resist spreading the news about just where he'd spent the last two days, his students might have thought him heroically risen from his sickbed to teach them. As it was, every man of them knew it was passion, not the ague, that roughened the young magister's voice and brightened his eyes. Other than a tendency to snicker when he used the words "come" or "bed," the students managed to comport themselves fairly well. If Theron Campion had chosen to attend that day's lecture, there might have been an incident; but, wisely, he did not.

Anthony Lindley was there, sitting by Alaric Finn, with whom he'd struck up an improbable friendship. Justis Blake was there, his heavy face unreadable, stolidly taking notes. Peter Godwin and Benedict Vandeleur were there, and all the rest of the paying students, except for Henry Fremont.

I N A SMALL ROOM ABOVE A PAWNSHOP, HENRY FREMONT woke at last to the sound of bells telling him that he was very late for Doctor St Cloud's lecture. First panic filled him, and then the knowledge that his head was full of knives, his mouth of dry leaves, and his stomach of cockroaches. By the time he'd disposed of the latter in his chamberpot and sluiced out his mouth with the small beer his roommate had thoughtfully left him, he'd remembered that Doctor St Cloud was a hypocrite and a lecher who cared more for his pleasure than for his students. After he'd staggered down to the yard and pumped a bucket of frigid water to wash his face in, and eaten an end of dry bread, he'd pretty well pieced together the events of the previous evening and begun to wonder what he was going to do now.

He couldn't stay at University, that was clear. He'd been betrayed and humiliated, not only by St Cloud, but by the men he'd considered his friends. They'd been laughing at him—he could see that now—laughing at his pain. Even Blake. Even Lindley, who was sticking closer to that madman Finn than his Northern stink. Briefly, Henry considered throwing himself out the window or into the river, but that was just the hangover. He wasn't entirely worthless—he remembered someone telling him so last night, someone who had found him kneeling by a gutter, spewing up beer. He'd lent Henry a handkerchief to wipe his face and a shoulder to support him to the door of the pawnshop. A stranger—tears came to Henry's eyes—a stranger had cared for him when his so-called friends deserted him.

Henry leapt to his feet, hung onto a chair until his vision cleared, retrieved his jacket from the floor, and turned out its pockets. His purse was there, with two brass minnows in it and a stub of charcoal and a fine cambric handkerchief, very foul, and a square of pasteboard engraved with the name *Edward Tielman* and an address on Fulsom Street.

SOME FEW HOURS LATER, A TALL, SKINNY FIGURE LIKE a fence-post in a gown could be seen trudging through the Middle City, stopping from time to time to ask directions of a shopkeeper. His hair was plaited into a long rat's tail secured with black thread, his face was pink around the purple glory of his bruised cheek, and his eyes were as clear as Bet's infallible hangover cure could make them. His linen was clean, his suit brushed, and his gown sponged and pressed by the soft-hearted laundress who lived across the landing. He had no very clear idea of where he was going or what was going to happen when he got there, but at least he no longer wished he were dead, and that was something.

The address on Fulsom Street was not a shop or a lodging, as Henry had expected, but a largish private house, with steps climbing up to the door and a polished brass knocker shaped like a dragon's head. His curiosity roused, Henry rattled it, and was answered almost immediately by a poker-faced individual who could only have been a manservant. Feeling rather out of his depth, Henry thrust the card at the manservant and said, "Don't say your master isn't at home. He's expecting me."

The manservant stood aside to let him enter a narrow vestibule papered in cherry and white stripes. "As it happens, sir," he said woodenly, "Master Tielman is *not* at home. But he has directed me to show you into the library, should you care to wait."

Henry, haughtily, did care to wait. He was led to a cozy room lined with open cases, offered brandy, which he declined, and left with Tielman's books. When Tielman came into the room some time later, he found Henry sitting cross-legged on the hearth with a pile of books beside him and a folio volume open on his lap.

"Is that Rafael on birds you have there or *The Lineage of the Noble Houses?*" Tielman inquired pleasantly.

Henry jerked violently upright and glared malevolently at his host. "Do you always creep into rooms without warning," he snarled, "or is it just poor students you try to catch touching your precious books? You shouldn't have had me wait in the library if you didn't want me to read them."

Tielman held up his hands. "Not guilty, I swear it. They're here to be read. I'm glad you found something to your taste." He sat in a well-loved armchair and cocked his feet on the settle. "Stay there if you like, and finish what you were reading. I've asked Fedders to bring in chocolate and some bread and cheese. Unless you'd prefer beer?"

Nonplussed, Henry said he'd take the chocolate, and sat fidgeting on the hearth rug pretending to follow out the bloodlines of the House of Tremontaine until the manservant came in with a large tray, which he laid on a table at his master's elbow before withdrawing.

Edward Tielman picked up a large block of chocolate with silver tongs and began to grate. "Milk or cream?" he asked.

Henry shuddered. "Water," he said. "And sugar."

"Of course." Tielman whisked a steaming stream into one cup, ladled three spoons of sugar into it, and held it out to the lanky student.

"Look," said Henry, ignoring the cup. "You want something from me. You must. Nobody invites a stranger to his house, last seen pissed as a newt, and feeds him chocolate and bread and cheese without having a reason for it. You don't even know my name."

"It's Henry Fremont," said Tielman promptly. "And you're perfectly right, I do want something from you. Are you going to take this cup or not?"

Henry hesitated, closed *The Lineage of the Noble Houses*, and took the chocolate from Tielman's hand. Then he accepted a hunk of bread and cheese, and before he knew it, he was sprawling among the books he'd pulled from the shelves, his gown discarded in the heat of the fire, drinking chocolate and disputing the historical roots of the City Council. He'd all but forgotten that this was something other than a social afternoon when the library door opened and Fedders said, "Lord Nicholas Galing, sir."

Henry jerked upright so suddenly that he knocked over his cup, which was blessedly empty. By the time he'd righted it, Lord Nicholas had shaken his host's hand and was standing over Henry like a hound over a rat, waiting to see if he'd bite.

"This is Henry Fremont, Galing," said Tielman. "He's at the University, studying with Doctor Basil St Cloud of History. Master Fremont, my friend Lord Nicholas Galing."

Fremont glared up at the young lord. He had an overwhelming impression of richness: rich clothes, rich brown hair richly curling over his forehead and the nape of his neck, a generous mouth, richly colored. About St Cloud's age, Henry guessed, but the clothes and the calculating expression made him seem older. Typical bloody noble, popping in without warning, expecting to be toadied to. Except it wasn't without warning—Tielman must have set it up. "I'm supposed to jump to my feet, I suppose, and say I'm pleased to meet you and have you any boots I could lick? Well, I'm not, and I'm very comfortable where I am, and I don't like the taste of boots."

Galing turned to Tielman with his brows raised. Tielman laughed.

"He's bright, he's observant, he has an excellent memory, his politics are impeccable, and he has a strong, if somewhat unsubtle, sense of right and wrong. He is also unbelievably rude."

"That would explain the colorful cheek," said Galing as Fremont goggled at Tielman. "Couldn't you have found someone with a little more address?"

"He's better off without that," said Tielman. "We were having chocolate, Galing. Would you like some?" Galing nodded. "More chocolate, Master Fremont?"

Between rage and curiosity, Fremont could think of nothing to say but, "I don't like being played with." The words did not adequately express his feelings, but he gritted them out with all the venom at his disposal.

Lord Nicholas settled himself in a cushioned chair across the fire and said, "We're not playing, I promise you that. I need your help. You are in a position not only to refuse, but to tell everyone you know that I've asked, thereby effectively disarming me. I can't afford to play with you—you're in the position of strength here."

While Fremont was digesting this speech, Tielman made two cups of chocolate with scalded milk, spiked them with peppermint liquor, handed one to Galing, and settled down to see what would happen next.

"What if it's something I don't want to do?" Fremont said at last.

"Then I'll just have to ask for your word that you won't talk about it," Galing answered.

"You'd trust my word?" Fremont asked incredulously. "I'm a potter's son, you know."

"And I'm a steward's son," said Tielman, "for whatever that's worth. You were talking last night like a man whose sense of honor has been outraged, suggesting that you do in fact have a sense of honor. Which no one wishes to outrage further."

"In my experience," Galing added helpfully, "potters and stewards are far more truthful than nobles."

A log fell into coals, sending up a spume of sparks. Tielman took a fresh log from the basket, threw it on the fire, and moved it into place with the poker.

Feeling at a disadvantage, Fremont retrieved his gown, got to his feet, and shrugged the black folds around him. "Very well," he said. "I'll listen to your proposal, and if I don't like it, I'll promise, on my honor, not to talk about it. I don't want any more chocolate, though."

"Barley water's what you need after last night," said Tielman wisely. "I'll ring for it."

Fremont found a very hard chair some way from the fire and occupied it in silence until the barley water arrived. He drank it down and said, "Tell me."

Galing and Tielman exchanged a glance; Tielman raised his cup to Galing and smiled. "Your deal, Galing, I believe?"

"I've promised Master Fremont not to play with him,

Edward," Galing said easily. "I wouldn't want my word to weigh less than his." He leaned his elbows on his knees, cupped his chocolate in both hands, and studied the dimpled surface. "I'll be as frank with you as I can," he said. "I need an agent in the University."

"An agent? You mean a spy?"

"I mean someone who can observe without being observed, who can ask questions without occasioning comment, who has a good mind and a good memory. Spy," he said thoughtfully, "is a nasty word, but I suppose it's accurate. Let's say I need a spy, then."

Henry thought this over. "Fuck you," he said deliberately.

Galing cast a cold eye over Henry's bony form. "I'd rather you didn't," he said. "Edward, are you *sure* he's the right one?"

"I'm sure," said Tielman firmly. "Listen, Fremont, it's like this. There's been trouble in the Northern provinces—nothing very big, nothing very particular: rumors of secret meetings, deer guts left on a noble's doorstep, farmers making dire predictions, that sort of thing. Lord Nicholas wouldn't have thought it worthy of notice if a Northerner had not presented a petition at City Sessions, demanding that the kings be reinstated."

"Even that," said Galing, "would not be significant, had he not killed himself."

"So he couldn't tell what he knew," Henry murmured, interested in spite of himself.

"Very likely," said Galing. "He was wearing a pin carved like an oak leaf in his hat, like a badge. And he came from the North. We did learn that much."

This was history coming to life with a vengeance. "Did you torture him?" Henry asked.

Galing shot him a look of disgust. "No. We did not torture him. He was very proud of being a Northerner."

"Like Finn and his friends," Henry said, light dawning. "You want me to see whether the Northerners at University are connected with this trouble you're talking about, and whether they're planning any trouble down here of their own."

Tielman smiled. "I told you he was bright," he said to Galing.

"You did. And he is. But that's not the whole story. You're a student of ancient history?"

Henry frowned, defensive at once. "What of it?"

Galing closed his eyes briefly. "What do you study in ancient history?"

"You're playing with me again," Henry warned angrily, and then he saw where this was leading. "You think," he said slowly, "that the Northerners are plotting to restore the monarchy, and that such a plot might be likely to show up among the ancient historians, or"—he corrected himself—"that the plotters would find adherents there. But they'd be fools to attach themselves to Doctor St Cloud, you know. His lectures are the first place anyone would look."

"You don't say," Galing drawled. "Tell me more of this Doctor St Cloud. Do you have reason to suspect that he yearns for the kings to come again?"

Fremont wasn't willing, despite his spleen, to go that far, but he did admit that Doctor St Cloud was king-mad. "He said the nobles were fools to separate the kings and the wizards. As long as the wizards kept them in line, the kings were fine. Why, Anselm the Wise was one of the greatest thinkers of his age. Of course, he signed those laws limiting the wizards' powers, but it's clear he was influenced by Tremontaine. . . ." He caught Tielman's amused look, flushed and muttered, "Well, you see the kind of thing he tells us."

"I do, indeed," Galing said with suspect sympathy. "We must keep an eye on this Doctor St Cloud. And the Northerners. So. Will you do it?"

Henry hesitated.

"We'd pay you for your trouble, of course," Galing said.

Henry glared at him. "I thought you weren't going to outrage my honor. I don't want your money." Yet he knew he could use it, if Galing insisted, with the rent overdue and his only warm jacket full of holes. And it wasn't as if he'd be doing any harm, not if Doctor St Cloud was innocent. Innocent! Why, he was dallying with the King-Killer's own great-great-grand-something! No sedition there. Whatever Henry thought of St Cloud's morals, he was sure that the magister had no more notion of current politics than a baby—he certainly wasn't politicking for the Horn Chair with any degree of sense. No, Henry decided, there was nothing for these men to find out about Basil St Cloud except dates and theories. He might even prove the young doctor blameless of royalist plotting.

Henry Fremont took a deep breath. "What, exactly, would I have to do?"

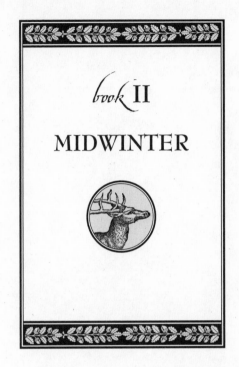

book II

MIDWINTER

chapter I

NOT LONG BEFORE MIDWINTER, BASIL ST CLOUD
came home one dismal afternoon to a slip of paper
under his door: a summons to dinner that evening at
Doctor Leonard Rugg's. *"Eels at 6:30,"* it read, *"with Cassius and
Elton. Do honor us. L.R."*

He stood in the open door facing his cluttered worktable and
thought he would rather work. Then his somnolent ambition
woke and counseled him to follow his self-interest for once and
take his scolding for neglecting his students. Besides, pride whispered, it might be good for Campion to call in Minchin Street
one night and find his lover engaged elsewhere.

So Basil sent the scruffy boy off to Rugg's with a politely
worded acceptance, and set out for Rugg's lodgings determined to
swallow whatever the acerbic metaphysician might serve up.

Leonard Rugg's chambers bore witness to the popularity of
his lectures. He had a sitting room and a study as well as a bed-
room and a chilly closet, where his manservant Barkis slept beside the casks of beer. Among his other duties, Barkis did basic
cooking over the sitting room fire: toast and hot water for

chocolate and punch. Anything else was sent up by the landlady or, on state occasions, by the cookshop on the corner. As the cookshop's specialty was jellied eels, jellied eels is what Rugg commonly served his guests when he was moved to entertain— jellied eels and a very decent Ruthven claret.

The stairwell smelled faintly of eels and more strongly of a smoking chimney. As St Cloud ascended the steps to Rugg's door, he was uncomfortably conscious of notes unanswered, appointments missed, and conversations avoided or curtailed to make time for Theron Campion's seductive tutorials in the pleasures of the flesh. Elton and Cassius—and Rugg, above all—were undoubtedly offended at his recent behavior, and Basil hardly knew how to appease them. He would not apologize for doing what he so badly wanted to do, for following a joy he had not imagined knowing.

It was therefore in no very comfortable mood that Basil knocked at Rugg's door. When Barkis let him in, he was not surprised to see the three friends already gathered around the fire like the Three Wise Men of Huffington, glasses of wine in their hands, an empty bottle at their feet, and a second open beside it.

The astronomer lifted his glass in greeting and Cassius said, "There's ten coppers I owe you, Elton. I never thought he'd come."

"I only bet on sure things," Elton said. "I'm glad to see you, Basil, and so is Cassius, for all his sour face."

"Of course I'm glad to see him," said Cassius. "I never said I wasn't."

Their host stood up, glass in hand. "Don't stand in the door, man—it's cold. Come in. Barkis, another glass here, and a new bottle. My learned friend looks dry."

It was as if they'd all dined together yesterday. St Cloud relaxed a little. Rugg filled his glass with clear, red Ruthven and regaled the company with a salty tale about the Harris Chair of Rhetoric and his newest lover.

"Illiterate, I heard," said Cassius when the laughter had died down. "A pickpocket from Riverside."

"Why do you immediately presume he's a pickpocket?" Elton

objected. "I acknowledge that most pickpockets live in Riverside, but it's absurd to say that everyone in Riverside is a pickpocket. He might be a swindler or a gambler or a housebreaker or a petty thief or a swordsman—"

"Or a whore," Rugg finished. "Which seems by far the most likely. I think we should eat now. Barkis, the eels."

The conversation over the jellied eels was largely political. Elton was at daggers drawn with Sanderling of Astronomy over the subject of the movement of the spheres. Doctor Sanderling subscribed to the ancient belief that all heavenly bodies visible in the night sky revolved around the earth. Elton, who had studied mathematics along with astronomy, had come up with a theory that the earth, and possibly everything else as well, revolved around the sun. Cassius supported him on the basis of mathematics, Rugg on the basis of friendship. St Cloud privately thought the entire question uninteresting and unimportant, the relative antics of the sun and earth having no discernable effect on human history. But he was entirely in sympathy with Elton's methodology.

"That's the problem, isn't it?" he asked rhetorically, his fork poised over his plate. "The old guard just won't accept that there's anything new to be learned by looking at the heavens or reading old documents or experimenting with systems of numbers, as Cassius did in that monograph there was such a flap over last year. They think all the important facts are already known, and all that's left for a scholar to do is refine methods of interpreting them. Which is absurd."

Cassius swallowed his mouthful. "Exactly. Scholarship, particularly scientific scholarship, should be based on making fresh discoveries, not on the incessant mastication of old ones."

"Especially when those discoveries are wrong," Elton agreed. "All the gyrations the College of Astronomy has been going through year after year to make their theories fit the observations, when it's all right in front of their noses. Why can't they just accept that it's not their instruments or observations that are at fault, but their stupid, outdated theories?"

"Because they'd have to accept that they were blind,

narrow-minded ninnies," said Rugg. "You can't blame them for declining to admit that their lives have been thrown away on the study of stupidity."

"Yes, you can," St Cloud objected. "Why would any *real* scholar persist in pursuing falsehood when he could pursue truth? Take Crabbe, for example. He's wasting a good, analytical mind on yet another commentary on Delgardie when what he *should* be doing is combing the archives at Halliday House or Hartsholt's warren up North, looking for diaries and letters that would tell us what was *really* happening up there after the Fall."

"As you have," said Rugg dryly.

"As I have," agreed St Cloud. "Oh, I haven't done research in the noble houses, not yet. There's no real need: I've found plenty of original documents in the Archives. And let me tell you, until Anselm's grandson, Iron Tybald, the kings weren't as bad as Vespas drew them, nor the nobles as spotless. It all makes sense when you know exactly what the kings did in the North before the Union. When I finish my new book . . ."

"Well, that's it, isn't it?" Cassius interrupted him. "When you finish your new book, how do you propose to get it past the censor?"

"The kings were deposed two hundred years ago, Cassius. There's never been a serious claimant to the throne."

Rugg frowned. "Wasn't there a Herriott raised an army once?"

"Sixty farmers, stark naked and carrying sharpened sticks," Basil said, "don't constitute an army. Herriott himself was barking mad. And that was eighty years ago. It's time we taught the truth, not politically convenient fictions invented by an embattled and cautious Council in our great-grandfather's time. Nowadays, surely, they have nothing to fear."

Rugg held up his glass for Barkis to refill. "Actually, that's what we wanted to talk to you about, St Cloud."

"The truth?" St Cloud asked casually, although his blood had begun to race unpleasantly. "Or Herriott?"

"Politics," said Elton. "You know you were never any good at them."

St Cloud carefully laid down his fork and wiped his greasy

mouth on the hem of his gown sleeve. "I'm the youngest doctor in the University, Elton. I can't see that my lack of interest in politics has done me any harm."

"It didn't," said Rugg, "as long as it was obvious that all you were interested in was ancient history. Not a flashy subject, ancient history. Half of it is fairy tales and the other half, by your own accounting, is lies. If there weren't a richly endowed chair in it, I doubt it would still be taught. You can learn all you need about the ancients in metaphysics and rhetoric, if you ask me."

"Then I don't see why I can't say what I like," said St Cloud. "Not that I agree with you, of course. I can't see how we can hope to call ourselves educated men without understanding where we come from, the bad and the morally ambiguous as well as the good. But if the Governors feel as you do, then I should be able to preach the return of the kings on street corners and risk raising nothing but derision."

Cassius sighed. "Well, that's just the point. As long as it was nothing but dramatic lectures filled with highly-colored incident, slender monographs on the ancient roots of obscure laws, and *The Origins of Peace*, you were a brilliant academic scholar. What you turned up was pleasantly titillating, like listening to your grandfather reminiscing about the deviltry he got up to when he was a boy. It didn't have anything to do with the real world."

Elton glanced at St Cloud's frozen countenance. "Cassius, you're an ass. He'll be too angry now to hear anything we say."

"No, Elton, I'm not," snapped St Cloud. "I am angry, but Doctor Cassius has said nothing more than I've suspected. As long as their contempt has encouraged the Governors to allow me to teach and publish as I wish, I am grateful for it. I am at a loss, however, to see why you are telling me this now."

The three men exchanged a look, and then Rugg said, "It's this Campion business, St Cloud. It won't do. Sullies your purity."

Between fury and astonishment, St Cloud could hardly speak. "Purity?" he sputtered. "How can you speak to me of purity, Whoremaster Rugg? The School of Mathematics will have to invent fresh numbers to tally your mistresses."

"Damned self-righteous prig," Rugg muttered, pouring himself more wine. "Don't know why I bother."

"You had it coming, Rugg," Elton said. "Listen, Basil. Theron Campion's mother is the widow of a duke, lectures in the College of Surgery, and has enough power and influence to endow a chair in Mathematics—for women, too. Oh, yes, it's a done deal; the Governors couldn't block it, though they tried. His cousin is a duchess. Campion himself is, or will be, a very powerful and rich man some day. They already call him the Prince of Riverside! Becoming this man's lover is a political act, Basil, whether you mean it to be or not, and it's not a wise one. It taints you with intrigue and patronage when your chief strength was a complete and obvious unworldliness."

Basil stood suddenly, sending his plate crashing to the floor. "Unworldliness? How dare you? My chief strength is, or ought to be, the originality of my research, the rigor of my arguments. It makes no difference whether I'm a nobleman's lover or a ravisher of lapdogs as long as I'm a better scholar than Roger Crabbe. Which I am."

There was a moment of silence while Basil glared at the three men and they stared uncomfortably back. Basil decided he might as well leave now, having heard and said every word he could imagine the subject warranted.

"Doctor Rugg," he said stiffly, "Doctor Elton, Doctor . . ."

"Oh, sit down, Basil," said Elton wearily. "Of course you're the better scholar. What your liaison with Campion means is that now you're going to have to prove it."

"My book won't be ready. I've found new material . . ."

"Bugger your book," said Rugg. "You don't need a book. You need drama, you need spectacle, you need—"

"A challenge," Elton finished for him.

Everyone looked expectantly at Basil. He sat down slowly to think about it.

Academic challenges, like swordsmen's challenges, had grown rare of late. The last one St Cloud could remember was when a Fellow of Law had debated a full-fledged Doctor before the University Governors for the right to be made a Doctor without having published. He'd lost, of course. He was a brilliant speaker, but that was not enough. Words draw no blood, and the final judgment rested with the Governors, who rejected his claim. Rules, after all, were rules; and the other magisters, who had duly published theses in their seasons, had made no objection.

Basil said, "If it's all about politics, as you say, what's to keep the Governors from deciding against me out of hand, as they did with that poor Law Fellow?"

"Well, it's a risk," Elton acknowledged. "But once the debate is all out in the public where everyone can hear, if you've got proof that Crabbe is talking out of his hat, they'll have to give you the Horn Chair. You're popular; there'll be an outcry if they don't."

"But our subjects are so different," Basil objected. "His specialty is the same as Tortua's: the fall of the monarchy and the rule of the Council of Lords. Mine is hundreds of years earlier. What can we possibly debate about?"

Elton leaned forward eagerly. "Methodology, of course. Methodology is going to be the real subject of every debate at this University for the foreseeable future. If you can just catch him out on some small fact, something that you've come across looking for something else—you know the kind of thing."

St Cloud nodded slowly.

"Then," said Cassius, picking up Elton's thread, "you can launch into a disquisition on primary sources and pure data, and leave Doctor Crab-cake to hide his head in the sand."

Basil thought a moment. "What do I do?"

Rugg was delighted to explain the procedure to him, and did, at some length, while Barkis cleared away the debris of the meal and another bottle of claret met its fate. Soon St Cloud's head began to spin with wine and the formal rules of academic challenge. "Time was," he said meditatively, "that apprentice wizards cried challenge upon each other, the loser to end his life as a crow or a mule or some lesser beast."

There was a dense and irritated silence. "You might want to keep away from the wizards," said Cassius at last.

Rugg nodded. "In fact, I forbid you to mention them. No, just listen, Basil. I'm your senior and your friend, and I know what I'm saying. Start talking about wizards, and your job becomes that much harder."

"Astronomically," Elton agreed.

"By a magnitude of ten," put in Cassius, not to be outdone.

Rugg ignored them. "No one will know how brilliant your argument is if they're laughing themselves sick over your premise. Promise me, Basil. Promise you'll keep away from the wizards and all their works."

Basil looked around at his friends' faces, crimsoned by wine and firelight and earnestness. "I can't promise about the wizards," he said at last. "But I'll stay away from magic, if I can. I don't want to shame you. And I do want to win."

Rugg sighed. "That'll have to do, I suppose. Now. Debates are traditionally in the spring, at Festival time. That means you'll have to challenge Crabbe as soon as MidWinter's over."

"Spring!" Cassius complained. "Where's the drama if you challenge him three months before you debate him? Everyone's going to be bored to numbness with the whole affair by then."

"It gives the other man time to prepare," Elton pointed out.

"Or leave town," said Cassius.

The meeting broke up very late, with all of the participants quite drunk and very fond of each other in a conspiratorial kind of way.

"Never liked Crabbe," Rugg confided loudly as the fire burned low. "Humorless bastard—stick up his arse, eh? Glad to do him one in the eye."

"Inn—innov— New thinkers got to stick together," Elton declared. "Scratch each other's backs. Would you scratch my back, Basil?"

"To the bone, Tom," Basil said earnestly. "Day or night. Just ask. You, too, Leonard, Lucas. You've saved my life. Do anything you like."

"Get rid of Campion," said Elton. When Basil stiffened angrily, he waved a languid hand. "Sorry. No harm in trying. It's out of love, you know."

ALONE, FOR ONCE, BASIL WATCHED THE MOON TRACK its way across the panes of the high, slanting window over his bed, doubling itself when it passed over an imperfection in the glass.

Keep away from wizards. If they only knew.

"Secrets fester," he murmured to the moon. "Knowledge must be brought to light." He rolled over, fumbled under his bed for the box that held the Book and, pulling it out, held it in his hands. If only he could bring its secrets to the light, he thought, he'd break his promise to Rugg in a heartbeat. But the meaning of its spells was locked as tight as the dead mouths of the wizards who had uttered them.

Basil lit a candle, held a page near it, then up to his slanted window. But neither flame nor cold moonlight could illuminate the sense of those words, as thick and impenetrable as a night without stars. He ran his fingers lightly over the thorny, undecipherable lines. Their very incomprehensibility spoke to him of powerful rites crafted by masters of wind and soil and human desire, who encoded their wisdom in a secret language to keep it safe. The magic was real. It had to be real. He could feel it in his fingers when he turned the soft skin pages, still miraculously supple after so many centuries. He could see it in the recalcitrance of the words, which never seemed so foreign as when he tried to transcribe them.

Basil shook his head. He'd had too much to drink, that's what it was. Magic wasn't real. Not now. But to these vanished wizards, trained in its spells, steeped in traditions and rites and knowledge passed down from master to master, oh, to them it had been real as sunlight. Of this he was sure. The book told him that, at least.

The book told him that, but what would it tell others? The intangibility of his proofs was one reason to pay attention to Rugg's caution against revealing the wizards as the new focus of his studies, let alone its source. Another was the tangible and utterly embarrassing fact that reading the book inevitably sent Basil into erotic daydreams that were as violent as they were explicit. Thinking of the book was tantamount to thinking of Theron and what Basil would like to do to him. Basil did not dare show

Theron the book. And tonight had made it clear that there was no point in telling Elton or Cassius or even Rugg about his discovery.

It was too soon to show his hand, he told himself. He didn't know enough about it. He must study Arioso's notebooks, collate the commentaries, see what he could find out about the wizards who had put their names to the spell-book's notes and conjectures, research the crest on the document box, turn it all into history: documented, analyzed, safely in the past. When he'd done all that, he'd write a book about it, and that book would be the most important historical analysis of the age. With it, he could win the Horn Chair, even without Rugg's precious debate. He'd dedicate it to Theron.

In the meantime, however, there was a great deal to do.

chapter II

THE YEAR DREW ON TO MidWinter, THE White
Days between the old year and the new. It was a time of
holiday for every soul in the city except the tavern-
keepers and the Watch. The Hill swarmed with tailors and seam-
stresses, with purveyors of fancy goods and wine, with carts from
the country bearing sheep and geese and deer and pheasants to be
served up at MidWinter feasts. At the University, the MidWinter
Brand went from door to door, collecting from each student his
(and occasionally, her) statutory stick of wood for the Last Night
bonfire in the Great Court. The honorable magistrates of the
City Council sat in conference with civic-minded nobles of the
Council of Lords, planning public entertainments.

Traditionally, the Last Night of the old year, which began the
festivities, was a night of bonfires and mayhem, presided over by a
University student chosen by his fellows. He was called the Little
King; his court were his Companions. Magistrates still sweated in
their cozy beds over tales of the bad old days, when Last Night
left behind it ravished maidens, abducted children, corpses in the
street, shops stripped bare of their wares and their furniture, and a

handful of formal challenges to the death. The City Council had finally abolished the Little King and tried to abolish the selling of liquor or the lighting of open fires for the ten days of the festival. That was the year the City had learned the true meaning of the word mayhem.

Now there were civic bonfires in the major squares, tended by the long-suffering Watch, and fireworks at midnight over the river. The whole city spent the night drinking and dancing in the streets, and if a dog was blown up by a firecracker tied to its tail or a few windows were smashed, well, a few nights in the lockup were enough to clear the taint of it in time for the new year.

Justis Blake's first year at University, he'd gone home for MidWinter to his country village, where they saw the old year out with fire and song and the little children fell asleep by the bonfire on the village green. He'd been homesick enough to endure his friends' teasing and the trouble and expense of going home. This year, however, he had decided to stay.

On the morning of Last Day, Doctor St Cloud lectured to no more than half of his usual audience. Which was a pity, Justis thought, sucking warmth back into his stiffened fingers, but only to be expected right before the holiday.

"In the archives of the University," St Cloud was saying, "there is a curious manuscript, written by one of the minor wizards attending on King Laurent. This wizard, who did not feel it necessary to sign his name to his private musings, conveniently spent many pages mourning certain ancient rituals, which he describes as you or I, when we grow old, might someday describe our University exploits."

Everyone chuckled. Justis glanced to where Finn was sitting rapt, his bony face sharpened to a fine point of concentration. Beside him, Lindley scribbled furiously. They both wore roughly-carved wooden leaves pinned to their hat brims, and there was a lovelock plaited into Lindley's copper hair. They'd begun floating about in a cloud of roses and musk shortly after the day Lindley had discovered his adored master with Lord Theron Campion. Vandeleur's opinion was that he'd settled on the Northerner out of pique, but Justis remembered how Lindley had looked when

Finn was holding forth on little kings, wizards, and deer. It had been the look of a thirsty man offered drink.

Blake returned his attention to the lecture. "Now, the wizard's account of MidWinter presents a neat problem of scholarship," said Doctor St Cloud. "The name 'MidWinter Festival' was bestowed on the White Days by law shortly after the Fall. It took a great deal of rereading and cross-referencing to determine that the wizard's Royal Hunt took place during the same time. Luckily, 'White Days' is a term of great antiquity, so I looked for a passage where the two terms fall together. And I found it." St Cloud took a small tablet of notes from his pocket and ran his finger down it. "Ah, here it is. 'This year, the White Days were gray, nor could the King's Wizard break the clouds, so that the Royal Hunt perforce took place in utter darkness.'

"So," St Cloud said, "I reread the wizard's memoir with an eye to the Royal Hunt, and this is what I learned. During the White Days, the king went a-hunting deer, leaving a young man, chosen by the wizards, behind him on the throne. This Little King ruled during ten days of license, when apprentices ruled masters and servants ordered nobles to do their bidding."

"Ten days is impossible," Peter Godwin shouted from the back bench. "Why, there would have been chaos."

St Cloud looked up. "I may have misread the passage. Perhaps you'd like to see what you make of it, and report what you have discovered, let us say, First Day morning?"

Godwin was silent.

"Never mind, Peter," Vandeleur soothed. "The manuscript will still be there when you've recovered from your hangover."

Finn turned on his bench and glared. "*Some* of us," he said pointedly, "are interested in what Doctor St Cloud has to say, and would thank you to shut up."

There was a good deal of angry murmuring at this—the students were excited and ready for their holiday, and Finn was not well-liked. Someone bounced an apple core off his hat—one of Godwin's cronies, probably—and the lecture might have come to a noisy end had not St Cloud burst out laughing.

"I'm flattered, Finn. And encouraged." He surveyed the

restless students. "The purpose of the Royal Hunt was not simply sport and venison for the royal table. The killing of the deer was a ceremony intended to bring back the sun and ensure an early spring. There's an old Northern poem about it, very exciting, full of hunts and betrayals. But here's the interesting bit." He consulted his notes. " 'Without his due of blood,' the wizard writes, 'the Sun dozeth in his winter quarters, and the frozen soil holdeth the grain locked in its stony clods.' " St Cloud looked at them and smiled. "In these degenerate days, the Sun must eke out his due of blood from broken heads and bloody noses. Try and make sure they aren't yours. Dismissed."

There was laughter, applause, shouts of "Good Festival, Doctor St Cloud," the clatter of boots on the steps from the gallery, the scraping of benches, and a blast of air tinged with the smell of roast chestnuts as the students tumbled out into the narrow street. Full of holiday cheer, Blake slapped Henry Fremont on the back and offered to stand him some roasted chestnuts.

"Don't *do* that, you great ox," snapped Fremont. "You'll break someone's rib one day, and, like as not, it'll be mine."

Justis laughed. "Undoubtedly. Do you want chestnuts or not?"

Fremont shifted the pouch hanging from his shoulder. It was new, Justis noticed, made of good leather, and worth the price of a good dinner with wine. "Nice," he said appreciatively. "MidWinter gift?"

Fremont glanced down at the pouch as though he'd never seen it before. "That's it," he said brightly. "My father had a good year, sent me a purse. I fell prey to temptation in Tilney Market. Don't worry, there's plenty left to pay my tick at the Nest, and for roasted chestnuts, too, and even a MidWinter apple. Want one?"

Justis nodded amiably and followed Fremont to the vendor's cart, where a tray of MidWinter apples shone a deep, sticky gold. As a liar, Fremont was about as convincing as a wolf got up in a fleece, as his mother would say. The thought made Justis suddenly, dizzyingly homesick. He bit into the apple. Sweet, warm caramel and tart, cold apple flooded his mouth with the taste of home. It was all he could do to thank Fremont for the treat and find his way to his cold, dark room, where he could sniffle in peace.

O N THE HILL, KATHERINE, DUCHESS TREMONTAINE, looked to see that all was in order for her Last Night party. The bonfire was laid ready to light. There was, as always, plenty of food. She wore a splendid new dress and a cheap pearl necklace her mother had given her: one old, one new, as was the custom. Katherine did not love tradition for its own sake, but there were things that had always meant a great deal to her, and Last Night was one of them. She liked to have her chosen family around her; they were her link to her future and her past. Her mother was long gone, and so was the alarming uncle, her mother's younger brother, who had left her the duchy. She liked to remember them both on Last Night.

So in a small room in Tremontaine House, tonight three candles burned. One was in front of a miniature, a portrait of a woman with soft brown hair and worried eyes. Katherine stood before it, fingering the pearl at her neck. Another candle illumined a bundle of papers tied with tape. She did not need to open them, she'd read them so many times. Marcus had helped her to collect them after the old duke had fled: letters he'd left behind, a curious mix of the deeply personal—invitations, love notes, hastily scribbled theories about the world—and daily trivia: guest lists and menus and bills. In the early days of her duchy, she had consulted them as if they held the secret of just what she was supposed to be doing there. There were also the few letters the vanished duke had sent home from Kyros, again a disparate lot: a request for money, a description of the house he was building, a request to see the little daughter he'd left behind. The duke had disliked sitting for portraits; those that existed, Sophia had in Riverside House.

The third candle burned on a table in front of a mirror: an invitation, of sorts, to the spirits of this night, of this House, to attend the festivities, to cast their gaze on the current duchess and see what they made of her tenure in their place. When she was a girl, Katherine had tried the little spells that country girls know in front of mirrors on Last Night, hoping to glimpse her

True Love's face looking over her shoulder, or boldly calling up ghosts.

Fleet light, last night
Old year out
Show what is past
As I turn me about

But the Duchess Tremontaine did not turn her in a circle to see vanished sights. She looked directly into the mirror, and saw them all in her own face: the centuries of noble ancestors, bound to this city and to the land that sustained them . . . and, like a caddis-fly, her own brief life so far: the people she had loved and learned from, feared and desired, who had all in some way left their mark on her.

She turned from the mirror, leaving the candles to burn, and looked out the window. In the drive below, horses were kicking up gravel, pulling up to the door with the first of many carriages. She heard children shouting, and the voice of her oldest friend, Marcus, who had chosen the name "Ffoliot" for himself because he liked the pattern the letters made. Marcus was laughing, and Katherine laughed too and went downstairs to join them.

L AST NIGHT FELL AS CLEAR AND BRITTLE AS THE ICE that skimmed the river. It was the kind of night where a shout is visible and hot air dances over open flames. Sundown was marked by a tocsin on the Cathedral bell, echoed by the bells of the University, Sessions Hall, and the Council Chamber as the Brands' Procession set out from the Cathedral. First came the High Priest, the Mayor, and the Crescent Chancellor in an open carriage, and behind them the other chancellors of the Inner Council—Raven, Dragon, and Serpent—accompanied by as many members of the Council as cared to come out, mounted on horses caparisoned with golden bells. Then came the City Magistrates, their horses decked in holly wreaths, and a company of priests on foot, carrying banners embroidered with suns and deer and boar and sheaves of wheat and other signs of plenty. The end of the procession was brought up by the three MidWinter Brands—a noble, a student, and an apprentice, holly in their hats, carrying the flambeaux with which they'd light their respective bonfires.

The nobles' bonfire in the cobbled yard in front of the Council Hall was attended mostly by secretaries, minor officials of common blood, and the luckless lord told off to be that year's Brand, who was forced to be late for the glittering Last Night parties on the Hill, with their smaller, private bonfires.

Justis Blake, standing among his friends at the mouth of the Great Court, heard all this and more from Vandeleur, who had attended city Last Nights in his mother's arms and ever since.

"The Crescent chooses all three Brands from the civil rolls," he informed Justis as they stamped their feet and waited for the procession to come round. "With a silver pin, they say, blindfolded, completely by chance."

"If you believe that, you'll believe anything," said Fremont. "All the artisans and merchants want one of their apprentices to be MidWinter Brand. It's supposed to bring good luck; it certainly brings customers. And none of the nobles want the job—it means they have to spend the night being polite to nobodies. It stands to reason there must be a brisk trade in bribes and favors."

"Can't you give it a rest, Henry?" Justis asked wearily. "It's Last Night. We're supposed to be bidding the old year and its worries farewell."

Fremont's answer was drowned in a shout from the end of the street. The blackness was punctuated by bobbing torches and everyone began to cheer. From the center of the Court, a group struck up the chorus of a traditional Last Night song, old as the hills and at least as dirty, and soon the air shivered with it. Justis found himself bawling along with the rest, tuneless as a cat in heat and ignorant of everything save the chorus, which he sang twice as loud because he knew the words.

*It's one for luck and two for love
And three for beer and brandy.
Four times a night*

I can do it all right
And the sun comes up in the morning!

The leading carriage passed, glittering in the torchlight as if each gilded curlicue were a tiny, separate flame. The three men it bore, massive in furs and velvet, tossed posies of scented herbs into the crowd. One of the posies struck Blake's forehead, but he wasn't quick enough to catch it. He caught the flask Vandeleur tossed him, though, and took a swig of what it contained.

"That's *three*," Fremont said. "Maybe later, we'll get lucky and have a taste of *two* and *four*."

E VERYONE AT THE DUCHESS TREMONTAINE'S LAST Night family party was eating except its newest member, who was spitting up.

"Ooh," said his mother, "that was a *good* burp!"

"Diana," her brother Andrew objected, "do you absolutely *have* to do that in here? It's disgusting!"

Her twin sister Isabel, pregnant as a whale, waddled over to take the baby from her. "Oh, Andy, you were ten times as disgusting, wasn't he, Mother?" The baby settled into her arms. "There, my little cuddle-bunny, yes."

"Andrew was not disgusting," said his mother loyally. "He was a lovely baby. You all were."

"Except for Alice." Andrew poked his youngest sister with a sugar stick. "I remember, she threw up all the time."

But in the last year, Alice had stopped crying when he teased her. She snatched up a stick of her own, shouting, "Guard yourself, evildoer!"

"Oh, well done," applauded the duchess, who was giving the child sword lessons. "Nice form, Alice."

Alice's brother drew back with all the dignity of his thirteen years. "Alice is such a child," he remarked to his sister Beatrice, who was sixteen.

"So are you." She turned her back on him to fuss over the baby.

Their father waved a mug of steaming ale expansively. "You are *all* children," he said. "Lovely children."

Alice drew herself up. "I am not a child. I am a swordsman. Will I get a sword for New Year's, Papa?"

Marcus Ffoliot crouched down to look his youngest daughter in the eye. "Well, that depends, doesn't it? This is Last Night, and it's ten whole days 'til the New Year begins. Those ten days are very important."

"Why?"

Marcus had not had a traditional childhood. He looked over at his wife for help. Susan smiled and said in a storyteller's singsong, "Because the old year is dead, but the new one's not begun. The doors are open between old and new, and anything can happen."

Her oldest daughter, Diana, full of the authority of new motherhood, said practically, "You have to be good for ten whole days, then you get First Night presents. Last Night isn't for new things, it's for getting rid of the old. Did you give alms today?"

"Yes," answered Alice. "We went with Nurse to give away our boxes of old clothes and things. I gave away my red ruffled blouse," she added virtuously, spoiling the effect with, "Swordsmen don't wear ruffles."

"Papa!" Andrew whined. "You're not *really* going to give her a *sword?*"

"Oh, no," said Marcus mildly, catching Katherine's eye. "I'll let the duchess do that."

"But only if she practices hard these ten days," Katherine added.

Andrew rolled his eyes. "If *you* get a real sword, *I'm* leaving home."

His sister Isabel hugged him. "That's all right, you can come live with Carlos and me."

He pulled away from her. "And another baby? No, thank you!"

Beatrice said, "Don't worry, Andy, she's not getting a real sword. They're mad, but they're not that mad."

Alice swung her candy stick in an arc. "Maybe Jessica will get me one. She sends *excellent* presents."

It was Katherine's turn to roll her eyes. "Indeed. And she never asks if you've been good or not."

"I hope," said Susan mildly, "she doesn't send any more of those rather *curious* carvings."

"I hope," Beatrice breathed a prayer, "she sends *silk*."

"I hope she sends swords," Alice muttered.

Diana's husband, Martin Amory, was a banker. With the birth of his son, he was feeling expansive. "Come on, Alice," he said. "What do you want besides a sword? How about a new necklace?"

His wife put her arm through his. "No, dear," said Diana. "That's what *I* want."

Her twin looked at them enviously for a moment. Her husband, Carlos the musician, was out playing for a larger party elsewhere on the Hill. Katherine would pay for him to be with them at Tremontaine House, of course, but they'd agreed that that was no way to make his reputation. Still, it would be nice if he could be with her for the bonfire. Isabel helped herself to another piece of marzipan and looked up to find her twin at her side.

"Another year," Diana said companionably.

Isabel nodded and put her hand to her huge belly. "I'll feel better when this little one's decided to come and join the rest of us."

"Yes," said her sister, "you will. Do you want me to rub your back? Sit down and put your feet up."

Isabel eased into a chair. "I feel like I might pop at any moment."

"Ooh!" Diana shivered deliciously. "A baby born at MidWinter! How spooky. It's said they can see ghosts."

"Theron always said he could."

"Where is he, anyway?" Diana asked acerbically. "Off lighting a few fires on his own?"

Isabel laughed. "That was last year. Sophia's not here either. She's probably been deluged at the infirmary, and he's escorting her."

Predictably, her words seemed to blow open the door, ushering in the Lady Sophia and her son. Like everyone else at the party, Theron was dressed in festival splendor. His shirt was green silk, his waistcoat a fantasy of winter ivy and gold thread, his coat a richly patterned brocade of copper brown with gold piping. An emerald drop hung from one ear. He circled the room, kissing his relations by blood and by adoption. He admired the baby extravagantly and congratulated Martin. Diana waved from the corner: "Hoo-oo! Theron! I'm the one who did all the work!"

Grinning, he came over. "Just because you couldn't get anyone else to do it for you." She kissed him anyway, because it was Last Night.

"Isabel!" He sprang back from her pregnant sister. "Do you think it might be twins?"

"I know," she sighed from the chair; "I look like a pumpkin."

"At least," he said, "I can finally tell you apart."

"Bah," said Diana, "you always could. We had to work extra hard to fool you."

"Why, thank you." He bowed. "That's the nicest thing you've said to me all year."

"Well," she smiled poisonously, "you've got ten more days to deserve something better."

⌐

THE MIDWINTER PROCESSION CROSSED THE GREAT Court, past the heap of logs and sticks the University Brand and his cohorts had been building for a week, and out the far side on its way to the Sessions Hall. The magistrates waved cheerfully at the singing students, many of them joining in for a chorus or two. The priests, singing their own MidWinter hymn, moved through the jollity like pebbles through a cow. They paced slowly and deliberately in the magistrates' wake, their ungloved hands patchy with cold.

"Are they deaf?" Justis bellowed into Vandeleur's ear.

"You could say that," Vandeleur bellowed back. "I think they're just so full of shit their ears are plugged."

A passing priest scotched this theory by shooting a furious look in their direction, bending Vandeleur and Justis almost double with helpless laughter.

"Look, look, you asses," screeched Fremont; "they're lighting the fire. Look, or you'll miss it."

⌒

ALL RIGHT!" THE DUCHESS KATHERINE CLAPPED HER hands, and the whole room looked up. "It's almost time for the bonfire. If you don't have your lists all written, there's pen and ink laid out on the table."

It was the same every year. She always left plenty of time for them to collect their thoughts, time to savor the heavy paper, the different colored inks (some of them scented), the old-style quills cut from the feathers of geese and swans and even peacocks. Beatrice snatched up one of the latter, and a bottle of violet ink. Andrew found a crow's quill, and the gold.

Theron had already spent time alone in his rooms, composing his thoughts and his words carefully. Some years he wrote them as a poem, but this year he had drawn up a simple list—of his regrets, his mistakes, the things he wished the old year's flames to burn away. Ysaud was chief among them; he'd even made a little packet to throw on the fire: a ribbon she'd given him and a lock of her hair, all wrapped up in a poem he'd written her once. He'd noticed that Katherine had taken down the painting by Ysaud that had hung in the front hall. It was kind of her. He felt for the packet in his pocket, then went to tell Alice how to spell "aggressive."

⌒

WHEN THE UNIVERSITY BRAND LAID HIS TORCH TO the piled wood, a great shout went up from a thousand throats, and then there was silence while they waited for the fire to catch. Far from the center of the Court, Justis strained to see the pale, smoky harbingers of the fire that would burn away the griefs and cares of the old year and rouse the Sun from his long drowsing. It felt no different from the same moment in his village—the sound of breathing in the dark, the anxious murmurs soon hushed, the sense of time suspended, waiting on a tiny tongue of flame to release it.

First came the crackling of new-caught kindling, and then a joyous shout sounded: "Death to the Old!"

Justis plumed out a breath he hadn't been aware of holding and added his voice to the general roar: "Death to the Old!" Briefly, he thought of Doctor St Cloud, watching with the other doctors from the steps of the Great Hall, and wondered whether the traditional phrase disturbed him. Then he wasn't really thinking any more, but fighting his way to the fire with the twist of paper upon which he'd written his year's regrets and bitternesses.

T HE TREMONTAINE BONFIRE WAS SOMETHING TO BE- hold. The wood was all seasoned, with great logs sent up from the country expressly for the purpose. It was piled high behind the house in the garden overlooking the river (the duchess's gardener having assured her that the peonies loved the ashes).

It was tradition at Tremontaine House for the youngest child to bear the brand to light the fire. When they were growing up, that meant it had always been Theron—a fact bitterly resented by the twins, who had come into the world a scant six months before him. But Theron in his turn had been supplanted by Beatrice, and Beatrice by Andrew, and Andrew now by Alice, a fact Andrew pretended mightily not to care about.

Alice marched importantly to the fire, her blazing brand held high. Theron had always hurled his into the center; but Alice was a careful child. Delicately she touched the flame to the bits of dry straw that stuck out at the bottom, watching them catch before moving on. Only when she had circled the entire fire did she step back and throw her torch as far into it as she could. Her mother let out a sigh of relief that only Marcus heard. He squeezed his wife's waist and kissed her, a small outlet for the joy he felt rising in him sharp and strong as grief, his love and gratitude for the family he'd never imagined he would have. Now that Alice was growing up, he wondered if Susan might manage just one or two more babies. Why should Is and Di have all the fun?

The whole staff of Tremontaine House was gathered there, too; people were singing MidWinter carols and throwing their past year's griefs into the flames. Katherine was embracing everyone and wishing them a healthy new year. New people began to arrive—friends and relatives paying calls, bearing fresh twigs and herbs to throw on each fire they visited. The Talbert cousins were among the first; as Katherine's nearest kin, her brother's children, it was only civil. Theron saw Charlie Talbert approaching and braced himself for another spate of horse-talk. But Charlie only saluted him on both cheeks, wished him a good year, and went off to flirt with Beatrice Ffoliot, whom Theron hoped knew better than to take Charlie seriously. Theron found Sophia indoors, settling Isabel in a chair. The girl looked tired and unhappy.

Theron bowed. "She blossoms like the MidWinter rose."

"You're an idiot," Isabel groaned. "Carlos was right, I should have stayed home. Theron, are you going to Lord Godwin's?"

"I suppose. We were invited."

"Well, honor them with your presence long enough to find my husband, will you? The beautiful bastard behind the keyboards? And tell him I'm staying here tonight."

Sophia squeezed her hand. "That will be best. I will send Molly in, to put you to bed."

Sophia looked magnificent in a gown of black velvet with white lace and a collar of pearls. It was one of the few times in the year that she bothered to dress according to her rank, and Theron always took considerable pride in escorting her to the Last Night parties, as if she were some foreign princess, stately and proud, exotic in her rich simplicity, her dark hair piled high. Once, when he teased her about vanity, she replied very seriously, "Your father always told me I must look my best before them all." *Them*—the nobles of the city—the people he belonged to, and yet did not. As for his own dress, Theron did not follow fashion: he paid his valet to do that. But he did love beauty, and the sleek fit of a good coat.

ODWIN HOUSE WAS BRIGHTLY LIT, THE FRONT HALL crowded with people coming and going. The past three generations of Godwins had each produced a Crescent Chancellor; the family was important, and everyone came to pay their respects.

Theron followed Sophia into the ballroom. A fire roared at one end of it, for people to cast their twigs into. The room was very warm, but one old man, splendidly dressed, sat close to the fire. He was wrapped in quilted silk, and the skin on his ringed hands was as thin and fine as a moth's wings. With a rustle of satin and velvet, Sophia Campion knelt at his side and put one of her hands on his. He turned to look at her, and Theron marveled at the beauty that still clung to him. Here was an ancient king for Basil to admire! Michael, Lord Godwin, went back to Theron's father's time. Legend even had it that he himself had once fought the swordsman St Vier.

"Lady Sophia." Lord Godwin smiled. His voice was papery too. "I know that you, at least, are not going to start shouting 'Death to the Old!' "

"No, indeed. Theron and I are come to wish you good health."

Lord Godwin looked up. "So this is Tremontaine's boy."

"Yes, my lord," answered Theron, staring. His father would be nearly this old, if he had lived.

Lord Godwin took in Theron's long hair. "A University scholar. Getting old for that, though—you'll have to marry him off soon, my lady."

"Yes," said Sophia gallantly, "but your daughters are all spoken for, sir."

The old man chuckled. "I've a great-granddaughter or two floating about somewhere—but I don't know what their mothers would say about it. Have to ask them; I'm no longer in the business. Lovely to see you, my dear; come and call on me again, sometime."

Theron helped his mother to her feet. She tucked her arm into his, and as they walked away, he bent his head down to hear her say: "Your father told me Lord Godwin was lovers to your great-grandmother. But I am not sure I think so."

"Someone should write a history," said Theron dreamily, "a secret history—someone should ask him, or it will all be lost."

His mother dealt him a sharp look. "Some things are meant to be lost. History is for knowing wisdom, not gossip."

He thought of Basil again, and forbore to answer her. Instead he left her talking with an old acquaintance, and went off to the musicians to deliver Isabel's message to her husband.

After reassuring the startled keyboardist that his wife was neither giving birth nor dying, Theron went looking for food. He found a table with roasted meats, and was helping himself to venison when someone touched his arm. It was his cousin Gregory Talbert, Katherine's older brother, Charlie's father. Gregory was a florid man who now headed the house of Talbert. Theron did not like him, and he suspected his father hadn't either, or he would not have passed Gregory over in favor of Katherine for the duchy. Lord Talbert was not stupid, but he was annoying. He greeted Theron warmly, adding, "It is so nice to see you out and about!"

"I've not been ill," Theron said, surprised.

"No, indeed. But at this time last year, shall we say you were a bit hard to find?" Theron flushed. He'd spent as little of the festival as possible on the Hill, rushing back to be with Ysaud. Talbert knew it, too: "I hear you were having your portrait done," he said.

Theron refused to hide behind the duchess's skirts, but he was not above playing her in a family hand. "Yes," he said blandly, "Katherine wanted it painted." Invoking her usually shut the Talberts up. But not this time.

"I hear," said his cousin, "that it didn't work out. Now don't get starchy with me, my boy—I'm just trying to be a little helpful. It's nothing that isn't common knowledge, after all."

"Is it?" said Theron starchily. "I didn't know you listened to gossip."

"Oh, I don't, my boy, I don't! But people will talk. Plenty of us have sat for portraits to her, but few have been invited to stay . . ."

Theron could feel his temper rising. "Excuse me," he said, but his cousin laid his hand on his arm with surprising strength.

"No, my boy, you listen to me. You may not like it, but what you do is noticed, and what's noticed is discussed. That is the world, and there's an end to it." Miserably fascinated, Theron allowed himself to be drawn off to the side. "It's one thing to enjoy tavern girls or your school friends or whatever you like, in moderation. But to disappear into the clutches of a notorious woman—and then, when she's finally finished with you, to mope about in Riverside without showing your face on the Hill in Society . . . It's not good. My sister has never understood about Society, but then, the Duchess Tremontaine doesn't have to. And that Ffoliot fellow"—Theron's jaw clenched—"I beg your pardon, but he's not one of us."

"He might have married your sister," said Theron meanly, goaded beyond endurance, "and then where would you be?"

"Where would *you* be, you mean, if she had produced an heir? No, dear boy, don't try to outface me. I am older than you, and I know the world. You do not come to see me, and I have not forced myself on you. But this is something you need to hear."

"What is? That people talk about me? Believe me, I know that. Why else do you think I stayed in Riverside after the—after Ysaud? To avoid having to walk through a room full of types like you, all gossiping about my private affairs."

"And I tell you," the older man hissed in his face, "if you want to keep them private, then act as if they're private. Live whatever life you want behind closed doors, but live one also in plain sight for people to see, one that's *normal*."

Theron stepped back, his mouth open. "Normal?"

Lord Talbert took his interest at face value. "It wouldn't hurt you to spend more time with other young men of your own kind. You're not a boy anymore. Now, I know Charlie and his friends are always glad to see you . . ."

Theron didn't know whether to black his cousin's lights or laugh in his face, but he knew both would get him in trouble. "Yes," he said unsteadily. "Yes, I'll have to try and do that."

"Good man." With another squeeze of the arm, Lord Talbert turned away, and then turned back. "Oh, and the hair." One last squeeze. "Think about cutting it."

Theron thought about Basil making a curtain of it for them

to kiss in. "Thank you, cousin," he said through gritted teeth.
"Happy New Year."

In search of a drink, Theron nearly ran into one of the
Godwin boys—Peter, it was, with his scholar's hair pulled back in
a curly little tail, and with him, the geography student Lord
Sebastian Hemmynge, eyes bright with drink.

"Campion!" The other noble students greeted him like a
long-lost brother, and he returned their embraces. "We are dying
of a surfeit of aunts and grandmothers," Hemmynge declared,
"and people who don't know Placid from a broken pocket watch.
The University bonfire's on in the Great Court, and there will be
whiskey and music and girls—and, of course, lots of fine rhetoric.
Will you join us?"

"Nothing," said Theron heartily, "that I would like better."

And fifteen minutes of warm farewells found them out the
door and heading down the hill with their bright torches, singing
at the top of their lungs on the way to the University.

J USTIS DIDN'T KNOW HOW MUCH TIME HAD PASSED SINCE
the bonfire had been lit. Benedict Vandeleur's flask of spirits
was nearly empty. Alaric Finn was pulling from a skin of new
beer; Anthony Lindley, who had no head for drink, had been
sick. He still looked a little white around the nose, but he'd recovered enough to dance at the edge of the space cleared by the
bonfire's heat. He had braided dozens of bright ribbons into his
red hair and tied them off with brass bells that glittered as he
whirled like flying sparks.

Justis reached behind his head to pull off the cord confining
his own sandy hair and shook it free. It felt wonderful.

"Pretty," a strange student said, and pulled Justis's head down
to his for a kiss. Justis let himself be lost for a moment in the
warmth of the stranger's lips, the tang of ale on his tongue, and
then he disengaged himself, laughing.

"You're pretty, too," he assured his admirer. "But I prefer hens
to cocks. Don't be offended."

The student shrugged. "Don't know what you're missing," he

said cheerfully, and staggered off in search of a more congenial partner. His hair slithered across his back in a mass of tiny braids.

A hand gripped Justis's arm and tugged him around to face a fellow historian—not someone Justis knew well. Cortney, he thought his name was. "Here. Have one of these." He thrust a hard and lumpy object into Justis's hand. It was a wooden leaf on a string.

"Where'd you get this, Cortney?" Justis asked.

"Get it?" Cortney blinked slowly. "I didn't get it. It came to me. I looked down, and there it was. They were." He indicated his own chest, which was decorated with a similar leaf. "I gave you the extra one."

"Why?"

"I like you, Justis. Don't know why." Cortney frowned. "Hang on. I do, too. You're a decent man, Justis Blake. Not as bright as some, but decent. I want to shake your hand."

He held out a plump, chapped palm, which Justis, much moved, clasped with his own, and pumped energetically.

"If I may interrupt this touching moment," Vandeleur said behind him. "Finn's making an ass of himself—over there, by the fire."

The crowd in the Court had cleared somewhat as the students spread their merrymaking to the surrounding streets and taverns. Justis had a clear view of Finn's wiry figure spiraling the bonfire, holding a stick that looked suspiciously like a linkboy's unlit torch.

"He better keep his mouth shut," Vandeleur remarked. "He's drunk so much his breath'll catch fire if he gets too close."

"What's he think he's doing?" Justis asked uselessly. "He's going to get burned!"

By twos and threes, the students remaining in the Great Court stopped whatever they were doing and watched Finn approach the fire, some calling out for him to come back, some urging him on. Blake headed toward the fire, shouting, "Don't go any closer!"

He'd hardly taken three steps before he was surrounded by a small group of Northerners, all wearing oak-leaf badges and dozens of ribboned braids.

"Don't, Justis." Anthony Lindley was kneeling almost at Justis's feet. His face was flushed and sweaty and stuck with tendrils of hair and loose ribbon. "You mustn't try to stop him. He's going to start the Hunt."

"What hunt?"

"The Royal Hunt, Southron." His informant was a vaguely familiar blond with wide-set eyes—Greenleaf, his name was. "The Hunt that feeds the Land."

"The Land wants him to." Lindley's voice was reverent.

Justis spread puzzled hands wide. "It's what we've always done back home," Greenleaf explained with ironic kindness. "To make the Sun come again. A primitive ritual, but it seems to work."

"He'll lead us to the wood," said one of his friends, "and we'll hunt the Deer, and all will be as it should be."

By this time, Lindley had taken in Justis's tumbling hair and the leaf lying on his breastbone. "I see you bear the token. You'll soon understand."

Justis tugged at the leaf, intending to remove the token and then himself from his disquieting company, but was distracted when a gasp went up from the assembled students. He looked up to see Alaric Finn dart up to the bonfire, thrust his torch into it, and dance back again, waving the lighted brand triumphantly over his head.

"To the Wood!" Finn shrilled. "For the Hunt and the Sacrifice and the Feast of the Sun!"

Lindley scrambled to his feet and tossed back his tinkling braids. "The Wood!" he cried. "To the Wood!" And he held out his hands to his scarlet-faced lover, who embraced him one-armed. The students, Northern and Southern, opened a path for them, stamping and cheering and picking up the chant, "To the Wood! To the Wood!"

Without actually having decided to join them, Justis found himself running through the streets surrounded by young men with loose, flying hair and loose, flying gowns, shouting, "To the Wood!" at the top of his lungs. At one point, the man coursing next to him veered to one side, grabbed at a hanging shutter, and, after a brief struggle, tore it free.

"Wood!" he shouted. And the entire pack obeyed him, tearing apart a shack some hapless merchant had built against the side of his shop and running on again, each man carrying a stick or a plank, pursuing Finn's torch and his hoarse cry: "To the Wood!"

As they rounded a corner, the torch stopped, and with it the panting, wild-eyed pack of students. Justis wiped his streaming face against his shoulder, suddenly conscious that his lungs burned, his legs ached, and his hands prickled with splinters from the board he carried. He heard a thick, aristocratic voice drawl, "What in the Seven Hells is this?"

As if in answer, Anthony Lindley's clear tenor cried aloud: "The Deer! The Deer! Behold the Deer!"

Justis squinted. The light of Finn's torch danced on the astonished faces of three richly dressed young men standing at the mouth of the street. Two of them looked familiar. Before Justis could collect himself to think why, Lindley pointed at one of them, a long-haired beauty in green and gold, and cried again, "The Deer!"

The chosen young man's eyes flashed with reflected light as he gaped at the panting, growling pack. Then he darted down an alley with Finn behind him, and Greenleaf and his Northerners and Lindley and Vandeleur and Fremont and cautious, decent Justis Blake, shouting "The Deer! The Deer!" as they harried their quarry out of the city.

~

THERON LAUGHED AS HE RAN. HE KNEW THE STREETS and alleys of University—hadn't he been finding his way around them since he was old enough to walk? *I'll lead them to Riverside*, he thought, *and lose them there.* He grinned to think of the University crowd staggering helpless amidst the filth and carnival of a Riverside Last Night. They were on the broad Riverway now. Their torches threw his shadow up wild against the warehouses. In another minute, he would gain the lower bridge; he'd be home free.

But suddenly he was in a daze of light and shadow, howling faces, and the heat of upraised fire. They had come round him, somehow, cut off his access to the bridge. Someone thrust a flask at him—he seized it, took a long pull of some honey-sweet liquor, cast it away, and wheeled back around, toward the North Gate. It was like the games of tag he'd played with the twins at Katherine's on summer nights, roaming the lawn in all directions. But this was the dark night of the year, and maybe they would all keep running till the sun came up.

Ahead, through the gate, the cold night air was sweet and pure. The scent pulled him: trees were there, and clear-running streams, and the cry of owls. Theron broke through the gate with the pack behind him.

Hardly anyone was shouting now. His own breathing was loud in his throat, and he could hear gasps and grunts in his wake. His feet sucked up midwinter mud, but so did his pursuers'. He wondered what had become of his noble friends from the Hill. Were they among the panting pack, or had they fled? Over the fields they all went, under moon and star, toward the tangle of the wood.

Something happened when he found himself amongst the trees. The torches were the only bright-colored thing in the black-and-silver world of the year's longest night. He couldn't tell tree from shadow of tree; he fought his way forward through stripes of illusion. But no longer did he lead them; he felt that he was being driven now, driven deeper into the wood, farther from the safety of the city. The spinning shadows made him dizzy. He closed his eyes and flung himself forward, hands outstretched, and felt before him nothing, a space, a clearing in the oak trees.

He was trapped. The men and their burning brands filled in the spaces between the trees, surrounding him with a ring of fire. He flung up his head, his nostrils flared, seeking a way out.

Around him the men began to sing, and to dance to their rough music. They were holding pieces of wood in their hands: torn-off shutters, bits of barrels, the spokes of a cartwheel. They flung them at the center, where Theron stood, so that he had to dance himself to avoid them. He understood words:

The Horn, the Horn, the King of Horn
Bless the day that he was born

Build the Fire around him high
New King in and Old King die!

The pile of wood grew at the center of the circle. Theron half-danced, half-staggered back into the arms of one of the men. It was Alaric Finn, who caught him and flung him across to another man, shouting, "The King! The King!" The next man caught him and held him tighter and longer—Theron felt the man's desire pressing hard against his thigh. He struggled and the man kissed him, biting his lips, before the shout went up and he was spun away to the arms of another—good god, it was Henry Fremont, hair disheveled and long face flushed. Fremont didn't kiss him. He gripped Theron's shoulders hard and stared at him with furious eyes, then flung him into the powerful arms of Justis Blake, who picked him right up off his feet and swung him around and around. Next was red-headed lovesick Anthony Lindley, who had fled from the sight of him naked that day at Basil's; this time, Lindley looked him full in the face and whispered, "Welcome, my lord." It was worse than a kiss. Theron shut his eyes—but the bright flames of the torches burned through the lids. He heard the singing:

You who bear the brand
You who bear the flame
Cast away the old
Let the new year reign!

He struggled in Lindley's arms—they were both holding him now, Lindley and the proud Northerner, Alaric Finn, between them—and a tall man was holding the honey flask to his lips, tipping the sweet burning liquid down his throat. Everything was orange and black, even the people—*Ysaud would love this*, Theron thought. He seemed to have stumbled into one of her paintings, and now he was trapped in it.

Someone shoved a burning torch into his face. He pulled his arm from Lindley's to grasp it, and Finn cried, "Light it, my lord! Light the fire now, you bollocks, and bid the Sun return!"

Theron hurled the brand into the center of the pile of scavenged wood. A great cry went up around the circle; all the torches were flung in, and the fierce honey liquor went round. He heard singing and shouting. As the flames rose up, the men fell back from the bonfire. Some retreated into the shadows of the trees; he heard sharp cries of pleasure, mixed with howls that might have been bloody murder but were not.

No one held his arms; now was his chance to escape, to return to civilization and warmth and safety. He looked up, and froze at what he saw.

Across the fire, across the circle, a figure stood very still amidst the trees. It was green as new grass, and brown as old leaves. It stepped forward into the firelight and smiled at him.

It was the King Man: the man from his dreams, walking free as dreams may on this night of all nights. Theron recognized the heavy brows and thin-lipped mouth, the powerful shoulders and the bearskin that hung from them. And, exactly as in his dream, the man held out the cup and said, "Will you drink, my lord?"

Theron shook his head, *No*, but the King Man still came forward, walking through the fire, which settled at his feet.

"The old year is dead," the King Man said, "and the new not yet begun. The door is open between the worlds. The old kings are dead, and the Land cries out for a new one."

Theron stepped back, but there was a pool of water behind him now, a flat pool of water silver in the moonlight. He was afraid to look into it, afraid he might see the horns spring from his head.

Again the King Man offered him the cup. "I tell you this. You will drink before the year is out, from the pool or from the cup, it makes no matter. Between that time and this, however you run, you will always run to me." He reached down and took a fistful of brown oak leaves from the forest floor, and cast them in Theron's face. Theron smelt old earth and fresh mold, the debris of a hundred centuries; he tasted the land in the back of his throat, and clutched at the forest as it rained around him.

"Now, run!" The voice rumbled through his bones, and he ran.

H IS PILLOW OVER HIS HEAD, BASIL ST CLOUD IG-
nored the noise of pounding as long as he could. There
were plenty of drunks out tonight. He'd seen them as he made his
way home from the festivities in the Great Hall, none too sober
himself. Best to stay behind closed doors.

But then he realized that the door being pounded on was his.
He rose and dragged himself to where he knew the door was, fumbled with the lock. His nose was assailed by wood smoke and
dead leaves, and the sharp tang of a man he had lain with many
times this year.

He clasped the man to him. "Theron," he whispered. But
Theron said nothing. Basil pulled him in, and flung open a shutter so that a little starlight could enter.

Theron's hair was unbound, tangled like a skein the cat had
played with. His gaudy festival clothes were muddy and torn. He
stared at Basil mutely, his eyes wide and helpless.

"My dear, what is it?"

Theron shook his head, opened his hand. An oak leaf,
crushed and dry, crumbled to nothingness.

"It's all right," Basil said. "It's all right." He smoothed the
hair back from his lover's face. Theron's breath was pungent with
liquor. His lips were rough and cracked, but his mouth was still
eager. Basil closed his eyes and saw himself falling into a sea of
old green—holly leaves, bright against the midwinter snow, and
ivy that grew up around him, twining around his legs, growing up
to his forked crotch with the inevitable power of life.

His fingers were clenched in Theron's hair. Slowly he released them and looked down into his lover's face, where Theron
knelt at his feet. The boy's face was a mask of passion. The edges
of his mouth were stained with blood and seed. He did not look
entirely human.

Basil searched himself for pity or concern and did not find
them, only the hot flush of power over the creature he had before
him. All questions of wealth and poverty, of Hill and University,
of Theron's father and Basil's father, dissolved into nothing before that power. It was more than desire. There was something almost sacred about it, bright and consuming as the flames of a
bonfire.

He began the slow removal of Theron's clothes. They were so wet, it was like peeling the skin from fruit. He uncovered the vine etched into Theron's chest. In the starlit darkness, it was like the shadow of leaves on his pale skin. Theron was trembling with cold, but Basil laid him down on the floor. In giving his lover ease, Basil took the boy's seed back into himself and never lost a precious drop.

Basil rose, intending to light a candle, to stir up the fire, but the power that had burned in his body was not yet done with him. The circle was not yet closed. *Bindings run in threes*, he thought, not knowing where the thought came from. It was as if he and Theron had just made some new thing between them, something that neither man could contain alone. It belonged to both of them, and must be passed back and forth between them as long as they both should live, growing in strength, always too much for either one to hold for long, always desiring outlet and renewal in the other.

Basil felt himself about to burst with it. He put his hands under Theron's arms, murmured, "Come, my lord, my dear . . ." and on the bed he sank himself deep, deep into his lover's body and filled it with the thing he could not name, that he had taken from him and now gave back, renewed and potent.

Theron cried out then, a loud keening wail that Basil thought must surely wake the city. He was deaf to his own shout of triumph, but he found himself lying across the other man. His lust was spent, but words rose in his mind, words that must be said.

"Now," Basil whispered hoarsely; "now the old year is surely undone, and the fires are burnt out. Bind up your hair, my princeling, and fast for the white days passing between the old year and the new. Live on my love, as I shall live on yours."

Theron twisted under him, looking up at him mutely.

"Why do you not answer me? Answer me! The circle is complete, and bound in completion," Basil heard himself say, and knew that it was true. "I charge you, Theron— No, wait." Formally, he said: "Son of Tremontaine: Alexander Theron Tielman Campion, I charge you, speak!"

Theron gave a great gasp, filling his lungs as though coming up from deep water. "The hunt!" he cried.

Basil cradled him in his arms. "Hush," he said. "The hunt is over, you're with me. You did well."

"You know? How did you know?" Theron asked fiercely. "They were your men, those students; did you set them on?"

Basil's bonfire cooled to embers, his certainty fogged. "What do my students have to do with this?" he asked, bewildered. "What are you talking about? How did I know what?"

"About the hunt—those fucking barbarians—I was hunted, Basil, hunted like an animal—and they were your men, your men!"

"The King's Hunt." Basil leaned up on one elbow and looked at him. "I don't know; I was just being poetical, I suppose. Are you saying my students chased you tonight?"

"They were there—all of them—and those Northerners besides!"

"Yes . . ." It was hard to rouse himself, but Theron seemed genuinely upset, and history was all he had to offer. Basil considered the precedent. "I've heard that the village lads up around Hartsholt still bear the brand deep into the woods, and choose one of their own to run out before them. You should be flattered: it's always the bravest and handsomest they choose."

"Let them choose one of their own, then, and leave me alone!"

Basil stroked his lover's arm. "Shh. Don't you know, you are their own? In another age, you would have been their king—as you are mine."

Theron gripped his hand, stilling it, forcing Basil's attention to his words. "Tell me now. And tell me true. Did you put them up to this?"

Basil looked at him in real confusion. "I? How could I? Why would I?"

"I don't know; to see how it worked!"

Basil recoiled, offended. "I'm not teaching in a village school. We don't act out scenes from history as part of my lectures."

But Theron gripped harder. "What scene, Basil? What history were we all acting out for you?"

Basil twisted in his grasp. "Don't blame *me*. It's a tradition, I didn't invent it. The king is hunted—was hunted—for the good of the land. I wish I knew exactly how, and why. Maybe the Book of the King's W—" He caught himself just in time. "Maybe there are books I haven't read yet, that tell us more than Northern folk tales do. I do know that a few generations after the Union, in Laurent's day, they kept a young deer on the palace grounds. It was brought up by the royal children; the king's daughters would put garlands on its head. When the king's son came of age, they'd let it loose. He and his Companions would hunt it down on Last Night, and he always killed it with his own hands."

"That's in Vespas," Theron said. Distracted at last, he curled into Basil's arms. "I always thought that was a terrible thing to have to do, to hunt down an animal you'd cared for."

"That may have been the point. I think the deer was a substitute for the man himself. There's an ancient epic all about how the king *was* the deer, quite literally. Which could just be poetic license—unless you believe that the wizards somehow transformed him into an animal. Since that's impossible, it must have been a man they used to hunt—maybe a man clad in deerskin, or crowned with horns."

"Did they kill him when they caught him?"

"No. They made him king." Theron's head was heavy on his breast. "*He that was the deer has killed the deer,* it says in one poem, a fragment, probably a praise-song for a king. You love poetry; untangle me that one, and I'll make you an honorary historian."

"Your students hate me," Theron said sleepily. "They blame me for taking you away from them."

"You're mine," Basil murmured into his hair. "I will not let anyone harm you. You are my heart's delight, and the source of all my joy." He felt Theron's breathing grow regular. He tucked a corner of blanket up around his bare shoulder. Theron twitched, and coughed, and coughed again. Basil reached across him for the cup of water he kept by the bed, and raised him up and offered it, saying, "Will you drink, my lord?"

Theron whimpered, more asleep than awake. Poor child, god knows how much wine he'd taken tonight, or worse. Basil put the cup to Theron's lips himself, and watched him drink, and laid him down again.

chapter **III**

S AVE FOR LAST NIGHT AND FIRST NIGHT, THE White Days had no names, no designations. They flowed together like the long nights, blurred by excess and its consequences. It was dark or it was light; one was more or less drunk or hungover; one was looking for a lover or enjoying one or, occasionally, sleeping.

At least that was how it seemed to Justis Blake, stunned by his first city experience of the turning of the year. The mad hunt through the city, the fire in the oak grove and what he had seen there, had shaken him. He remembered waking up at dawn almost lying in the warm embers of the fire, twisted up against the back of a man whose face was so black with smoke he couldn't even identify him. His clothes were tucked between his knees. With pounding head and frozen fingers he'd scrambled into them, found a stream to wash the taste from his mouth and assuage his raging thirst, and stumbled back to the city through the frosty morning, shivering in his bones.

He'd spent the afternoon in bed, swearing he'd never drink again. He should have known better, he told himself. Men did

things when moved by whiskey and crowds they'd never do sober
and alone. He'd allowed himself to be caught up in the heat of
the moment, and was paying for it with a head filled with hammering dwarves and the uncomfortable knowledge that he
wouldn't be able to write his mother all that he had done on Last
Night.

"You were pissed," Benedict Vandeleur said when Justis tried
to explain all this to him. "You went out with the boys in the
woods and did some things you don't remember very well and saw
boogie men and now you feel like the bottom third of the Sixth
Hell. Serves you right. You should have come to Mother Ginger's
with me. The girls don't charge on Last Night, and it's a lot
warmer than an oak grove."

"It would have to be," said Justis gloomily. "You're probably
right, Benedict, about all of it. I was certainly drunk."

"Of course I'm right," Vandeleur said. "Now, get out of bed
and put your head under the pump and I'll show you how a real
city man spends the White Days. And not a word about ancient
history or oak groves or any of the rest of it until the term starts
again, or I swear by all that's holy you can look for a new roommate."

Justis laughed, wincing when the dwarves picked up the pace
of their hammering. But he got out of bed and dunked his head
and the headache went away, just as Vandeleur had said it would.
They went together to Mother Ginger's, and Justis kept his
mouth shut on the subject of ancient history and oak groves. He
thought about them, though, and his thoughts were not altogether comfortable.

⁓

JUSTIS BLAKE WAS NOT THE ONLY MAN IN THE CITY TO
feel the effects of the Last Night hunt. The Northerners who
called themselves the Companions of the King staggered into
The Green Man to warm up and heal their heads with toasting
the dawn of the Hunt. Robert Coppice, Third Companion,
climbed onto a table with the help of Burl, his Fourth, and proposed a solemn toast to the shivering, hungover crowd: "Here's to

our Hunt, boys, and a royal Deer to bring the Sun to the North Country!"

As they knocked back beakers of cider they pieced together their memories of the night. "Theron Campion." Coppice carefully shook his head. "Who would have thought it? Still, he gave us a good run, a mighty good run . . ."

"He did that," Burl agreed. "I thought I was going to bust a gut with running. Almost as good as the chase Finlay gave them in my grandfather's time, to hear the old ones talk."

"Did you see the horns on him?" a boy named Farwell said softly. "I did, I swear I did."

Greenleaf and Smith, First and Second Companions, had been oddly silent since their return from the woods. But at Farwell's words, Greenleaf nodded and asked eagerly, "You saw that, did you? What else did you see?"

"What didn't we see?" Hob chuckled. He was a natural scientist, but had thoroughly enjoyed himself nonetheless. "The Hunt was good, but the mead was even better!"

The First Companion quelled him with a glance. "Let Farwell answer."

"Just the horns," Farwell whispered. "But it might have been the trees . . . the branches, you know."

Greenleaf nodded. "I, too, saw the horns on him. And when I kissed him . . . Oh, lads—" His voice cracked; his companions saw that he was struggling not to weep. "Oh, my brothers, the time is truly upon us. We have been faithful servants of the Living Land, and it has not been in vain. The king will come again."

Someone snorted. "In Lord Theron Campion?"

"Hush," said Coppice, mindful of his rank. "The First Companion is speaking. He's Master of the Hunt and Keeper of the Mysteries. He knows."

"There are signs," Greenleaf went on. "I saw them, and Smith saw them, too."

Will Smith finally raised his head. His cheeks were scratched, his hair was full of twigs. He looked like he'd been dragged through a hedge backward, which was close to the truth. But his eyes were clear blue flame. "It was a great mystery," Smith said hoarsely. "Around the fire, I saw the ancient tales live again. There was the Deer, the king that will be, and from the woods there came a man, dark and fell, with power lying like a mantle on his shoulders." He glared at Hob. "Other years I have drunk deep of the mead, and seen nothing like this. This was true seeing."

"We will watch, and we will wait," Greenleaf said. "If the signs hold true, the king will reveal himself with the year's turning, springing from amongst us as the new grass springs from the earth. A wizard will bind him, as the kings of old were bound, and the Companions will honor him and call him brother. The old order will be restored, and the Land will rejoice and we will rejoice with it—" He choked on the words, tears running openly down his face.

Coppice put his hand on Greenleaf's shoulder and kissed him, as was his right. "Rest," he told his friend. "It was a long night. And the days are long until spring. There will be time to speak of this."

His arm around his lover Lindley, Alaric Finn glowed with pleasure and returning warmth. "You saw the Deer," he crooned in Lindley's ear. "You saw him first, and you knew him. You are truly one of us."

OUTSIDE THE UNIVERSITY, THE LAST NIGHT hunt had other consequences. The City Council was besieged with complaints from property owners who had lost shutters and wagons and sheds to the rioters. And Lord Nicholas Galing's man brought him a letter from Henry Fremont.

Something happened last night. Northern royalists in the wood. At the bonfire, too. Finn's friends. Finn started something, about the kings. Don't think he's the leader, though. Who'd follow Finn? If he didn't have a brand, I mean. Anybody'd follow a Brand on Last Night.

Nicholas laid the letter on his knee, took a sip of wine, picked up the cloth packet the letter had been attached to, and slit through the dirty folds with his paper-knife. Cloth and string fell apart to reveal a roughly-carved wooden oak leaf like the brooch Arlen had shown him, threaded on a leather thong.

He grinned down at this MidWinter's gift with pure joy. "Thank you, Henry," he murmured, and returned to the letter with renewed determination. He needed it. Henry Fremont had been neither calm nor sober when he'd written it.

I just got back. Want to get it all down before I forget.

Just what had really happened wasn't very clear. Fremont mentioned running through the streets, chasing a Deer (with a capital "D") into the woods, a bonfire, men dancing. Nicholas huffed impatiently and read on until, swearing, he reached for the bellpull and rang it as though it were Henry Fremont's scrawny neck. He told the manservant who answered to take a chaise to an address in University Town, roust Henry Fremont out of his bed, if necessary, and bring him back within the hour.

When the servant had bowed himself out, Nicholas reread the passage that had caught his attention.

Theron Campion was the Deer. Lindley's revenge for Campion stealing St Cloud from him, I think. Not that Lindley ever had a chance. He's with Finn now anyway. But the point is, Lindley and Finn said T.C. was the King, and T.C. ran, and we chased him and when we caught him we passed him around the circle and called him King and he did not object.

It wasn't much. As it stood, it was little more than drunken babble, but it was definitely worth pursuing. Nicholas scribbled a note to Tielman, then crumpled it up and threw it on the fire. Time enough to consult Ned when he had more facts, and the time to think what they might mean. The names, though: Lindley and Finn and Campion. He ought to send those to Arlen, as a little MidWinter's offering of his own.

What was taking so long? Where was the damn boy?

In spite of all the manservant's best efforts, it was almost two hours before Henry Fremont was shown into Nicholas Galing's study. A day's rest hadn't seemed to do his hangover much good. His long face was the greenish-white of a fish's belly, his pointed nose was raw, and his deep-set eyes were watery and bloodshot. But he was shaven, neatly dressed, and tolerably in command of his senses. He glowered at Nicholas and said, "I'm sick as a dog, as

I told your man when he woke me. He didn't seem to think you cared."

Nicholas gestured to a chair opposite his own. "On the contrary, my dear Fremont, I do care. Very much."

Fremont's air of sullen suspicion did not change, but he took the offered chair. "You want to ask me about the letter, I suppose. Well, I can't tell you any more than I've written there. It was a very confusing night."

"I'm sure it was," Nicholas said dryly. "Let's not worry about that right now, shall we? I'm interested in something that happened before Last Night."

"Nothing happened before Last Night," said Henry sullenly. "Nothing very interesting, anyway. You have my letters. Why ask me about them now? Shouldn't you be out with the other nobles, eating apprentices and fucking apricots? Or is it the other way around?"

He really didn't look well, Galing thought. He'd undoubtedly caught a cold cavorting in the wood, and served him right. Aloud, he said pleasantly, "You didn't mention this in your earlier letters." He handed Fremont a page with one sentence underscored. "What does this mean?"

Fremont squinted red-rimmed eyes at the page. "Plaguey cheap pen," he muttered. "Can't read my own . . . Ah—'revenge for Campion stealing St Cloud,' is that what you mean? Seems clear enough to me. Lindley wanted St Cloud in the worst way, got his nose put out of joint when St Cloud took up with Campion instead. Naming Campion the Deer could have been his way of getting back at him. But that's not the point I was trying to make. My point was. . . ."

"Yes, I know what your point was," Galing interrupted him. "It's an interesting one, and we'll talk about it later. What I want to know about at the moment is this affair between Doctor Basil St Cloud and Lord Theron Campion. How long has it been going on?"

Fremont stared at him. "Who cares? It's just two men in bed—that's not politics, that's gossip. You didn't tell me you were interested in gossip."

I can't hit him, Galing reminded himself. He won't tell me

anything if I hit him. "Two men in bed is indeed politics," he said patiently, "if one of them is a king-mad ancient historian and the other is a descendant of the last king's sister."

"Yes, of course he is." Fremont grimaced. "I hadn't thought it through." He sneezed explosively and wiped his dripping nose on his sleeve. "I don't suppose you've got a handkerchief?"

Galing rang for a handkerchief and a lemon toddy. While Fremont was using the former and absorbing the latter, Galing coaxed from him all he knew about Doctor Basil St Cloud's liaison with Lord Theron Campion. It wasn't much, but it was enough to make Galing curious about young Campion's politics.

In short order, he packed Fremont off in a chaise with blankets and a basket of food and wrote a polite note to Lord Arlen, containing what he thought Arlen should know about the events of Last Night. Then he flipped through the invitations for MidWinter festivities piled on his mantelpiece, selected the one that promised the greatest opportunities for unbridled gossip, hastily changed his clothes, and set off for Lord Davenant's all-day card party.

When Galing emerged from Davenant House some hours later, he was the richer by two pressing invitations to intimate suppers, a respectable sum in gold, and a confusing portrait of Lord Theron Campion, heir to Tremontaine. According to the men at Lord Davenant's, Theron Campion was without shame and easily offended, spoiled and generous, overeducated and ignorant, boorish and charming, unattainable and easy as a wink and a nod, a fribble and a philosopher. Not very conclusive.

The most fruitful conversation he'd had was over a hand of Constellations he'd played with the Lords Condell and Filisand and young Lord Clarence Randall. Galing himself had proposed the game as the four men stood eating steamed river clams from a huge silver bowl on a sideboard. He'd chosen his partners carefully. Filisand was the Raven Chancellor, Condell enjoyed a reputation for knowing all the best gossip, and Clarence—well, Lord Clarence was newly on the town, rich, and not very skilled at Constellations.

Galing introduced the topic of Theron Campion as Lord

Filisand accepted a pack of cards from a servant and broke the seal between his thick, red fingers.

"Theron Campion?" Lord Condell pulled at the frill of lace edging the sleeves of his admirably tailored coat. He was a handsome man, all porcelain and gilt like a mantel clock, and every bit as alive to the time of day. "You're not thinking of pursuing *him*, are you, my dear? Because, if you are, you might wish to reconsider. He's lovely, I agree, but sadly unsteady."

"What Condell's trying to say, Galing," said blunt Lord Filisand, shuffling the cards, "is that you don't want to get mixed up with the Campions. Sadly unsteady! That's very funny, Condell. They're all mad as swordsmen—including the widow."

"Lady Sophia isn't a Campion; not by blood, anyway," Lord Clarence pointed out. He was very young and eager, like a half-broken colt, and flush with the triumph of being asked to play Constellations in such exalted company.

Lord Filisand began to deal out the deck. "She's mad anyway. What would you call a woman who presented herself at the Surgical Theatre not a month after her husband's death, gravid as a sow, declaring that she was going to be a surgeon?"

"Courageous?" offered Lord Nicholas with deliberate provocation. "Determined?"

"Mad," said Filisand firmly. He picked up his cards and pursed his full-lipped mouth over them. It made him look rather like a river-pike, if river-pikes wore yellow velvet.

"Unwise, certainly," Condell temporized, "if Lady Sophia were a woman who cared what is said of her. As she is not, and was backed by the Duchess Tremontaine, laying siege to the College of Physic wasn't an unreasonable way of getting what she wanted."

"Sounds a redoubtable woman," said Galing, sorting his hand. "And young Campion takes after her, you say?"

Lord Filisand snorted. "Takes after both parents; that's the trouble. No morals. No shame. No sense of civic duty. Only time the old duke took his seat in Council was when he had some scheme to upset things. Whatever else you may say about the Duchess Katherine, she's conscientious. And she's discreet in her amours, if she has any. Unlike the old duke."

Galing examined his hand. "And unlike his son?"

Lord Condell pouted thoughtfully. "I wouldn't say Campion is indiscreet, precisely. I can't actually furnish you with the names of any of his lovers. Except Ysaud, of course."

Lord Filisand laid down the Sun. "I open, I think."

Galing sat up straighter, a hound on the scent. "Land, I'd forgotten that bit of gossip. So Ysaud was really his mistress, was she?" He threw down the Hunter.

"More likely he was hers," tittered Condell, covering the Hunter with a Comet.

Lord Filisand discarded a minor star and snapped, "Are we here to play or to gossip? Lord Condell takes the first constellation. Lord Nicholas, do you care to lead?"

Galing led the Six-pointed Crown and lost the constellation to Condell's Eclipse, a tyro's error. But his mind was not on the cards. As it happened, several years ago he'd had occasion to give Ysaud a commission—six small paintings to illustrate a favorite book. He'd discussed them with her, approved the sketches, visited once to check on her progress and been told that if he came again, she would paint over the canvases. There had been a lively argument, which he had let her win. He'd seen her only once more, when he'd gone to view the paintings. It was time, he thought, to see her again.

THAT NIGHT, ANTHONY LINDLEY AND ALARIC FINN slept curled together, naked in Finn's narrow bed. There was a half-bottle of cheap wine on the floor beside them and a plate of crumbs and apple cores from their supper. The University Clock struck two as the rickety wooden stairs shook under the booted tread of six City Guardsmen and the door groaned under the blows of their truncheons. Finn shouted for the unknown torturers to go away and buried his head under the pillow. A moment later, the cheap lock burst with a crack, and his tiny room was filled with the flare of a torch and large, unsmiling men who hauled him and the whimpering Lindley out of their nest, bundled them into their gowns, and dragged them, barefoot, dazed, and shivering, out of the room, down the stairs, and into a box-like carriage with straw on the floor and no windows.

The carriage drove to the Chop, where more Guards escorted the shaken, bewildered pair to a stone cell furnished with a straw pallet, a blanket, a bucket with a lid, and a tin ewer of water.

Time passed. Lindley shivered and clung to Finn, who had little comfort to offer him. At one point, the banded oak door opened and some clothes were tossed in. The boys dressed and waited some more. Lindley might even have dozed, exhausted by terror, with his head on Finn's shoulder. And then there were guards again, and torchlight scorching their eyes, and a tall man with a deep, silky voice, saying, "So you are the young men who like to hunt deer on Last Night. Come and tell me all about it."

T HE SAME MORNING THAT SAW LINDLEY AND FINN IN the Chop saw a note from Katherine delivered to Riverside House requesting Theron's immediate presence at Tremontaine House. Sophia read it, shook her head, and rang for Terence, who said woodenly that Lord Theron's bed had not been slept in that night, but he'd no doubt return in time for the duchess's sledding-party. Which he did, barely. He was still wearing the brocade he'd put on for Last Night, sadly ripped and soiled. He was unshaven, scratched, and glowingly happy from two nights and a day of per-fect love.

The Campion butler, a retired swordsman named Sly Davy, had been standing by the door at Lord Theron's private entrance, ready to open it as soon as he appeared. "Happy MidWinter!" Theron greeted him cheerfully.

Davy twisted his scarred face into a truly hideous scowl and muttered, "Maybe for some." Since he was always full of dire warnings, Theron swept on past him with a grin.

But he stopped at the sight of his mother, who'd been waiting for him in the antechamber. She took in his appearance with tightened lips and lifted chin. When he saw how angry she was, his face fell. "Oh, dear. You didn't know where I was. I should have sent a note, shouldn't I?" When she didn't respond, he tried a smile. "Just let me get cleaned up and changed, and I'll do whatever penance you choose."

"Bathe and shift your clothes you must," Sophia said stiffly. "You are disgusting. It is not I who will punish you, however, but the duchess, who sent this morning and is waiting for you still." She blinked, and Theron saw a tear slide by her nose. He held out his hand, and her uncharacteristic restraint dissolved.

"Pestilent boy!" she cried in her mother tongue. "Brother of goats! I've heard such things, I don't know what to believe. What have you done? Katarina is furious, and I am ashamed of you, and of myself for being your mother."

Theron put himself to the task of calming her, which wasn't hard, her tempers being as brief as they were rare. He wrote a contrite note to the duchess promising to come as soon as he was decent, and rushed up the stairs, stripping off his filthy coat and shirt as he went. He burst into his room where Terence was waiting with a bath before the fire and the razors laid out. "The suit is ruined," he announced, "and I'm as filthy as a dockman. Can you turn me back into a duke's son again in less than an hour?"

Terence, who was fond of his rackety and generous young master, frowned sternly. "I might contrive, sir, if you do as you're told and don't distract me."

Not much more than an hour had passed before Theron presented himself to his mother, clean and rosy and freshly clothed in fine blue wool. Sophia embraced him warmly when she saw him, but all she said was, "Where is your hat? You'll catch your death, going out with wet hair."

Theron bit back an objection and stepped into the chair waiting at the door without saying that he'd rather walk to the Bridge where a carriage waited to take him up the Hill to Tremontaine House.

The sledding had ended with the short MidWinter day. When Theron came into the tall and glowing entry-hall, children of both sexes and every age between five and fifteen were running up and down the long, shallow sweep of the grand staircase, screaming at the tops of their lungs. Marcus's wife, Susan, stood at the bottom with her hands folded at her waist, watching them.

"We just came in," she said in greeting. "They'll all collapse soon. Katherine's in the library, Theron. If I were you, I'd leave your high horse at the door."

Theron kissed her round cheek. "I'll leave it here for you to keep an eye on. Is she very angry?"

"Livid," said Susan calmly. "Andy, watch that little boy. He'll be over the banister in a minute."

Theron composed himself and entered the library. His mind and body were still flushed with love; and the hot bath and careful grooming, the crisp, fresh linen and the hot brick in the carriage had done nothing to dispel his sense of well-being. He had no idea what the duchess was in a tear about, but he'd find out soon enough. I'll give up anything but Basil, he thought.

Katherine's cheeks were still scarlet from the sledding. She looked Theron up and down and smiled icily. "Transformation," she said. "From young thug-about-town to noble scion of Tremontaine. It's wonderful how you do that, Theron."

A cold spot grew in his spine. "Cousin," he said formally, "whatever ill you have heard of me has gravely upset Sophia. She can't even get the words out."

"Don't you think," Katherine answered civilly, "that it's time you stopped hiding behind the affection we all feel for your mother?"

He felt the blood leave his face. She was a woman, she was his kin and his superior in rank. He could not strike her. "Are you going to tell me what I've done, or just insult me?"

"I am waiting for an apology."

"For *what*, in god's name?"

She drew a deep breath. "Theron. You've never lied to me—and believe me, I would know. That leaves only the equally unsavory possibility that you were so outrageously drunk on Last Night that you have absolutely no memory of leading a gang of drunken students on a rampage through University and out the North Gate, terrorizing citizens and pulling down property as you went." Her clear eyes gazed at him, leaving him no grace.

"I don't—" he stammered. "It wasn't like that."

"What was it like, then," she said snidely, "the Battle of Pommerey? At least you don't deny it. That's a good place to start. Which is nice, since quite a few people saw you at the head of your little army. Some of your scholarly friends have been picked up for questioning; I'm surprised you don't know that. Your intelligence isn't very good, I guess, or you just don't care. But you may thank me, when you've a mind, for keeping you out of the Chop along with them. Or if you've no mind to thank me for anything, thank the House of Tremontaine. By god, Theron!" she exploded. "It's not as though we ask much of you. You have your books, your studies, even your colorful assortment of sweethearts—nobody says a word, we deny you nothing—all we ask is that you keep our name clean. And you repay us by making yourself into a civic menace!"

She stopped, hands clenched on the back of a chair, waiting for Theron to say something. Theron returned her glare for glare, choked on the unfairness of her accusation. All he ever did was worry about keeping the family name clean. He'd pulled back a hundred times from serious misdemeanors of the kind his friends indulged in; he even went to boring parties on the Hill when he'd rather be studying or lying in the arms of someone he loved. But what could he tell her? *I didn't lead them; I was being chased.* Or maybe, *I didn't start it. They did.*

"There's more—" he began. "More to it than that."

"More?" she asked, nostrils flared. "How much more?"

He drew his shoulders back. "Speak to Peter Godwin. Or to Sebastian Hemmynge. They were there, too; they saw. You have no regard for me or for my word. Ask them."

"I may," she said. "Meanwhile, have you any objection if restitution is made to the city out of your Highcombe revenues? I hold them in trust, and I want to be scrupulous."

"Of course." It wasn't as though the students actually responsible could pay for anything, he knew. Dimly, he wondered what sort of damage had been wrought in the chase through the city streets. Wood, probably, for that awful bonfire. He had known nothing but the exhilaration and terror of the hunt.

"Good. And I do trust your word. I will have it, in fact, that for the remainder of the holiday you will confine yourself to Riverside House."

"What? Oh, no."

"Oh, you are free to attend all the parties you've already accepted invitations for, or to go about on visits with your mother."

"What purpose would my going out in society serve, if I've already been exposed as a thug?"

She looked surprised. "But you haven't been, Theron. That's what I've been telling you. We've made sure that as few people as possible know of your involvement in this."

"Thanks to Tremontaine." It came out more bitterly than he'd meant.

"If you like," she said dryly. "Have I your word?"

"I— No. I cannot give it." Katherine waited, eyebrows raised. "I have a friend—a lover, at University. Not . . . one of the rampaging gang. A magister. He would take it very ill if I were to abandon him now."

"You may write him a note."

"He wouldn't understand. He thinks—he believes a nobleman is master of his own life. And, unlike you, he believes me a man grown."

"Does he, now?" Her contempt was palpable. "Well, we wouldn't want to disappoint him."

Theron had been in trouble with her before, but it hadn't been like this: she'd never fully unleashed her cold, pure power on him as if he were an adult, an equal, an enemy. "Katherine." He held out a hand toward her. "Please. I am sorry—most heartily sorry—to have offended you and . . . to have done what I did on Last Night. I promise, it won't happen again, or anything like it."

"See to it." She turned away, her business done—but then relented. "Theron." She leaned across the table to him. "You may piss away the duchy if you like—I don't have to threaten to deprive you of Tremontaine, you know as well as I do what steps you might take to lose it. But don't make us all ashamed of you."

His eyes pricked with foolish tears. "I think of you," he said, "more than you know."

She held out her hand, and he took it and kissed it, without flourish.

～

LORD NICOLAS GALING HAD NOT SENT A NOTE TO SAY he was coming, and perhaps he should have. But he felt that the less time Ysaud had to prepare herself and her studio against his visit, the more he would have the advantage. What advantage, he was not sure—but it was always nice to have one. Especially where Ysaud was concerned. He was just pleased that she was still in town and working during the MidWinter Festival, instead of off enjoying the hospitality of some patron's country house.

It was a gray day, and late. She'd be running out of natural light at any moment. He was counting on it. Meanwhile, Galing threw another stick on the fire her servant had left him with. Nothing but sticks—no logs. Tiresome, and vaguely insulting—but one couldn't mind that with Ysaud; it was a part of doing business with her.

"Would you care to see my latest?"

He straightened swiftly. The artist stood in the doorway behind him, letting in a draft. The small woman, dressed in a gray robe lined with squirrel fur, was not troubled by it. "I doubt it would appeal to you, though: nymphs. I'm doing a whole frieze of them."

"Oh? For whom?"

She smiled. "You'll see. It will be very grand: a staircase. I'll cartoon it, and let some apprentice do the painting."

He followed her into her studio. It looked as if it had been a ballroom once, with long, uncurtained windows and tall mirrors lining the walls to make the most of the light. It was cluttered with canvases at various stages of composition and a model's stand and a sofa and closed stoves set up in the marble fireplaces—hardly elegant, but workmanlike and warm. As it would have to be, if Ysaud's models were as naked as the work on the easel. She was right; it didn't appeal to him. "Not your usual," he said.

The artist shrugged. " 'My usual.' What's that?"

He looked closer. "This is nothing but shapes. Lines and shadow."

"Well, it *is* going to be a frieze. I see it as a timeless dance. Beautiful women—with nowhere to go." She laughed.

"It's all . . . form," Galing concluded. "There's no drama. Usually your pictures imply a story, even if you're not referring to an actual historical event."

"Oh. You mean like this?" She strolled over to a large canvas facing the wall, and pivoted it on one corner till it faced Lord Nicholas.

He was looking through a frame of dark, painted leaves: oak, mostly, and some holly, densely layered. The scene at the center was a glade: pale moonlight, and a bonfire with dancing figures flashing black and gold around it. The figures were naked, young, the leap of their long hair echoing the leap of the flames. The leaves crowded around them, hiding shadows: a stag, a bear, a wolf, a boar. Except for the shadows, it might have been a rustic Last Night—or a group of drunken students dancing in the wood.

"This is new," he said, careful to hide his excitement.

"A few months. I thought it might be in your style."

"Why mine?"

She grinned at him, her pointed face foxy. "Lord Nicholas, really. I remember your specifications perfectly well."

"Truly," he went on, ignoring her reference to his last commission; "it's quite wonderful. Have you got any more like it?"

"Nearly two dozen. But not for sale."

"Oh? Private commission?"

"Hardly. Where would anyone put them all?"

"What are you going to do with them?"

She frowned. "I'm really not sure. It was enough just to have done them. For now."

She pulled out another. Even with the huge windows and the mirrors, the fading light made things look powdery and illusory. Curiously, the paintings seemed more alive than any other thing in the studio. The second canvas was a more reasonable size. It showed a man's torso, lit by moonlight, rising from behind a holly bush. The head was out of the frame—but beyond the figure, on the ground, was the shadow of a stag's antlers.

Galing felt his skin crawl. "What is this?" he breathed.

"You mean, *who?*" she said smugly. "That's just it, isn't it? Nice-looking fellow."

"Oh, come." He was suddenly annoyed. "Everyone knows who, if it's last year's work. It was all over town."

"Be nice." She considered another canvas, then made a great show of putting it back unseen, and instead opened a portfolio and presented him with a demure sketch: a young man, fully dressed in antique clothes. His face was arresting: she'd captured an odd mix of the sensual and the austere. Galing studied it for a long time.

"You know my young friend, then?"

Galing could not swear he'd never seen Lord Theron Campion. It was more than likely that they'd been at the same balls or parties—he might even have spoken with him. But he certainly had never seen him through the eyes of the artist.

"I know of him," said Galing mildly. "This is quite remarkable. May I see the final work?"

"It didn't come out. I painted over it. This was the best of the studies."

"A historical piece. One of the old kings?"

"Yes, he was good at kings."

"I expect it's the hair. The old kings always look like today's scholars to me."

"Oh, if it's hair you like—" Ysaud wrestled with another canvas, propped it against the wall for his inspection. But the light really was going, now; all he could discern was a pattern of light and dark. She brought forward a branch of candles, and the scene sprang to life.

A pool in the forest, flat and bright. A man knelt by it, naked from the waist up. He seemed to be gazing into the pool; his face was hidden by a fall of hair, some of it braided with ribbon. His arms were braced against the pool's edge; his hands were tense. What he stared at so intently, reflected back from the water, was the muzzle of a deer. A stag.

It all really happened, Henry Fremont wrote. *Theron Campion was the Deer . . . they said Theron was the King . . .*

And Galing had further intelligence, now, forwarded from

the Chop. They had not wanted him in at the questioning, but at least Arlen had sent him this:

Question: *I know you hunted the deer on Last Night. But why did you call him the king?*

Prisoner: *I did not. I never did.*

Q: *Your friends did. Why?*

P: *The deer is the king. The king of the year.*

Q: *The old year, or the new?*

P: *Neither, both; it's kind of complicated, please don't—*

Q: *Why is the deer the king?*

P: *It has always been so.*

"Well, well," said Galing. "He had some bizarre ideas, your noble subject."

"Don't talk nonsense," the painter said. "It wasn't his place to have ideas."

"You mean you—oh, come, Madam Ysaud, really. You paint to sell, or so you've told me. Often. Your time is valuable, not to be wasted, I remember. Why create a dozen, two dozen canvases for nothing, for no one? Campion can afford them." He paused, smiling maliciously. "Was that the cause of your split? not a lovers' quarrel, but a lover's commission? Did he refuse to pay up? Didn't he like the work?"

"You go too far," she said, and turned away, leaving Galing and the painting in darkness. "I should not have shown you any of these."

Galing's ears pricked at her tone. She was uncomfortable, perhaps frightened. He needed to know why. "You still haven't told me," he reminded her. "Where do these come from?"

"From him, from Theron."

This was promising. "Then he *did* suggest these—these bizarre images. How? What did he say?"

He'd followed her to the center of the room, where she stood islanded in light. She cocked her head insolently at him. "He didn't *say* anything, Lord Nicholas."

"Books, then; did he show you books?"

"Oh, honestly. What would I want with books? He showed me his body. It spoke to me, and this is what it said. I used to watch him when he was asleep—and other times. The pictures grew up around him."

She was lying, he thought; or she was a little mad. Or the whole thing was an absurd coincidence. Which didn't seem likely.

"So what did he think of these pictures he 'gave' you?"

"He hated the whole thing. But he was in love with me. He complained nonstop about posing, but he'd do anything I asked him to. Here, look at this."

A young man lay spread-eagled on his back, at the heart of an oak grove. The pure white of his skin was streaked with scratches, as though he'd been running naked through the wood. His head was tilted back, his throat exposed as though waiting for a lover's kiss—or for a knife.

"He enjoyed that one," she chuckled; "a little too much: I had a hellish time getting the shadows right, just there . . ." She pointed to where a scattering of oak leaves and shadows hid his private parts. "Shall I show you why?"

Without waiting for an answer she delved into another port-folio and offered up a drawing in reddish chalk: the same man, but his pose was held by ropes binding his wrists and ankles to posts—probably bedposts, Nicholas thought. In the sketch, there was no mistaking the face of the young nobleman, though in the painting it had been obscured. The figure's eyes were still shut, his head tilted back, but his member was fully erect. A painted vine embraced his chest and hip as if it loved him.

"Distracting," murmured Nicholas.

"Not to me. Here's another."

Campion again, unbound this time: asleep, or maybe only sated, in the middle of a rumple of sheets, one arm flung luxuri-ously away from himself.

"Did Lord Theron understand," Nicholas breathed, "just what you were doing?"

Ysaud smiled affectionately at the sketch. "About half the time, he did. He couldn't stop me drawing, could he? But the paintings never show his face, except in one or two decent, historical ones. Those I could sell, actually. They couldn't possibly offend anyone: in fact, some nobles think it's an honor to pose for those. You, Lord Nicholas, you'd make a very nice Duke Tremontaine—the historical one, I mean, the King Killer—a man in his prime, in command of his power . . . much better than poor Theron, despite his lineage. Though if we go back far enough, you're all interbred, I suppose. I see it all the time in the old portraits: a modern Karleigh nose on an ancient Lord Horn, and so forth."

"I would be honored to be the King Killer—some day. With young Campion as King Gerard?"

"Tremontaine would never forgive me. You don't paint a family that important as one of the great villains of history." She glanced up at him with bright malice. "Really, Galing, do you know nothing of politics?" Galing smiled and shrugged. "You know, he came to me at first for a sitting," she went on. "His cousin, the duchess, admires my work. She owns a couple already—a *Rosamund's Bower*, I think, and a swordsman genre piece. The duchess wanted a portrait of her heir apparent. One thing led to another."

"I'm sure it did. But how did he like you doing *these?*" Galing shook the handful of drawings.

"Oh, those. Those are for you."

"For—me?"

"Yes, don't you like them?"

Galing felt the blood pounding in his veins. She knew perfectly well just what he liked. "You are remarkably generous, Madam Ysaud."

"Not at all." She pulled another few sketches, rolling them up before he could see what they were. "A compliment to a friend. Here, I'll wrap them up for you myself."

chapter IV

THERE WERE NO CLASSES DURING THE WHITE DAYS.
But Basil warned Theron that he intended to spend
most of them working on something important.

"Don't you want me?" Theron asked, hurt.

Basil smiled. "Do I look as if I don't want you?" He took
Theron's face in his hands. "Understand, my dear; this is my one
time free of lectures, free of students—time to get some real work
done."

The truth was, he found it easier to resist poring over the
book of spells when Theron did not visit. He didn't tell him that;
nor did he tell him that he was looking for proof of something he
could use to call Roger Crabbe a liar—something that didn't involve wizards and magic. He still hadn't told Theron about the
academic challenge. Sometimes he hardly believed himself that
he'd earnestly committed to it with three of his closest friends,
and that, come the new year, they would be expecting him to
have something to debate, something fresh and exciting, something tied in to his latest work on the Northern kings and their
successors. Seduced by the wizards' book and his noble lover, he

had fallen behind on his true work, the slow steady plumbing of source texts and notes for the book he was going to write. He should be strict with himself, for once. "Besides," Basil said, "I thought your days would be full of parties. Family. That sort of thing."

"They are," Theron said glumly. "Well, they don't have to be—I can get out of the worst of them—but as you're so busy . . ."

"Not every day." Basil kissed him, nearly poking his eye out with the quill he'd stuck behind his ear. "I'm not busy every day. But if we spent the White Days all in bed—what could we hope for in the new year?"

Theron scowled. "We are meant to spend the White Days in self-improvement, conducting ourselves as we mean to go on in the coming year. So you will be working hard, and I will attend more parties. Charming."

"Think rather," Basil traced his cheek, "that we are storing up virtue. Getting it out of the way, if you like."

Theron tried to think of it that way. He also remembered Katherine's warning and even, to his annoyance, his cousin Talbert's humiliating lecture at the Godwin party. Very well, he would be the model heir, escort his mother to all conceivable gatherings on the Hill, and leave no one to wonder where he was spending the rest of his time. It was one thing to be notorious with Ysaud. He had no desire to let the Hill crowd know about his scholarly lover.

THAT EVENING, THERON CAMPION STOOD IN HIS WARM room in Riverside House while Terence dressed him. Fine linen against his skin, followed by layers of more linen, stiff with embroidery, then brocaded silk, rounded with collar and cuffs of lace. His long hair was brushed and oiled and clipped in a golden buckle, a heavy gold chain laid around his neck. It weighed him down, but it had been a gift from the duchess, and he thought it would be expedient to wear it. He had eaten nothing for hours; come rushing home from Basil's after his mother had already dined, with barely enough time to bathe and change for the

Montague ball. His consequent pallor and his hair gave him an antique air his lover would have approved of.

The ball was already crowded when Theron and Sophia arrived. He left her with a group of noble ladies presided over by her old friend Lady Godwin, then swam and bowed his way through the brightly dressed throng toward the refreshments. A hand at his elbow stopped his progress: "Young Campion! Pried you away from your books, have we?"

He was in a knot of men he'd known since he was a child, men he'd played at swordsmen with, men he'd ridden with, men he'd gone drinking with, even men he'd kissed. Now they wanted to talk about politics and the latest gossip. He wondered what they'd make of Basil, or Basil of them. Contempt and incomprehension all around, he suspected; it was hard even to think of them in the same breath.

Everyone was laughing—someone must have made a witty remark. Theron smiled mechanically and took a glass of wine from a passing tray. He began to feel much better after he'd downed it.

A fragile-looking girl with dark hair came into view just past the swirl of pattern in the padded shoulders around him. Her hair was severely upswept, exposing delicate ears. The shadowy tendrils that escaped onto her neck served to enhance its frailty.

Ralph Perry followed Theron's look. "Ah!" he said archly. "The true purpose for our sojourn in these parts: the flowers in the garden of maidenhood, ripe for the plucking."

"Perry!" Clarence Randall expostulated. "I hope you don't mean my sister!"

"Plucking," explained Perry smoothly, "is a very considerable enterprise, involving ladders of contracts, baskets of jewels, and books of vows."

"*Is* it your sister?" Theron asked Randall.

"*It's* not the cat, you rogue!"

But in the end, he achieved his introduction to the young beauty. Lady Genevieve Randall smiled shyly; she was fresh from the schoolroom, and had been told that it was better to play up her freshness and innocence than to pretend to a sophistication she lacked. Her skin was fine and flawless, with a ripe-peach glow;

Theron had to stop himself from reaching out to touch it just to feel it under his fingers. Even her shoulders, bare in their calyx of lace, were round and shone faintly golden in the flattering candlelight.

But he might take her hand if he asked her to dance, and so he did. They trod the measures of a slow *pas*, and he was careful to exert no pressure of the fingers that might alarm her. He could not help looking, though, at the wisps of dark hair at the base of her neck as the two of them moved back and forth, gravely dipping and bobbing. A sheen of moisture appeared on her upper lip; he wished he might bend down and lick it off.

Her mother met them as they came off the dance floor. Lady Randall knew all about him; it was a mother's business to know what there was to know about men of marriageable age. She inquired first after his mother's health and then after his studies and his cousin the duchess, to let him know that she understood both his own priorities and his standing in the world's eyes. Theron took pains not to say anything particularly original, so as not to alarm her. His efforts were rewarded by a motherly smile and the information that the Randall ladies received in the mornings, should he care to call.

⁓

COMING DOWN THE STAIRS FROM THE CARD ROOM, Lord Nicholas Galing stopped and stared at a young man with clubbed hair bowing to a majestic lady in purple and feathers. There was something about the tilt of the young man's head, the slope of his nose, the set of his shoulders that tugged at Galing's memory. The young man straightened and turned toward a group of young bloods in their first season.

"Dammit, Galing," said the Duke of Karleigh at his shoulder. "Warn a man when you're stopping, won't you? Damn near sent me arse over teakettle."

"I do beg your pardon, Karleigh. Do you know that boy in gold brocade?"

The old man followed Galing's gaze to the clump in the corner. "Puppy with the long tail?" he asked jovially. "That'd be the

Lady Sophia Campion's boy—I misremember his name. Something outlandish. Theodolite?"

"Theron," Galing murmured. "Lord Theron Campion."

His body had recognized him if his mind had not, telling him with certainty that he had seen this man naked and desired him. As who would not? he thought as he threaded his way through the crowd toward his quarry. Ysaud had taken good care that anyone looking on those paintings would long to possess their subject. It would be the height of imprudence, of course, especially if Theron proved to be mixed up in the Northern affair. Lord Arlen would not approve. Still, the boy was very beautiful.

Galing stepped into Campion's line of sight and bowed. "Lord Theron Campion, is it not? I believe we met last year, at the Filisands' Daffodil Ball." It was a safe bet; everyone on the Hill attended that one. Galing saw the puzzled frown on Theron's face, but, gamely, the boy pretended to remember.

"Oh, yes. How are you?"

"As you see." Galing smiled self-deprecatingly, winning a polite smile in return. "We spoke then of University. I see you still attend."

But this time he had pushed it too far. The handsome face closed up. "That's common knowledge." Poor young thing! His every thought was reflected on his features for the world to see. Galing could see what the appeal was for Ysaud, and how she would have played with him. His manners were atrocious. Galing couldn't resist trying if he could overcome them with charm.

"Ah," he said, "but common knowledge is so . . . common."

This amused the boy. "It is, at least, a basis from which to start," he agreed. "Now: we have established that I study at University."

"And your subject is—?"

"Rhetoric."

Galing burst out laughing. "The elements of speech, in fact! And I've just put my foot in it."

A rueful smile. "You have, rather. Though it was a prime use of antanaclasis: the repetition of a word whose meaning changes in the iteration."

"I see. Far over my head. Now, me, I would be more likely to study something a bit less . . . strenuous. Geography, maybe, or history. Who would you recommend for history?"

Lord Theron frowned. "Well, Doctor Wilson isn't very strenuous. But Doctor Roger Crabbe, in Farraday, enjoys a following among the nobles."

Galing noticed with interest that Lord Theron did not think of himself as a noble. "Really?" he said lazily. "I've heard Crabbe is a bit of a bore."

"He's not especially known for his originality." Theron paused. "You might prefer Basil St Cloud, then. He's in LeClerc. Just remember, visitors must sit in the gallery so they don't bother the serious students. Alternate mornings at nine." Theron surveyed Galing up and down, from his polished shoes to the fashionable embroidery on his collar. "Too early for you, perhaps."

"Perhaps." Really, the boy was practically begging for a setdown. But Galing wouldn't give him the satisfaction. He wondered what Theron had made of that quick survey of his body. He thought of what the young nobleman was hiding under his shirt collar, and took a steadying breath. "But perhaps not. I may see you there some day?"

Theron said quickly, "Oh, I'm not a historian."

"I may see you elsewhere, then."

"At another MidWinter ball, no doubt." The clear, light voice was cool, reserved. He couldn't be bothered to flirt—not with Nicholas, anyway. It rankled, knowing what Nicholas knew of the boy's body, abandoned and louche on the paper locked in his desk. Playing the prim little scholar with all his might, this son of a notorious rake, cousin of a public scandal, heir to a title that was a byword for madness. Nicholas could not resist. "I'm surprised you don't give a ball at Riverside House," he said; "though it would be hard to surpass the parties of the last duke there."

He had scored, and handsomely. The boy's face paled with rage. "If ever," he said tautly, "I do make the attempt, I will be sure to invite you so that you can check it for accuracy. You don't look old enough to remember them, but perhaps I am mistaken."

Galing showed his teeth. "Yes. I'm afraid you are."

So there was to be no amorous pursuit, Galing thought as the boy turned and walked away. No loss; it was another sort of chase Nicholas had in mind, with higher stakes and graver consequences. If Lord Theron proved to be involved with royalists in any way, bringing him to justice would be a positive pleasure.

A little while later, Galing saw Campion again, dancing with a girl like a porcelain figurine, all soft dark hair and stiff white lace. Ysaud was small and dark, too. At least this time he'd chosen one who wouldn't bite.

T HERON WAS ABLE TO DANCE ONCE AGAIN WITH Genevieve Randall. A third time would have aroused comment, and so he took many other partners, including a bouncing blonde whose dancing he enjoyed thoroughly, although her flirting alarmed him. He never knew how to respond to noble girls who flirted with him; he was always sure that he would say the wrong thing. One thing he particularly liked about Genevieve was that she didn't flirt. She answered his questions in a soft, pretty voice, and laughed when he ventured a mild joke. After handing his last partner back to her mother, Theron went in search of the Randalls again, thinking that he might talk to Genevieve and look at her, even if he couldn't dance with her. But the Randalls, mother, daughter, and son, had gone, as well as the bouncing blonde. No longer hungry or thirsty, Theron suddenly longed for bed, the warmest bed he could find, which was in a small room on Minchin Street.

K NOWING HIS LOVER WOULD NOT COME TO HIM THAT night, Basil set himself to the long-delayed task of sorting through the papers that had migrated in unrelated piles from his bed to his worktable. A phrase in his own hand caught his eye: "Anselm the Wise was beyond doubt the last of the kings who was entirely sane. He was also the last of the kings whose chief wizard-advisor was trained in the North."

Was that true? What about Anselm's heir's wizard, what was

his name? Ranulph? Abandoning the table, Basil rooted through old lists, diaries, letters, until, some hours later, he established to his satisfaction that Ranulph had indeed been the first Southern-born wizard to pursue his training entirely at the University. It had been part of Anselm's new rulings, he remembered, that the wizards "make themselves of Use to the Kyngdome, All its People, through our Schole of Studye, by teching their Practices and oder Wisdomes there." He was speculating happily on why Southern-trained wizards might not have turned out as powerful as their Northern-trained teachers when footsteps on the stairs outside stopped at his door. The latch lifted, and a perfumed gentleman appeared in the shadows.

"Oh. Am I disturbing you?"

"No." Basil shuffled his notes together, closed the inkwell, rubbed his cramped fingers. "No. I was just winding down. You look cold. Come in by the fire."

"There isn't any fire. You've let it go out."

"So I have, so I have." Basil peered in the wood-basket; it was empty. "Sit down and take some brandy while I fill this. Here," snagging the quilt from the bed, "wrap this around your legs. I won't be a moment. Did you know that the University as we know it could be said to have been established by Anselm's wizards?"

"I don't want to hear it just now," said Theron petulantly.

For the first time, Basil looked straight at him. "Oh, my dear," he said. The boy looked like a doll, white face and glittering eyes above an elaborate costume.

"I'm tired," he said. "Please let me lie down."

"Are you all right?"

"Yes—but never mind the fire. Just come and warm me."

Basil undressed him, save for his chain and rings, and covered them both with every blanket he possessed, as well as both his scholar's gowns and Theron's rich cloak. "There," he said when the boy stopped shivering. "Better?"

"Yes. I'm sorry; I should not have disturbed your work. But I'm cold and weary and my cheeks ache from smiling. All I want is to rest quiet and warm."

Basil said, "Why must you go out at all? Can't you just stay home and read a book sometimes? It's too much, all this running back and forth, staying out late and leaving early. Lord knows what you'll do when term begins again."

"I have to go. I can't just disappear into University, into my studies, however much I want to." Theron had never told Basil about his conversation with his annoying cousin Talbert, much less about the Duchess Katherine's latest threats. They were a side of his life he did not see any reason for Basil to have to encounter. But he tried to explain it simply. "Someday I must take my place among the nobles of this city. They have to know me. My mother put up with a great deal of nonsense from these people over my birth and my inheritance. I owe it to her, and to my family, to do the thing properly."

"You speak as though you were not one of 'them.' "

Theron gave an embarrassed shrug. "I am, by birth. Someday I shall take my seat in Council. . . ."

"But you don't look forward to it."

"There is so much I want to study first! So much to learn!"

"But, Theron . . ." Basil fingered the chain around his neck. "Theron, you are no scholar."

"*What?*"

"Not a real one," Basil went on gently. "Not by temperament. You must know that."

"Not a scholar?" Theron tried to make light of it, but Basil could hear the pain in his voice. "When I've spent almost as many years here as Master Tortua?"

"Oh, yes, you've amassed a great deal of knowledge, and you are well read. But scholarship—scholarship is a discipline, Theron. It is a single-minded pursuit of a construct of reality, a dedication to discovery and analysis. Your mind is bright and quick, quicker than many. You have a great range, and a great sense of the world."

"But I'm a cuckoo's egg in the University nest," Theron finished bitterly.

"Hardly a cuckoo." Basil smiled. "A nightingale, perhaps; or a swallow. It will serve you well, this knowledge, in years to come."

Theron turned his face away, but Basil kept on. "Why can't

you be proud of what you are? A great noble, from the seed of kings . . ."

"*Damn* your kings! Sometimes I think you take me only because Alexander Ravenhair's not available!"

"Hush." Basil gave the chain a tweak. "I am trying to tell you something important. The kings no longer rule. You nobles have taken their place, and must strive to be better than they were."

Theron sighed, burying his face in Basil's chest. "I know. I do know. But it is hard, being two people all the time. I wish I could . . . hire someone else to go to parties for me—to remember people's names and families, and to be charming when I don't feel like it."

"You mean a wife?"

Basil meant it ironically, but the young nobleman answered seriously, "Yes. I'll have to marry someday, for the title and the lineage and all. Already they are circling, the mamas with eligible daughters. I don't know what I will do! Marry, I suppose, and get it over with."

"The kings didn't need wives," Basil said dreamily. "They had their wizards."

"Oh, really?" Theron sounded annoyed. "How did they reproduce?"

"You've read Hollis. The wizards chose their women for them. The early kings' lives were brief and turbulent; during his reign, a young king was sent out in the autumn to give his seed to the land—in other words, I suspect, to beget as many children as he could while he reigned."

Theron murmured, "What an extraordinary amount you do know. So tell me, Basil: in the end, did the wizards corrupt the kings, or was it the kings corrupted the wizards?"

Basil opened his mouth to explain about the South and Queen Diane and the influence of the nobles, and realized that he knew a better answer. "Neither," he said. "Both. There was no corruption as long as they loved one another."

Theron drew back. "Now, love, my dear—love is one thing I think you are *not* qualified to lecture on."

"Whatever do you mean?"

"I mean," said Theron edgily, "it is 'not a word to pass between your father's son and mine.' "

Basil sighed, twisting Theron's chain in his fingers. "That was before."

"Before what?" Tantalizing, Theron held the chain out of his way.

"Before I—before the—it was a long time ago."

"Weeks." Theron drizzled the links of the chain onto Basil's chest.

"Weeks. I'm a quick study. I love you."

"What?"

"I love you. Mind, body, and soul, I love you. I can't help it."

Theron stretched and grinned. "Have you ever loved anyone else?"

It was not what Basil had wanted him to say. "No," he answered, rather sharply. "Never."

"Never?" Theron tweaked the chain. "Not very experienced, are you?"

"I never pretended to be. I've had other lovers, of course."

"Really? How many?"

Basil tabulated his actual conquests, added the ones he might have had if he had cared to try for them, and answered, "Eight. Or so."

"Eight. Or so. And you never told one you loved him?"

"You're different; the way I feel about you is like nothing I've ever known."

"You're serious. You really mean it." Theron crushed the chain between them in his embrace. Their two hearts thudded against it. They breathed in each other's scent. They stayed thus for some time, perfectly happy. Then Theron formally placed the chain around his lover's neck. "You are the lord of my heart," he said. "We are even now, love for love."

⌒

ALARIC FINN WAS SITTING IN A CELL IN THE CHOP, chin to knees on a straw pallet, watching the light fade slowly from the small barred window. He had been questioned twice since he'd been taken—once roughly by a stolid Guardsman, once courteously by a magnificent man with silver hair. The humiliating thing was that he had told the courteous gentleman everything he had withheld from the Guardsman. He'd been so gentle, so intelligent, so understanding, that it had seemed only reasonable, only natural, to confide in him.

Not, Finn thought miserably, that he had known very much to tell. Most Northern customs and rituals were not really secrets, after all. Everyone north of the foothills knew that the Companions of the King didn't have anything to do with politics or anything like that. It all had to do with the Land, giving the Land its due of blood and life so that it would sustain the people living on it. Any Northerner could have told the courteous gentleman about how it was necessary to feed the Land with hunting and dancing and loving. Any Northerner could have told him how the Companions who came South continued their rites in this gentler land, hoping to possess it and be possessed by it, renewing the Union begun by Alcuin so many centuries before.

Any Northerner could have. But only he, Alaric Finn, had actually done it. And he'd told him what little he knew of the Inner Mysteries as well.

Again he heard his voice, speaking almost without his will, telling the silver-haired gentleman about the Hunt, the Trial, the Deer, the Little King. These things may not be secrets in the North, his heart told him, but in the South, among the king-killers, the apostates, one did not speak of them. Still less did one speak of the men who led the rituals, who named the Hunter and loosed the Hounds. And he had named them— Roland Greenleaf, Will Smith—and watched the gentleman's secretary write it all down.

At the end of the interrogation, the gentleman had smiled slowly, gently, as a great cat might smile having caught its prey. "You've been most helpful, Master Finn. Thank you. Nonetheless, I'm afraid you must stay with us some time longer, perhaps until spring. It depends on the state of the road North. We shall not, I think, meet again."

Finn would have liked to have been released. But now, having had time to realize just what he'd done, he was glad to be in prison. It was right for him to be punished for betraying his friends, his country. Not to mention his lover, Anthony Lindley, who had taken so naturally to the ways of the North. And what about his brothers, the Companions of the King? What would Greenleaf say when he knew?

He groaned and hid his eyes against his knees. He could never go home again, never face his father, who would have preferred death to telling a Southron the smallest, most unimportant detail of his life; never kiss his mother or embrace his brothers with a heart unshadowed by shame. All his life, he'd been taught that every man is tested, as the Little Kings were tested. A man who failed the test was less than a man, and cast out of the company of all true men. Sitting there in the dark, with the damp of the ancient stones creeping into his bones, Finn realized that he had met his trial in the person of the courteous gentleman, and had failed it utterly. He was without honor, without hope. And the weeks were long until spring.

book III

WINTER TERM

chapter I

WHERE LAST NIGHT WAS ROWDILY PUBLIC, First Night was spent with intimates in quiet preparation for the year to come. Quarrels were made up and presents were exchanged. The streets were silent and the new moon swung unmarked among the stars. On the morning of First Day, time fell again into its accustomed cycle, and lives disrupted by the license of the White Days were put to rights again.

At LeClerc, Basil St Cloud lectured on the legal powers and responsibilities of wizards under the Treaty of Union. The students yawned and shifted on the benches. When Basil described how Alcuin had traded Northern titles for Southern forestland to be deeded to his wizards, he glanced at Finn's usual bench, expecting an outburst. Another student was in his place, industriously taking notes. Basil wondered if the boy had gone home for MidWinter. A pity, if he missed the challenge—it was just the sort of thing to thrill his romantic Northern heart. Lindley was absent, too. But this wasn't the time to consider the whereabouts of amorous students. Basil had other things to worry about.

When the bell released the students to their noon meal, St

Cloud gestured for the inner circle to stay behind. In the absence of Finn and Lindley there were four of them, ranging from little Peter Godwin, who was barely fifteen, to Benedict Vandeleur, who might be twenty. He wanted to tell them exactly what he intended to do that afternoon, but Rugg had warned him against gossips. So all Basil said was, "Be outside the Nest before two, just you four, and Finn and Lindley, if you can find them. I have a thing I must do, and I would be glad of your company."

Vandeleur and Justis Blake exchanged glances, and then Vandeleur said, "Before two, you said, outside the Nest. You may count on us, sir."

Basil nodded, hesitated, decided that to add anything would be to say too much, swung his bag up on his shoulder, and marched out of LeClerc. His students stared after him in bewildered silence until Fremont said, "You may freeze your noses off here if you like. I'm going to the Nest, where I can be curious in comfort."

Flush with the quarter's stipend and MidWinter gifts, they ordered venison stew with dumplings and hot punch and also some hot potatoes for their pockets to be brought to the table just before two.

"So where is love's young dream?" Henry asked, unwinding a bright new woolen muffler from about his throat.

Vandeleur shrugged. "If you mean Finn and Lindley, last I saw them, they were making asses of themselves at the University bonfire. Way they were carrying on, they probably spent the holiday in bed."

"Surely they'd be done by now," said Peter Godwin.

Blake remembered two figures dancing half-naked and ecstatic in the heart of the wood, and said uncomfortably, "One of us should go look for them."

Henry snorted. "I wouldn't bother. Do you really want Finn here? I don't."

"But Doctor St Cloud does," Blake objected. "He said to find Finn and Lindley, and that's what I mean to do." He got up. "Save me a bowl of stew, Vandeleur. I shouldn't be long."

Looking beyond him, Peter Godwin said, "Don't bother, Blake. Lindley's just come in the door. Can Finn be far behind?"

It was indeed Lindley, but a very different Lindley from the love-flushed and braided dancer of Last Night. This Lindley was hollow-eyed and dressed in rags under a torn academic gown. His red hair hung lank, his narrow cheeks were bruised under reddish stubble, and he stank. The historians stared at him as though he were the ghost of murdered Hilary.

"Great god!" breathed Vandeleur at last. "Where in the Seven Hells have you been?"

Lindley frowned. "All of them, I think. Is that stew?"

"It is," said Godwin. "I'm not sure I want to sit next to you while you eat it, though. No offense meant, but you smell like a midden."

"There are worse things to smell like," Blake said pleasantly. "Sit here, Lindley, and tell us about it. I was just about to go and look for you."

Before Lindley could answer, two men appeared behind him. Their hair was bound in a dozen braids down their backs and their cheekbones were high and sharp—Northern men beyond doubt. One of them spun Lindley around, fisted a hand in his clothes, and shouted, "It was you, wasn't it? You told them about Smith and Greenleaf. I'd like to . . ."

The second man shoved him aside and took his place. "Where are they, eh?" he snarled into Lindley's stark face. "Where's Greenleaf and Smith? And Finn? Where's he?"

By this time, the historians had recovered themselves enough to take action. Blake and Vandeleur tackled the Northerners while Godwin took charge of Lindley, who looked ready to faint. Almost immediately, the tavern-keep bustled up, armed with his usual fistful of tankards, suggesting that the young gentlemen take their dispute outside. The Northerners departed, muttering and casting black looks behind them, and Basil's students resumed their benches and their stew, all except Lindley, who stared at his bowl as though it contained snakes.

Blake touched him gently on his shoulder; he shrank pitifully from the touch. "You'd better tell us where you've been, Tony."

"The Guard came and took us to the Chop. They put me in a cell and asked me questions about Last Night. I didn't answer them. They let me go this morning. That's all I know." He lifted his eyes, their dense blue luminous in his filthy face. "Don't ask me any more questions. Please."

There was a shocked silence. Then Blake took a deep breath and said, "Fair enough. Why don't you go to the baths, get some sleep. I'll stop by in the morning and see how you're getting on."

"I don't want to go home." Lindley began to shake like laundry hung in the wind. "It's dark at home. No candles."

Someone got up—Henry Fremont—fumbled in his new pouch, slapped a silver coin down on the table, muttered, "Get candles," and shoved his way to the door as if the place were on fire. Peter Godwin, looking troubled, met Fremont's contribution, and soon there was a small pile of coins in front of Lindley.

Benedict Vandeleur scooped up the coins and tied them in his handkerchief. "I'll buy the damned candles. Blake, Godwin, get him home and stay with him until I get there."

"What about two o'clock and Doctor St Cloud?" Godwin asked.

Vandeleur looked harried. "We've better than an hour yet. I'll think of something. Go!"

They asked Lindley no more questions then, but it all came out soon enough, in Lindley's narrow room, between coughs, while Blake bathed his burning face and Godwin looked helplessly on. He'd been questioned and questioned again, then left to cool his heels in a cell for days with nothing to eat save thin gruel and cold water.

"I don't even know if Alaric's dead or alive," he wailed. "They wouldn't let me see him or answer any of my questions. This morning, they told me I should be more careful of the company I kept, and let me go."

Godwin caught Blake's eye over Lindley's head, his mouth twisted with unsympathetic mirth. Blake frowned at him and said gently, "I'm sure he's alive, Tony. They'll let him go, too, as soon as they realize he's guilty of nothing but being a damn fool."

Lindley was not comforted. "But he *is* guilty. He betrayed them, you see—Greenleaf and Smith. He must have. I said nothing. I would rather have died than betray them. What they're doing is important: keeping up the old ways, the reverence for the land. . . . This city, here, it's all so dead, so cold, so artificial. No one believes in the Southern gods any more, including the priests—everyone knows it's all for show. We need something real to love and honor. We need the kings."

Blake hardly knew what to respond. The man was clearly half out of his mind with fever. "I wouldn't be too quick to condemn Finn, Tony. If they tortured me, I'd tell them anything they wanted to know, just as quick as I could. Any sane man would."

Lindley gave a barking laugh that turned into violent coughing. His skin felt hot and dry under Blake's hand, and he was shivering. Blake thought uncomfortably of prison fever and how it must be close to two, and where was Vandeleur with those candles? Then the door opened and there was Vandeleur, a blanket thrown over his arm, followed by a buxom young woman in a feathered hat and a man's greatcoat, carrying a basket.

"It's almost time," he said without preamble. "I've brought candles and some food and Odette. She's promised to sit with Tony until I come back. If we run, we'll just make it. Come *on!*"

WHILE HIS STUDENTS WERE TENDING TO LINDLEY, Doctor Basil St Cloud was sitting alone in his rooms, surrounded by the books and papers, staring at the Book of the King's Wizard and finding it easy, for once, not to think about Theron. By nightfall, he would have challenged Crabbe to a duel of knowledge.

There was nothing to worry about, he told himself. In fact, it should be almost childishly easy. Roger Crabbe was an ass. His books and lectures were as full of false facts as a hive is full of bees. Crabbe wasn't interested in actual truth. He was interested only in catering to popular prejudice, of proving into infinity the viciousness of every king back to the dawn of time. Rugg was right. There was no obvious need for Basil to bring up the wizards.

Yet how could he not, when the assumption that they were monsters was what held together Crabbe's whole net of falsehoods? If the wizards had indeed been manipulative charlatans, then it followed that all the kings might well be corrupt tyrants at worst, at best gullible fools and madmen. But if the wizards were true . . . then the early kings, too, could be seen at last for what they truly were: dedicated rulers serving the land hand in hand with those who knew it best.

Furthermore he, Basil St Cloud, had the proof incontrovertible that they served true magic in their time. He had the Book of the King's Wizard.

But the Book, inscrutable and indecipherable, was a two-edged sword.

It lay before him, open to A Spelle to Un-Cover Hidden Trothes. That wouldn't help, Basil thought, even if he could read it. Irritably, he flipped to A Workyng of Confusion. Below it, For if Ye wold Turn the Tong to Fyre caught his eye. That one, now . . .

Basil slapped the book shut, folded it into its wrappings, laid it in the box, closed it, and slid the whole under the bed. The greatest scholarly discovery of the age, and as useless to him as so much rotting fruit. Fury choked his breath like cold water. He slammed his fist into his papers, tearing the topmost sheets and toppling a stack of old books onto the floor. The noise brought him to himself: he picked up the books, smoothed the papers, and rubbed his smarting hand.

It wasn't as if he didn't have at least a dozen other sources that contradicted Crabbe's received "wisdom"—Karleigh's diaries and the Montague notes were the least of what he'd found. Let Crabbe say almost anything about the reigns of Alcuin's heirs, and Basil had him.

Basil got up and examined himself in the hand-sized mirror he used for shaving, knotted a clean neckcloth at his throat and tucked the ends into the bosom of his coat. No muffler—it looked sloppy. He wished he had a brooch for his hat, something ornamental—a deer's head, perhaps, or a leaf like those some of the students were wearing. He brushed the felted wool against his sleeve, set it on his head, and left the room, locking the door behind him.

H IS STUDENTS WERE WAITING FOR HIM OUTSIDE THE Nest, looking very young and solemn. Finn and Lindley were still missing. Never mind: four was enough. St Cloud took cold air deep into his lungs and said, "We're going to Farraday. I'm challenging Doctor Crabbe to a formal debate."

Henry Fremont gave a long, impressed whistle; the rest of them pricked up their ears like horses itching for a gallop. "I don't want any trouble, now," St Cloud added hastily.

"No, sir," said Vandeleur, grinning. "Of course not."

"It would create a disturbance," Godwin agreed.

"We won't lift a finger," Blake assured him. "Unless they lift one first."

"Not even then," said St Cloud, equally warmed and alarmed by his students' enthusiasm. "Doctor Rugg will be there as my witness, to see that it's all done in form. You are here because he suggested that I bring you."

What Rugg had said was, "Crabbe's the kind of man to be impressed by an entourage—just your nearest and dearest, and no one who can't keep his head." On reflection, it was just as well that Finn and Lindley weren't there. Flushed and determined, they all set off for Crabbe's hall, united in the feeling that they were no longer just studying history, but making it. St Cloud's challenge might not shake the land or even the city, but it would certainly have an effect on how every subject was taught at University. Each one of them knew that this wasn't just Basil St Cloud against Roger Crabbe, but Research against Theory, Observation against Authority. As he pushed through the winding streets, Justis Blake was suddenly aware of the irony of an ancient historian raising the banner of a new and progressive methodology: the Past in service to the Future in opposition to the Present. It made him almost as happy as the prospect of the ruckus St Cloud's challenge was undoubtedly going to raise.

Doctor Crabbe's lecture having begun at two, the street outside Farraday was empty when St Cloud and his guard arrived, save for Doctor Leonard Rugg, his ample form wrapped in fur under his gown, looking as bright and eager as First Day morning.

"The hall's pretty full," he said. "You'll have a good audience. Do you remember the formula?"

Basil, who was wishing himself back on his father's farm, closed his eyes, searched his memory for an endless moment, and said, "I challenge you, Roger Crabbe, on your facts, your reasoning, and your conclusions. The matter shall be debated between us at the Festival of Sowing, as the Governors shall witness."

"You need to say what you're challenging him on! And that last part is Crabbe's," Rugg said. "Blake, you're trustworthy. Tread on his foot or something if he looks like answering his own challenge. Get him out of there as fast as you can, and take him to— oh, the Four-Cornered Hat, and I'll meet you when I've done my part. Ready?"

St Cloud was already at the door, which, like many doors at University, was carved with oak and holly leaves entwined. Wizards once touched this latch, he thought as he put his hand to the worn bronze deer's head.

The door opened miraculously—one of his students had ducked in before him, he realized. He edged past the intent bodies of Crabbe's students, who glanced at him curiously. Crabbe was talking about the fall of the kings. His voice was clipped and slightly nasal—as ugly as the falsehoods he was feeding his students. It would be a joy, Basil thought, to blast that lying tongue with a cleansing fire.

"King Gerard put great trust in his wizards," Crabbe was saying. "That trust was his greatest, some would say his only weakness, he and his cronies being otherwise so very adept at terrorizing his subjects. Only the nobles dared to oppose his despicable practices, but Gerard instructed his wizards to keep the nobles busy, and he believed them when they told him that the plague that broke out in the Horn and Montague lands was their doing. Gerard also trusted the wizards' fabled knowledge of men's hearts to warn him of any plots or disaffection, and he seems to have been so credulous as to have trusted in their magic to protect him from any actual attack. How shocked he must have been when the Liberator, Duke Tremontaine, walked jauntily past them all and stabbed him through the heart."

That was wrong. Basil knew it—everyone knew it, it was

even in Vespas; Crabbe was just being flip and arrogant, because he thought details didn't matter. True, Gerard's wizards had been weak—but the nobles had not "walked past them." The last king's court wizards had all been carefully invited to a great feast, and then locked into the banqueting hall, its doors bound "in thrice-three locks of iron, gold, and lead," as one old ballad put it. After the death of their king, none had left that hall alive; they were burned there, with their books of magic—all except for the one Basil had in his keeping. Which did, indeed, contain notes "On the Bynding of a Renegado, with Thrice Times Three About Him." Crabbe was being flippant, of course, but his prating was intolerable, and Basil raised up his voice in the hall to say so:

"I challenge you, Roger Crabbe, Doctor of this University, on your facts, your reasoning, and your conclusions." The words poured strong and clear over his tongue. "The wizards were true wizards, and their power was true magic."

Gasps and shouts, silenced by Crabbe's lifted hand. He scanned the hall, his eyes narrowed, his tight mouth lipless with rage.

Leonard Rugg's rich tones rolled out across the room. "Should you care to accept the challenge, Doctor Crabbe, you must say, 'The matter of the wizards shall be debated between us at the Festival of Sowing, as the Governors shall witness.' Then you appoint a second, and he and I will present the whole thing formally to the Governors. My advice," he went on in a more confidential tone, "is to say it and get it over with before there's a riot."

Belatedly, St Cloud realized that the hall was buzzing like a hive of wasps working themselves up to an attack. The pulse thudded in his throat.

"Very well," said Crabbe, his voice tight with rage. "The matter of the wizards shall be debated between us, at the Festival of Sowing. And the University Governors will judge between us, who is the traitor and who the true scholar." He turned to Rugg with furious courtesy. "Will that do, Doctor Rugg?"

Rugg glared at the little history Doctor. "I'm willing to stretch a point," he answered, "for the sake of expedience. And your second?"

"You must excuse me, Doctor Rugg, if I hesitate to embroil any of my colleagues in this nonsense without warning or permission. I will furnish you with a name tomorrow, or perhaps the next day."

Justis Blake's voice rumbled in Basil's ear. "It's time to go."

Basil nodded absently, his whole mind concentrated on the compact, truculent figure of his rival. He was as single-minded as a terrier after rats. He'd be a vicious fighter, too, full of tricks and dodges.

Blake's large hand gripped his arm and tugged at it urgently. "Come, Doctor St Cloud! Please!"

Reluctantly, St Cloud allowed Blake and Vandeleur to guide him through a gauntlet of jeers and shoves. The other students went before and behind, protecting him from the worst of it, shoving back a bit, but on the whole, behaving themselves. When they reached the street, St Cloud wanted to wait for Rugg, but the students, more shaken than they would admit, hustled him directly to the Four-Cornered Hat. It wasn't familiar territory, but it was where Doctor Rugg had said to go, so in they went, and found an empty table, and sat down and called for ale for themselves and brandy for Doctor St Cloud and Doctor Rugg.

Silence fell, awkward and unaccustomed among such a garrulous lot. St Cloud glanced from face to shocked face. "I would have warned you," he said frankly, "had I known. But it was the inspiration of the moment. Like Sebastian Fire-Blood, I seized my enemy's weapon by the blade and turned it against him."

Henry Fremont snorted. "That's bitter comfort, seeing as Sebastian Fire-Blood lost his hand."

"He won the battle," said St Cloud. "That was what signified. And that's what signifies here."

Justis exchanged a look with Benedict Vandeleur, who shrugged—he wasn't about to make a fool of himself stating the obvious. But Justis didn't believe, seeing St Cloud's dazed and exalted face, that the young magister had any real notion of what he'd just done or what it meant in the real world. Scholars weren't much given to practical concerns, after all. So he wet his throat with a gulp of ale and said, "A battle isn't an academic debate, sir, nor the other way around. Academic debates draw no blood. On the other hand, there's a law against talking about magic. People will take notice. And spring is a long way away."

"I mean them to take notice," St Cloud said stoutly. "The truth about the wizards and their magic must emerge eventually. Truth can't be stifled forever. It's better brought out in an academic debate than in some more violent manner."

Peter Godwin raised anxious hazel eyes from his tankard. "Do you really think so, sir? Won't it upset things?"

"Of course it will upset things," said Rugg from behind him. "Bastard. Little tick."

"I beg your pardon," said Basil stiffly.

Rugg sat down in front of the brandy and took a gulp. "Crabbe," he explained. "I was a whisker from challenging him myself. 'Will that do, *Doctor* Rugg?' And you should have heard what he said once you left. Tick."

Henry Fremont snorted and then yelped as Vandeleur's boot connected with his shin. St Cloud smiled. "You've hit on it exactly, Rugg. Crabbe is a tick, sucking ideas from other men and claiming them for his own. I must be careful not to ignore his head, lest it fester in the wound."

"And just what do you think you mean by that figure?" inquired Rugg testily. "You're a wonder, St Cloud. Do you realize that you've just committed yourself to proving a fact the nobles have been moving the earth to disprove these two hundred years? And I'm your second. We're both likely to be clapped into the Chop for treason. Or laughed out of University, which would be worse. I thought I had your word you wouldn't do this."

Basil looked the irascible metaphysician in the eye. "You had my word I'd try. I'm sorry, Leonard. He left me no choice. I know what I'm doing."

Doctor Rugg threw up his hands in despair and applied himself to his brandy. The door of the tavern opened to admit a group of students and their teacher. St Cloud caught a glimpse of a red ribbon-bow in one student's long, fair hair. *Girlish*, he thought disapprovingly, then realized that the student *was* a girl, that they were all girls—no, not so young as most of his students. Women.

The magister turned, searching for an empty table, affording Basil a clear view of a hawk-nosed, olive-skinned face and a mass of dark hair braided into a heavy crown.

"Doctor Sophia Campion," said Doctor Rugg, amused. "Would you like an introduction?"

"No," Basil snapped. "I would not. What's *she* doing here?"

A buxom woman with brassy hair was leading the female physicians to a table that had been occupied a moment before by a group of young men. "Fraternizing," said Rugg. "Just as we do at the Nest. I told you she was odd." He glanced around at St Cloud's students, who were gaping as though they'd never in their lives seen a woman before. "Those are not women," he told them. "Those are surgeons. They'd sooner cut you up than kiss you. And there's not one of them a day under twenty-five."

"I knew that," said Vandeleur unexpectedly. "When the Governors let women attend lectures, they stipulated they had to be of legal age." Everyone stared at him. He shrugged. "My sister wants to be a mathematician. She's sixteen."

Ignoring this byplay, Basil studied Theron's mother, trying to find his lover in her vividly foreign face. She was explaining something to one of her students, shaping the air with her hands, touching the woman's arm, tapping a finger against the table, never still until the woman spoke, when she leaned forward to listen, all attention. *Like Theron*, Basil thought, and was suddenly overcome with restless desire. He drained his brandy and stood up.

"Where are you going?" Rugg asked. "We have a lot to talk about. Strategy. Plans. Meetings with the Governors. You've put a match to dry tinder, Basil. You must help contain the fire."

"Later, Leonard." It came out more brusquely than he'd meant, but that was better than pleading. "Come to my rooms to-morrow afternoon—we'll plan then, as much as you like." He looked with affection at the concerned faces of the students who had witnessed his challenge. "You have my gratitude, all of you. No finer scholars and friends could exist the length and breadth of University."

He turned to leave.

Sophia Campion, chancing just then to catch his eye, was astonished to see a handsome young Doctor of Humane Studies turn scarlet and give her a sheepish smile before fairly fleeing the room. Then one of her students claimed her attention, and she forgot all about him.

chapter II

Henry Fremont's note informing Galing about the challenge was short and not particularly informative: *Doctor St Cloud has challenged Doctor Crabbe to a debate about the wizards.*

Galing looked at the back of the paper, but there was nothing more. It was not like Fremont to let a chance escape to expand Galing's knowledge. His reports were commonly as full of ancient history as modern news (*context*, Henry said), and ran to several closely written pages. Whatever else Galing might learn in the course of this investigation, he was learning a great deal about history. But not today. What about the wizards was St Cloud intending to debate? Why had Henry suddenly grown so coy? He laid the letter on the thick stack of Henry's reports and buried his shapely hands in his curls.

This favor Arlen had asked of him, this matter of tracing and diagnosing a troublesome rumor, was more complex, more obscure than Nicholas could have imagined. No sooner did he root out one stem of it than two others would spring up to claim his attention. First, there were the Northerners, the Companions of the King. Troublemakers, malcontents, full of superstitious customs and beliefs. Now that their ringleaders were safely stored in the Chop for easy reference, that should be the end of it. But it wasn't the end, not by a long shot. The world of the Companions was beginning to creep into the drawing rooms of the Hill. While their wives danced, the older nobles discussed in shocked whispers how the Duke of Hartsholt's "revolting peasants," as Condell insisted on calling them, had burned Hartsholt's steward in effigy up north in their MidWinter bonfire. Even Lord Hemmynge, who was more interested in horses than politics, knew that the women of Harden had made a show of stuffing their mattresses with valuable goat hair, rather than spin it for sale on their lord's estates; they called it "Alcuin's Bed," and said they slept easier on it than the old king had. The past was rising; people were talking, and even nobles with no Northern holdings were beginning to say that something must be done.

Under the circumstances, it made Nicholas uneasy that a young Doctor of History was proposing to trot out theories about wizards in a public forum. It made him even more uneasy that the heir to Tremontaine was so consistently attracted to lovers who delved into the past.

But when he imagined explaining his unease to Arlen, he could all too easily imagine Arlen's response: "Historians talk about wizards. Painters love exotic subjects. Young men are romantics. Where is your proof?"

Right now, all Galing had to go on was Greenleaf and Smith in the Chop, Ysaud in her studio, and Doctor Basil St Cloud in his lecture-hall, all babbling, in their several ways, about wizards and deer and mystic sacrifices. And the subject of the Northern boys' hunt, of Ysaud's paintings and St Cloud's passion, was Theron Campion, heir to Tremontaine.

If Galing could only show some connection between Campion and the North!

He pulled out the transcript of the prisoner Greenleaf's interrogations and leafed through the pages. His eye caught on a phrase, repeated several times over several days:

The kings must come again. The land withers and dies without their blood; the people weaken without their seed.

Galing dropped the transcript with a sound of disgust. Green-leaf was clearly mad. Magic kings and wizards were the stuff of old wives' tales, not of political uprisings. To become king, Campion would need allies behind him, followers, an army. There was no sign, in University or anywhere else, of anything so tangible.

Still, he thought, the key to his proof must lie somewhere in the great mass of historical information with which Henry had burdened him. It was significant that Theron was descended from the sister of Gerard the Last King. True, the nobles had signed a document relinquishing any claim to the throne by right of blood for themselves and their descendants. But a signature is merely ink, as an oath is merely breath to a man with sufficient motive to break it. It was not difficult to imagine Theron Campion break-ing his ancestor's word to set himself upon the very throne his an-cestor had broken.

If there was anything going on—and Galing could not swear absolutely that there was—Campion must be at the center of it. There was nothing for it, then, but for Galing to scrape a closer acquaintance with the fellow and see if he could discover what he was up to. It was a pity about that exchange he had allowed himself at the Montague ball, but he could always apologize, if Campion even remembered it.

Rising from his desk, Galing went to the case that held his collection of curious books. He unlocked the delicate iron grille, opened it, abstracted a leather case, and pulled out Ysaud's sketches. Theron Campion's narrow face looked up at him out of a fretwork of leaves that shadowed but did not hide his eager body. Horns branched from his temples. Ysaud had scribbled a ti-tle across the corner: "The Summer King."

Arrogant bastard, Nicholas thought, and returned the sketch to the folder.

⁓

THERON CAMPION WAS ATTENDING A BIRTHDAY PARTY when he learned of Basil's challenge, and he was not pleased.

It was the birthday of Lady Genevieve Randall, the girl he'd admired at the Montague ball. Now that term had begun again and he felt he had proven to Katherine that he had no more New Year's madness up his sleeve, Theron was much less inclined to go to parties on the Hill. But the invitation had been delivered personally by the Randall son, Clarence; Theron had a vague feeling that having made a fool of himself in Clarence's company in a whorehouse at the Harvest Feast gave the Randalls some rights to him now. And besides, the sister was very pretty. So he allowed his valet to pour him into something tight and stylish with dozens of tiny buttons, and went to celebrate with the Randalls.

Sebastian Hemmynge and Peter Godwin were there, too, along with the usual marriageable girls and eligible young men. Theron realized he hadn't seen his erstwhile companions since the night of the Deer Hunt. He wondered if they, too, had been scolded and kept home. Had they even been there in the grove? He really did not know. When he tried to picture that night, the images made him queasy. He had no desire to ask what the other men remembered.

The party took the form of a rustic feast, with the servants all dressed as country folk from the Randalls' estates, serving bread and cheese and cider and preserves from their home. Supervised by mothers and married sisters, Lady Genevieve and her guests danced and even played at forfeits and blindman's buff. Theron had to redeem his forfeit by kissing "the prettiest girl in the room," and politeness dictated that he choose his hostess. With everyone watching, he tilted up the chin of the blushing girl, and brushed the lightest of kisses across her lips. Her hand trembled on his sleeve. He looked into her eyes, and felt his rod stiffen like a schoolboy's. "My token," he cried breathlessly, to cover his throbbing pulse. "You've got to give it back now. Unless you want another kiss!"

Everyone went "Ooh!" and Lady Genevieve fumbled to release from her wrist the ribbon from his shoe that he'd thrown into the forfeit ring.

"Isn't she going to have to lace it back on for you?" a bold girl cried. (After the party, her mother slapped her for it.)

But Theron was just as glad to be able to bend down and lace his shoe himself.

The dances were country dances. Genevieve's eyes sparkled and her pale cheeks were flushed, and tendrils of dark hair escaped from her chignon in the most alluring fashion, clinging to her sweating neck. Theron partnered the girl twice, but swung her about and touched her hand countless times as the lines of dancers met and parted. When they played at blindman's buff he tried to track her by her laugh, but found instead that he had his arms around the waist of the bold girl, who made a great fuss refusing to be kissed, and so he made her sing a song, instead.

He was heading to the punch bowl to get a glass for her when he overheard the words "St Cloud," and stopped in his tracks. Peter Godwin was gesticulating with great animation to his friend Hemmynge. Theron forgot all about the girl.

"It was magnificent!" Godwin was saying. "He stood up right in front of the entire room and said the wizards were real! You should have seen their faces! If we hadn't been there, who knows what they might have done to him, right on the spot."

Theron moved closer. Peter saw him and froze. Godwin had not been one of the bearers of chicken last fall, but he'd certainly heard all about it. "Oh," young Godwin said stiffly. "Hullo, Campion. Lord Theron, I mean. I was just telling Seb about the challenge."

"Wonderful stuff," Hemmynge raved. "I might have to switch to history! Nothing this interesting ever happens in geography! Can you get me a good seat for the debate, Theron?"

"I really have no idea," he said stiffly, and turned away.

⁓

I CAN'T BELIEVE YOU DIDN'T TELL ME." THERON HAD looked for Basil at the Blackbird's Nest, but found him hunched over his books on Minchin Street in an atmosphere of dust and ink and musty paper. "You challenge Roger Crabbe to an academic duel, it's the talk of the taverns, and I find out from bloody Sebastian Hemmynge! Who found out from baby Godwin, and only because they both happened to be at the same birthday party."

"Well, you know now," Basil said mildly.

Theron stormed on. "I am not accustomed to getting my University gossip at third-hand on the Hill, Basil. You are much to blame."

"Because I do not supply you with gossip, my lord?"

Theron stopped as if he had been slapped. "That was not called for."

Basil saw with surprise that Theron's face had gone quite pale. Stubble stood out dark on the young man's cheeks, and his eyes were big with hurt. Wearily, Basil pushed his chair back from his worktable. "I am sorry. It just never occurred to me—I don't think of University politics when I'm with you."

Theron sat on the edge of the bed. "Because you love me. You love me so much you don't bother to tell me anything important. Wonderful."

"You always object when I try to tell you about history."

"This isn't history, this is *real*." He caught himself. "I don't mean history isn't real, but—don't you see there's a huge difference between telling me about dead kings and wizards, and telling me something you have decided you will do?"

"They are both real to me," Basil said quietly.

"I know. I know they are." Theron came and put his hands on Basil's shoulders, and nuzzled his hair—a peace offering. "What are you studying? It looks like a laundry list."

"It's clothing, actually. The paper was used as the lining for a cookery book, but I think it's an inventory of clothing for the royal compound, and I'm hoping—wondering, really, if it might not be—well, something about wizards."

"Wizards? In a cookery book?" Theron kissed the top of his head. "Basil, you are wonderful. I'll leave you to it, then."

He paused a moment, and Basil said, "No, don't go. It's not important, just interesting. Look: 'Ten robes of brown wool, with cloaks of fur, according to their natures.' And this: 'Bear Dress—Master WG.' That *could* mean Master Wizard G. . . . Don't go, Theron."

"I have to go," Theron said mournfully.

"Why?"

"Because I'll never get all these buttons undone and done up again!"

Basil said huskily, "I'll do that. Lie down, my love, and I'll do it all."

WHEN THERON RETURNED TO RIVERSIDE THE NEXT day, Lady Sophia showed him an envelope. "Who are these Randall people?" she asked him. "The Lady Randall invites us to a musical evening together to their house. You know I detest musical evenings. Are these people I know, Theron? Must I go?"

Her son bit into an apple. "I don't think you know them; they're newly come to town, to marry off the daughter, probably. There's a son my age, who's in the Perry crowd. I don't see why you can't decline."

"Ah. Is it the daughter who plays the viol? The Lady Genevieve, it says?"

Theron looked over her shoulder. "Why, yes." He imagined Genevieve with a viol tucked between her knees. "I'll tell you what; I'll go, and give your regrets in person. I'll tell them you had to perform a sudden triple amputation, or lance a large boil."

Sophia laughed. "Come here, my darling, your buttons are crooked."

chapter III

NICHOLAS GALING WAS FEELING DISCOURAGED
and frustrated. Henry Fremont hadn't sent him word in
days and Theron Campion was proving annoyingly
elusive. He was never with the other young nobles of his age group,
and Nicholas had no mind to go chasing him at University. Galing
was full of suspicions and instincts and empty of hard facts and
tired to death of the whole subject of wizards and kings. So he took
himself, as he sometimes did, to a public bathhouse. There was
nothing like a good sweat to clear the mind.

He was lying in the steam room on a scratchy piece of towel-
ing, sweaty, sodden, and blissfully empty-minded, when two
young men came in and established themselves on the marble
benches. Their voices boomed and rattled off the tiles, the words
running together almost incomprehensibly. Nicholas caught a
word—"magic"—then a name—"St Cloud"—then a laugh. He
came to attention, and was rewarded by a whole sentence: "I'll
give him this: he has balls, does Doctor St Cloud, to unseal that
wasp's nest after so many years."

"He's right, of course," said the second man. "He must be. There'd be no point forbidding all mention of magic if it wasn't a real threat. I wonder how he'll prove it?"

"Make lightning flash out of a blue sky?" the first man suggested. "Grow corn on the Great Hall steps?"

"Make all the Governors' robes disappear—that's what I'd do."

"That's because you haven't the imagination of a ten-copper nail," the first man said, disgusted, and the conversation degenerated into bickering.

Assuming that his informants thought themselves alone, Nicholas lay still until they'd sweated their fill. Feeling weak and wobbly from the heat, he ignored the blandishments of the bath-boys and the massage-men, and had a cold plunge before drying himself and scrambling into his clothes. It was late—nearly mid-night—when he emerged, clean, neat, and blazingly furious at the world in general and Henry Fremont in particular. Still, he needed information more than he needed to wring young Master Fremont's scraggy neck. So he procured a chaise and directed it to take him to Edward Tielman's house on Fulsom Street.

Late as it was, Felicity herself received him in the library. He was startled to see her heavily pregnant—he hadn't thought it so long since their last meeting. Her belly was like a cauldron among the folds of her gown, but her face was thin and there were dark circles under her eyes.

"Ned's very occupied," she told Galing after the first pleas-antries were over. "He's seldom home before midnight and leaves first thing in the morning. I'm thinking of having his portrait painted so the baby will know what its father looks like, except he'd never find time to sit for it."

Galing accorded this sally a sympathetic smile. "I'll look for him at the Council Hall, then, if you'll excuse me. It's rather urgent I speak to him."

"Of course," said Felicity, rather sadly. "But do come by again for a late supper or something. Ned and I miss you, and I, for one, am not getting about much these days."

Nicholas bowed and murmured politely and was on his way

out the door when voices in the hall heralded Edward's timely return from the Council Hall. Felicity heaved herself out of her
chair. "I'll tell him you're here and send him straight in. Don't
keep him up too late, will you, Nick?"

The minutes ticked by, and Nicholas waited for Edward with
mounting impatience. He imagined Felicity reproaching her husband for coming home so late and extracting a promise to get rid
of his untimely visitor as soon as possible. It was odd, how child-
bearing could metamorphose a perfectly nice, tolerant woman
into a domestic tyrant. Nicholas knew a moment of gratitude
that he was not an eldest son, to shackle himself to a woman for
the sake of the family.

The hands of the library clock approached one. Nicholas was
reaching for the bell to summon someone to remind Tielman of
his existence when his friend himself entered. He was wearing a
dressing-gown over breeches and shirt. "I'm sorry, Nick; Felicity
said you were in a hurry, but I insisted on seeing her to bed before
I came up. She's more delicate than she'll let on, you know, and I
worry." He unstoppered a decanter, poured two glasses of red
wine, and held one out to Nicholas. "Now, what can I do for
you?"

Nicholas ignored the glass. "Did you know that Basil St
Cloud has declared that he will prove that the wizards had true
magic? In public forum?"

"Why, yes. I did. Didn't you? What happened to Henry?"

"Henry is obviously more loyal to St Cloud and his bizarre
notions than you thought," Nicholas snapped. "What I want to
know is why this Doctor St Cloud isn't in the Chop, debating the
reality of magic with Lord Arlen and his inquisitors."

Edward smiled. "Is that all? I thought you'd figured it out, or I
would have written you a report myself. As it is—look, I'm not
going to stand here like an idiot with two glasses of wine while
you glare at me. Take this and sit down and I'll tell you everything."

Nicholas was very close to knocking the glass from Edward's
hand and cursing him for a swollen-headed, jumped-up servant
who didn't know his place. But a good intelligencer must govern

his temper, so Nicholas took the wine and sat as he'd been told, and sipped before cocking his eyebrow at his friend. "Well, Ned?"

Tielman propped his elbows on his knees and twirled the wine in his glass. "Well. The Governors came to us as soon as they heard about the challenge, wanting to know what they ought to do about it. They were in a right old state, like maiden aunts exclaiming over a housemaid who's fallen pregnant. Should they dismiss St Cloud out of hand, should they refuse to hear the debate, they hadn't known anything about any of this, the University held itself above such matters, and could we please make it all go away."

"And you said?"

"Lord Horn said he would put it before the Inner Council, and let them know."

"And the Inner Council said?"

"Well." Tielman sat back and took a thoughtful sip of wine. "It wasn't quite the whole Inner Council—Lord Horn saw no reason for the Dragon Chancellor or the ducal houses to be bothered over so trifling a matter."

Galing gripped the arms of his chair. "Trifling?" he inquired as mildly as he could. "The Council of Lords didn't think so when they declared any mention of the wizards and magic to be unlawful. And it still is, as far as I know."

"Yes, yes, I know; which is why the Governors are in such a flap. But Lord Arlen made the point, and Lord Horn agrees, that subjects no one is allowed to discuss under threat of imprisonment are more likely to attract the wrong kind of attention than subjects anyone can talk about with impunity. You can't have secret societies when you don't have a secret for them to rally around. We're indebted to St Cloud, really, for bringing it all out into the open."

"Ah." Nicholas sat back with an assumption of ease. He was blindingly angry, and aware that his anger might impair his judgment. "Lord Arlen said that, did he?"

" 'Let the man do his best to prove it was real,' he said. 'I don't imagine he can do it, but if he can, I don't imagine it will mean much outside the University. Magic has nothing to do with the way things are run today; why shouldn't scholars talk about it?' "

"And those were his very words?" Nicholas couldn't quite keep the sarcasm out of his voice.

"Close enough."

"I take it you were there, then. At this little convocation of the cream of the Inner Council. And that despite the extreme erudition of the distinguished councilors assembled, no one thought to point out that it's not only about wizards and magic and ancient history. Such a debate calls the Council's own legitimacy to challenge."

"How so?"

"Because the overthrow of the monarchy is the foundation of the Council's authority!" Without knowing he was doing it, Nicholas drained half his wineglass. "Of *our* authority. Of the nobles' right to rule. Because, you blockhead, if the wizards were really tied to the land with real magic, and chose the kings to rule, then the nobles had no right to depose them!"

Tielman looked at him with affection, long and hard. "What a lot of knowledge Henry's managed to cram into your head after all. Far better than old Bracegirdle and our other tutor." He waved his hand. "You are right, I'm sure. But whoever was in the right of it two hundred years ago, it's a done deal now. And no amount of scholarly debate, however well-reasoned, can change that."

Nicholas struggled with his temper and subdued it enough to say, "I presume my investigation is closed, then."

"Has Arlen told you it is?" Edward inquired.

This was too much. "You know he hasn't. He hasn't told me anything. You're his leaf-crowned boy—you tell me."

"Oh, lord," said Edward. "You're really hurt, aren't you? Don't deny it—I knew you when your father gave your brother that horse."

"Edward." Galing's voice was tight and even. "I'm not a boy. And this isn't a matter of petty jealousy. I understood that I'd been given a job to do, a job that had some importance to the welfare of the city, perhaps of the country. To discover that it was so inconsequential that no one would even bother to call me off . . . Well, it came as a shock. I wouldn't have thought it of Arlen."

"No," Tielman agreed. "You wouldn't, would you?"

The fire popped and settled in the grate; Tielman stirred it with a poker and threw on another log. Galing thought a moment and said, "He's playing some damned endgame, isn't he? It's another of his plague-rotted tests. All I have to do is figure out whether he's really not paying attention to St Cloud's challenge, or only officially not paying attention."

"Sounds a bit complicated to me," Tielman said.

"The Serpent's a complicated man."

"He is that."

They sat for a moment, contemplating the fire and Lord Arlen's complexity. Then Nicholas said, "Look. Do you want me to keep pursuing this or not?"

"This?"

Edward sounded as if he might have begun to nod off over the fire. Now that Nicholas came to look at him, he saw that his friend's eyes were almost as shadowed as his wife's. "The possibility of a monarchist plot in the city," he explained.

Edward yawned and shrugged. "Truth? I don't know. This is Arlen's game, and Arlen plays his cards close to his chest. If he hasn't called you off, it's my guess you're still on."

This was Galing's guess, too, but it was comforting to have his friend's confirmation. It was so comforting that Nicholas turned down Edward's half-hearted offer of more wine and left the poor man to his bed and whatever joy he might get of his pregnant wife and went home. There he spent the rest of the night composing a careful letter to Lord Arlen, hinting that he had something to report concerning a highly placed member of the nobility, and would like to wait upon his lordship at his lordship's earliest convenience. It was time to flush the Serpent from his lair.

THE TIME FOLLOWING MidWinter is the dreariest of the year. Days are short, nights are long, and both are cold and wet with no immediate prospect of relief. Winter's Tail is what the old wives call it, dragging filth at winter's ass. It is a good time to sit by a roaring fire in company or with work at hand. It was a bad time to be poor and alone.

Which was why Justis Blake took it on himself to shame the softer-hearted members of the St Cloud coterie into calling upon Anthony Lindley with food and fuel and good cheer until he was able to fend for himself. His ten days in the Chop had left him very ill indeed, ill enough to need a physician to bleed him and prescribe no fewer than two noxious and expensive medicines. Henry Fremont, whose father must have had a very good year indeed, bore the greatest part of the expense, and furthermore gave up his new muffler to the sufferer. Since he and Lindley had hardly been close friends, he came in for a certain amount of teasing, particularly from Vandeleur, who pretended to scent a helpless love in Fremont's generosity. Fremont finally lost his temper and gained a black eye trying to box the notion out of Vandeleur's head. Which didn't, as Godwin pointed out, really prove anything one way or the other.

It was two weeks after the challenge, and Justis Blake's turn to play nursemaid. When he came into the Nest, Benedict Vandeleur greeted him with, "How's our little king-maker today?" and shoved down the bench to give his friend room to sit.

"Is that turnip stew? Can I have some?" Without waiting for an answer, Blake picked up Vandeleur's spoon and dug in, accepting with a nod the hunk of bread Vandeleur handed him across the table.

"You'd think the Chop would have given him a distaste for all that Northern flap," Godwin remarked.

"Or at least taught him the sense of keeping quiet about it," Vandeleur added.

Blake tried to say something around a mouthful of stew and bread, choked, coughed, and was thumped upon the back until he protested he was fine.

"Good," said Henry Fremont. "But if you were going to tell us that you can't expect a man half out of his mind with fever to display sense or discretion, you'll wish you had choked."

Blake grinned across at his irritating friend. "Shut up, Henry.

I wasn't going to say anything of the kind. He's better today. He said he needn't trouble us any more, that he can take care of himself now. He's grateful but embarrassed, is what I think."

"Fair enough," said Vandeleur. "I can't say I'm sorry. I like Lindley, but it's damnably inconvenient. Odette complains."

"Oh, does she now?" Henry sneered. "Is that because you make her visit him in your place?"

Vandeleur ignored him. "Lindley's changed. I can't quite put my finger on it, but he's not as soft as he was."

"He's got new friends, too," Godwin put in. "I met them on the steps last time I went to see him. A couple of weedy Northerners, looking like they'd been eating gooseberries—you know what they're like. After that scene in the Nest, I couldn't imagine what they'd been doing there, but Lindley seemed cheerful enough. He'd better watch himself, though, consorting with Northerners. It doesn't look good."

"Maybe they had news of Finn," Blake said. "Anyone heard anything?"

No one had. The general opinion was that he was still in the Chop, and what were things coming to, when a man couldn't raise a little riot and rumpus on Last Night without the Council getting in a twist over it? "He has only himself to blame, spouting off about kings and deer all over the place," Godwin said, a noble to the bone.

"Perhaps we should go and tell someone he didn't mean anything by it," said Blake.

"Should we?" asked Vandeleur. "I expect he's told them that and they don't believe it. We'll only make things worse."

A few days later, Lindley duly returned to Basil St Cloud's lectures, looking pale and painfully thin. When St Cloud tried to speak to him, he turned away the magister's sympathy.

"It was the making of me," he told St Cloud earnestly. "I had nothing to do for ten days but think about it, and I realized for the first time how important it is that everyone know the truth about the kings and the wizards. Truth is the greatest thing, greater than love or friendship. Love betrays you; so do friends. Truth is the only thing that never changes. Truth and the Land.

That is why your debate is so important. Doctor Crabbe is the enemy of truth. He must be vanquished."

He was very serious, as only a young zealot can be serious, and Basil was touched. "I intend to do my best, Lindley."

The young man's eyes glittered eagerly. "Will you let me serve you, magister? I'll search the Archives, take notes, carry your water and fetch your wood, if that would ease your labors. It is not right that you should work unattended."

"Thank you, Lindley," Basil said briskly. "I was just about to bring that up." He raised his voice. "Blake, Vandeleur, Fremont, Godwin. Don't leave. I need you."

When his students had gathered, he said, "You may think spring's a long way off, but you're wrong. There's hardly time for me to find the material on the wizards I'll need to convince the Governors that I'm not a dangerous lunatic. I'll need your help. I'll need you to go into the University Archives."

The students exchanged stupefied looks. "But, sir," Vandeleur objected, "there's nothing to find about magic in the Archives. They burned all the wizards' books. It says so—not only in the usual texts; it's even in the ballads and the poems."

"Ballads and poems tend to take the most dramatic view of things. *They* were nobles, Vandeleur, not academics. They only burned everything they found," St Cloud said. "They could not have found everything."

Justis Blake's heart had begun pounding as though he'd been running. This was scholarship with a vengeance, scholarship with teeth. This was the most important thing that had ever happened to him. "What are we to look for, sir?" he asked.

"Anything that might conceivably have to do with wizards. Look through lists, letters, books. Look for wizard-like names in the University Rolls and references to unusual weather or plagues or good harvests. I know there was a School of Arts Magical at University once: see if you can find out what the subjects of the lectures were. Universities hate to get rid of documents. There's bound to be something."

He studied their faces. Lindley was glowing. Fremont and Vandeleur seemed stunned—no doubt by the amount of work

involved. Blake looked almost as happy as Lindley at the prospect
of hours in the Archives, sifting through dusty papers. But young
Peter Godwin looked deeply distressed. Basil, who had temporarily forgotten the boy was a noble, said, "Never mind, Godwin. I
shouldn't have asked you. You're too young for divided alle-
giances. It's enough that you remain my student."

Godwin's voice was tight. "If I'm to remain your student, sir,
then I must work with the others."

"Thank you, Godwin. But I'd be a poor magister, to set you
against your family's interests."

The boy looked at him sternly, and in his set face Basil saw
the man he would become. "I'm not a child, sir, and I'm not a . . .
a reactionary. I want you to win. Not just for our own honor, or
yours, but for truth. My family will understand."

Basil pressed his shoulder. "Let's hope so. The rest of you, do
you agree to help me?"

"We do," they said gravely, feeling the solemnity of the moment and the undertaking. Then they grinned, and he slapped
their shoulders and told them he'd meet them tomorrow, with
their letters of introduction to the Master Librarian. And then
they left, all except Lindley.

The redhead unpinned the brooch on his hatband and thrust
it into his magister's hand. "Take this, for luck. And remember
that in your service, the service of truth, I would dare anything."
Then he darted off after the others, leaving Basil holding a
carved oak leaf.

WHEN LORD ARLEN CAME TO CALL AT TREMONTAINE
House, the duchess was sparring with her arms-master in
the Long Gallery. The butler announced the Serpent Chancellor
in a stentorian voice that might have been a mouse-squeak for all
the attention Lady Katherine paid it. She continued to dance the
arms-master across the hall, forcing him back with a series of
neat, quick thrusts. His foot struck one of the chairs pushed
against the wall and he went on the offensive. Katherine began
to give way; there was a little flurry of action, too fast to follow,

and the arms-master's sword spun into the air and fell clattering to the parquet.

"I wish you'd teach me that disarm, m'lady," said the swordsman, rubbing his stinging hand.

Katherine retrieved his sword and offered it to him, hilt-first. "If I taught you that disarm, Morris, I'd never have a chance of beating you, and well you know it. Thank you. It was a good bout."

Morris bowed and disappeared. Katherine picked up a loose scarlet gown, wrapped it around her shoulders, and turned to the two figures standing at the gallery's far end. "I'm not fit for company," she called to them. "Will you wait in the study while I change, Lord Arlen? It won't take long."

Arlen smiled. "No need to change on my account, dear lady. I do not intend to detain you for long."

"I see." Katherine came down the room and handed her sword to the butler. "See to this, if you please, and tell Molly to prepare a bath. I'll ring if we need anything."

They walked companionably through the beautifully appointed halls of Tremontaine House toward Katherine's study, as odd a pair as might be met anywhere on the Hill. Lord Arlen was tall and well made, his black coat tight across his shoulders, his hair burnished silver, his nose uncompromising, his face seamed like a mountainside. Beside him, the Duchess Tremontaine trotted like a stocky boy, her graying hair escaping from a tarnished buckle, her round cheeks patchily flushed with exercise.

"A handsome apartment," Arlen observed as she shut the door behind them.

Katherine snorted impatiently. "You did not sally forth from your private fortress to talk about my study," she said. "This is about Theron, isn't it?" Lord Arlen raised his brows meaningfully in the direction of the chairs flanking the fire. "Oh, sit down and stop playing off that air of mystery," she said irritably. "The boy means no harm. He's a young fool, and his mother spoils him."

Arlen sat and stretched his long legs to the fire. "Dear Katherine. I can always count on you to cut straight to the heart of the matter. I agree that Lord Theron is a fool. I only seek enlightenment about what sort of fool he is."

"Fair enough." Katherine took the other chair, drawing her gown closer around her. "He's given to enthusiasms," she said thoughtfully. "Mostly over people, some of them highly unsuitable."

"Politically?" Lord Arlen sounded bored, but Katherine knew the question was far from idle. They were old sparring partners, she and Arlen, battling amiably over the course of the city's development while Crescents came and went. Arlen distrusted change; Katherine welcomed it. Both loved the city and the country that sustained it.

Katherine mentally reviewed what she knew of Theron's friendships. "No," she said. "Not really. Not on purpose, anyway. I think politics bore him."

"Do they?"

"He always makes an excuse to leave the table when Marcus and I get going, and he's made it clear he'd rather do almost anything than sit in Council."

"A pity," said Arlen, "given the position he'll hold someday. But not, perhaps, surprising."

Katherine suddenly looked older. "I'd hoped he would prove to be more his mother's son than his father's; she raised him, after all, and she has a fearsome sense of responsibility."

Arlen smiled. "Fearsome, indeed. And I'd argue that his father did, too, in his way. But we digress. These . . . enthusiasms: does Lord Theron cherish them for unsuitable causes, too?"

"No," said Katherine decidedly. "Ideas, yes. Causes, no. And don't try to tell me that having ideas leads to treasonous impulses, because that horse won't run. He's casting around for a center to his life, but I don't for a moment believe this king business is it. Whatever kind of fool Theron may be, he's not dangerous, not in that way."

Arlen considered this, his chin resting on his steepled fingers. "Very well. I trust your judgment. But if he's not dangerous, he would be well advised to stop behaving as if he were. Since MidWinter, I seem to stumble over him wherever I turn."

It was the gentlest of playful thrusts. Katherine parried smoothly. "I'll just have to keep him out from under your feet, won't I?"

"That," said Arlen, "would be very nice." He rose. "The Tremontaine duchesses have been so much more satisfactory than the dukes."

"How thoughtful of me not to marry," Katherine snapped, out of patience. "Go away, Arlen. You've had your say, and I want my bath. All that ails Theron is too much freedom and too little discipline. He's a good boy at heart."

"His heart is not what concerns me, Duchess," Arlen said dryly, whereupon Katherine laughed and rang the bell and indulged in friendly small-talk until Farraday arrived to show Lord Arlen to his waiting carriage. When he'd gone, Katherine did not immediately seek her bath, but sat down at her desk, wrote a brief, emphatic note, sealed it, and directed it to Lord Theron Campion at Riverside House. Then she sat staring at the letter until her maid Molly came down to bully her upstairs and out of her sweaty clothes. She was very stiff indeed.

T HERON WAS AT HOME IN RIVERSIDE HOUSE WHEN HIS cousin's note arrived. He was in the library, a delightful cave of a room with heavy curtains, thick rugs and well-stuffed chairs, and books that seemed to breathe dust. It was a cold day; a fire roared in the grate, but still he had himself wrapped in a beat-up old quilt. He was reading a famous essay on the difference between power and persuasion. His mind kept straying from the main point, wondering hazily if anything in the essay would be of use to Basil in preparing his debate.

He was not pleased to be handed an envelope with the duchess's crest. Written herself, not dictated by a secretary; it could not be good.

It wasn't. Nor was it particularly informative. Visit her on Monday week. Matters of state to discuss. He turned the paper over, as if there were a translation on the back. *Matters of state.* What in the Seven Hells had he to do with matters of state?

Theron stretched, and swore again. It was no use trying to read anything serious now. He couldn't concentrate. He went upstairs to frame an answer, and found an old pile of invitations

he'd been ignoring. One was from Charlie Talbert, son of the odi-
ous cousin Gregory, inviting him to join some friends in a theatre
party. Poor Charlie had never been interested in theatre before,
but he was courting a girl who was mad for it. He'd begged the use
of the Tremontaine box from Katherine; presumably Theron
would be another ornament to the event. It was this afternoon,
after lunch and before his evening lecture. Theron shrugged; why
not? Maybe Charlie knew something of the matters of state. Or
his father had let slip something. He dashed off a note to Charlie,
penned a polite response to Katherine, and shouted for Terence
to find him something decent to wear.

T HERON COULD BE PERFECTLY POLITE WHEN HE RE-
membered to be, and he really did exert himself with
Charlie and his friends, so much so that Charlie's sweetheart,
Lady Elizabeth Horn, asked later what all the fuss was about the
Mad Duke's son, since Lord Theron had been pleasant, even if
his hair was somewhat ridiculous.

The play was dull, one of those comedies about lovers kept
from marrying each other by endless misunderstandings. But
Theron wasn't looking much at the stage. His eyes kept straying
to the Randall box, where the Lady Genevieve sat, surrounded by
suitable chaperones. Lady Genevieve Randall was dressed all in
white, like a nymph of winter, with silver drops in her ears and
brilliants glittering high in her soft dark hair and around her slim
neck. He found himself delighted by the way her hand flew to her
mouth at the comic scenes, the careful way she always turned her
head to reply to her friends' comments, the air of propriety that
breathed from her like perfume.

And suddenly he knew why he had come. Genevieve was the
answer to all his problems.

At the interval, he bought a bunch of white hothouse violets
from a flower-girl, and gained admittance to the Randall box.
Lady Randall was delighted to see him. Genevieve ducked her
head to smell his bouquet, and smiled up at him between her dark

lashes. His heart jumped in his chest, and he knew there would be no impediment to his desires.

"I wish," he said, to be sure, "that I could escort you to your carriage after the play. But I must dash off to attend a lecture."

"At the University?" the girl said.

"Yes. I study there. You must think me very dull."

"Oh, no," said Lady Genevieve. "It must be terribly exciting."

"It is exciting." Theron bowed, and took his leave.

He nearly danced back to his seat, and saw nothing of the final act. Everything unfolded before him in perfect sequence, like a well-made length of brocade rolling off the loom, flowers and ribbons and curlicues all patterned as they should be. He would not tell Basil, not yet. Basil had kept the challenge from him; well, he would keep his secret too, though in the end it was one that would please his lover well. A little social fuss, a legal ceremony, and everything would be in place, with Theron free to live the life he chose, as he chose to live it. How could anyone object to that?

chapter IV

SOME TIME AFTER INFORMING LORD NICHOLAS Galing of the debate between St Cloud and Crabbe, Henry Fremont wrote his patron one last letter.

I have thought about it, he wrote, *and I have decided that I am not cut out for a spy. I don't like being responsible for people going to jail, even irritating fools like Finn and Lindley and their Northern friends. I think Doctor St Cloud is an honest man and a great scholar, and I don't think he would give a bean-fed fart for a new king. All he's interested in is truth, and if you're going to put him in prison for that, then I don't want to be part of it.*

He'd signed himself *Your Humble & Ob'd't Sv't,* with an ironic flourish.

Nicholas swore long and fluently. After all he'd done for that miserable hat-rack, he had the brass-bottomed gall to quit? He deserved to be thrown in the Chop for questioning—or brought straight to Nicholas himself. It would be pure pleasure, Nicholas thought, to torture information out of the rude historian, and it would pay Arlen back for not asking him to attend the questioning of the Northerners. Feeling much more cheerful, he called for his servant to drag Henry out of his scholarly lair, considered the irritation of actually having to be in the same room with him, and decided not to bother. Instead, he dashed off a note to Lord Arlen: *My University contact broken; shall I make another? I must talk to you.* He scratched out the last line, wrote *I am ready to make a preliminary report on the Northern matter. Would tomorrow afternoon be convenient?* and sent it off with his servant. The servant returned without an answer, which did nothing to sweeten Galing's temper.

If Galing was still angry when he showed up at Lord Filisand's some hours later, none of his fellow guests would have known it. Dispensing smiles and embraces, he moved through Filisand's stuffy, overheated rooms looking for someone who was well-acquainted with Lord Theron Campion. The University was not Galing's world; he'd been a fool to try and enter it without knowing how it worked. But the Hill—the Hill was his native hunting ground. He'd caught Arlen's eye because of his ability to nose out noble secrets elegantly and thoroughly. And Lord Theron Campion of Tremontaine was a noble, whether he liked it or not. Nicholas knew in his hunter's bones that, no matter who else was involved, Lord Theron was at the heart of the whole affair. Thanks to Ysaud, Nicholas possessed the bait to lure Lord Theron. All he needed was to get close enough to set the trap.

Thus Lord Filisand's supper, a weekly evening of cards, food, and talk through which almost every man on the Hill passed sooner or later. Wives were not welcome, nor daughters, sisters, or even mistresses. Men came to gamble, to flirt, to discuss horses or swordsmen or votes on troublesome measures up before the Council—to enjoy themselves, in short, without having to worry about moderating their tongues or their consumption of brandy-punch. Ancient history had kept Galing away since MidWinter. Now he must make up for lost time.

"Absolutely tied to my bed," he explained solemnly to Lord Condell, who wanted to know where he'd been hiding. And then he winked, which caused Condell to call him a naughty man and tap him on the wrist with a fan of brown silk. The fan was new—clearly the latest cry of fashion. Galing noticed several men busily plying them against the fug. Even young Lord Clarence Randall had taken up the fad, awkwardly flapping a girlish scrap of pink lace before his sweating face. The boy looked like an idiot. A charitable impulse, inspired by having won a great deal of money from him at Davenant's MidWinter card party, sent Galing to his rescue.

"Hot, isn't it?" asked Randall plaintively.

"Lord Filisand suffers terribly from the cold," Galing explained. "And we suffer with him. The fans are an inspiration. It would do you more good, however, if you held it like this"—he adjusted the fan in Randall's fingers—"and moved it thus, from the wrist." He watched Randall critically, nodded, and said, "That's better. But may I say without offense, that your fan is perhaps a bit . . . delicate for your hand? A larger one would be more effective."

"It's my sister's," Randall confided. "I pinched it from the hall table." He eyed the spangled lace doubtfully. "Likely she'll have my ears for taking it."

"Surely not," said Galing, beginning to be bored, "if she left it lying about."

"She didn't. She left it behind because Campion gave her a new one. Had to carry it—manners, you know. Devilish attached to this one."

Galing was no longer bored. "What's a fan, more or less," he said carelessly, "when you have a lover to give you new ones?"

"That's what I thought," Randall agreed. He leaned forward to murmur in Galing's ear. He smelled of brandy-punch. "Theron Campion's spending a devilish lot of time with her, if you know what I mean. They're seeing *Fair Rosamund* at Kean's. Very romantic play, *Rosamund*."

Galing plucked the fan from Randall's hand and furled it neatly. "It is indeed, and one of my favorites besides. Let us abandon this amazingly hot room and refresh ourselves at the well of immortal love." Lord Clarence goggled at him. Unoffended, Galing laughed. "The play, man, the play. I propose we go to see *Fair Rosamund*."

They reached the theatre just as the third act was beginning. Lord Clarence led Galing to the Randall box and introduced him to his mother, Lady Randall, in a piercing whisper. Lady Randall looked only moderately pleased to see her son and his friend, and when Lord Theron would have given up his seat at the front of the box to Galing, she declared that she was feeling quite faint and would rather sit at the back. So Galing settled himself beside Lord Theron, fixed his eyes on the stage, and turned over ways of intriguing the irritating young heir of Tremontaine into a private conversation.

It wasn't going to be easy to get his attention. Every time Galing glanced away from the posturing actors, Campion was turned toward the Randall girl, his knee breaking the white foam of her voluminous skirts. Once he heard her murmur something; once he heard her sigh: Lord Theron's courtship seemed to be proceeding well. Remembering Henry's history lessons, Galing wondered how a queen might figure in his plans.

On stage, King Alexander Ravenhair, in a long black wig and a short tunic that showed his excellent legs, was hurling poetic defiance at the evil Wizard Guidry, who was listening with a patience remarkable in so choleric a personality. Galing chuckled. Startled, Campion glanced over his shoulder at him. Galing cocked his brow at the stage, rolled his eyes, and gnashed his teeth. Campion's lips twitched in unwilling amusement before he turned again to Genevieve. At the interval, he allowed himself to be distracted from her long enough for Galing to strike up a conversation about how a good actor might transform a bad play.

"Have you seen Mistress Sedley at the Buttery?" he asked. "Her voice is pure alchemy, able to turn the hoariest bombast into tragic gold. They say she's the Black Rose come again."

"Ah." Campion was politely interested. "There's a portrait of the Black Rose as the Empress hanging in the breakfast-room in Riverside House. I quite feel she's a member of the family."

"The Black Rose, or the Empress?"

"Oh, both. I always think of them together."

Galing was visited by inspiration. "I believe Mistress Sedley has chosen *The Empress* for her subscription performance. I usually take a small party to these events—shall I include you?"

Campion, with one eye on Lady Genevieve, professed himself flattered and begged Galing to tell him the date. Galing suspected that the boy was only being civil because of his audience, but it didn't matter: Galing could now claim acquaintance with him. And the young man's interest in the Randall chit added considerably to the value of Ysaud's paintings.

Nicholas settled back to watch the last act of *Rosamund* in a mood of happy confidence.

U NIVERSITY STUDENTS ARE A QUARRELSOME LOT AT the best of times. Young blood runs hot and rises suddenly to a boil in defense of its passion, whether it be a man or a woman, an idea or an ideal. Nearly every winter brought a cause to divide the University into factions that spat when they met in the street and occasionally blacked one another's eyes.

Older magisters reminisced about the academic feuds of their youth, when students threw rotten fruit at Doctor Darlington of Geography when he debated Doctor Russom over the earth's roundness, and carried Weedin of Rhetoric shoulder-high through the streets, waving his defeated rival's gown behind him like a banner. But not even the oldest of them could remember feelings running quite as high as over the ancient historians' debate.

In the King's Horn, where Governors, Chairs, and the older magisters were accustomed to drink undisturbed by lesser mortals, it was generally agreed that young Doctor St Cloud had gone too far. It was all very well to shake things up—that was what young magisters did, what they themselves had done in their salad days. But to declare the wizards were real and their magic true! First off, he couldn't possibly prove it, not by those so-called "new scholarly methods" of his, not by any methods at all.

Doctor Leonard Rugg walked into the thick of it one afternoon when he joined his old magister and sponsor, Doctor Polycarp of Metaphysics, for a friendly cup of the Horn's famous brandy-punch.

"It's a thing that shouldn't be proved, whether it's true or not," Polycarp was saying as Rugg approached. "Ah, Rugg, there you are. Take a cup, lad, and sit down. Doctor Standish and I were just talking about this challenge business. Standish, you remember Leonard Rugg. I know you're not much on metaphysics, but you ought to hear him on the Essence of Being."

Rugg disclaimed modestly, declared himself honored, dipped himself a fragrant cup of punch from the pewter bowl on the table, and installed himself in a comfortably shabby chair.

"It's a bad business," Polycarp went on. "Bad for the City, bad for the University. I don't know what the Governors were about to allow it."

"They can't refuse permission for an academic challenge," said Standish. "It's a bad precedent."

Rugg struggled briefly with the knowledge that he ought to keep out of this, and lost. "Just so," he said cordially. "It's what academic challenges are for, after all: to bring up uncomfortable subjects and put them to public scrutiny, find out the truth, whatever it may be."

"Truth!" Polycarp snorted. "The truth is, magic is nasty and unnatural, whether it's 'real' or not."

"What," said Standish, "is 'real' anyway, in this context? No one disputes that the wizards did *something*, something they made a great mystery of, something that did considerable harm. That's 'real' enough. I don't see that there's anything to dispute."

"Of course there is," Rugg said. "The harm came from the mystery. Remember what Arvin said: 'Truth is a lamp. Shuttered, covered, hidden, it illuminates nothing, and leaves us stumbling in the dark.'"

"Arvin wasn't talking about magic," Polycarp objected. "He was talking about metaphysics. In any case, we already know the truth about the wizards. From Vespas on down, the authorities are in absolute agreement. It's as if this Basil St Cloud has offered to prove that the sun rises in the west. It's pointless and useless and dangerous."

"That's what Doctor Crabbe says, certainly," Rugg began, "but—"

"St Cloud, too," Polycarp barreled on. "Dangerous, I mean, and ambitious. I wouldn't be astonished to learn that he means to throw over the faculty and the Governors and turn the University into a college for wizards."

Rugg looked at Standish, who was shaking his head in somber disapproval. "Well, I'd be astonished," Leonard Rugg burst out. "I've never heard such nonsense. In the first place, if magic isn't real, how could St Cloud teach it? And in the second, I know the man, and he hasn't an ambitious thought in his head."

Understandably offended, Polycarp puffed himself out like an owl. "Nonsense, is it?"

"Don't rise to his bait, Poly," Standish said. "He's one of them. I've heard your name, Rugg. You're St Cloud's second, aren't you?"

With the two old men glaring at him, Rugg was overcome with a complex mixture of defiance and fear he hadn't felt since he was twenty. "Yes, I am," he snapped. "What of it?"

Polycarp bristled. "Keep a civil tongue in your head; that's the Halliday Chair of Mathematics you're speaking to."

Standish said, "You tell young St Cloud that he's likely to end by being stripped of his position and his rank. It's a pity, as bright as he is, but he's only himself to blame, making a mockery of the University and her institutions. He can still withdraw, save us all a lot of grief. You tell him."

Leonard Rugg set his untouched punch down gently on the table and said, "I will, Doctor Standish. But he won't withdraw." He stood up. "You're quite right to be nervous of St Cloud. This debate will show the whole lot of you how true scholarship works against a moribund tradition that should have been put down along with the dead kings! What price the Halliday Chair then?"

He bowed and beat a strategic retreat.

⌐

L EONARD RUGG WAS NOT THE ONLY MAN TO JOIN BAT-
tle IN St Cloud's cause. Students quarreled with their magis-
ters and with each other. Catchwords began to appear: a sure sign of trouble. "Wizard's boy" was a taunt that could bring erstwhile

friends to blows. Some of the noble students, or their families, took umbrage at the subject of the debate and stopped coming to classes altogether. Peter Godwin might have been one of them, had his grandfather, Michael, Lord Godwin, not required his parents to let the boy follow his own loyalties without interference. This inspired Peter to examine his loyalty to St Cloud and his cause very carefully indeed.

"It's not St Cloud, really," he told his grandfather, with an air of astonished discovery.

The old man was amused. "It's not?"

"It's true he's a great teacher, and he never laughs at you the way some of them do and he makes you feel brighter than you thought you were. But that's not worth fighting for."

"Are you planning to fight?" Lord Godwin inquired gently. "If so, perhaps we should add swordsmanship to your course of study."

"Don't tease me, Grandfather. I'm serious. What St Cloud is going to debate has to do with our right to speak the truth, no matter who objects. And that's worth fighting for."

"Oh, dear," said Michael Godwin. "You'd better see your knife is sharp, then."

"It's not that kind of fighting," his grandson said.

～

PERHAPS IT WASN'T KNIFE FIGHTING, BUT IT WAS close enough. Coming out of LeClerc one day, St Cloud and his followers were set upon by a dozen Crabbites, none of them quite sober.

"Traitor!" they shouted. "Wizard's bumboys! Superstitious pigs!" And they let loose a volley of rotten apples and snowballs. One of the latter, packed around a stone, hit Benedict Vandeleur on the arm. He let out a roar and swung his fist at the foremost Crabbite, a bulky man with a wild shock of curls, who roared back like the bull he resembled and set himself to wrestle Vandeleur to the ground. Justis Blake swore, pushed Doctor St Cloud into the safety of the arched doorway, and launched himself into the melee.

It would have been more fun for everyone concerned if the street had not been freezing cold, with yesterday's snowfall churned to a frozen mush with mud and filth. Blake's knuckles stung and ached with each blow he landed. Beside him, Peter Godwin was sobbing with pain or anger, tears runnelling his muddy face as he flailed at his sneering opponent. Blake tripped the sneering man, who fell heavily back into the man Blake had been fighting, who reflexively punched him before he realized that they were on the same side. Blake laughed, seized them both by the scruffs of their gowns, and banged their heads together with a great crack. He was beginning to warm up nicely.

Suddenly, a Crabbite at the edge of the fight shook off his opponent and took to his heels, shouting, "The Watch! The Watch!" Two of his fellows followed him, dragging a downed friend between them. Blake heard the telltale whistle, close and drawing closer. He froze, as did his opponent, stared wildly around, and dropped into the mud, felled by a farewell blow to his jaw.

By the time the Watch sauntered onto the scene, the street was empty. Trampled mud, three mangled caps, a muffler, and a torn sleeve bore silent witness to the recent combat, but combatants there were none. The Watch shrugged, pocketed their whistles, and went back to their warm guard-house. It was nothing to them if the idiots all killed each other, as long as they cleared away the bodies after.

Inside LeClerc, Doctor St Cloud was rather helplessly stanching Peter Godwin's bleeding nose with his own handkerchief, while Fremont and Vandeleur revived Blake with a handful of snow. One man had lost his sleeve; a bruise spread like an inkstain across another's cheek. Lindley was nursing a sore jaw and scraped knuckles. They were all filthy, shivering with cold and reaction, and chattering sixteen to the dozen.

"Did you see the buggers run?" inquired Vandeleur happily.

"We showed them who were the better men." Godwin's voice was rather muffled by the handkerchief.

"They called us traitors!" Fremont was indignant. "Reactionary pigs!"

A chorus of agreement: "They're nothing but sheep! Parrots! Geese!"

"Silence!" St Cloud, who had been listening to all this with mounting impatience, lost his temper. "You are carrying on like small boys at a fair," he said into the astonished lull. "We are civilized men, are we not? We settle our differences with words, not blows; reasoned arguments, not curses. Are you dockmen, or are you scholars of ancient history?"

Glances were exchanged, sullen or shamefaced or amused. *Poor Doctor St Cloud,* Blake thought muzzily. *Who's going to tell him?*

Oddly enough, it was Lindley. His flaming hair was quenched with mud, and his narrow jaw sported a painful-looking lump, but he spoke clearly and proudly. "We are scholars of ancient history. We are scholars of truth. There are those who must silence truth at all costs. When they come at us with blows and curses, what may we do but answer them in kind?"

"Well said, Lindley!" exclaimed Vandeleur, astonished, and there was a murmur of approval from the other students. Lindley blushed scarlet and sucked blood from his knuckles.

St Cloud shook his head. "I am ashamed to be the cause of this," he said. But even as he said it, he knew that he was lying. There was something in him that gloried in the sight of these young men, battered and bleeding in his cause—something that accepted their service as its due, that counted each drop of blood shed as an offering. "But you have fought nobly, and I am proud of you for that, at least."

They all looked pleased with themselves. St Cloud considered telling them not to fight again unless attacked, decided that would be spitting into the wind, and recommended that they clean themselves up before going to the Nest, "to save Max the trouble of kicking you all out as vagabonds." This mild jest raised a laugh, so he went on, "I'll go ahead and bespeak a pie for you." And then he left them.

THE BLACKBIRD'S NEST WAS NOT IMMUNE TO THE GEN-
eral late-winter infection of change and upset. It was no
longer the cheerful haunt of humanities scholars out for a drink
and a good argument, but a kind of radicals' headquarters, full of
St Cloudites of all academic persuasions. Whatever they thought
of St Cloud personally, they all agreed that Truth was to be found
in the examination of empirical data rather than in the writings
of previous generations. There were contingents of astronomists,
physicians, and natural scientists of all kinds. And there were
Northerners.

There'd always been some Northerners at the Blackbird's
Nest: they were an insular lot, but not too insular to drink with
their fellow students from time to time. Now there were more of
them, making faces over Max's excellent beer when he ran out of
cider, and repelling friendly advances with stony silence. But not
Anthony Lindley's.

To everyone's astonishment, Lindley often forsook Historians'
Corner for the Northerners' table, and even took to wearing his
hair in the multiple braids they affected. Whatever unpleasantness there may have been between them over Finn, Greenleaf,
and Smith, had obviously been forgotten. He and the Northerners
were, as Fremont put it, thick as gruel.

"I wonder what he sees in them?" Peter Godwin wondered
one frozen afternoon. "It's not as if they have anything in common with him—they're all natural scientists and lawyers and
physicians."

"And they're all dreamers at heart," Blake explained. "They
share a vision of the ancient North as an enchanted land, and
they'd love to wake up one morning and discover that enchantment returned."

Vandeleur added, "There's hating Finn's guts. They've got
that in common, too."

"The incendiary Master Finn," said Godwin. "I do wonder
what has become of him. He can't still be in the Chop, surely."

Vandeleur shrugged. "They could have forgotten about him
or mislaid him, I suppose; but it's more likely that he took off
downriver as soon as they let him go. He did betray his friends,
after all, and, as far as I know, Greenleaf and Smith are still in

prison. The Northerners don't impress me as being as understanding and tolerant as our kindhearted Blake here."

Blake fetched Vandeleur a gentle clip on the head, designed
to demonstrate just how tolerant and understanding he really
was. Vandeleur shoved him back, and there might have been a
friendly scuffle had not Anthony Lindley joined them, tankard in
hand.

He endured his friends' jocular comments on his hair and his
choice of companions with a reasonably good grace. "My grandmother," he explained, "was from the North—well, her father
was. It makes a difference." But that was all, so soon the talk
turned to the ever-absorbing topic of their researches. They'd
been spending hours in the Archives every day, going through
boxes and document cases, unrolling scrolls, deciphering unfa-
miliar handwriting, breathing ancient dust. So far, they'd found
very little of obvious value, but Doctor St Cloud was pleased with
them, and they were not discouraged. Lindley was just describing
a book on Northern customs he'd found, illustrated with wood-
cuts, when a street urchin of indeterminate sex inquired shrilly
for scholar Anthony Lindley.

Henry Fremont, who'd been remarkably subdued recently,
beckoned the child closer. "You Lindley?" the child inquired.
"Scholar says Lindley'll give me a copper."

"Why," asked Fremont mildly, "should Lindley give you a
copper?"

The urchin held up a twist of paper, very dirty and mangled
at the ends. Fremont held out his hand for it. "Not without you
be Lindley, and not without you give me a copper," said the
urchin. "Scholar promised."

From the other end of the table, Lindley said, "I'm the man
you're looking for. Bring it here."

The child squeezed between the benches. "Where's my
copper?"

Lindley put the coin into the urchin's hand, accepted the paper, untwisted it, and began to read. "Be damned if I do," he said
aloud. "Where's that child?"

But the urchin had disappeared. "What is it?" asked Blake.

"Finn," Lindley answered shortly. "He wants me to meet him

in the oak grove outside the North Gate at dawn tomorrow. I don't know which is worse: if he thinks I don't know he betrayed Greenleaf and Smith, or if he imagines that I'll forgive him for it."

"Will you go?" Godwin asked.

"I've no desire to set eyes on him again. And you may spare me the lecture on tolerance, Blake, because you don't really know what's at stake here."

Blake shrugged. Lindley's self-identification with the Northern cause, whatever it was, was beginning to get up his nose.

"Don't be such a little prig, Lindley," said Vandeleur, disgusted. "It's hardly fair to condemn a man unheard."

"I agree with Vandeleur," said Henry Fremont unexpectedly. "People can do very stupid things for what seem, at the time, to be very sound reasons. Look at the Union, for instance. It was hardly a good thing for the North, in the long run."

"Don't try to change the subject," Lindley said. "I don't care what Finn's reasons were. What he did was unforgivable. He is less than a beast, for a beast has no choice in what it does, but acts from instinct only."

Vandeleur made one last try. "If the choice is between torture and betrayal, I think most of us here—yes, and most of your Northern friends, too—would choose to keep their limbs intact, even at the expense of their honor."

"I wouldn't have told them anything, no matter what they did to me."

Blake lost his temper. "But they didn't do anything to you, did they?" he inquired savagely. "When they heard your Southern accent and your Southern name, they put you in a cell to think over your poor taste in lovers, patted you on the head, and let you go. You loved this man, Tony, or at least you led us to believe you did. The *honorable* thing for you to do is hear what he has to say."

Everyone stared at Blake, who glared back. What was it about scholarship and learning, he wondered, that seemed to wither the hearts of University men, leaving them incapable of loving anything as imperfect and fallible as an actual human being? Now they were going to laugh at him for getting so heated about the feelings of a man none of them particularly liked, and he was going to have to thump them.

But Godwin turned to Lindley and said, "Blake's right."

"Couldn't have said it better myself," Vandeleur agreed.

"In fact," Fremont pointed out, "Finn's behaving very honorably. He could have just slunk off down the river without telling anyone."

"Oh, very well," Lindley said. "I'll go. But I won't go alone."

Blake stood up. "If what you're trying to say is that you're going to turn Alaric Finn over to your Northern friends, I swear I'll tie you up and keep watch over you all night. Revenge and kings and such are very romantic, but we live *now*, in the modern age, when men settle their differences in a civilized manner."

"You're a damn do-gooding busybody," said Lindley hotly. "A sanctimonious, preaching, clod-hopping—"

"Watch it, Lindley," Godwin said, alarmed at the look on Blake's face.

"—mama's boy," Lindley finished.

It was enough. "You're lucky I'm a damn do-gooding mama's boy," Blake said, as steadily as his pounding heart would let him, "or I might forget that you're smaller than I am, and still weak from prison fever, and feed you your teeth, one by one." He turned on his heel and, with considerable dignity, left the Blackbird's Nest.

"You're an ass, Lindley," said Vandeleur, and followed him.

Lindley looked after them with a strange expression, half-frightened, half-triumphant. "So the ox has a temper after all."

Fremont cast his eyes to the smoky ceiling. "You'd try the patience of a stone, Lindley. You're right, though. Blake is a do-gooding busybody, and I'm grateful for someone other than me pointing it out. I tell you what. You don't snap my head off, and I come with you to meet Finn tomorrow, just in case he gets melodramatic and tries to persuade you to fly with him or some such nonsense. That's what you're afraid of, isn't it?"

"I'm not afraid," Lindley began, then: "Yes. I guess so."

"I'll come too," said Godwin, all agog with the romance of it all. "I'd like to hear what Finn has to say for himself. However"—with a level look that would have made his grandfather proud—"you have to swear you won't tell your Northern friends about this."

Lindley looked from one stern face to the other and nodded.

"Swear," said Fremont, not to be outdone by a noble's whelp.

"By oak and holly, by blood and bone, I swear I'll tell no living man of our meeting. Will that do?"

It would, and the three friends drank to it and parted.

IT WAS STILL DARK WHEN THEY MET AT THE NORTH GATE next morning, and as cold as the Ice Maiden's breath. Godwin and Fremont were heavy-eyed and sullen, Lindley haggard and grim-faced.

Once, the oak grove had been visible from the North Gate, and the path had lain through wide meadows grazed by cattle and ponds noisy with water fowl. But the city, like a fountain with the wind behind it, had spattered inns and smithies for the convenience of travelers among the farmsteads, which were followed in time by city-folk hungry for a bit of green. Now the grove was at the city's edge: in another generation, it would be within city bounds, if not swallowed altogether.

Snow had fallen in the night, although it was hard to tell until the little band came past the outermost houses and saw it spread like a featherbed between them and the grove. Remembering MidWinter, Fremont shivered and opened his mouth to suggest a retreat to the nearest inn and let Finn and his confession go hang. But Lindley stepped out into the feathery snow with Godwin beside him. What could Fremont do, but step out after them, or admit that he was afraid of a stand of trees?

A half-hour's hard slogging brought them to the eaves of the grove, where the going grew rougher still. Snow hid stones and logs and uneven ground; to brush against a branch was to bring a numbing avalanche upon their heads. Soon all three were soaked to the skin and chilled to the bone.

Through chattering teeth, Godwin said, "Let's go back. He's not here."

"He is," said Lindley.

"He is not," snapped Godwin. "We were fools to come so far. No man has come here this morning—ours are the only tracks in."

Henry cursed and turned to retrace his steps, but Lindley said, "He's here. I know it. Come and see. It's only a little further," and pressed on without a backward glance.

Undecided, Fremont and Godwin hung fire, then turned again to follow the beacon of Lindley's hair through the black maze of branches. He was right—it was only a little further. Another two or three minutes brought them to the edge of the glade, where they saw Alaric Finn.

Henry knew at once that he was dead. Live men do not have blue lips and bluish-white skin like fine marble, nor do they lie unshivering, naked, and half-covered with snow. It was a little longer before he took in the wide scarlet stains that haloed Finn's outstretched hands.

A retching noise told him that one of his companions was reacting badly. Godwin, it must be, since Lindley was kneeling by the body.

"Is he alive?" Fremont croaked hopefully as Lindley laid his hand upon the snow-covered chest.

"No." The single syllable hung in the air like a bird. "He has poured his blood upon the land, and the land has drunk of it."

"Ah," said Fremont, and turned away from the macabre tableau to help Godwin, who was almost as pale as poor Finn, but trying very hard to act the man.

"We should tell someone, shouldn't we?" he said, his hazel eyes round with the effort of not looking at the glade, his voice pinched. "There's an inn, not a hundred paces west, right on the Northern Road. The coaches stop there; they'll know what to do."

Fremont risked a glance over his shoulder. Lindley's fiery head was bowed to his lover's chest. "You go," he told Godwin, his lips stiff. "I don't want to leave him alone."

Godwin nodded and fled. Fremont squared his shoulders, stalked into the glade, touched Lindley's back. The fabric of his gown was stiff with frost. "Godwin's gone for help," he said. "There's a log over there we can sit on while we wait. I've got some lucifers. We might try to make a fire."

Lindley didn't even look up. He took Finn's hand, gloved with blood, and tried to raise it, but the arm was locked with death or cold. He bent his head to the hand and kissed it.

Henry swallowed. "We should leave him as he is, don't you think? In case there should be an inquiry?"

"There will be no inquiry," said Lindley. "It was a lawful sacrifice. See? Here is the knife." He opened his hand to display a penknife—Finn's penknife—unpleasantly stained from blade to haft. Lindley's palm was smeared scarlet where he'd clutched it.

"Where did you find that?" Fremont demanded.

"Just here." Lindley dropped the knife by Finn's right leg, then wiped his hand across his own cheek, leaving an untidy smear. He bent once more, to press his lips against the slack, blue mouth, and then he rose and followed Fremont to the log and watched quietly while he fussed with damp tinder and leaves and his lucifers until a distant crashing heralded Godwin's return with the ostler and two barmen from the Nag's Head and a plank to tie the body on. Then it was all large men trampling the snow and exclaiming and asking questions that Henry was shivering too hard to answer, and a parlor in the Nag's Head with hot wine punch and their coats and gowns steaming in front of the fire.

The host of the Nag's Head was not best pleased to be saddled with a corpse, naked as a frog and a suicide to boot, as likely a haunt as the host could imagine. If it had just been Lindley and Fremont who brought it to his attention, he'd have left them to drag the body away as best they could. But young Godwin was a noble's son. So the host set up a trestle for the corpse in the woodshed and sacrificed a horse-blanket to cover its nakedness and provided young Lord Peter and his friends with a parlor, a fire, bread and meat, and blankets to wrap themselves in while their clothes dried. He gave them an hour to recover themselves, and then he tapped at the parlor door to inquire what they intended to do with the poor young man's body.

This was just what had been puzzling Henry Fremont while he toasted and rubbed some feeling back into his numbed hands and feet. He'd asked Godwin and Lindley, of course, but they were of no help. Godwin wanted to leave it all in the hands of the host, along with a gold piece for Finn's burial. Fremont thought the host likely to keep the gold for himself and tip Finn behind a rock in the grove for the foxes and rats to gnaw.

This conjecture drove the blood from Godwin's cheeks and tears to his eyes, and he refused to take further part in the conversation. Lindley, on the other hand, thought the grove a very good resting-place for Finn's body, and the foxes and rats his natural mourners. "Flowers will grow where he lies, fair as he was fair, and his flesh will hallow the grove."

"That's very poetic, Lindley," Fremont said. "But he's not going to hallow the grove, so you can just shut up. Be sensible for a moment. Did he have family? Friends? Anyone who might claim his body for burial?"

"A Companion of the King has no family, save his brothers to whom he is sworn," said Lindley.

"What in the Seven Hells is a Companion of the . . ." Henry interrupted himself hastily. "No, don't tell me. I don't want to know. Can you get word to them, tell them he's dead and wants burying?"

"He is forsworn," said Lindley. "He is without honor, without brothers." His dense blue eyes were flat as buttons. "Without life."

So it was all up to Fremont, who'd never organized anything more practical than a formal argument in his life, to answer the host's questions and decide what must be done. The host, with one eye on Peter Godwin, was moderately helpful. He provided a chaise to convey the young gentlemen to their homes in the city, and agreed to keep their poor friend in the woodshed until they might make provision for his burial.

"No longer than a day or two, mind, and don't go thinking to leave him here forever while you go about your business fancy-free. I don't doubt Lord Godwin won't like to hear how you left a man to rot in my woodshed without a backward glance."

Henry thought of several clever things to say calculated to let the host of the Nag's Head know just what kind of a blackmailing, boot-licking, ignorant blubber-head he was. But tweaking the host's nose, though excellent sport in itself, would not get

Godwin and Lindley home nor Finn buried. So Henry said they were all very much obliged and poked Godwin, who gave the host the contents of his purse and his solemn word as a Godwin that Finn would be out of the woodshed as soon as may be.

⁓

THAT NIGHT, ALONE IN HIS BED WITH A BOTTLE OF wine, Henry Fremont thought over the events of a long and unpleasant day.

Lindley had remained steadfast in his refusal to tell the Companions of Finn's death. "You made me swear by oak and holly that I'd tell no man of our meeting. That oath binds me still."

Fremont and Godwin had plied him with every argument they could lay tongue to, but nothing could move him. Disgusted, they'd left him in the middle of the street and gone to consult with Blake and Vandeleur, pulling them out of the Nest to the neutral territory of the Bramble Bush. There they sat down with tankards of watered ale and talked over what was to be done.

There were two issues to be considered. The first, and most pressing, was how to get Finn's body out of the Nag's Head woodshed and decently interred. The second was to decide whether or not to tell Doctor St Cloud about what had happened.

"Not," Vandeleur said. "He doesn't even know Finn was in prison. It would be too much, what with the debate and all."

"I don't think we should tell him any of it, ever," said Godwin. "It would upset him horribly."

"Perhaps," Blake said. "I think he'd rather know the truth, however upsetting. But I agree he doesn't need to know it now."

So that was one decision made. The question of Finn's body was harder. Long into the afternoon, they considered ways and means with as much care as the Governors brought to a Fellowship appointment. Finally, Vandeleur said, "Look. All we know about his family is the name, and that they live in Finnhaven, which is about as far North as you can get. We've determined that a message couldn't possibly reach them before the host at the Nag's Head loses patience. We agree that we could just scrape enough together to get him buried ourselves, but that still leaves the question of his family. I really don't know what's best to do."

"He might have kin among the Northerners," Blake pointed out, not for the first time.

"Are you going to ask them?" Godwin inquired sarcastically. "We've already decided they'd rather cut off their braids than talk to us."

Throughout the conversation, Henry had been struggling with complicated emotions. If Alaric Finn had been a traitor, he himself was another. He did not have to be a metaphysician to realize that the argument that he had sent Lord Nicholas little but his lecture notes and a few pieces of common gossip anyone might have heard in any tavern in University was pure sophistry. He had given Lord Nicholas Finn's name, and Lindley's, and now Finn was dead.

"I'll ask them," he'd heard himself saying. "If you three are frightened of a bunch of mop-head Northerners, I'm not."

He blushed now to think how astonished his friends had been at his offer. But they'd accepted it quickly enough, and now he had to do it or face the fact that he was not only a dupe and a traitor, but a coward to boot.

Having gotten so far, Henry Fremont corked up the wine, got out of bed, and composed a short and careful note:

Alaric Finn, Historian of the School of Humane Sciences, has died in the oak grove, by his own hand, of remorse. His body lies in the woodshed of the Nag's Head Inn, west of the oak grove. Whatsoever his life, his death was all honor.

He signed it, *A Friend,* folded it, put on his gown, and went out to find a boy to deliver it to the King's Companions at the Green Man.

chapter V

KATHERINE, DUCHESS TREMONTAINE, DID NOT avoid formality and ritual when they served a purpose. To receive her cousin and heir, she wore a gown of green and gold, the colors of her house, woven with its emblem, the swan on the waves. She had invited two other people—his mother, Lady Sophia, and her steward, Marcus Ffoliot—to attend the meeting, but she had not told them everything, and so she was the only one formally dressed. Marcus recognized the trappings of authority; Sophia merely complimented her on her lovely robes.

Theron stood before the duchess's desk until she invited him to sit down. Then he sat on the edge of his chair. No use pretending this wasn't going to be awful. He only hoped she would give him a chance to explain whatever crimes against the state he was supposed to have committed this time.

Her dress was formal, but her speech was not. She came straight to the point: "Theron," the duchess said, "people are watching you."

"I know." He tried not to sound childish. "I wish that they would not. But I suppose it's unavoidable. Even my cousin Talbert was warning me—"

"This does not concern Talbert and his gossips. I mean the Serpent and his people."

"What!" Theron half-started out of his chair. "But I've done nothing! The Last Night chase was a student prank; they must have figured that out by now. What right do they have—why on earth would they—" But the part of him that knew the City, knew the reason. Basil, the dead kings, the debate . . . They must know about him and Basil; half the University did. Did the duchess?

Katherine said, "I know you too well to suspect you of any kind of scheming. But they do not. Everything you do takes on double meaning, Theron, and I don't know where it will end. I think it is too much to ask you to suddenly overturn all your habits. You'll have to settle down someday, but I can't expect you to change overnight. And so I think it best that you leave the City for a while."

Oh, God, he thought, half-wanting to laugh, not Highcombe! Not with Basil's father there! He had no desire to go the country at all, but to be banished to Highcombe would be too much.

"I've pulled some strings," she went on, "and gotten you an appointment to an embassage." She smiled at Sophia. "To the Kyrillian Archipelago. I thought you might like to see where the other half of your family tree springs from."

For a moment, he was seeing them all through a veil of gray ash. Sophia was out of her chair, her hand on his pulse. But he looked past her at Katherine.

"I cannot," he said. "I cannot leave at present. I am going to be married."

Katherine leaned back, the wind knocked out of her sails. "Re-eally? To whom?"

"To Lady Genevieve Randall."

"Randall?" Sophia asked, bewildered. "The music people?"

"How nice. But, judging from her face, you don't appear to have told your mother about this."

"I was—I was going to. Today."

"Well, that's good, considering that you are underage. You will need the consent of your guardians."

"I think that she is very suitable," he bulled on. "The Randalls are an old family; they were created right after the Union. It's Lady Genevieve's first Season."

"Not bad," said Marcus. "Tell us about it."

"I've been paying her court these last weeks," Theron explained, "and I have reason to believe neither she nor her family would object to a formal offer. If you give your consent, I can propose very soon. She's young, so I think they'll want to wait on the wedding until the fall." And by fall, he hoped to see Basil established in the Horn Chair, the challenge and debate behind him, once more ready for love. "I do want to see Kyros, of course—it was terribly kind of you to think of it—maybe we could go there for our bridal trip. But in the meantime, do you think it might please the Council if I were married instead of exiled?"

Katherine said, "Are you offering me a bargain?"

"No, cousin." He was beginning to enjoy himself. "I intend to marry Lady Genevieve whatever happens. I grow tired of waiting to settle down, as if it were some sort of terrible weight that will eventually descend on me. I'd rather choose the time myself, and get it over with all at once."

There was a heavy silence, and then his mother said plaintively, "Theron, you don't know what you are saying."

He ignored her, holding Katherine's eyes, willing her to agree. He wished he knew what she was thinking. She'd recovered from her surprise and was looking particularly ducal. "Let me think about it," she said. "It could do very well, and I'll wish you every happiness. Marcus, will you look into the Randall family?"

———

THE CARRIAGE RIDE BACK TO RIVERSIDE WAS A QUIET but not a comfortable one. Sophia was thinking, Theron could tell that. He watched the high, blind walls of the Hill give way to the lighted windows and shuttered shop-fronts and chocolate houses of the Middle City, and prepared to take his medicine like a man.

He wasn't surprised when his mother waved away the chairs waiting by the Bridge to carry them home and strode out through Riverside's maze of streets with the linkboys trotting behind. If he was the Prince of Riverside, she was the Queen, at home here as she'd never be on the Hill, or even the University that she had bullied into accepting her. Voices called out to her as they walked: goodnights and greetings that she punctiliously returned. Once she stopped to reassure herself that a beggar's sores were nothing more than mustard and gum before giving him a copper and directing him to the dormitory she maintained behind the infirmary. "It's free," she told him. "They'll give you a blanket and soup, so go ahead and spend the coin any way you like. Just don't sleep in the street tonight. And if you want to beg in Riverside, you'd better see Battered Bob in the morning for permission."

The walk from the Bridge calmed them both to a degree, and it was more in sorrow than in anger that Sophia turned to her son and said, "What I do not understand is why you have not told me of all this earlier."

They had just entered Sophia's sitting-room, a comfortable apartment in the narrowest of the connected houses that made up Riverside House. It was dominated by a life-sized portrait of the late duke as a young man and a smaller one of Sophia, richly dressed and obviously pregnant.

Theron bit his lip. He'd deceived her, if only by omission; his sole recourse was complete honesty. "I was afraid you'd try to talk me out of it," he said.

"You were correct." Sophia sank into her favorite shabby chair and gazed up at him with dark, steady eyes. "I will still try to talk you out of it. If I succeed, I shall myself explain to Katherine that you have thought better of your plan."

Theron dragged a puffy leather ottoman to her feet and settled himself on it. "It's a very good plan," he said earnestly. "I have thought it over carefully. I must marry sometime; we are all agreed on that."

"Of course. But I had always hoped you would marry for love."

He took her hand. "My perfect mama. But I cannot be like you in every way."

She snatched her hand back. "This is not a jest," she said hotly.

"I'm sorry. Your love for my father is legendary. But I must make my own legend some other way."

Sophia was not mollified. "And the girl? Are her feelings to be considered?"

He shrugged. "Oh, I assume her feelings are that she will like being Duchess Tremontaine some day, and having beautiful houses to live in and parties to give. That is what the world knows being my wife entails."

"You sound as though you despise her already," Sophia said grimly.

He looked at her in surprise. "I don't despise her. I quite like her. She is pretty and has a nice laugh."

"Oh, dear."

Theron got up to pace, reeling off his points as though he were in a classroom debate. "After all, what is a noble marriage? I grant you the obvious: we must find each other attractive. Which we do." He blushed faintly. "But how much of our time will be spent alone in each other's company? Awake? Precious little. Most of our days will be full of our individual work and occupations. I'll have my seat in Council, which I do intend to take up, eventually. There will be meetings, dinners—which she will arrange. Highcombe, and the other estates. And, of course, my studies; I won't let everything go. She will have her own amusements; doubtless her tastes are already formed, and I won't interfere: cards, gowns, music, sewing, friends, whatever she likes.

"What I really need her for is to take care of *people*. I'm tired of having to know everyone, of endless parties and connections. It wears me out just thinking about it! Genevieve knows them all already, knows their consequence and their place. She has a quick understanding of how things work, and I need that." His voice was getting shrill, his movements agitated. "I cannot keep it all in my head—I've more important things to think about—"

"Theron," his mother interrupted. "You need not be duke, if the thought of it is such a burden to you."

He stopped in mid-stride. "But you have always intended me to be. You and Cousin Katherine; it's quite obvious. You chose to stay in the city to raise me to it. You promised my father. And now that I've figured out a way to make it work, you balk and want to talk about love." He lifted his head haughtily. "I do think, madam, that it—"

She said, "Ah, I see I have come down in the world."

"What?" he demanded.

"First I was 'mama,' then 'Sophia,' but now I have descended all the way to 'madam.' "

"I'm sorry." Abruptly he curled up in a miserable heap at her side. "I am just trying to explain. No one seems to understand."

"Well, I will try. Why don't you tell me about it?"

He tried, he really tried, to explain just how difficult it was, trying to live up to everyone's expectations. "Cousin Katherine wants a politician," he said at last. "My noble peers want a sportsman, you want a loving, faithful husband. You all want me to be like you. I can see the good in all these things, so I'm doing my best, but it's hard."

Sophia took his face in her hands and searched it with dark serious eyes. "And you, my son. What is it you would like to be?"

He looked away. "Left alone. That's why I want to marry Genevieve. She will give me time, room to discover who I am when I'm not trying to please my family."

Hurt, she released him. "So you marry her to please me?"

"I marry her to do my duty by my family. That should please you anyway," he said petulantly. "You're always talking about duty and responsibility."

"Am I?" Sophia smiled sadly. "And from this you have learned to marry a young woman you do not love so that she may shield you from the demands of your position? I have not taught well, my son, or you have not listened."

"That's not fair, Mama," he said, sounding very like the child who had been told he might not hit the twins back because they were girls. "You *like* teaching surgery and bringing women into University and taking care of beggars."

"That is not the point. It is there to be done, and I have the knowledge and the money to do it. That is the point."

"Oh, Mama." There was a world of affection as well as impatience in Theron's exclamation. He made as if to rise, but Sophia restrained him.

"You say you want this girl to take care of the demands of society on you. But are you quite certain she is able to? She is just out of the schoolroom, almost a child, far younger than you. How do you think she will be able to do what you yourself cannot?"

"Because she has been bred to it, as I have not," he snapped; then, appalled, he put his hand over his mouth and shook his head. "I don't mean to find fault, Mama. Forgive me. But . . . you don't know these people as I do. It's what they learn, these girls: how to run a household, how to get on in society. It's all they teach them, really; it's what their 'schoolroom' lessons consist of. Her mother's a knowing one; if Genevieve has any problems, she can just ask her. It will be fine."

"One more question, my dear. What about the man you stay with at University—the young doctor?"

"Basil," Theron murmured. "Basil St Cloud. I will continue to go to him. I love him."

Sophia made a helpless gesture. "Then why do you marry this Randall? Surely you may live with whomever you please and adopt an heir as Katherine has done."

"Cousin Katherine is a law to herself," he said. "That's not what I want. I want to be like everyone else—to have a proper house, a proper wife. Basil doesn't signify: half the married nobility on the Hill have lovers. Look at Lord Condell and David Tyrone! Their wives don't care—they have lovers of their own; Condell's wife has been with Flavia Montague since they were girls. It's a time-honored custom. Everyone does it. My father did it."

"Your father," said Sophia gently, "was also a law to himself. And when he had lovers, he had no wife. After he married, he was absolutely faithful—not because he was too old and ill to stray, but because he did not wish to."

"Mama—"

"Hush. You have been honest with me; I can be no less. You are my son. I love you even when I do not understand you. It is right and natural that you have opinions that differ from mine.

But I would be a poor mother indeed if I did not tell you that this marriage to Genevieve Randall is a terrible mistake. You know nothing of what marriage is, or can be. I am afraid that you will be very unhappy—both of you. I hope that you will change your mind."

She spoke gently and sadly, and when she had finished, she rose from the chair in which she had sat at her husband's bedside, kissed her son on the brow, and went to bed.

chapter VI

BASIL ST CLOUD GREW USED TO THE CONSTANT
company of his inner circle of students—"your body-
guard," as Rugg called them, only half joking. Basil's
students closed ranks around him whenever he appeared in public. Paradoxically, the more they were with him, the less they demanded of him. It was as if, having become a Cause, Basil was
relieved of the petty need to actually say anything or engage with
anyone. When he or they were not in the Archives, Basil grew
used to sitting in the Blackbird's Nest, half-listening to his students' joking and arguing with one another. Their voices turned
to a comfortable music while he thought about whatever was pre-
occupying him at the moment: where Theron was, or what
Crabbe was reading right now; whether a connection could reasonably be drawn between the Wizard Guidry as described in
Hollis, and the "Guidry" mentioned in a pre-Union heroic
stanza; a nasty remark Crabbe had made at a historians' dinner
five years back. Most dangerously, he thought about the Book.

He was making progress. He'd applied everything he knew of
scholarship to the Book of the King's Wizard: the rules of rheto-

ric, logic, analysis. His students had found things, too, that helped more than they knew. Sometimes, deep in the night, he imagined himself on the brink of discovery, of comprehension, of mastery. And imagining this, it was a short step to imagining himself standing before Roger Crabbe, casting a spell from the Book, casting it successfully, and Crabbe's face turning purple when Basil succeeded. Delicious as that image was, he shouldn't even think of it. He knew better than to try any of the spells. He had not the training for such things. Best stick to what he was already master of, and that was scholarship.

Anthony Lindley's voice cut through his musings. "Of course it's important, Godwin, you idiot. Everything's important, when there's so little to go on." Basil focused on the boy and smiled. He was more Northern than the Northerners these days, tricked out in braids and an oak leaf, spouting obscure Northern folklore as to the manner born. He'd always been a dedicated student, but his research was showing flashes of true brilliance. It was a pity he'd been so ill at the beginning of the term. He still looked unwell—too thin and excitable. Basil knew there'd been something between Lindley and the dour-faced Northerner who'd once been amongst his most fervent students.

"What ever happened to Finn?" Basil asked the table at large.

Frozen in mid-conversation, four startled faces looked up at him.

"Finn?" Peter Godwin repeated stupidly.

"Yes," said Basil. "Alaric Finn, our resident expert on Northern customs and traditions. Last I saw of him was right before MidWinter break. He hasn't changed disciplines, has he?"

"No." Lindley wore a curious look on his face. "That he did not change."

"Not that I'd blame him," Basil hastened to say. "Ancient history's no path to a decent living—you all know that, don't you?" Dumbly, they nodded. Afraid he'd offended them or seemed to be complaining about his income (which they paid, after all), he added quickly, "And I really thought Finn had the feel for it. Perhaps he had trouble with his fees. There's many a promising man has been forced to abandon his studies for lack of funds." Basil looked at their uncomfortable faces, then down at the beer-ringed tabletop. "You know I'd never refuse knowledge to anyone just for the want of a few coins. You'll come to me if you have problems, won't you?"

"He went home!" blurted Henry Fremont. Even patient Justis Blake looked at him oddly. "Finn, I mean. His family, or something."

"Ah." Basil nodded. "I'd like to go North myself, someday. It's strange to have read so much and never seen the forests of Redding or Guidry's Well. Which I suppose," he said, rising, "is my cue to go back to work, so I can earn my way there."

His students were never so glad to see him go.

But at the door to Minchin Street, Basil met Theron come to look for him—and all thoughts of any glory but the present were put aside. They lost themselves in a trance of sensation and release that lasted all the afternoon. When Basil knew where he was again, the room was dark, his throat was raw with shouting, and his body heavy and stiff with drying sweat.

"I hate to say this," said Theron from beneath him, "but I'm thirsty."

Basil groaned.

"Cold, too," Theron went on. "And I can't breathe."

Basil grunted and rolled away from his lover's body, groaning again as the chill air hit his sweat-matted chest. The mattress shifted as Theron got up; more cold air signaled that he'd taken the sheet with him. A moment later came the scrape and sizzle of a lucifer; candlelight banished the shadows to the corners and revealed Theron kneeling by the hearth, building a fire. He was wrapped in the sheet, his hair in his face. Basil's heart contracted painfully: that beauty, that passion, that power belonged to him, to him alone, to use and to enjoy. The time was coming to release it to the Land, to sow new life in the woods and fields.

He rose and put his hands on Theron's shoulders. "The time approaches," he said.

"Are you worrying about the debate?" Theron asked.

Basil stroked his lover's hair. "The debate?" He had to think for a moment. "Oh. No, I wasn't thinking about that." He tipped Theron's head back, ran his palm down his throat.

Theron shook him off briskly. "Not now, Basil. Look at you—

you're half-mad with hunger. What you need is food. And a drink." He scrambled to his feet and began to look for his clothes.

Basil wrapped himself in Theron's abandoned sheet. "Perhaps," he said doubtfully.

"And lights. And people to distract you. We'll even go to the Nest," he offered magnanimously, but Basil put his hands over his face.

"No! God, no! My students will be there."

"All right, all right." Theron pulled his lover's hands away. "Come with me to Riverside."

All Basil's dreams of power and passion dissipated before an utterly mundane and unscholarly anxiety. "I won't get killed?" he asked, only half teasing.

Theron smiled. "Not if you're with me, you won't. I'm the Prince of Riverside."

"In that case . . ." Basil laughed.

Theron was pulling on his breeches and his linen shirt. "I'll take you to a place I know." He thrust a bundle of clothes into Basil's hands. "Here, get dressed. No, not in your robe—leave it off, just wear your jacket. There's no scholars where we're going! This place is small and quiet, with very good whiskey. After, when you've cheered up, we can go round the corner to where there's dancing."

Alarmed, Basil said, "I don't dance."

"You don't have to," Theron said indulgently. "But it's fun to watch. Lights. Music. Very engaging."

"Lead on."

In nearly ten years in the city, Basil had never crossed the Bridge over to Riverside. Why should he? The district had nothing that he needed—except old trunks of books buried amidst the ruins of its tattered townhouses, and the trunks Foster Rag-and-Bone had brought to him. He felt immensely bold, walking arm in arm with his lover, their hats pulled low over their faces against discovery and the biting wind. They went along the University side of the river, then past the Council Hall, where lights still burned.

"You walk this way every day," Basil said, unexpectedly moved.

"Pretty much." Theron pulled Basil closer. "Here's the Bridge. It's old—maybe even pre-Union. They never widened it for carriages, just foot- and cart-traffic." They stopped for a moment, considering the stones. Then Theron raised their torch, and raised his other arm, inviting: "Shall we?"

And they crossed the water onto the island.

Basil felt Theron change, or thought he did. He was like a farmer who's just crossed onto his father's land—which, in a way, was it exactly. His step was sure, navigating them down streets and around potholes it was too dark for Basil to see. He gestured and pointed to places where things had happened to him involving people with strange nicknames, until Basil was dizzy with his history.

They ducked as they went down narrow stairs to a tavern in a cellar, dark and warm, that seemed to expand forever underground.

"Hey there, Liz!" Theron greeted the proprietor.

She lifted her hand to her bosom. "It's him! Back from the dead!" He raised his eyebrows, and she explained, "I heard love put a spike through your heart while you were getting your portrait painted."

"Old news," Theron said curtly, "and very stale. Almost as stale as that pie you serve. But I've brought my new friend, and told him you have good stuff here. Don't make a liar of me, eh?"

"You want the oak cask?"

"Of course I want the oak cask."

The whiskey that came from it was rich and fiery. Basil blinked tears from his eyes. His lover grinned. "Better? This is the real thing—Northern firewater, straight from the mountain streams."

"Is there anything," the magister asked quizzically, "you haven't tried?"

"Nothing that's any good"—Basil smelled the spirits on his breath as Theron leaned forward—"that I wouldn't share with you." In the tavern, there, they kissed, and Basil nearly swooned with the heat and the fumes and pride and embarrassment and disbelief that this was really happening to him.

"Tremontaine!" a voice near their ears whispered.

Theron's hand went to his knife. But when he saw who it was, he only said, "Louie, what is it? Can't you see I'm busy?"

A ferret-faced young man with one ear missing said, "Yeah, but—how busy is busy? I've got a new shipment in, see. You get first pick."

"Not interested."

"You'll pay twice as much—three times—on Lassiter's Row, I'm telling you."

"I know." Theron beamed. "But I've got a new friend," he squeezed Basil playfully, "and I'm spending all my allowance on him. He likes books, though, not emeralds; right, my sweet?"

Basil looked from the radiant prince to the shadowy dealer. "If you want to buy me a stolen emerald, I'm not stopping you."

"Hush," said Theron, over Louie's protest of, "Stolen? Who said stolen? What sort of trash you bringing in here, T?"

"Aw, Louie . . ." Theron fished out some coins from his waist-band. "Get us all another round, will you?" Then he murmured to Basil, "Bad form, my dear. They're as touchy as first-years defending their mothers. Certain words do not get used."

Louie came back with the drinks, and Basil had to listen to the young men reminiscing about a series of fights they'd once been in with kids from other streets. He wondered how Theron had found time for all these exploits while attending so many classes as a boy. It must have been before he'd moved on from street fighting to taking all those lovers, that was it. You found time for all sorts of other amusements when your life didn't depend on your studies . . . but, no, he wasn't going to think about Crabbe and the debate. Basil knocked back the last of his whiskey and concentrated on the conversation.

"You still see much of Nora?" Theron asked.

"Nora with three kids and a dockworker husband?" snorted Louie. "Not if I see her first. You should come round more often, T, you're missing what's new around here. I'll save you something special. You still like a hit of smoke now and then?"

"Ah, no." Theron grimaced helplessly at Basil. "I was only doing that because of . . ."

"Say no more. Well, I'll let you get back to your books!" And Louie passed on to another acquaintance who might, perhaps, like a deal.

"Well!" Theron said brightly. "That was entertaining."

Basil said, "At least now I understand something you said once. That first night we had together? You said you weren't really a dutiful son. I've always thought you were, though, despite it all. But now I see that it is my good influence—my very good influence—that has kept you from all sorts of mischief. When are you going to introduce me to your mother?"

"When you need a goiter excised, and not a moment before. Come on, let's move on."

"To the dancing? I'm not sure I'm ready for that. Buy me another whiskey."

"Sensible man." Theron kissed his brow and waved to the barmaid. "You are a very good influence."

THEY COULD HEAR THE MUSIC ALL THE WAY DOWN THE street, pouring out of a hall that was as bright as the other had been dark. Basil's feet were not quite steady, probably because Theron was hanging on his neck, breathing fumes and kisses into his mouth. Basil started to worry about whether anyone on the street would see him staggering and laughing with a beautiful student; then he remembered that they were in Riverside, not on the streets of University, and that what he did here was no one's business. The music was even louder when they opened the door, meeting the hot blast of people sweating, the reek of spilled beer, and a cacophony of fiddle and pipe and drum.

Theron held out his arms. "Dance with me!"

Basil knew all of the steps from village fairs: simple swings and stamps and twirls. But it seemed so ridiculous to him. "Ah, no. Let's have some more to drink."

"I don't want to drink; I want to dance!"

"Well, you can't. Not with me."

"With someone else, then?" Foxily, Theron eyed the crowd. "How do you like that redhead with the huge knockers? Think she'd be fun to hold? Or the boy with the unconvincing mustache—if it's a boy at all—you never know, down here."

Basil's fingers dug into his arm. "If you dance, you dance with me."

"But you won't!" Theron complained. He bounced on his toes to the beat. "And I've got the music in me, now! If you won't do it, find me someone who can. Look at them all. Come on, Basil, let's play the Wizard Game! Pick me out someone to hold—a partner for the night—"

"How dare you!" Basil flung him away, miraculously missing the people in the tight-packed room.

"What? How dare I what?"

"Don't make a mock of me!"

"Of your wizards, you mean, and their peculiar fancies? Don't you think it would be fun? I wouldn't do anything, only dance—"

"How dare you make a game of it? I study truth and share it with you, and you—"

"I know what you do! Do you think I don't listen to what you're always talking about? Do you think I'm stupid, Basil?"

"I think you're spoiled. I think you presume. I'm not some sort of toy—"

"You are my toy as much as I am yours in this!"

"Love is a game to you, then?"

"Not love, no, but our bodies—like a dance—"

"I said I don't dance! You heard me; you just don't like it when I don't leap to dance to whatever tune you happen to be playing."

"Well, then." Theron looked at him haughtily. "Why don't you just run on back to your scratchy paper mistress?"

"I'm not your servant." Basil heard his voice, hot as his face and hands. "If I go, it's only to spare myself the shame of being seen with you."

"Ashamed to be seen with the Prince of Riverside?" Theron was frostily amused. "Then shall I ask one of my loyal subjects to see you safely home?"

Heat was replaced by chill. "Don't bother, my lord. I think that I can find the river from here. And if one of your *subjects* wants the few coppers I have in my purse, I will gladly give them." He made Theron a stiff bow, and stalked to the entrance and out into the night, scarcely noticing how his set face and clenched hands cleared a path through the revelers.

Theron watched this exhibition. As the door slammed shut, he shook his head, as if coming out of a trance. He was moved to follow his lover and beg his pardon. They'd both had too much to drink.

As he hesitated, he noticed a stocky young man standing by the door, looking around as if lost. His face was a little too sweet, and Theron wondered if he knew just where he was. He looked like he might be wanting the Apricot, instead. It was a chance, Theron thought, to be helpful. Basil would take a deal of soothing and coaxing before he'd be ready to make up the quarrel. And suddenly Theron was tired to death of soothing and coaxing and ministering to the tender pride of a mayor's son who lusted after dead kings.

He snagged two beers from a server and approached the young man.

"How kind." The stranger's voice was a pleasant tenor, younger than the lines around his eyes.

"I wonder," Theron asked politely, "if you were looking for anything particular in here."

"In fact, I was." The man gestured to the dais where the band played. "There's a singer I came to hear. I work on the river; we don't get much chance for such things."

"Oh, a riverman! Now that's something I've always wanted to know about."

"Have you?" The stranger's eyes were amused. "Well, it's mostly hauling freight and watching the banks go by. Oh, there we go!"

The singer had come on, a tall red-headed woman in a tight dress. Theron recognized her: "the Sizzler," they called her, for a number of reasons, not least of all the peculiar hissing purr in her voice, which lent a certain punch to even the most innocuous of lyrics. He had been a big fan of hers when she first appeared a few years back, had even tried his hand at writing her some verses. Now the Sizzler sang an extremely clever song about the city's lack of charity, and then a risqué one about a shopgirl setting terms with a noble who wanted to sleep with her. Theron clapped and shouted with the rest of the crowd, but he kept his eyes on the riverman. Who kept his eyes on the singer. And when she'd finished her set, the Sizzler made a beeline for them, encircling the riverman in her scented arms. Over her shoulder she said to Theron, "And you, young Tremontaine, you can just keep your hands off my Felix!"

Theron said stiffly, "I hope I may buy someone a drink without being accused of assault."

"I know you," the singer continued, unmollified. "And if you make any more scenes in here, I'll write you some songs will make you wish you'd never been born—aye, and sing 'em, too, where plenty of folk can hear them. How would you like to have your latest folly cried all over town?"

"Now, Sally." The riverman was grinning. "I can protect my virtue without your help."

"That's as may be," said the singer. "I know this one, Felix, and you'd better watch out. Go with anyone, he will, with no thought in the world save his own pleasure. Last I heard, some painter woman was leading him about by a ring through his nose. Ready to die of love for her, they say, though I take leave to doubt it. And now a blind man may see he's making that handsome young man's life a misery. So you just leave my Felix alone, do you hear?"

Theron felt his face grow hot, and hoped it didn't show. *Leading him about by a ring through his nose.* It was not how he would have described his affair with Ysaud. But he could just imagine the song it would make.

"When I start chasing rivermen," he said stiffly, "I'll make sure Felix is not on my list. Fine as he is."

The woman looked at him, and then, disconcertingly, began to laugh. "You *don't* much care, do you? Well, if a river*man* is what you're after, Felix won't give you much joy!"

"Spitfire," said Felix lovingly. She quirked her mouth at Tremontaine. "Don't stare. 'Tisn't manners."

Now that Theron knew she was a woman, he could see that

she was not as young as he'd thought; well over thirty, certainly. Handsome, both for a woman and a man, and as easy in her man's clothes as Katherine.

"I beg your pardon," he said stiffly.

"No need. My Sal put you out a moment since; consider the honors even." She turned back to the singer, and the two of them moved on to the dance floor.

Nonplussed, Theron drained his beer and thought of going on to the Brown Dog to dice or to the Apricot, or even home to a full night's rest for once. But the singer's words had stung him more than he'd admit. He thought of Basil, hurt and angry in his shadowy room, imagining his lover in the muscular arms of a young riverman, or worse. How he'll laugh, Theron thought, when he finds out the truth! Almost without conscious decision, he struck out for the Bridge, his boot-heels ringing over the cobbles, his breath steaming as he hummed the Sizzler's last chorus.

HENRY FREMONT WAS MODERATELY PLEASED WITH himself. The act of notifying the Northern contingent of Alaric Finn's death had gone far to lull his pangs of conscience. He still could not entirely justify his letters to Lord Nicholas, but he was inclined to be proud of his reparations for his misdeeds. He'd given away the leather pouch and fancy jacket he'd bought with the money Galing had paid him. He couldn't bring himself to part with the books, but he vowed he'd lend them to anyone who asked, and he'd given most of his ready cash, as well as his new muffler and a blanket, to Lindley. He'd even walked all the way out of the city to the Nag's Head to make sure the Northerners had gotten his message. They had—or at least the body had disappeared from the shed and a purse containing two silvers been left in its place. And he was working for the magister day and night, wizard-hunting in the Archives. Henry still had nightmares—only to be expected, he thought, after such a shock—but on the whole, he thought he'd brushed through the incident pretty well.

So it was with a quiet heart that Henry sat in his room one

night, candle lit, book open, catching up on the reading for Doctor Rugg's course, which he'd fallen behind on. When he heard a knock at the door, his first thought was that it must be Blake, come to tempt him away to the Nest. Well, Blake could knock his knuckles raw; tonight, Henry meant to be virtuous.

"Bugger off!" he shouted, when the knocking renewed. "I'm busy. I'm sleeping. I'm not in."

The latch rattled, and the door opened. Henry turned in his chair to blast Blake for disturbing him, but it wasn't Blake. It wasn't anyone he knew, although he'd seen him at the Nest, or someone very like him. As tall and nearly as thin as Henry himself, his visitor wore his long hair in dozens of tiny braids down his back, and his face was as bleak as a week of rain.

Henry swallowed sudden nausea and cleared his throat. "I don't believe I know you," he said weakly.

"But I know you," said the Northerner. "You are Henry Fremont, of the College of Humane Sciences." His Northern accent was thicker than Finn's, but Henry could not miss the irony of his tone. "You are also, by your own calling, a friend. I have come to see whether you are a friend of Alaric Finn's, or a friend of ours."

Feeling very much at a disadvantage, Henry stood up and tried to get a grip on the situation. "I don't know that I was, strictly speaking, a *friend* of Finn's—more a colleague, really, but we won't fuss over terms. I don't know who you are—apart from being Northern, of course—and I don't know anything about Northerners—apart from the ancient variety—so it would be foolhardy of me to call myself your friend, in the personal sense, anyway."

"Enough," said the Northerner. "If you are not our friend, you are our enemy. And therefore I have this to say to you, Henry Fremont. The Land has been deprived too long of blood and honor. It thirsts, Henry Fremont; it hungers. It needs a king again to feed it properly. Until that day comes, it will accept whatever sacrifices it may come by—even the poor, thin blood of such a Southron fool as you."

Henry listened to this speech with mounting indignation, and by the time the Northerner had come to his ringing conclusion, he was almost as angry as he was afraid. "That puts me in my place, doesn't it? Well, let me tell you something, Master King's Companion. It's not too bright of you to go around threatening people who might, if you'd keep your mouth shut, be more sympathetic to whatever you're up to. I'm an ancient historian, you idiot. I know the Northern kings weren't barbarians, and I know that their Companions were much more than a bunch of drunken, rutting, strutting thugs."

The Northerner looked amused. "Do you call me a thug, Southron?"

"If the hat fits—or should I say, the leaf? You're really something, with your little secret society and your badges and your silly, girlish braids. If I'd known how you were going to behave, I'd have left Finn to rot in the grove, as Lindley wanted us to, and be damned to the lot of you."

Henry stopped, appalled at what he'd said, waiting for the Northerner to draw the long knife gleaming at his belt. But the braided man just stared at him silently, mouth stern, pale eyes slitted. "Yes," he said finally. "That would have been best. You know nothing. You understand nothing. You are no threat to us. But take good care, Henry Fremont. Ignorance is not always innocence."

He did not close the door after himself.

chapter VII

A S THE DAYS AND WEEKS WORE ON TOWARD SPRING,
the first stray tepid breezes brought a tentative thaw to
the land. In the oak grove and in the gardens of the
Hill, snowdrops showed their heads above the damp ground. In
the city streets, gelatinous mud sucked at the boots of the rich,
worked its way into the shoes of the poor, and caked upon the
floors of taverns, shops, council chambers, and tenements. There
was an outbreak of ague among the mathematicians, and a big-
bellied mercer's daughter brought suit in City Sessions against a
Fellow of Astronomy who she swore had promised to marry her.
The Council of Lords was much concerned with the unrest in the
North, and how to bring the Duke of Hartsholt to a better sense
of his duties without setting a precedent that might threaten
their own power some day.

Basil St Cloud did not notice the weather. Sunk deep in his
studies, he hardly knew whether it was day or night. His lectures
and Theron were the only punctuation in days spent prying
the secrets of the past from the papers and books his students
brought him.

Basil was beginning to believe that he had been mistaken in his theories of the Northern kings. The more he read, the more evidence he found suggesting that the oldest kings, the Northern kings, had indeed been a little mad. The way the wizards spoke of them, the deeds they did of battle and of love; the way they knew things and the way they heedlessly sacrificed themselves . . . these were not the sane and reasoned acts that Basil admired in their successors. Since several sources suggested that it was the wizards who controlled that madness, it then followed that the union of the wizards and kings must be critical to the prosperity of the Land. So much was clear. What was less clear was why the Northern kings had been mad in the first place. Had the wizards chosen only madmen as their Little Kings? Or had they deliberately driven sane men to madness? The evidence pointed that way: a Little King was wholly under the tutelage of a single wizard from the time he was chosen until he stood his trial. But why? No source that Basil could find would say.

And then the kings rode south. If the wizards ruled the kings either by choosing madmen or driving them mad, it followed that once the kings began to marry women and to father heirs who were not chosen by wizards, the ruling family would begin to grow sane at last. Look at Laurent, Peregrine, and of course Anselm the Wise, the greatest of them all, who formally curtailed the wizards' power over the throne and its workings. But by this reasoning, Anselm's heirs should have continued to grow, if not wiser and saner, then certainly no madder than their fathers. Which was abundantly not the case.

After Anselm, the place of the wizards in the royal court became less well-defined. Wizards came and went in the royal households of Anselm's heirs as advisors, as spiritual guides, as supernatural guards, finally as spies and inquisitors; as everything, in fact, but tutors to the king's children or mentors to the king's heir, as they had once been.

That was something, but was it enough to account for the great decline that took place over the hundred years between Anselm the Wise and his Wizard Querenel to Iron Tybald and his flock of sadistic wizardly councilors? There had to be something else as well. Was it something to do with the book of spells and the lost language, or the shift of the Wizard's College from North to South? Were the wizards spreading themselves too thin, caring for the two lands at once, when the roots of their magic lay in the North? Or could it be that, with Anselm, the king had sundered the old bond between them by refusing to let his son take a wizard as his lover?

It galled Basil that he had no documentary answers to these questions, but he knew enough to form some theories, and his instincts told him that his theories were near the truth. Whether the kings liked it or not, their fates were entwined with the wizards. When the kings withdrew from the control of the wizards, they began to lose control over themselves; when the wizards lost their traditional purpose, they also began to lose their wisdom and their abilities. In the end, the very last kings—Iron Tybald, Hilary the Stag, and finally Gerard—turned to the wizards again, to strengthen them, to heal them, to protect them from a realm that had grown to hate them. But it was too late. Guidry's Book survived, but the key to unlock its wisdom had been irrevocably lost. So the kings were mad again, the wizards useless . . . The nobles had been right: there was nothing left to do but wipe out the whole boiling of them, kings and wizards both, and start over again.

It made perfect sense. If only he could find enough concrete proof, even the Governors would have to accept his reasoning. So Basil applied himself to sifting studiously through the flotsam and jetsam of ancient history. But studying ancient history meant studying power and ancient kings, meant studying the Book of the King's Wizard, meant studying Theron. Meant pinning Theron to the mattress, meant touching the Book when he touched his flesh, touching flesh when he touched the Book. Almost impossible these days to unknit the strands that bound them all together. And all of them seemed to be leading him to some great conclusion, a final knowledge that would not only defeat Crabbe but change all of history as it had been studied. Spending time on anything else was almost unbearable. Every moment spent away from his books or his lover was a sojourn in a trackless waste.

His books were faithful enough, but Theron was increasingly

occupied with lectures, with family gatherings, with various appointments on vague matters of business too dull to tell his lover about. It was not remarkable for him to appear an hour or even two after his promised time, penitent, affectionate, and eager.

Which was why Basil was sitting in the Blackbird's Nest one foggy afternoon when he should have been working. As they'd kissed and parted that morning. Theron had said that he would come to the Nest at noon for a bite and a word before Doctor Tipton's rhetoric lecture. "I'll buy you a beer," he'd said. "We'll sit and talk. We haven't talked properly for ages."

NOON CAME AND WENT. BASIL, COLLECTING A BATCH of notes from Blake and Godwin, hardly noticed how the time passed until they left for their afternoon lectures and he realized that Theron was still not there. He had half a mind to leave himself, let Theron learn his lover had better things to do than cool his heels waiting for a thoughtless boy to remember him. But the Archives were dank and smelled of mildew and mold, and the Nest was warm and bright, and the mulled ale he was drinking was fragrant with hops and cloves. He ordered another, and was still waiting for it when Theron arrived, breathless, on the tolling of the University bell. He was two hours late.

Theron flung himself onto the nearest bench. "Sorry! Beer? No, wait—it's two already—I must get to Tipton's rhetoric—"

"Theron, what is that you're wearing?"

The young noble's black robe was open over a pair of tight-fitting striped yellow breeches and an embroidered waistcoat. He looked ruefully down at his splendor. "Sorry—had to go see the lawyer this morning, no time to change—"

Basil laughed. "Well, cover them up, and maybe no one will laugh at you. Lawyer, eh? Nothing's wrong, I hope?"

"Oh, no. I think it will all be fine. Thanks, Basil, I'm off—"

"Wait." The black whirlwind froze. "Tell me if you're coming to Minchin Street tonight." There was a note of command in his voice that brought a speculative smile to Theron's lips.

"Will you be there?"

"Will you?" Basil insisted.

"There's a party," Theron began apologetically.

"There have been other parties. I'll be up late."

Theron looked his lover full in the eyes, then nodded. "Yes," he said. "I will come."

⌒

T HERON TOLD HIMSELF HE WAS NOT NERVOUS. THE difficult part had all been done: the contracts, the lawyers with their endless talk of rights and property, duty and dowries. Marcus and his aides had handled the bulk of it, but the family (in this case, Sophia, Katherine, and Marcus all united) had agreed that it would be good for Theron to attend some of the ne-gotiations himself, so that he had a true understanding of what was at stake. It had been hard for him to pay attention. He could not bring himself to care about the fine points of income from land he'd never seen, or which pieces of the family jewelry his wife would be entitled to wear. His thoughts kept straying to Basil, hot in bed and cool at his desk, rising this morning from the papers he was examining as Theron dressed to kiss him again and again as though setting his seal on him until next they met. The lawyers with their endless arguments had made him late, but he'd gotten away in time to meet Basil at the Nest before Tipton's lecture. After all, Theron was there to observe, not to negotiate; he had perfect faith that his people would not let the Randalls get one brass minnow more than was their due.

But tonight was different. Tonight he was on his own, with business only he could take care of. He dressed in green the color of his eyes, with starched white linen at his neck and wrists. He put rings on his fingers, a diamond at his throat. He went to the ball where all had agreed that he would ask Genevieve Randall to marry him.

He found her sitting with a group of girlfriends, including Charlie Talbert's fiancée, Lady Elizabeth Horn. Ever since Theron's pursuit of Genevieve had become known, the Talbert cousins and their circle had made a point of befriending the pretty Randall girl. He supposed once he was married they would all be coming to the house. Genevieve could entertain them; she seemed happy in their company. When they saw Theron, Lady Elizabeth nudged her. Genevieve looked up, her clear face lit with a smile. The other girls shifted their billowing skirts to let him approach her, and he held out his hand across the sea of flounces that remained. He marveled, as always, at how light and tiny her bones were. Tonight, her hand was cold.

He said, "Will you dance?", noting that it took her a moment to acquiesce. Then he drew her away from the crowded ballroom, leaving the girls to whisper with delight.

"Oh!" Genevieve looked back at the brightly lit room, as he led her into the shadows of a quiet corridor. He had never been alone with her before; it had never been permitted. But no one came after her. He turned her, and it was like a dance, so that she was facing him, her back to the wall. He did not let go her hand, and he felt it warming in his grasp.

"You look beautiful," he said. "I thought so the very first time I saw you."

She smiled. "I remember. It was at the Lassiters' ball. I was wearing my willow cream silk, and I was afraid it made me look sallow."

"No. You had your hair up very high." With great care, he reached out his hand and touched one lock of hair over her ear and raised it up. "Your ears were exposed, just like this, and I wanted to kiss them."

"Kiss my ears?"

He showed her. She stiffened when she felt his lips, and then she laughed, and then she leaned into his arms. Her ears were pierced, hung with huge pearl drops. He sucked one into his mouth, tasting her and smelling her at once. He made a noise in the back of his throat, and her tiny fingers gripped the cloth of his jacket. He worked his tongue around her earlobe, feeling the pearl clatter against his teeth. She clung to him harder.

He had never kissed a noble girl before. She smelt of powder and perfume, gold wire and silk and her own sharp sweet sweat. The tops of her breasts glowed like twin moons pushing out of her gown, held there in perpetual temptation by her corset. He kissed her parted lips, and then he pulled away.

"I think," he said, "if we were married, we would"—he paused for breath—"we would enjoy one another."

Her mouth quirked gently. "Would you eat *all* my jewelry?"

He said, "Perhaps. Will you marry me?"

"Everyone wants me to."

"I want you to."

"Well then, I will. Yes."

"Yes?" He looked into her eyes, where his mother told him the truth resides. She looked back at him, bright and clear and young. Theron nodded. He took a ruby ring from his finger. "This is mine," he said, "and my family's." He slid it over her forefinger, where it was still too large. "You keep it. Wear it for me."

Shyly, she kissed his finger where the ring had been. "I will like being married to you," she said, keeping her eyes on his hands.

"I hope so."

"They tell me you are wild," she confided to his hands, "but I don't think so."

"It's true. I am wild, or I have been."

"Oh," she said, glancing up swiftly. "I don't mind. That is—it sounds as if you've had an exciting life."

He smoothed his thumb over her fingers. "I will try to make you happy," he heard himself say, just like a bad romance.

She looked into his eyes, her face aglow. "When we are married," she said, and he said, "Yes?"

"When we are married, there is one thing I would like."

"What is it?"

"I was thinking . . ." She dropped her eyes and blushed. He waited. "I was wondering, perhaps, if I might see your hair unbound."

Swiftly he raised his hand and undid the clasp. His long hair came tumbling down around his shoulders, down his back, a smoky waterfall. Like a child who cannot resist a sweet, she reached for it, tangled her fingers in the silky mass. "Oh," she cried. "How I would love to brush it!"

He almost laughed. Instead he said, "Well, help me gather it back up, or I will start behaving as if we are already married, and I'm told contracts have been broken over less."

It felt good, the way she ran her hands through his hair, smoothing it out, neatening him up, her fingers fumbling at the clasp in the dark for a moment before it closed.

"Don't lose the ring," he said. "Your parents have to see that you've accepted it from me, and then they can announce our engagement."

"I know," she said; "it's next week. The Montague banquet, Mama thought, because everyone will be there."

"Next week? Why not tonight?"

"It isn't proper. They always wait a few days before the formal announcement, in case—well, to give people time to get used to it, I suppose."

"Or in case you want to change your mind?"

"Or you change yours," she said.

"I wouldn't dare. My lawyers would have me killed."

To his surprise, she looked alarmed. "Is there trouble? With my dowry?"

He said gently, "If there were, I wouldn't be here now, no matter how beautiful your ears."

But everyone must have known, and the announcement would be a mere formality, for the heir to Tremontaine danced with the Randalls' daughter three times that night, and three times more, and the other girls flirted ferociously with him, now that he was safely bound, while their sweethearts and brothers welcomed him as one of themselves at last, drinking with him so deeply that he forgot all about a promise he had made to a man on Minchin Street.

⁓

B ASIL WOKE AS DAWN WAS SILVERING THE CITY. HE was slumped over his table, cramped and cold and weary. He was aware of a sullen rage burning in him like a banked fire, and the unwelcome fact that he had a lecture to give. He pulled together his notes, jammed a hat on his head, and stopped by the Nest for something hot on his way to LeClerc.

His lecture that morning was more discursive than usual, its subject being the fabled wizard Guidry. A forest of legends and

stories had grown up around the name, obscuring everything
but the undeniable fact that a wizard named Guidry had served
every king of the North from Simon Thunderer to Alexander
Ravenhair, spanning some two hundred years.

"Later historians have assumed," St Cloud said, "that the
original Guidry, Simon's Guidry, founded a dynasty of wizards
who shared their master's name as they shared his statecraft and
magical pre-eminence. But there's an earlier source. You will remember that Hollis mentions a *True Chronicle of the Wizards and
Their Deeds*, written before the Union by one Martindale. The
True Chronicle was very popular in the early years of the Union
and was among the first books to be printed. Bits of it are quoted
by Hollis and Placid, but Fleming states absolutely that no copies
survived the Fall. Now I have found one, and very interesting it
proves to be."

Massed on their benches, St Cloud's inner circle turned to
each other with mouths agape. Who had managed to turn that
treasure up? And why hadn't he claimed his victory? But Blake
and Vandeleur and Fremont and Godwin and Lindley all looked
equally astonished. Basil saw no need to tell them that the gift
had come from Theron Campion, a penitent Theron, making up
with him after the Riverside debacle.

"I found it at home," Theron had said, "propping up a table
leg, can you believe it?"

Basil believed it more likely that the boy had taken it from
the Riverside library, but he had been too thrilled to do anything
but thank him and kiss him for his gift. Now that Theron had
failed him again, he wondered if he could expect another such
find. He wondered if it was worth it.

"According to Martindale," Basil continued his lecture,
"Guidry lived two hundred years without growing old. The description is a striking one." Basil referred to his notes. " 'Tall as a
bear, and thick of neck and thigh like unto a forest tree was the
Wizard Guidry; hair and leaves grew upon him close, ancient in
wisdom and love of the Land. Power ran in his seed and strength
in his hand, and whatsoever Little King he chose, that one endured his trial and survived to be chained with gold and give
his blood and bone to the Land.' " Basil looked up. "Martindale's

style is colorful, of course. Hollis did not scruple to call his prede-cessor 'a golden-tongued rogue,' which Delgardie and his crew took as evidence that Martindale, who saw at least one wizard Guidry with his own eyes, was a liar.

"Now. As we know from our copious dealings with the gen-tleman, Delgardie's definition of a liar was simply someone who did not see the world as he himself saw it. So what are we to make of Martindale's assertion that after two hundred years choosing and guiding the kings of the North, Guidry did not die, but hid himself away in a magical grove where he would sleep until the Land was in need of him?"

Here St Cloud paused, as if waiting for an answer, savoring the attention of his acolytes. They were a good group, strong-hearted and devoted to the truth, to the Land, and to him. One of the most promising, young Lindley, stood and said, "That it is a great mystery, magister, and like all mysteries, both true and beautiful. I would that I might live to see his return."

The laughter began even before he finished this quaint speech, breaking the spell that had begun to gather. Basil laughed as heartily as any before saying, "It is a mystery, Lindley, but I sus-pect Martindale has taken poetic license in this passage to signify that Guidry's magic will live forever, perhaps in the lost Book of the King's Wizard. Which teaches us something about poetic li-cense and about the ephemeral nature of books."

All in all, it was an exhilarating morning, but an exhausting one, after a long and fruitless night. Afterward, Basil was of two minds whether to return to his books, or accompany his students to the Nest and spin out the heady feeling of power that buoyed him. He was still trying to decide when he came out of LeClerc, surrounded by his informal guard: Blake, Vandeleur, Fremont, Lindley, Godwin. An unlikely group, he found himself think-ing—more townsmen than countrymen, but passionate, each in his way, and ambitious. They would have made good wizards, in a different time and place.

"Watch out there," Vandeleur snapped.

"What shall I watch for?" a lazy voice drawled. "The Lord High Doctor of Scholarship? I'll step aside for none less, University boy."

Basil came to himself with a shock, saw Vandeleur and Blake confronting a small group of young men with cropped hair and lace at their throats—nobles out slumming.

"Lay off, Perry," said one of them. "Won't find out anything if we don't ask politely."

The young man made a scornful gesture and stepped aside; St Cloud and his entourage moved forward, only to be blocked by another of the group—a sturdy young man, square-faced and flushed above his foaming lace. "Beg pardon," he said. "I'm looking for a teacher, and I thought—well, are you Doctor St Cloud? My mother wants—that is, I'm so interested in—in the kings and all. I'm Clarence Randall, by the way. My father's Lord Randall. A Northern title, you know." He stuck out beringed fingers, seized the magister's hand, and pumped vigorously.

St Cloud merely looked at him, and at their joined hands, which Randall was still pumping. Randall, oblivious, chattered on. "I've wanted to attend your lectures ever since I heard about the challenge. Felt shy about looking you up, not being used to University ways. But here you are, dropped out of the sky. So. May I come?"

Several thoughts went through Basil's head at once. He loathed cocky, stupid, presumptuous young puppies like Clarence Randall; his challenge was making him known beyond the University, just as Rugg and Cassius and Elton had said it would; he was in no position to send young Randall off with a flea in his ear.

"Lord Clarence," he said, temporizing. "I don't know if you realize the term is almost over. You'd be plunging into deep waters indeed, were you to begin your studies now. Still, if you read my *Origins of Peace*, you will have the bare bones of it. If you want to know more, you are free to come to me next fall, when I will begin a new course of lectures."

"*The Origins of Peace*, you said?" Randall turned to his friend. "Remember that, will you, Perry?"

Perry laughed. "Remember it yourself. Whence the sudden interest in ancient history, Randall? I'd have thought cards and drinking more your line."

Randall turned positively crimson. "Oh, it's some notion of my mother's."

"Ah," said Perry. "I see. Then you'd best ask Campion to remember it for you. He's interested in history, too, and he's practically a member of the family, eh, Campion?"

It was only then that St Cloud realized that Theron had joined the gaudy crowd, a crow among peacocks in his black scholar's robe. As Perry spoke, Basil caught his lover's gaze past Randall's head. Theron's green eyes shifted, veiled themselves under the heavy oval lids. He put his arm around young Randall's broad shoulders. "I'll remember anything you like, my dear," he said, "as long as I don't have to do it in the middle of the street." And he led the boy away.

Simple bewilderment rooted Basil to the spot, followed close by rage. Someone was repeating his name; Justis Blake. St Cloud shook him off impatiently and strode off toward Minchin Street. A dry, soft breeze ruffled his hair. Winter had masked itself as spring today. There'd be another frost—there always was—to slick the streets with ice and blast the early crocuses. But true spring was not so far behind, bringing the end of the term and the Festival of Sowing and his meeting with Roger Crabbe upon the Great Hall steps. He'd been wasting his time on dalliance while his honor hung in the balance. Well, he'd dally no longer.

Back at Minchin Street, Basil sharpened his pens and mixed fresh ink and prepared to marshal his arguments concerning the wizards and the reality of their magic. He knew just what he had to say, and how, but he wrote and crossed out sentence after sentence, wrote and crumpled page after page, until at last he found himself sitting amongst a snowdrift of spoiled sheets, plagued by the memory of Theron's face turning from him. He knew that Theron was hiding something important. Confronted, Theron would undoubtedly lie about it, try to charm or kiss his way out of an explanation. Basil thought he could bear anything better than Theron's false protestations of love and innocence.

But what could he do? He was no nobleman, to command Theron's obedience. He was no dockside bully, to beat the truth out of him. He was powerless, he had nothing—

Basil stared at the mess of papers spread out on the desk before him. He felt as if the words were laughing at him, giggling like schoolchildren as they hid and revealed themselves amongst the crumpled pages of notes and transcriptions. *Truth*, they read, and *wizards* and *spell* and *If Ye wold* and *If Ye Dare. . . .*

He went to the bed and dug out the battered document box, and lifted out the wizards' book. He turned to *A Spelle for the Uncovring of Hidden Trothe*. He mouthed the strange words through, and then began again at the beginning, aloud.

Having begun, he could not stop, though the mysterious syllables clashed and slid in his mouth like rough pebbles. His voice rang strangely in his ears, and the meaning of what he read crouched half-seen at the edges of his understanding. When he came to an end, he was dizzy, and his pulse thundered in his ears. The countryman in him half expected to see his candle burning black, and shapeless shadows seething in the corner behind the fire. But his room looked as it always had: homely, cluttered, shabby, prosaic. Basil rubbed shaking hands over his face, then wiped them dry on his robe before touching the Book again. He'd done it wrong, that was all. Perhaps he should try again.

The door opened behind him. "I've been having the most excruciating evening," Theron announced. "I've been conversing with debutantes, flattering dowagers, and listening to politically minded nobles discourse upon taxes. Comfort me, my dear, before I explode from an excess of respectability."

He wore full ball-dress. His hair was oiled and pulled back into a glossy club held by a jeweled clip. Rings weighed down his hands and a pearl hung from the lobe of one ear. He was flushed and a little unsteady. He held out a hand to Basil, who ignored it.

"Aren't you glad to see me?" Theron asked plaintively.

Basil laid the book on the table. "I did not expect you tonight. I was working. You interrupted me."

"You've never minded being interrupted before." Theron closed the door and stepped into the room, stripping off his cloak and tossing it into a corner. "And you won't mind it this time, either." He came up behind Basil and put his arms around his chest. He smelled sweet and complicated, of perfumed oil and wine and desire. He leaned over Basil's shoulder and rubbed his face like a great cat. The pearl in his ear brushed Basil's cheek, smooth and hard as glass.

The pearl seared Basil's flesh like a torch, ice and fire at once.

Basil shook Theron off. "That earring is a woman's jewel," he said, knowing as he spoke that it was true. "She gave it to you tonight, from her own ear as you begged it."

The flushed face turned pale. "Nonsense, Basil."

"Nonsense, indeed. Do you think I don't know you?"

"No." Theron stared back at him with glittering eyes. "You don't. You don't know me at all."

Basil breathed in deeply. It seemed to him that he could smell Theron's every emotion as clearly as he could smell the woman he'd been with. "It does not become you, my lord, to lie. Not to me."

Now two spots of color, like red bites, stained his lover's cheeks. "Because I am a lord? Or because you are so fond of truth?"

"Both," said Basil calmly. "And more besides. You, with the blood of kings, and I with—what I have. Now, come here." He held out his hand as if coaxing an animal from the woods. "Come here and tell me about your latest conquest."

Theron started back violently, the pearl swinging against his cheek. "No! Dammit, no! You have no right—"

"Theron, I have every right," Basil said in the same sweet, reasoning voice. "You are mine. You have said so a hundred times. Did you think it was just a bed-game?"

The young nobleman drew himself up proudly. "You presume on my love."

"Yes," Basil answered. "I do. Oaths have been made, and pledges spoken. Seed has been spilt. What's done cannot be undone."

Theron was staring at him with a kind of horror. "You speak as though you really think you own me."

"You are mine, Theron. And you have betrayed me. I know that, too." Basil laughed ruefully. "You told me once you wanted to make a study of me. But you are no scholar, remember? It is I, my dear, who've made a study of you. And I know what I know."

"What do you know?" Theron hissed, his fists clenched. "You understand nothing of the world beyond these walls. All you know of love is what I taught you! Study me?" he sneered. "How could you do that—when all you see when you look at me is the mask of one of your dead kings?

"You never wanted me at all—you wanted Anselm the Wise, or Francis the Brave, or Alexander Ravenhair—but they've moldered to dust in a wood somewhere, so you had to make do with what turned up and reminded you of them. You don't see *me* at all, do you?" He was shouting, but his arms were wrapped tightly around himself. "You don't see me, you don't know me, you don't know who I really am! I tried to tell you, over and over, but you ignored everything that didn't fit your history books! Whatever you loved, Basil, it wasn't me—and I was a fool to love you."

Basil listened in silence. The words should have cut deep, but they did not. He heard instead how Theron's misery was a form of love, how it was he who was breaking the young man's heart. The knowledge of his power worked in him like desire, potent and delicious. He had never known a joy quite like this, fierce and dark with the knowledge of just where he might inflict the most pain. He had not known Theron could be hurt like this.

"I do love you," Basil said with steady truth. "I love you and I know you. The land will have what that land will have, Theron. 'A man proud and willful and arrogant. And loving and passionate, with the gift to make men love him, and women, too.' Yes, it's Hollis on King Alexander—and it is you to the life. And always will be. Ask anyone."

Theron's hand was on the latch.

"You're running away, now," Basil said. "That, too, is who you are. But you will not run forever. Sooner or later you will stand and face your trial." It was all coming together; all the little hints and clues contained in his papers and books, pieces of a pattern as inevitable as it was compelling. "Be careful to know yourself when the time comes," he warned the Little King. "The man who fails the test will run for the rest of his life, with the beast still in his heart."

Theron said nothing. He flung open the door, and slammed it behind him. Basil heard his feet clattering down the stairs.

He had left his cloak in the corner of the room. Basil picked it up and inhaled the scent of him. Power was sweet, as sweet as knowledge. Together, they were mastery and achievement. Doctor Basil St Cloud lifted the Book of the King's Wizard from the table where it had lain all the while, and carefully folded the cloak around it, until it was wrapped in layer after layer of his lover's rich garment. He put them both under his pillow, and lay down to dream.

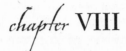 chapter VIII

B Y THE TIME LORD ARLEN FINALLY SENT FOR HIM,
Galing had reached a state of high frustration. His servants had caught the brunt of his temper, to the extent
that his manservant would have given notice, if he hadn't been
sure that Lord Nicholas would get over it eventually, just as he always did.

Galing's irascibility was not to be wondered at. In his own
mind, he was absolutely sure that the Tremontaine heir was involved in some plot. Henry's reports, Ysaud's paintings, his own
conversations with Campion, all pointed toward a man of unusual arrogance and romantic ideas, a man who could easily be
flattered into accepting a crown. All Nicholas needed was the
weight of the Serpent's authority behind him, and he'd soon
know who was planning to win that crown for him. He had written to tell Arlen that he had something important to report; he'd
even sent a note to Edward. And Arlen had left him hanging for
weeks. It was all he could do, when the summons came, not to
fling it back in the messenger's face.

Accustomed by now to Arlen's ways, Galing endured the

opening pleasantries of the interview, answering inquiries about his mother's health and which swordsman he intended to back at the exhibition fights with what grace he could muster. Arlen never came straight to the point. Very well, Galing wouldn't either; but as the discussion of swordsmen dragged on, he grew increasingly impatient. Perhaps Arlen was leaving the opening move up to him. In any case, he could wait no longer. "I've been seeing something of Theron Campion," he said slyly. "An original young man."

"Is he?" Arlen drawled. "I find him quite conventionally ill-behaved. Unsuitable lovers, low interests, carousing: what's so original about that?"

It was now, Galing thought, or not at all. "I was thinking more of treason."

"Were you?"

The fire crackled. Lord Arlen sipped his wine and gazed into the flames, offering Galing ample opportunity to study his hawk's profile. Nicholas felt put-upon. Did Arlen want a report or not? Everything's a test, Edward had reminded him last autumn when all this started. A test of what? Patience? Persistence? The ability to have two conversations at once?

"I beg your pardon," he said stiffly. "I thought you summoned me to discuss a possible royalist plot in the city. If you prefer to gossip about swordsmen and waistcoats, I am, of course, at your disposal."

"Treason is a serious charge, Galing," said Arlen. "I presume you have some solid reason for making it?"

Nicholas unpacked his notes and laid what he knew and what he'd guessed before the Serpent Chancellor. Arlen listened gravely, looked at the papers Galing handed him, asked a question or two, and when he was done, said, "I must congratulate you, Galing. You have the makings of an excellent intelligencer, can you but curb your impulse to reason in advance of your data. All this"—he tapped the sheaf of papers lying on his knee—"is very interesting, very useful. Thank you. You need do no more."

Galing was too good a card-player to show surprise, but his temper took a moment to subdue. When he thought he could trust himself not to say anything that might jeopardize his future career, he ventured, "It is good to hear that the matter of the Northern rebellion has been resolved so quickly."

"Not resolved, precisely; simply confined to the North. My agents are investigating the activities of the society calling itself, rather incautiously, the Companions of the King. Thanks to you, the leaders of the University branch—Masters Greenleaf and Smith—are safely out of harm's way. As to the Northern branch— well, my agent currently describes it as an association of young men, young and unmarried, who gather in the woods from time to time to celebrate elaborate rituals that draw equally from local folklore and a youthful taste for mysticism and indiscriminate copulation. We're watching them closely."

"And the trouble up North?"

Arlen shrugged. "As I think I said this autumn, the Northern farmers are always unhappy. They are unhappier than usual just now, but steps are being taken to cheer them. You are not to trouble your head over them."

"What about Campion?" Voices are harder to control than expressions. Nicholas heard a pleading note creep into his tone and clenched his hand in vexation.

Arlen didn't seem to notice. "Campion is to wed Lord Randall's daughter in the fall, and will take his bride to the Kyrillian Archipelago on a diplomatic embassy to the Parliaments."

"But Ysaud's paintings . . ."

"Mean nothing. Madam Ysaud is a well-known eccentric, with no more interest in politics than my cat. My dear Galing, you haven't got a case. Outside of the Last Night incident, there is no connection between Theron Campion and the Companions of the King or indeed any other faction, political or otherwise. What that leaves us with is a cause without a focus and a focus without a cause—in short, with nothing." He nodded kindly at Galing, who was dumb with fury. "Your concern does you credit, Galing, but I assure you, there's nothing in it."

"I don't believe that," Galing said.

Lord Arlen's lids descended in a slow blink: he was getting annoyed. "The matter is closed," he said. "There is no evidence."

"There's lots of evidence," Galing insisted. "There's the Hunt, and the fact that Campion led it to the oak grove; there's his relationship with St Cloud, who seems hell-bent on proving the wizards weren't frauds."

"Those incidents are not evidence," Arlen said coldly. "They are coincidence magnified to significance through the lens of ambition. Where is young Campion's army? Where are his allies? When would he have planned all this? And with whom? As I understand it, you are suggesting that Theron Campion is somehow destined to restore the monarchy. Under the circumstances, to believe in such an eventuality one would have to believe in magic." Arlen paused. "Have you come across anything in your studies, Lord Nicholas, to convince you that magic actually exists?"

"Of course not," Galing answered promptly. It would have been foolish to give any other answer to Arlen's question, even though he'd begun to wonder privately whether there might not once have been something very like magic practiced in the courts of the ancient kings. But his private reflections, he thought, were not Arlen's concern. Nor were any questions he might think to ask or friendships he might choose to foster in pursuing his own private ends. Which included, just now, putting a definitive stop to whatever Theron Campion might be up to. "You're perfectly right, Lord Arlen," he went on smoothly. "I do beg your pardon. It's—well, disappointing to spend so much time on something and see it all come to nothing."

"Of every twenty paths an intelligencer explores, only one or two will lead to a clear destination," Arlen said kindly. "You must shrug and go on to the next project."

Galing looked up eagerly. "I will, sir. Gladly. And what is the next project?"

"Gently, gently," said Arlen, smiling. "I have nothing in hand just now calling for your special talents. Go home, attend to your affairs, forget all this tedious ancient history. And leave young Campion alone, eh? He's too highly placed to be hounded to no purpose."

"Of course," Nicholas murmured, falsely submissive. "And St Cloud?"

"Let St Cloud's own words dig his grave." Arlen leaned forward, caught Galing's eyes and held them with his predator's steady gaze. "Let it be, Nicholas. And if you cannot, tread carefully. I would hate to lose such a promising ally."

Galing nodded, rose, made his farewells, and left Lord Arlen's house. He had no intention of letting it be. And he would not tread carefully. The best way to cross thin ice is not to feel your way, but to run lightly and quickly to the other side. It wouldn't do to pursue the boy; he'd wait and see if Campion showed up for his theatre party. If he didn't, well, his absence would provide Nicholas with a good excuse to call. The hunt was up, the quarry running. Soon enough, he'd bring him to bay.

TWO DAYS AFTER HIS QUARREL WITH THERON, BASIL was in a pitiable state of nerves. He had cast a magic spell from the forbidden book and it had revealed truths to him that, on reflection, he'd prefer not to have known. Or perhaps common sense had revealed them, and Theron's own behavior, which had been very odd of late, and that was not magic at all, only delusion and coincidence. And then there were the dreams, vivid as life, which he could not remember when he woke, save for disconnected images of men with pelts and dainty cloven hooves, of his own hands turning to brown-furred paws, of a bright pool of water and oak and holly and a bone-handled knife. He felt restless, uncomfortable, out of joint, as though his skin were not his own. He could not work.

There were two possible explanations for all this. Either he was growing as mad as the kings had been, or else he was in sober truth becoming a wizard. The impression that his thoughts and words were not entirely his was very like madness, certainly. But it had all been true, hadn't it, what he and Theron had said to each other? Theron had never admitted that the pearl had come from a woman; but neither had he denied it.

Madman or wizard? Basil wasn't sure which explanation frightened him more. And there was no way of knowing which was the more likely without seeing Theron again. Their encounter had been so strange, limned by jealousy and colored with rage, that it seemed more like a painting or a play he had watched than a conversation in which he had taken part. Talking to Theron would at least make it seem concrete, palpable, subject to discussion. He would even apologize, if he had to.

But would Theron speak to him? Or was he too angry? Had all their winter's loving pleasure been undone by one evening?

If it had been only the quarrel, Basil might have waited Theron out a little longer. But there was the Book, and his dreams, and Basil needed to know, finally, whether he was mad or not. So he went out in search of his lover, beginning with the places where rhetoricians were known to gather.

No one had seen Campion at the Ink Pot or the Blasted Vine or the Bramble Bush. Basil ducked into the Gilded Cockatrice, where the noble students liked to drink overpriced claret.

The Gilded Cockatrice was a large, high-windowed room above a bookseller's; an ancient presence-hall, perhaps, or a petty court, its ceiling carved with strange beasts and half-human creatures holding up the mantel over the great hearth. It was always a noisy place, but today the noise was deafening: at the other end of the room, noble students were knocking back drinks and toasting something, which seemed to involve jumping up on a table. Basil looked around. He didn't see Theron, but Cassius, of all people, was sitting near the door with a glass of ruby wine in front of him.

Basil accosted him. "What are you doing here, Cassius? I thought you hated this place."

"I was invited for a drink," Cassius said shortly. "What's your excuse? You should be home working on that challenge!"

"I'm looking for Lord Theron Campion," Basil said tersely. "Is he in here?"

"Not anymore," Cassius said. "He left—that is, he's probably at the Nest. Hurry up, you just might catch him—"

A voice raised itself above the general roar: "I've got one, I've got one! To Campion: Netted at last—may we all be spared the same sad fate!"

"Well said, Perry! Man deserves better. How about this? To

Campion: May his bride's maidenhead prove as tight as his lover's arsehole!"

There was a brief, shocked silence. "Hemmynge, you fool," said someone.

Basil surveyed the crowd: faces turned up to him or down to their cups and tankards, flushed, pale, round, hollow-cheeked, waiting for him to react.

"Idiots," Cassius muttered, taking Basil's arm. "Never mind, old fellow, let's go—"

"It is traditional," said Basil, raising his voice to lecture-room pitch, "to toast a man on the occasion of his betrothal." He took the cup from Cassius's lax hand and lifted it to the room. "To Lord Alexander Theron Campion of Tremontaine. May his dedication to his name and his lineage prove true and just." He put the cup to his lips and drained the excellent red wine to the dregs.

Silent bewilderment greeted his toast, breaking into murmurs that followed him as he turned on his heel and strode down the steps and out into a bright, cold afternoon. Basil felt no anger as he walked through the narrow streets, just a slow bleeding away of mind and spirit that could only be stanched by the sight of Theron Campion on his knees before him.

I F HE WEREN'T BUSY WITH THE DETAILS OF GETTING married, Theron thought, he would go mad. Anything to distract him from what had happened between him and Basil! He could not believe what he had heard himself say. The words had come out of his mouth without his thought, without his foreknowledge, as though he were reading lines fresh-written, still wet with ink.

The worst thing was, he knew that they were true. He and Basil had loved each other, yes, but as shadows love one another, each yearning toward a shape that was cast by something real, yet never looking beyond the shadow's form. The year he'd studied metaphysics, he'd read about something like that. All his study, though, all his reading and thinking and discussing—all these years of work, and where had it left him? The same fool he would have been if he'd spent them learning surgery, or dog-breeding, or how to tell the difference between goose-turd green and peapod green taffeta! He'd learned nothing that did him any good. He fell in love and gave his heart and felt safe, and then he found out that he'd gotten it all wrong. Furthermore, everyone around him had known all along that he'd gotten it wrong and were only waiting to tell him. Though he still wasn't sure how he had failed this time. Basil had been everything that anyone could wish for in a lover: beautiful, brilliant, devoted . . .

Fortunately, Theron mused, this time would be his last. He would marry Lady Genevieve, and maybe he'd be faithful to her after all. God knows he wanted her right now. Her inexperience only meant that they could spend a long time working on the basics. She struck him as a quick learner. Once she got the hang of things, he did not imagine that they would soon tire of one another. The fact that he did not love her yet probably counted in her favor. Probably, he could only have a decent life with someone he was not foolish enough to fall in love with from the start.

The engagement had been formally announced at the ball where Genevieve had given him her earring. The wedding was set for autumn; it was too late to plan a spring wedding, and everyone would be in the country during the summer. He would probably go to the country, too. The city was always rife with fever in the summer, and it wouldn't do to have him die before his nuptials. He thought he'd go to one of the Tremontaine estates, maybe with the twins and their babies. Di and Is could spend the warm months giving him pointers on how to be married; they'd enjoy that. He would certainly not go to Highcombe, even though all the people there who'd known him since he was a sickly baby would want to congratulate him on his betrothal. He would not risk running into Basil's terrible father, the cock of the Highcombe walk.

Theron was now a welcome visitor at the Randalls'; indeed, it turned out he was supposed to be paying visits almost every day or it would be remarked on. He wished that he could go to the country right now; the number of things that turned out to be expected of him were a little bit more than he had bargained for. His Talbert cousins were giving a dinner for the newly betrothed couple, and Katherine was making him go over a list of invitations to distant relatives. She was even sending announcements to Jessica, wherever in the world she might be, in hopes that she might arrive home by the fall. He wondered what on earth Ysaud thought of the whole thing; surely she had heard.

And Basil? Did Basil know? Someone must have told him, by now. He wished that he had been able to tell him himself. It would have been hard, but at least he would have been able to explain that it was not in despite of their love, but rather, in a weird way, because of it. Perhaps he should write to him. Perhaps he should not. He still had classes to go to. But he would avoid the Blackbird's Nest. Tony Lindley and that crew would be thrilled.

The dreams were back, too; he knew they were the same ones, though this time he was not himself at all. It was as if the dreams no longer bothered to draw him to themselves; instead, they had a part for him and he walked into it. He was a man with braided hair strung with beads and bells. Other men, his brothers, watched him from the shadows of the leaves as he walked toward that same damned grove. He was very much afraid, and it was important that he let no one know it. He wanted what was there, although he did not know what it was. It was like an itch in the part of the back you cannot reach. It was like trying to remember the thing that would save your life.

B ASIL SAT IN HIS ROOMS ON MINCHIN STREET. HIS door was locked and his worktable was bare of everything but a single, fat, leather-covered book. Basil laid his hand upon the oak leaf stamped into the cover. It was time.

He was very calm. Theron had betrayed him. That was unimportant: lovers betrayed one another. Kings had even betrayed their wizards—often, if there were any truth in his researches at all. Alexander Ravenhair had betrayed the great wizard Guidry by falling in love with Rosamund of Brightwater and wanting to marry her. But the wizards always managed to bring their kings to heel in the end, even if the end, like Alexander's, was death.

The problem, of course, was that Theron was not yet king. Basil had pieced it all together over the long winter nights, a phrase here and a hint there, with the commentary on the spells to help give it all context. He'd started something at MidWinter, lying with Theron when he'd returned from the Hunt, and now the time had come to take the next step. Imprisoned in the city, lost in a labyrinth of stone and mortar and dry, dead wood, he had no connection to the Living Land as the Northern wizards had before him. But he had his dreams and he had his learning, and the ability to analyze data and reason from premise to conclusion. He'd reasoned long and hard, and he had concluded that he and Theron had come together because they had been brought together: by fate, by magic, by the Land that desired, after all these centuries, a wizard and a king to serve it.

Sudden tears blurred Basil's sight. It was too much. He was unworthy, unprepared, untaught. He would never understand the words of the spells he cast, never be a true power-master like Guidry, whose own hand had inscribed the words he studied, or even Pretorius or Ranulph, though their power had been weakened by the South. But his study, his devotion, had taught him what the spells meant and why, deep down in his bones and blood where mere words had no meaning. By some process past his understanding, Basil had become a wizard, and worthy or not, it was his duty, his holy obligation, to set the young king to his trial and bind him at last to the Land.

The Spelle of the Great Tryal was long and complex. Basil read it through once and again, emptying his mind of thought and emotion, filling it with images of green leaves and running waters, of a young man with long dark hair and a stag leaping like a breaking wave through the forest branches.

The third time, he read it aloud.

Theron was on the Hill, in the Randalls' gilded drawing room. He had brought Genevieve a book of colored prints of flowers, since she had said that she liked gardens. Also a book of poetry, since she'd asked him about some he'd quoted to her in a letter. She'd had the ring he'd given her sized to fit her hand. It was one of the Tremontaine rubies, and looked a bit garish on her because her bones were so small and red was not really her color. But it was important that she wear it throughout the engagement. He might, perhaps, have chosen more thoughtfully, but he'd been raised with tales of the ducal family rubies and they meant something to him.

Lady Randall had sent Genevieve to fetch an embroidered cushion that she was almost certain depicted the same flower as one in the book (though Theron knew Genevieve well enough by now to tell that, despite her docile acquiescence, she was sure it did not); meanwhile Lady Randall was discussing the benefits to one's health of drinking vinegar, something he had often heard his mother deride as a fad of the overfed rich. He was being charming and agreeing with her, because he'd found he had no choice—and anyway, what did it matter? It was almost funny. Genevieve brought the pillow, but it was nothing like, and her mother sent her back across the room to look again.

Then Theron smelled green leaves and running water, although the windows were closed and the Randalls' house far from the river. The scent was so strong, he lifted his head and gave a small cry.

The next thing he knew, he had fallen to his knees.

"My dear, what is it?" Lady Randall stood over him, trying to reach beyond her corsets to help him to his feet. Theron's body felt heavy; his sex was a weight between his legs. For once, he had no words to answer. Lady Genevieve hurried to his side in a rustle of skirts.

"No!" he cried hoarsely, arm upraised to fend her off. "Don't—"

The girl's scent filled his nostrils. He tried to stumble to his feet, but his hands still sought the safety of the floor. Her flurried petticoats were attacking him with sharp rustling sounds like something coming at him through the underbrush. The scent of woman overpowered him. He wanted to run toward the scent, but away from the sounds.

He flung up his head and found his balance. "I must go," he gasped. "Please, let me go—"

They were speaking, but he could not understand them. He ran, kicking aside the presents he had brought her, to get to the window, the fresh air. He fumbled with the latch, got it open, and breathed deep. It was the way out. He took it: stumbling over the sill and out through the garden, head high, nostrils flared to catch the scent of danger, running.

⏤

THERON NEVER REALLY REMEMBERED FINDING HIS WAY home to Riverside. It took a long time; he slid from shadow to shadow, afraid to let himself be seen. He moved by scent, away from the gardens and perfume, past the treacherous shops and soapy houses and bitter bloody tanneries, to the clear swift scent of the river and the stone that spanned it, crossing the river to the streets his feet knew in the dark. Night had fallen. Riversiders slipped through the streets to do their arcane business in the city: thieves and cutpurses, whores and rogues of all stripes. They walked past his still and breathing form without even seeing him. At the small, private door of his house he paused, stroking the wood, smelling its oaken grain and the iron that bound it. He peeled his clothing off as he went up the stairs. His own odor of fear and exertion rose to his nostrils; he fell asleep wrapped in the scent and heat of his own body.

Theron woke just at dawn, alert to the singing of the birds. The sky was cool and gray. There was a thirst raging in him so fierce that he poured cold water into his washbasin and drank from it. He pulled on a loose robe and found pen and paper.

"Dear Lady Randall," he wrote, "My behavior yesterday was inexcusable to anyone, but doubly so to one I esteem so highly. Nonetheless I pray you will excuse me more gracefully than I excused myself, and even find it in you to praise me for my swift withdrawal from your fair company, since I was overcome by a malady which, had I stayed, would have inconvenienced every-one." He smiled; he wasn't a rhetorician for nothing. Rereading his letter, he found that he barely recognized the hand. The letters were awkward, ill-shaped. Frowning, Theron rang for Terence. He was famished; he'd had no supper the night before.

"Breakfast," Theron commanded. "Whatever there is, but quickly."

He went back to his letter, a fresh sheet of paper, forming the letters carefully like a penman's exercise: hooks and pots and cir-cles and swirls . . . and found that what he had made was a series of spirals, like a maze. He cast it into the embers; it was flaring brightly when Terence came in with a tray. "Sausages, my lord." The smell filled the room like blood and death. Theron gagged, and reached his washbasin in time to vomit violently into it.

He dictated his note of apology to his mother's secretary; in return, the Randalls sent him a basket of hothouse grapes, which he ate with gratitude. His mother took his pulse, and looked at his tongue and under his eyelids. His pulse, she said, was tumul-tuous. She did not generally believe in bleeding, but he was so hectic that she thought it might do good and help him back to an appetite. Theron wanted to tell her that he would eat as many fruits and salads as anyone cared to bring him, only meat and cheese revolted him; but he felt simultaneously agitated and list-less, reluctant to speak. Sophia sent for her bowl and her lancet; they arrived on a tray, covered by a white napkin. "Hold out your arm, my love," she said, and he did. The steel lifted, flashing bright and sharp, and he gave a full-throated scream that the whole house heard. Sophia stood very still. "Theron," she said softly. He was pressed against the far wall, half twisted in a cur-tain.

"No," he begged, "no, don't cut me, no—"

She soothed him back to himself, and made him a very strong posset, and stood over him while he drank it all down and fell asleep. In his dreams, he was running, always running—and he woke with his muscles aching in unaccustomed places.

BASIL ST CLOUD UTTERED THE LAST OF THE HEAVY, edged words of the ancient spell and fell silent. The air rang around him, as if lightning had just struck nearby, and sparkling rainbows danced in his vision as the echo of his spell faded into the ancient walls.

He found he was standing in the middle of the floor with the Book in his hands. He did not remember rising from his desk. A trembling took his legs and hands, and he hastily sank onto the bed. He was not entirely sure, now, what he had done, or even if it had been entirely he who had done it. The power that had risen in him, had it been his or the Book's, or even Guidry's sleeping in those oddly supple pages until his desire woke it? He couldn't think about it just now, with his head afire. Slowly he closed the Book. And then he slept.

The next day's dawning found Basil St Cloud stretched fully dressed across his unmade bed. He woke with a burning thirst and a sense that the ground had been overnight cut from beneath his feet. He remembered that Theron had betrayed him. And he remembered that he had cast another spell on him.

The book lay by his hand. He opened it to *The Spelle of the Tryal Royalle. By the whyche the True Kynge may be Knowne, or Loose Hymself in the Wode.* He did not remember, now, exactly why he had chosen that spell, or what effect it could be expected to have. It was madness to have cast it. And what had he to show for it? Limbs as weak as damp cloth and a headache like the rumbling of carts and no proof that the spell had worked, or even the possibility of such proof. Unless Theron died, he thought dismally. Or somehow showed himself to be the king.

Whatever his spell-casting may or may not have done, whether he himself were mad or sane, certain things remained unchanged. Theron had abandoned him for the comforts of a noble marriage with his own kind. There was Roger Crabbe to face in a month's time and all the Governors and Doctors of the University to persuade that magic was, or had been, real. And lectures to give and students to train in the pursuit of truth.

Slowly as an old man, Basil St Cloud rose and brushed down his clothes and rinsed his mouth with the rusty water from the yard pump and went out in search of breakfast.

Genevieve Randall wrote to Lord Theron every day, little bulletins about her new perroquet, or the sculpture-viewing party he had missed, or the plans for her wedding dress and her attendants. The world she inhabited seemed small and serene; a nice, safe place to be. When at last Theron felt himself well enough to go out, he dressed with care and set out for the Hill.

Riverside was alive with sharp-bladed sunlight and the buffeting scents of fresh air. Every flash of light caught his eye and made him jump: sun on a windowpane, the ornament on someone's hat, even a speck of mica embedded in stone startled him as he went by. But he was determined to go on. When at last he achieved the Tremontaine stables across the Bridge, he sank into the recesses of his carriage with relief and kept the leather curtains down until they'd reached the Hill.

Lady Randall and her daughter were at home, as they usually were at this hour. Lady Randall, splendid in mole-colored satin, held out a plump hand to him. She smelled of some heavy, floral scent with civet in it. Teeth clenched against nausea, Theron touched her hand to his lips, then turned to Genevieve. There was a faint crease between her blue eyes; her rosy mouth was grave. She exclaimed over his pallor, wondered whether he was quite recovered.

Listening to the high, soft voices, Theron felt as if he'd entered a different world: the colors of their sitting room were so bright, so pure; the smells of dried roses and beeswax so unlike the wood smoke and spice of the Riverside house. They offered him chocolate to drink, but all he wanted was water.

"Such a temperate young man," Lady Randall joked approvingly. "Or is it, my lord, that you'd prefer something stronger?"

Theron sipped the water gratefully. It tasted of metal, very different from the stone well at home. "No, thank you. This is very good."

She rose, businesslike and cheerful. "If you are quite comfortable," she said, "I've been meaning to have a word with

the housekeeper. I'm sure Genevieve will be glad to entertain you."

He had brought his betrothed a little token: a dove carved
from tourmaline. It fit into the palm of his hand; he drew it from
his bosom and held it out to Genevieve, to show her how soft it
lay there. She made a pretty noise, jumping up in a rustle of
taffeta, and bent over his hand to look more closely. He felt her
breath on his upturned fingers. A wisp of her dark, feathery hair
stroked his wrist. Theron gasped, and clenched his fingers on the
bird. She laughed, and pulled at them with her own fluttery fingertips. He could taste the smell of her on his tongue, suffusing
his mouth. His breath came in panting gulps, his body prickled
with sweat, and he began to tremble with the strength of his desire. He knew it was not yet time to touch her, but he had forgotten exactly why.

"Show me the bird," she laughed. "Theron, give it me!"

"I'll show you," he said hoarsely. "Give me your hand—"
And he drew it down to his desire, and closed his eyes. She
tugged against his grip, whimpering.

The door opened, and they sprang apart.

Lady Randall took in the sight of their faces and said, "Are
you well, Lord Theron? You look quite flushed. Please, sit down.
More water?" He heard the tone of her voice, like boiling sugar
syrup, more than he understood the words. He put his nose in the
glass of water, smelling it deeply to bring himself to coolness and
stillness, and drank.

"Lord Theron brought me a bird, Mama," said Genevieve,
much too brightly.

"That was very kind of him. Not a live one, I hope!"

"No," Theron said. "It's made of stone." Carefully he opened
his hand. The carving was washed in sweat. He wiped it with his
handkerchief, and put it on the table.

"What a sweet man you are," said Lady Randall, "to come up
here so soon after your illness with such a nice token. It's what
the poet says, isn't it? 'Two birds in one nest, is always the best.' "
He forced his eyes away from the twin doves of her plump breasts,
rising above her tight, brown bodice. "But I do think it is impor-

tant for you not to tire yourself. Genevieve, have you thanked
Lord Theron for his gift?"

She darted a glance at him, a flash of blue like a bird folding
its wings. "Thank you," she whispered. "I will cherish it."

Theron's carriage was sent for, and once again he drew the
leather curtains so that he could have privacy for his needs. As
the wheels jolted over the cobblestones of the city, he dreamed in
a haze of woodland glades and soft-breasted birds and delicious,
undying pleasure.

A S THE DOOR CLOSED ON LORD THERON, LADY
Randall turned to her daughter, who was staring at the little dove with something like loathing. Lady Randall took a deep
breath and began: "My love. Now that you're betrothed . . ."

Genevieve began to weep in the overwrought, gusty way her
mother particularly disliked. Lady Randall cast her eyes to
heaven. "Genevieve! Stop that at once. It's all very well to be
sensitive and high-strung, but not if you're going to carry on over
a kiss like a serving-girl."

"He didn't kiss me," Genevieve sobbed. "I wanted him to
kiss me."

"Well." Extracting a lace handkerchief from her tight
sleeve, Lady Randall gave it to her daughter, and silently cursed
randy young bucks who couldn't wait until the wedding feast
was over before drinking the bridal cup. She had not planned to
have this discussion for weeks yet. When Genevieve had
reached the sniffling and mopping stage, Lady Randall said, "I
won't ask you what he did—you're perfectly all right, after all,
and you *are* betrothed. If he frightened you, I blame myself
entirely for not having explained—certain things to you before now."

Whereupon Genevieve's mother launched into a general description of the joys of the marriage-bed, with particular attention to how pleasant it could be for the bride, especially if the
groom was experienced.

"At least we know Lord Theron is experienced," Genevieve observed with unbecoming asperity.

"My love!" Lady Randall raised a shocked hand to her throat. "I hope you've not been listening to backstairs gossip."

"He told me himself, when he proposed. I said I didn't mind. And I don't. It's not that." Her color rose. "I rather liked that."

"Ah," said her mother doubtfully. "Then what has occurred to distress you?"

Genevieve lowered her eyes to the damp cambric balled in her hands. "Well. He behaved . . . *oddly*, Mama. Not at all as he did before we were betrothed."

Lady Randall shrugged. "My love, all men behave oddly between the betrothal and the wedding. And he's been ill, remember? You must not make too much of it."

"No, Mama. But when he left us so suddenly that time he took sick, he acted so strangely. And his letters . . ." She picked at the handkerchief.

Lady Randall studied her daughter's face, dry now and fast returning to its usual charming color. "To be frank with you," Lady Randall said, "his family has a great reputation for . . . eccentricity. His father's life was very irregular, and his grandfather lived very much out of the world. Luckily, the Tremontaine men have always shown great good sense in their choice of wives. Why, the last duchess—the current duchess's great-aunt—was only a Tremontaine by marriage. Her husband's—indisposition—allowed her the entire guidance of his land and fortune."

She waited hopefully while Genevieve took this in, with all its implications. The expressive features passed from bewilderment to comprehension to dismay. "Mama!" The blue eyes were very wide. "I don't want to be married to a madman!"

Lady Randall realized she'd made a tactical error. "I never said a word about madness," she said severely. "I only said he might be eccentric. And there's nothing eccentric about his being over-eager—it's a tribute to your beauty, my love. You ought to be flattered. Why, there are married women who have to turn to other lovers for that kind of passion. Think how lucky you are, to be gaining both position and pleasure in one man." She gave her daughter's unquiet hands a dismissive pat. "Better? Good. The seamstress will be here soon with your bride-gown. Run up to your room now, and bathe your eyes. They're a little swollen."

Like the good daughter she was, Genevieve obeyed, leaving the handkerchief balled up on the sofa behind her. When Lady Randall opened it, it fell into shreds. She shook her head. Bridal nerves, she thought. He probably put his hand on her breast. These Campions are sadly flighty. It is to be hoped he doesn't make her too unhappy.

book IV

SPRING

chapter I

SPRING CAME TO THE CITY. THE DAYS WERE GROW-
ing longer. The snow had melted from all but the dark-
est and most stubborn of corners. Crocuses sprang from
muddy crevices and, in back gardens, tender leaves began tenta-
tively to unfurl. Fellowship examinations loomed, turning students' attention to their studies. Basil St Cloud cut the number of
his lectures from four a week to two, and released his students
from their archival burrowing.

"This is all wonderfully useful," he told them, turning over
the latest batch of offerings. "I haven't the words to thank you."

"There's no need to thank us," said Lindley. "It's our duty."

"Besides, we've learned a lot," Blake said.

"And sneezed a lot," Vandeleur added.

"And disturbed the ancestral homes of countless spiders,"
Fremont went on.

"And mice," Godwin finished, not to be left out.

St Cloud laughed. "Well, you can leave them in peace now.
I've come to a point where I need to go down there myself. It's no
reflection on your abilities, my friends: there are rooms students

can't get into, even with a magister's permission. You've done well."

Vandeleur, who had not enjoyed the Archives, insisted that they celebrate their deliverance from spiders and dust in a blow-out at the Spotted Cow. "Just think," he said. "Out of University, sewing-girls by the dozen, and the best music in the city. Come on. It's spring."

Lindley, predictably, declined. And Godwin was expected at home. So it was just Vandeleur, Blake, and Fremont, and a high time they had of it, spending their last coppers on salmon and roast potatoes and good wine like men of taste, and dancing with all the prettiest girls. At least Vandeleur and Fremont danced. Justis spent most of the evening in earnest conversation with a brown-haired milliner's apprentice. She was country-bred, plump as a partridge in all the right places, with eyes as bright as a running brook and a sweet, soft laugh. Before the night was out, she'd told him all about her parsimonious mistress, who made her apprentices buy their own wood or sit sewing in the cold, and her mother in Swinton, and all her brothers and sisters, working back home to keep the farm. They danced twice and when they parted, she'd kissed him sweetly on the mouth. Justis was in love.

After that night, the inner circle of St Cloud's followers began to drift apart, and Henry Fremont found himself very much at a loose end. He went to lectures and he haunted the Nest, where he did his best to keep up Historians' Corner with Godwin and a few other students who fancied themselves as academic radicals. But he still had plenty of free time left over in which to worry.

The Northerner's visit had frightened Henry badly. In the lonely deeps of the night, he fretted over past crimes: his and the Northerners', actual and possible. What if the Companions of the King really were plotting to bring back the monarchy? What if Lindley, despite his oath, had told them of the meeting in the grove? What if Finn had not killed himself after all, but been a bloody sacrifice to their precious Land? What if, by some mischance, they discovered Henry's role in this series of imprisonments and betrayals?

And then Henry would remember Finn lying in the snow, a marble statue inexplicably toppled and sprinkled with scarlet paint, and the knowledge that he had been responsible gnawed at him like a rat. The end of it was that he decided to find Justis Blake and tell him all about it.

Justis was not particularly pleased to be found. Being a practical man, he had quickly realized that he could not keep both himself and his lady-love in fuel and food on the few silvers his father allowed him each term. So he compounded with a paper-seller in Lassiter's Row to set up a table in his shop for five coppers a week and became a public letter-writer.

And that was where Henry found him, solemnly taking dictation from an elderly lady in a red flannel shawl, who wanted to tell her son that she couldn't attend the birth of his third child.

The old lady described the misery in her back and legs that kept her from walking the twenty leagues to Endersby and the poverty that kept her from buying a place on the coach; Justis scribbled and suggested deletions and emendations. Henry fidgeted among the stacks of paper and board. Finally, the letter was written to her satisfaction and sealed with wax, three coppers were counted out into Justis's inky hand, and she was hobbling out in search of a post courier.

Henry folded his lanky frame into the client's chair. Justis frowned. "Go away, Fremont. I'm working."

Henry cocked his eye at the empty shop, the bored young man keeping it, and the window, fast darkening with dusk. "No, you're not. There's nobody here, and it's going to be dark soon, and that boy is aching to put up the shutters and have his supper. There's a little place around the corner with a nice smell coming out the door. Come talk to me, and I'll buy you whatever's making it. Come on, Justis. If you eat lightly, you can take what's left to your sweetheart."

Justis hemmed and Justis hawed, fearing that this unprecedented generosity was likely to come at a high price, but in the end, he went with Fremont, and listened to his story between bites of roast beef and dried pease porridge.

He'd been right. The price was high. Fremont's description of his seduction by Galing and Tielman made his teeth itch, though he was unsure which of that self-righteous trio angered him the most. Fremont, he thought, who had sold his honor for a few silver coins and a chance to feel important. Galing and Tielman were just acting according to their stations. Fremont had chosen to betray his friends.

Which is what he told Fremont, once he came to a halt. Fremont, who rather thought he should be praised for his honesty, began to justify himself, and Blake said, "Don't, Henry. Please. You did what you did for reasons that seemed good to you at the time. If they seemed good to you still, I doubt you'd be asking me for absolution. Well, I can't give it to you. Of course you hold yourself responsible for Finn's death. I do too."

Furious, Fremont called Blake names and offered to fight him. Blake kept eating calmly, leaving him to sputter himself to a standstill. Finally, Fremont poked at his untouched roast beef, drained his pot of beer, sighed heavily, and said, "You're right. I'm a worm, and I shit myself whenever I think what those Northern madmen might take it into their heads to do to me. What am I to do?"

"Land, Henry, I don't know. It depends on what you want to accomplish. If you're afraid of the Companions, you'd better slip out on a south-bound boat and go study foreign history at the University of Elysia. Personally, I think they're all flash and no fight, but then, I haven't gotten three of them thrown in jail. If you want to mend the harm you've done, you can't. You can, however, warn Doctor St Cloud that the Council of Nobles isn't as uninterested in University politics as he'd thought."

Fremont went even paler than he already was. "I was only trying to help him," he said. "I was trying to prove that he was innocent of any connection with the Companions. And I think I succeeded."

"Then you won't mind telling him about it," said Blake serenely.

"What about Finn? I thought we'd agreed Doctor St Cloud wasn't to be upset."

Blake looked grim. "He doesn't need to know about that

right now. Just the bit about the Council." He wiped his mouth on his sleeve. "Are you going to tell him or not?"

"I don't know," said Fremont miserably. "I need to think."

"I don't," said Blake, rising. "I'm going to go tell him now. You can come with me or not, as you like."

Henry wiped his mouth and rose with him. What else could he do? There was no telling what Blake would make of his story to St Cloud. And a man must make his own apologies, after all— it was only right.

Justis smiled as though he'd been watching the progress of Henry's thoughts through a window in his head. "Good man," he said, and the two students went out into the evening air.

The streets of the Middle City were always crowded at this time of night. Shop girls, apprentices and clerks, merchants in fur-lined cloaks, and whores in second-hand velvet jostled one another on the narrow walkways, heading toward home or supper. Carts splashed through the mud; carriages and chairs conveyed the rich to their evening's entertainment. A curtained chair went by, carried by four stout men in brown livery: Lady Randall going to Riverside to take supper with her future in-laws.

It was full night, damply cold but without the sting of winter. At home, Justis thought, the willows would be blushing gold, the whitethorn buds would be swelling toward blossom, and the early lambs would be robbing his father's men of their night's sleep. Was farming a better life than learning? he wondered. It was certainly simpler, both practically and morally, and it produced something of undoubted worth. And it did not usually lead to fistfights and intrigues and corpses in the wood. Perhaps he should marry Marianne, take her out of this infernal city they both hated. His mother would like Marianne, he was sure.

Fremont had no such pleasant reflections to shorten his way, but trod the paths of self-disgust he'd worn into his soul. When they reached Minchin Street, he was almost eager to confess himself to Doctor St Cloud and receive either his forgiveness or his just punishment.

There was no answer to Blake's knock or his call, but the latch lifted when he tried it, and no outcry greeted the opening door or their timid entrance. The room was dark, save for one candle burning on a long table drifted deep in books and papers and a low fire smoldering in the narrow hearth. A man sat beside it, his hands folded around a book on his lap. When he heard the door, he turned, regarded Blake and Fremont blankly, and turned again to the fire.

"Doctor St Cloud?" It was a real question. The young doctor's face was gray, unshaven, his eyes red and strained. The room smelled of damp and ink and old, musty books.

"Go away," he said. "I'm working."

Fremont made a choking noise that might have been a laugh and might have been a sob. Blake glared at him, daring him to flee. Fremont glared back. "It's Fremont, sir," he said, holding Blake's gaze. "Fremont and Blake. We have something to tell you."

"It must wait until the test is done." Doctor St Cloud's voice, at least, was as it had always been, deep and clear and reasonable.

"I'm afraid it can't wait, sir," said Blake apologetically. "Not until the debate, at any rate."

Fremont decided to grasp the poker by the hot end. "It's about the debate, you see. Lord Nicholas Galing thought you were trying to restore the monarchy. He—"

St Cloud lifted his hand to stop him. "I don't often have guests," he said apologetically. "This is my only chair." He gestured toward the bed. "Please, sit. Who is Lord Nicholas Galing, and how did he come to be interested in me?"

For the second time that night, Fremont told his story. It wasn't as bad as the first time. To be sure, Blake was radiating disapproval as a tanner's yard radiates stink, but Doctor St Cloud listened to his every word with an eager intensity, nodding from time to time, asking questions when Henry faltered.

"Interesting," he said at last. "These nobles are a suspicious crew, imagining threats to their power and influence behind every bush and under every black robe. They have been so since Alcuin came South, and probably before. They disliked the kings. But the wizards they hated." He looked down at the fat leather-bound book he held in his hands.

Silence lengthened. Henry shifted his seat on the hard mattress, but Doctor St Cloud made no sign he'd heard. It was as if he'd forgotten the existence of his two visitors.

"Beg pardon, sir," said Justis Blake tightly. "Is that all?"

Doctor St Cloud glanced up. "Is what all?"

"Fremont here tells you he's been spying on you for some noble who is looking for evidence of a monarchist plot, and all you've said is that you find his tale interesting." Blake was clearly struggling to keep his tone properly respectful. "Aren't you worried?" he continued. "These men put Finn and Lindley in the Chop, and a couple of Northerners, too. We didn't want to tell you this, but you need to know. Alaric Finn is dead. He killed himself when he was released. The Northerners have disappeared. This is serious business, sir. I'd be worried, were I you."

Doctor St Cloud smiled gently. "Justis Blake. Dear, responsible Justis Blake. What a Crescent you would make, were you born noble. This news, for all its gravity, is the smallest of the ills that torment me. This is a time of testing for all of us—for you and for me, for Lord Galing and his master, for Theron Campion and his bride, for the parrot Crabbe, and for those Northern fools who call themselves the Companions of the King."

Fremont said, "If I've been tested, I've failed miserably. I might as well kill myself, like poor Finn, and be done with it."

"You've failed only if you think the test is over," said St Cloud. "The Feast of Sowing approaches, but has not yet come." With sudden energy, he pulled his chair up to the long table and laid the book on the papers. "Thank you for coming to warn me, Blake, Fremont. It was kindly and well done. You remind me that I have a great deal of work to do. I think I shall be forced to suspend my lectures completely until the challenge has been fought. Please tell the others."

He glanced encouragingly toward the door and watched as first Fremont, and then Blake, reluctantly rose from the bed and walked out to the stairwell. Fremont descended straightaway, but Blake turned in the door and said, "What will you do, sir?"

Doctor St Cloud scrubbed his face with both hands. "Work, Blake. I need to work. Now go away and leave me alone."

Feeling as though the world had gone mad and he the only sane man left in it, Blake slammed the door and pounded down the steps. He needed a drink; he needed to lose himself in Marianne's sweet body. Doctor St Cloud and the rest of it would be there in the morning, as his mother used to say. Tonight, he'd had enough.

THERON REMAINED IN THE SAFETY OF HIS BELOVED house. He did not think it wise to see Genevieve again. Her letters, coming to him scented with her skin, sent him to his bed for relief. The thought of her dark hair lifted off her neck made him shiver. The wedding was a good idea. In a few months, he could satisfy himself on her whenever he wished. He wished it could be sooner. Perhaps they could move it up. How long could it take to plan a wedding, anyway?

Meanwhile, he prowled the odd and twisting corridors of the Riverside house, looking for diversion. There was something he needed, but nothing interested him. He could not read. He tried poetry, science, even sensational romances, but the words were only words, sounds represented by hard black shapes; he could not seem to get them to cling together and make sense. He could, he thought, listen to music. He would like that. But Sophia kept no musicians. So he drifted out into the streets of Riverside, looking for some.

Toward the end of the day, the island began to come awake. Theron wandered past tavern doors, listening for the sound of someone playing. At the Awl in Owl, an old blind Northern harper, who made music when he wasn't too drunk and his harp wasn't in pawn, had struck up a tune. The tavern stench of people and beer and boiling grease was too strong for Theron; but he leaned against an outside shutter, glad of the cool air, listening. He wanted to weep for love of the music and love of the people who were united with him in listening and loving it, too. A man came out of the tavern and nearly pissed on his boots in the twilight. When the man saw him, he swore and pulled out a knife, but Theron said, "Hush. Hush," and drew silver from his purse, and gave it to the man to give to the harper.

He dreamed that night of a wild harping, a tune like the

blind man's but more filled with ornament, played by a man with gold around his wrists. Theron and his companions danced with knives, a pattern that allowed for no misstep. At first it was hard, but then it was easy. They knew they were being watched, and held their heads high, flashing their braided hair in the torch-light, their bodies nearly naked, their skin oiled and shining. Under a canopy, a group of men dressed in furs stood watching them dance. He felt the eyes of one upon him, heating the oil on his skin.

In the morning he was exhausted. He lay in bed until nearly noon, and then decided he should go to the Randalls', and then decided that he should not. Instead he wrote Genevieve a letter all about his longing for her. He judged it quite fitting and poetic until he read it over and discovered it contained obscenities. He went down to the library, and word by word, copied out a love poem by Aria. He had discovered that if he wrote each word without looking at the next, he could do it clearly. At the end of the poem he added the line, "He speaks for me," and signed it.

The next day, Genevieve wrote back to say she liked the poem, and wondered if he could tell her more about the author. He decided that a literary engagement would do very well, in-deed—for one thing, it would be nice if she knew something about poetry when they were married. Theron took himself up to the bookshops of Lassiter's Row to find something suitable. He found an Aria nicely bound and asked to have it delivered.

"Will you inscribe it, sir?" the bookseller asked. Theron took the pen, and could think of nothing to write but, "For G with love from TC." Who was TC? he wondered. Did those lines and curves really represent him?

"The pen, sir?"

He had been drawing on his own hand, *TC*, covering himself with the letters. "Oh," he laughed, and the man laughed with him, and Theron left, blushing.

To steady himself, he walked into a jeweler's he knew; Katherine had taken him there to choose a ring for himself when he turned eighteen, a setting for one of the Tremontaine rubies. The jeweler recognized Lord Theron. He was sufficiently up on the gossip of the nobility to congratulate him on his engagement.

"And if you're looking for a gift for the happy lady, my lord, we have a few little trinkets that I can show you."

Theron looked at lockets and rings and brooches, but nothing caught his fancy. The jeweler smiled, and made a respectful quip about young love. "Well," he concluded, "another time. But meanwhile I will show my lord something very splendid—a piece of work such as doesn't come along every day." He unlocked a leather case and brought it forth for inspection. "Weeks, my man was, working on this." It was a collar, a necklace, all in well-wrought gold, each piece shaped and carved in a pleasing harmony of curves and curls. Its base was hung with moonstones like drops of water. Or tears, Theron thought, or the semen that glistens on the tip of a man's tool.

"I'll have this," he said. "For my bride. A bride-gift. It's appropriate. Please have it sent, and put it on my account."

"Will that be the duchess's account, my lord, or would you prefer to open your own account now for your new household?"

His new household? Yes, he'd discussed all this with Marcus, with Katherine, and with lawyers. On his marriage, Theron's revenues would be increased, properties signed over to him; Genevieve's family, of course, was providing some of them. His wife would want to buy jewels for herself, and she might buy them here, on credit. "My own account," he said, "please."

He went home and wrote to Marcus that he had exceeded his current funds. He dug the bill out of his pocket. The necklace cost the same as a carriage, more than most people earned in a year. *Far* exceeded his current funds, and could Marcus please see that the bill was covered by advancing money from his Highcombe rents—no. He drew a hard black line through the name, and the pen spluttered ink all over the page. Not Highcombe. He'd not ask Basil's family to pay for his bride-gift. He put his head down on his ink-stained fist, and rubbed the place where it ached, the temples from which Ysaud had painted springing horns. He wanted Basil. Basil needed no gold, no jewels; Basil was a fur coverlet in a wooden bed; Basil was a chest full of rare books; Basil was nights and days that flowed into each other without boundary.

"Lord of my heart," he wrote, "lord of my pulsing blood—I

live to offend you and to make good the fault. I live because of you. The woods are thick, but I will find you and kneel at your feet, and you will return me to myself. Please advance me the revenues of whatever you can find that is not already my father's, something that is mine or will be mine when I have tied myself to the Land."

W HEN MARCUS FFOLIOT READ THERON'S NOTE, much blackened with crossings-out and insertions, he set out at once for Riverside. It was an uncharacteristic thing for him to do; it was as if Theron's own impetuousness had infected him. And, indeed, after a little walking had given his fancy a chance to cool, Marcus altered his direction and went instead to a much closer house, the house of his eldest daughter, Diana.

He found her in the nursery, which gave them the pleasure of adoring a very small baby together.

"You've heard," Marcus began, wiping drool off his shoulder, "Lord Theron is getting married."

"Mother told me. It's odd; he seems so young."

Her father smiled. "He's older than you were when you married Martin."

Diana shrugged. "Theron isn't practical. Always with his head in a book, or else helplessly in love with someone—I was going to say, someone unsuitable, but clearly this girl's not unsuitable. Do you want your lambie?"—this last addressed to the restless baby, who was gnawing on her sleeve. "Da, get his lamb, would you? It's on the chest."

"He's trying to be practical. But, as you say, it doesn't come naturally." Marcus handed the lamb to his grandson.

"Yum, yum, my sweetikins! What's she like, his intended? She doesn't paint, I hope?" Diana added acerbically.

Marcus chuckled. "I don't know. Perhaps you should ask him. You and Isabel, I mean."

His daughter smiled a private smile. "Is this a *duchess* perhaps or a *Sophia* perhaps?"

"It is a *Ffoliot* perhaps. I don't want to bore you with

details—" She grinned; this was longstanding family code for *It's none of your business* "—but I think he is not altogether sure of what he wants. He seems to be trying both to please and to annoy his elders. We are useless appendages, my dear, fit only for signing over large sums of money. Which I admit I am very good at. But perhaps—well, you're near his age. And you're already married. Theron might benefit from your experience."

"*And* we know all his tricks. If this is just another stupid crush gone too far, we'll have it out of him before dinner."

THERON WAS GLAD OF THE INVITATION TO VISIT WITH the twins. It kept him from thinking about going to the University. It was as if parts of the city had become closed to him—marked DANGER as clearly as if he'd seen a map printed with the sign. He wanted so badly to see Basil; but where Basil was, it was not safe for him to go. In the streets of University, someone would notice him, and ask him a question he could not answer; they would see what he was, and what he was not, and men with bells and torches would harry him through the wood by night. On the Hill, there was the danger of Genevieve, and his cousin the duchess. And between the Hill and Riverside were shops where jewels could be had at a price he could not pay.

Isabel lived in the Middle City, well across the river from University—below the Hill, beyond the docks, in a district of small shops and artisans. Her husband, Carlos, was a musician; their rooms were far less grand than the little house Diana's banker had bought, but Isabel's place was closer to Riverside. He supposed that was the reason they'd chosen it to meet with him.

The girls smelt warm and milky when he hugged them. "Ooh!" Isabel tweaked the braid in his hair. "Love-knot?"

Blushing, he undid it with his fingers. He kept finding them—he must be doing it without thinking, weaving little braids in when he was trying to read or write.

Diana asked, "Are you going to cut your hair for the wedding? Oh, where are my manners?" She held out a formal hand.

"Please accept our sincere best wishes for your future happiness. Now tell us everything!"

The rooms were sun-washed, white-walled, clear of all but the most basic furniture, though what there was was well-made. Theron recognized the carpet he'd sent, in a place of honor on the dining-table. By far the most costly and beautiful thing in the place was an elaborate keyboard, Carlos's instrument. "Is he out?" Theron asked. "I'd love to hear some music later."

Isabel glowed. "He should play you his new variations, then. I think they are absolutely beautiful, but he's still fussing to get them perfect for Lady Montague's spring revels."

Theron nodded.

"Tell us about your bride," they demanded. "Is she pretty?"

"Very."

"I do wish that we could meet your lady first. Da has, but he won't say a word. I suppose you've been giving grand suppers up at Tremontaine House for her family and all."

Isabel said wistfully, "If only we were younger—we could dress up some night as serving maids at supper and spy on the whole thing!"

"Wicked, Is. We'll see her at the wedding."

"And after— Oh, Theron," Isabel took his hands, "you will bring her to dinner at Katherine's with us? Family dinners, I mean?"

He tried and failed to imagine the small, quiet Lady Genevieve sitting at table with Katherine in a brocade loose gown pitching breadcrumbs at Marcus, while the twins and Sophia discussed nursery diets.

Holding his gaze, Isabel's eyes filled with tears. "Is that what this means, then? That you're going to go all lordly and grownup and leave the family?"

"How could I?" he whispered. "You are my family." He kissed her cheek. Her sister's head was on her shoulder. "I'll still come to dinner, even if Genevieve doesn't care to," he said. He looked at the two women, mirrors of each other even to their motherly gowns, coifed hair, and ringed hands, standing with their arms around each other's waists, as they always had. "How can you ask me such a thing?" Theron demanded. "You're the ones who did it first—went out and found husbands and left us all."

They looked at each other, and only they understood what the look meant.

Isabel said abruptly, "There's fruit and cheese and barley water; I didn't think anyone would want chocolate at this hour."

The food was set out on the table like a still life, with pearl-handled fruit knives and painted plates. Just as they were sitting down, there was a yelp and a cry from the other room. Isabel's hands flew up to cover the stain seeping through her bodice.

A child came in carrying the squalling infant, which was half as big as she was. Isabel unlaced her bodice and put the baby to her breast.

Theron gazed on the nursing child, at its perfect little fingers and the almond-shaped eyelids closed in bliss as it suckled. The most precious thing in the world, warm and soft and alive, new with possibility. He wanted to hold the baby close, to defend it against all comers. He wanted such a one of his own getting. If only he had started sooner—if he had married Isabel, or Diana, it might be his child now that the woman held to her rich, round breast. He would create one soon, he and Genevieve; he would remember, when his life throbbed and pulsed within her at last, that when it burst into joy, its purpose was to make such a child, his child.

There was a heavy step outside the door. Mother and child sat very still, defenseless, lost in a milky feeding world of their own. Theron closed his fingers around a knife, and stood waiting for the door to open, for the intruder to reveal himself. He breathed softly, quietly, ready to spring.

The door opened slowly, slowly, and the man announced his presence by hooting like an owl. Theron tensed.

"Shh!" Isabel whispered; "she's nearly asleep!"

"Papa's home!" Carlos crooned, and Theron dropped the knife. "Shh!" the women hissed. The baby whimpered, then fell silent. Theron's heart was pounding; his skin tingled from the fight that had not happened. He had no name for what he felt: the love and the need to kill something, both at once, both focused on the sleeping child, and on Isabel, his old friend, now transformed under his protection.

He put a hand on Carlos's shoulder. "Take care of her," he said, his voice thick with this new passion.

Carlos never took his eyes off his wife and child. "Oh, *she* takes care of *me*."

Theron's hand tightened. "I mean it."

"Of course."

Theron embraced him. "I want to hear your music. But not now. Come to Riverside; I'll have the spinet tuned. Music is very good." And to the women he said, "Thank you for—for a lovely day."

Diana glanced up from the little head. "Oh, Theron—can you not stay? We'd so much to tell you."

"I'm sorry," Theron said. "I must go. Now." It sounded ungracious, even unfriendly, but that was better than staying and doing he knew not what.

Carlos said, "Please give Lady Sophia our fondest regards."

"I will. I'll tell her about the baby." He smiled helplessly around at them all. "Goodbye."

When the door closed behind him, the sisters looked at each other. "I'll put her back to bed," said Is, and Diana said, "No, let me."

"Let me," said Carlos, so of course they let him.

Isabel looked over her table, still neatly spread except for one fruit knife, which was lying on the floor. "He didn't eat."

"It's bad," said Diana.

"It's worse than bad. He doesn't love this one at all."

"He's miserable. He's so nervous I can barely stand to be in the room with him." Diana picked up the knife and an apple, and angrily began to peel it. "I wish we could just march up to that Randall chit and tell her to leave him alone!"

Isabel hugged her. "What should we do?"

"We should probably tell Lady Sophia."

"What? That he's not in love with his intended? I expect she knows."

"If only she'd cry off," Diana said.

"Why doesn't *he* cry off? Take back the proposal, say he's changed his mind?"

Her sister the banker's wife looked at her with patient exasperation. "Papa's already drawn up the contracts. Theron can't break them now."

"But Genevieve Randall can?"

Diana drummed her fingers. "It is the woman's right. But for a lord to reject his contracted bride—well, for all of the things that men may do to us with impunity, it should be comforting to know that this is not one of them."

"Hmm." Isabel fiddled with her laces. "I say, do it anyway. What's the worst thing that could happen?"

"For her? It implies that he has found fault with her—judged her and found her wanting somehow. No one else would be in a hurry to offer for her. It could ruin her life. It's an insult, anyway."

"In the old days, it would have meant a swordsman for sure. A challenge to Theron, maybe even to the death. Do the Randalls keep a swordsman?"

"How do I know? They could certainly hire one. But even if they didn't, it would make him look bad. People would start up again talking about how rackety the Campions are, and bringing up old stuff about Katherine, and—and Lady Sophia. The next time Theron picked a bride, the contract would be brutal."

"She *must* cry off!"

"Why should she? He's a catch."

"Maybe she's really very nice."

"I doubt it," Diana said gloomily. "He's always had abominable taste in women."

Isabel said quietly, "Di. Did you ever wish that you and Theron—"

Diana looked at her sharply. "Of course not."

"Oh. It's just that, that summer we were sixteen, you were on at him all the time, and at home you talked about him."

"Well, what else was there to talk about?" Diana asked fiercely; "Andy's cough? Theron had an interesting life; we didn't." She laid the apple on a plate, cut neatly in quarters. "Meeting Martin was the best thing that ever happened to me. I love banking."

Isabel deemed it wise to change the subject. "By the way," she said, "Mother told me they've invited Jessica to the wedding."

"No! She'll never come!"

"Of course she will—if the invitation finds her. She's out there somewhere, on that ship of hers. If anything would bring her home, I'd think it would be the chance to see her brother get married."

In the next room, music began.

Isabel said, "Let's eat."

chapter II

I T WAS NO GOOD, THERON THOUGHT; WHEREVER HE
went it was no good. The things he wanted were all wrong,
and he wanted them with a gut-twisting fierceness. He
wanted Genevieve for the easing of his body, and because he
thought she meant he'd have to give up nothing; instead, he had
lost the thing he valued most. Which was Basil.

He had a hazy memory of some kind of quarrel—Basil
wanted him to be king, that was it. And he'd been angry because
he thought Basil didn't understand who he really was. Theron remembered himself as being independent, a scholar, a thinker,
even a poet: a man of discriminating tastes. But he was none of
those things, now. Basil had been right after all. Basil had told
Theron the truth over and over about himself: he was his blood,
his blood, and nothing but his blood. And Theron had laughed,
argued, ignored what he'd heard.

Despite his fear of University, he would go back to Basil, and
agree to everything and end this torment. He would be whatever
Basil wanted him to be. Together they would rut like stags in autumn; he would find ease and comfort, acceptance and under-

standing. His was the blood of kings—*Mad kings*, a voice inside him whispered. *Are you ready, little prince, to do what they must do?*

"What must I do?" he cried aloud, and started at the sound of his own words.

Terence tapped on the door, and entered. "Yes, my lord?"

It took all his strength to keep from hurling something at his servant. "Don't come in," he said tightly, "unless I bid you."

"I thought I heard you call, sir," Terence said patiently.

"I did call, but not to you. Leave me."

"With respect, sir—"

"How can you respect me?" Theron demanded. "You clean my dirty clothes—my dirty body— What is this *me* that you respect?"

Taking a deep breath first, the servant replied, "My lord. Theron. Your nerves are in a perilous state. I would walk across the city to get you the remedy, but I don't know where it is to be found."

"Not," said Theron, "among my mother's medicines."

Terence stood there, his capable hands hanging empty at his sides. When his master said nothing more, he asked, "Is it the dreams, sir?"

"Dreams? What dreams?" Theron said.

Terence looked down. "As my lord says, I know his habits better than most."

Theron had told no one of the dreams. He suddenly wanted to spill everything to this calm, familiar figure. Terence was never shocked. Terence was competent. He would find a way, some way to relieve him of his burden, as he found ways to remove a grease stain from a jacket. He said, "Terence, I need a wizard."

His servant smiled at the joke. When Theron did not smile back, he said, "A wizard, sir?"

"Yes."

"What . . . sort of wizard, sir?"

Theron stared at him. "Get out," he shouted.

The manservant looked as if he would say something—but then, without a word, he bowed and closed the door behind him. In a fever of rage and despair, Theron pulled clothes from a chest and dressed himself and left the house.

D AY AFTER DAY, BASIL SANK DEEPER INTO HIS WORK. Martindale's history of the wizards, Karleigh's memoirs, Arioso's daybooks, the long lists of wizards and the pedigrees of the kings, the ballads and the legends and the festivals, the notes and fragments his students had found for him in the Archives: these were his whole world. And the Book, always the Book, tempting him with small spells of finding and persuasion to aid him in his task. Nothing else existed. Enemies, friends, false lover, all were as the wax that puddled and hardened at the base of his candlestick: the residue of flames long dark and cold. He ate only what the scruffy boy, unasked, brought him from the cookshop once a day, and slept only when the pen fell from his cramping hand and his heavy eyes pulled his head down onto the papers in front of him.

He hated sleeping. Sleep wasted time. Sleep brought dreams as sharp and bright as the stained glass in the Great Hall, dreams of rushing through the streets of University, late for a lesson, tossing his long hair back from his face, tugging his tunic straight, bending his head for his magister's salute, learning to bring fire from a stone.

"Guidry was the last to speak the Old Tongue," his magister said, his sorrowful eyes fixed on the green flame licking out of a hunk of turquoise. "He didn't want anyone to know all he knew. And now we know so little, with more lost every year. I wonder if he knows, Guidry the Deathless, wherever he is sleeping. I wonder if he cares?"

I care, Basil heard a voice whisper as he woke from that dream, and immediately went to drown the memory in clean water. But the pitcher was empty, the chamberpot full, the hearth cold, and the air colder still from the thin spring rain. Cursing, Basil huddled on a coat and gown, excavated a few coins from various caches, and left his room for the first time in days.

Some little thread of common sense told him that he was filthy and hungry and cold to the bone, that the Governors would judge against him unheard if they saw him in this state. So he went to the baths, and then to a quiet tavern he'd never visited before, which turned out to serve a very decent roast of mutton and young salad. On the way home, he stopped by the wood-monger's and ordered a bushel to be delivered to Minchin Street. Feeling more himself than he had since the night of his quarrel with Theron, he thought as he crossed Kingsway to Minchin, Of course it wasn't a spell. If there was magic once, there isn't any longer, and besides, I have no training. He's just tired of me, and I'm well rid of him.

At the street door, Basil smiled at the scruffy boy, who smiled nervously back and said he was sorry, but the gentleman wouldn't have it that the master weren't seeing no visitors, and if Doctor St Cloud wanted, he'd go for the Watch, for he didn't think anything short of that would discourage him. Justis, St Cloud thought ruefully, gave the boy a copper, and thanked him for his many kindnesses. The boy blushed and grinned, took the copper and said he didn't mind. Basil ruffled his greasy hair and mounted the stairs with a light step, ready to tease Justis for being a nurse-maid.

But it wasn't Justis sitting outside his door. It was Theron, his knees drawn up, his head down, his hair like a fine silk shawl draped over all.

The sight of him worked on Basil like a blow. He gasped and clutched the railing to keep from falling, to keep from running forward and taking Theron into his arms or striking him across the impossibly beautiful face he raised from his knees.

Theron was thinner than he had been, his cheeks gaunt, his eyes huge and liquid under bruised lids. He was dressed in brown and fawn, with a gold drop in his ear and a lovelock braided into his hair, and he looked haunted, hunted, hungry as a stag before the snow releases the grass in springtime. The air was thick with the smell of musk.

Basil worked his mouth, trying to find something to say. "Get up," he managed at last. "You're in the way."

Obediently, Theron scrambled to his feet, hesitating with his hands braced against the floor as if he wasn't sure whether he could stand upright. Basil thought he saw horns springing in the hollows of his temples where Basil had once kissed him. Then Theron straightened and moved politely aside, allowing Basil to come up the last steps, unlock the door, and open it.

"You may as well come in," Basil snapped. "I'm not inclined to quarrel with you on the public stair."

Theron bowed his head, stepped delicately over the threshold, and halted, his nostrils flaring as he tasted the air. He snorted, backed up a step.

Basil growled with impatience. "Come *in*, damn it! And close the door. I'm not your servant."

White was showing all around the greenish pupils, and the fine body was trembling in its fine clothes, but Theron closed the door as he'd been told. Then he paced forward through the wadded paper and spoiled pens and books, knelt at Basil's feet, and leaned his head against Basil's leg.

By this time, Basil was trembling as hard as Theron was. Triumph, jealousy, lust, and rage shook him as a bear shakes a dog in its jaws. He felt himself swell, answering the need straining at Theron's tight fawn breeches. He laid his hand lightly on Theron's head, burrowed his fingers into the silky hair, and pulled his head back and away to look into his startled face.

"You mistake your place, my lord. This is not the Hill, nor am I a noble maiden. I will bring you no dowry, no land, no sons." Deliberately, he tapped Theron gently between the legs with his booted foot. "Take this to her, my lord. It is none of mine."

Theron moaned and reached out to stroke Basil's thighs. Basil caught his groping hands and thrust him roughly backward. A part of him exulted in the success of his spell-casting. Theron was indeed transformed. In the old days, in the North, it had been a complete transformation: bone, sinew, and skin.

"I do not lie with beasts," Basil said. "Go from me until your time is accomplished and your crown is won. You must come to yourself before you come to me." Then Basil straightened, settled his weight into his feet, planted deep in the wooden floor, raised his arms, took the wind into his hands, and blew the Little King to his feet and toward the wild, where he must run until he tamed the beast within himself.

WHEN HE KNEW WHERE HE WAS AGAIN, THERON was standing on the embankment over the river. The University was behind him, and the ancient Council buildings. The smell of the river was wild. The green-brown water rushed past below him, on its way to the harbor mouth, where it released the detritus of the city, and the last of its memories of the great upcountry. He thought for a moment of leaping into the flood— not so much thought as felt his body poised for flight, to join the glory of that passionate, anonymous flow. But what he desired was more earthy, less exalted.

Theron remembered a place he knew, where a man could be had for the price of a drink, and headed down the river to the Apricot.

The Apricot had a low, narrow doorway off a street of tailors and leather-fitters, where men worked only until the light began to fade. In the glooming dusk, after they'd gone home, the tavern began to gather its custom. Theron paused in the doorway, his fingers still clenched on the solid wood of the door. The smell of all the men inside, the heat of them, made him giddy. They were waiting for him. But the noise, the constant motion in the close room, meant danger. He breathed deeply, filling his head with the scent, and plunged inside.

As quickly as he could, Theron made his way to the long counter where drinks were dispensed. He downed one of the small fierce glasses of clear apricot brandy the place was famous for, and then another. Around him, men were taking each other's measure. The musk of their desire was heavy on the air, rising with the fumes of the liquor: brandy and sex and sweat and old fruit in the sun.

He felt a hand on his leg. A man nearly as tall as he was, with a soft ginger beard, his breath cloves and apricot as he said, "Another drink, scholar?"

Theron spun him around, locking his arm behind his back. "Easy, sweetheart," the man gasped. "You do understand what we're here for, don't you? Do you know what this place is?"

Theron did not speak. He stroked the man's face, then forced him to his knees, pressing him farther down, until his head was touching the floor. He put his foot on the man's body. Then he turned away.

"You're a nasty piece of work," said a man in red. "I thought students were supposed to be mild. What are you studying, dear? Venery?"

He was in too close; Theron shoved him back, but the man closed in again, trying to bring his body's heat, the scent of his skin and his hair within Theron's bounds. It was intolerable. Theron shoved him harder. The man fell back, bouncing against another group of customers, who turned with irritated growls.

One of them took the man's arm: "What is it, Fred? This kid giving you trouble?"

Fred shrugged. "I guess he doesn't fancy me."

"You want Big Lou to throw him out?"

But Big Lou had found Theron for himself. Lou moved slowly, as though his bulk made him swim through air like deep water. But it was not his size that held him back; he was stalking, approaching the young student carefully, not to startle him. The Apricot gave Lou plenty of experience with men who were not as stable as they might be.

Lou held out his hand. It was huge as a ham, and empty. "Evening," Lou said. "Everything here to your satisfaction?"

"Everything," Theron echoed.

"I wonder," Lou said, "if you might be looking for those other longhair boys—the ones with the oak leaves in their hats?"

"Oak leaves?"

"Because I chucked them out, an hour or so back. We don't like seditious talk here—though I understand the brandy can drive a man to extremes."

"I am not here to talk." Theron handed him a silver coin: a man's wages for a week.

Lou considered it, and took it. "Is that another brandy for you, sir?"

Theron felt the drink burn along his arms, down his legs, right into his fingertips.

A man came up beside him, tall and swaggering. "Kiss me," the man said, and Theron wrestled him to the ground—a good fight, muscle against muscle, sinew against sinew, enough to rouse him, but not enough to satisfy. He felt the other men's interest, their breathing, their fury and admiration; he would stand against them all, and make them know their master, and bow to do him homage.

A circle had formed, like a clearing in the forest, with Theron at its center. A man, very drunk, rushed at him headfirst. Theron fought the urge to lower his own head and lock horns with him; instead he ducked his shoulder and took the blow there, sending the drunk reeling out of the circle. Another man danced in like a cat, sinuously prowling the edges of Theron's space, stalking closer and closer. Theron moved his hands until they caressed the man's body, a long and luxurious *pas de deux*, intimate and stimulating, teasing and inaccessible, that ended finally with the man curled up at his feet. Theron did not spurn him, but let him lie, and turned to face his next challenger.

There was betting going on, and kissing and stroking in corners where men went to hold each other and watch the fight. Theron threw down man after man, and cast them out. His desire grew, and he was lighter of heart than he had been in weeks.

When his true opponent came, Theron was ready for him. His hands locked on firm muscles, a solid strength that could stand against his. They stood perfectly balanced, and Theron trembled with the effort. The man was panting, sweating with desire—and that was what undid him. On a single breath he weakened, and in that breath Theron took him down, forced the man to his knees, and held him there for all to see.

He heard cheering as he took his prize.

⌐

THERON AWOKE ON A DIRTY MATTRESS WITH BITE marks on his shoulders and no money in his pockets, in a house he would never find again. He made his way out into the morning and home to Riverside, where he left his crumpled clothes by the bed and slept until afternoon.

Then he called Terence to bathe and shave him, and bring him chocolate and bread and butter and preserves and sweet rolls and an omelet and fruit and more chocolate. He apologized sweetly for his temper of yesterday, and said he was much better. He truly was. He felt light, his head clear, even his body free of its terrible sluggish weight of yearning. He dressed in tawny velvet and went to call on his betrothed.

The Randalls were glad to see him. Genevieve said he looked pale, then blushed at her familiarity. Lady Randall suggested that the young people walk in the garden together. Genevieve looked mildly alarmed, but Theron smiled encouragingly, and stood aside to let her pass without taking her hand.

In the garden, though, when they stopped beside a blooming cherry tree, she looked up at him and told him that the golden necklace he'd sent was the most wonderful gift she'd ever received, and they were going to alter her wedding gown so she could wear it. He looked down into the world of her sparkling eyes, the rosy flush of her parted lips, and knew she wanted him to kiss her. But he was afraid to break the fragile peace he'd earned himself last night.

He reached over her head to pull a spray of pink blossoms and handed it to her, saying that flowers or gold equally were inadequate to the task of adorning her lovely neck as it deserved. She nested the spray in her bosom and preceded him back to the house.

When Theron went home, he stuck his head into Sophia's study. His mother looked tired. He'd seen little of her these past days—some ruckus to do with her University women, and an outbreak of sickness across town. Indeed, when she noticed his velvet coat, Sophia gasped and grabbed at her papers: "Oh, no! We have a dinner tonight and I forgot?"

He came forward into the lamplight. "No, Mother. I was just paying a call at the Randalls'."

"Ah." She put the papers down. "She is well, your little girl?"

"Quite well."

"And you?" Sophia busied herself straightening papers as if he were already gone. Impulsively, Theron knelt at her feet and laid his head in her lap. He closed his eyes and breathed in the sharp smell of the herbs her clothes were stored in. "And you, Theron?" she asked softly.

"I don't know," he answered her. "From day to day, I really do not know."

His mother stroked his hair. "It's all right, my love. It's always been hard for you, these sudden changes in your life that you make. And you will make them. One minute you wish to be a swordsman, the next a scholar. One moment you are the world's greatest astronomist, the next a rhetorician." He laughed uncomfortably. "So maybe all this is for the best: you marry, you have a wife to love and keep—something that's always real, always solid, that does not change; something to build over the years whatever else happens, no?"

"Perhaps."

She heard the uncertainty. "If you change your mind, Theron, about this marriage—"

"No," he sighed.

"That is good. I know your moods. You can be difficult," she teased, twisting a lock of his hair. "Did you know? So charming, until you've had too much of it—like a little boy sick on sweets. And then you are moody, you do not talk at all. Everyone thinks, 'What is wrong? What's the matter with him, is he all right?' But then you come around all by yourself. I think about telling her that, your sweet bride, but she'll find out on her own. And she will love you anyway, just as the rest of us do."

It was a long time since she had sounded so loving and easy. Theron took her hand from his hair and kissed it. "Thank you, Mama. I'm sure I will be happy."

"Oh, no." She took his chin in her hand, and looked at him tenderly. "You are not sure at all. But perhaps that is good."

He leaned into her hand and murmured, "Mama. I have bad dreams."

"So do we all, my son," she said sadly. "Shall I make you a posset to help you to sleep?"

"Yes, please."

The hot liquid put him to sleep, but he was only shutting the door to one world of incomprehensible demands to open it on another. The world of his dreams was full of trees and torches. A man he knew was Basil, who looked like a bear, held him in his dark-furred arms and said, "You will be king. I have chosen you, and you will run for me, and stand the trial."

"What is the trial?" he whispered, his cheek against the man's warm fur.

The bear pressed a finger to his lips. "Oh, Little King, that is secret wisdom. No man knows that but the wizards, and the king who does not fail his trial. And when you have succeeded, you will not wish any man to know what you had to do."

"Do you know what it is?"

"I? Of course I do."

"How do you know that I can do it?"

"It is my business to choose wisely. I chose you for your trial, out of all the Little Kings that the land has grown for herself. My chosen always triumph."

"But how shall I triumph if I don't know what to do?" he asked plaintively. His heart was pounding. He had only moments left to ask the right questions. Already he could feel the tingling in his legs, the way his muscles were bunching and regrouping into powerful leaping haunches. He reached out his hands to beg for more time, and heard the wizard laugh.

"Pay attention to your lesson, Little King, and it will go well for you. Know yourself, always. There's many a Little King has failed by failing to know himself."

Theron woke and struck a light and stared down at his face in his washbasin. He saw there the stag's head of Ysaud's pictures: liquid eyes, proud muzzle, branching horns.

He cried out, and woke for real, and stumbled out of bed. He pulled on the white shirt that he had worn, musky with his desire for Genevieve, and a black scholar's robe, and soft leather boots that covered his legs like a second skin. Then he went out into the night.

I T WAS EARLY YET IN RIVERSIDE. THE EVENING'S ENTER-
tainments were just beginning. Theron could have found a man or a woman on the street and had them for a handful of coins. A few more steps would have taken him to the most fa-

mous brothel in the city, where on his family's credit he could have enacted any and all of the bizarre scenes that plagued his sleep. But Lord Theron Campion passed Glinley's and pressed on across the bridge, toward the Apricot.

The men came alert when he entered. "That's him," he heard them say, as they drew aside in fear or amusement, disgust or caution. He didn't know which and he didn't care. This was his turf now, and he welcomed the green flame of his fighting spirit as it licked through his veins. He stood on the table, and felt the belling cry burst from his lungs.

The tavern was silent. "Well, well," a man said. "Come to put us all in our place again, are you?"

The man was not beautiful, but he was graceful, with a dancer's body and a head of black curls, a red mouth, and swarthy skin. Theron wanted him. He nodded his heavy-branched head, *Yes, I am come.*

"Fine," said the dark man, "that's fine. But none of your pussy wrestling this time. That's for nanny boys." A few men laughed, and others blushed. "Can you fight," the dark one said, "like a man?" He raised his arm up over his head. From his hand, like a claw, sprang sharp cold steel.

The tavern erupted. Big Lou pushed forward through the crowd, shouting, "None of that!" The dark man was rushed outside, and Theron followed, at the heart of a knot of men urging on the fight. Someone had seized a torch from the doorway, so that their shadows crossed and wrestled with each other on the street.

"Campion!" He heard the word over and over, until he realized it was directed at him, and he turned and saw several men with hair as long as his own, done in dozens of tiny braids. They'd been among the men who had hunted him into the grove at the year's turning. One of them was smaller than the others, his hair reflecting flame from the torchlight. Theron knew him—a follower of Basil's.

"Lindley . . . ?"

The student pushed to Theron's side through the shouting, jostling crowd. "Have you got a knife?" he asked breathlessly.

"No."

"Take mine."

The handle was antler, the knife was sharp. Lindley was hastening him with the crowd around the corner to the dark courtyard of a deserted tannery. Theron could smell the residue of death and piss. It made him wild. In the circle of men, he sprang at his opponent. The knife felt good in his hand; when he was young, to prove he wasn't just a sickly boy who read books, he'd made one of the Riverside toughs take him into his gang. Sophia had put a stop to it, but not before he'd learned a lot.

The dark man pulled back sharply, surprised by his ferocity. Theron bared his teeth. With the knife in his hand he was hunter as well as hunted; he was man as well as beast. The power of the Land flowed up through his feet. He knew where his opponent's knife would be before he even moved. He heard the dark man's breathing as clear as words, telling him his body's thoughts. He smelt the man's fear. He wanted blood, he wanted dominion. He feinted and ducked and slashed, driving onward to his mark.

"Blood!" the men shouted. "Blood! Blood!"

If it had been a swordfight, it would have ended right there, or else gone on to the death. But this fight occupied a middle ground between formal ritual and mortal honor.

The dark man's breathing was loud and ragged. He was gripping his knife wrist where it had been slashed, and staring white-eyed at the Deer King, poised to move edgily away from his glittering horn.

Theron did not close the space between them. Instead he slashed his knife upward in the air once, twice, and a third time, his blade blue in the moonlight, black where the vanquished man's blood stained it. The man fell to his knees as if in prayer. Theron stood over him, breathing hard, the night air filling his lungs. He lowered the knife, and held it out to his side.

Lindley took the knife from him. "My lord," he said, "that was well fought. The Companions are witness."

Theron didn't hear him. His eyes were fixed on the kneeling man, his erstwhile challenger. The man's dark head was down, low to the ground. Theron parted his gown and lifted his shirt to his waist. He said, "Yes, I can fight like a man. Now show how you appreciate it."

His pleasure was fierce and exalted. All of creation spun around his dominion and his joy.

When he returned to himself, there was no color at all in the world, just moonlight and shadow. The man with the knife was gone, and so were most of the ones who had been there watching, though some stood by or coupled in the shadows. Lindley was supporting him, and another person he did not know.

Lindley said, "I'll get you water."

Theron rasped, "No." He shook himself free of the sustaining arms, and stood alone. He shivered at the cold wind on his sweaty skin.

Lindley, again: "Shall I see you home? To Tremontaine House?"

"No."

"Hush, fool." It was the other one who had held him, a person as tall as himself in a heavy cloak and a large felt hat. "No names, I think, and no direction. I can see our young friend to safety."

Lindley moved in closer to Theron, demanding, "Who are you? You're not of the Companions."

"No, indeed," the other said. "I am of the Blood."

"The Blood," Lindley breathed, not quite comprehending.

"Yes," said the other in silky tones, "the Blood of Kings. It runs as true in my veins as in his." Theron felt his arm being taken in a grip so sure that he did not think to flee. "Come, my young lord. Sophia will be worried about you—and if she isn't, she should be."

The walk back to Riverside seemed to take forever. He was tired to the bone; at times, he even thought he slept as he walked. His companion's voice wove strands of meaning through his exhaustion: "What a wonderful evening! . . . I won't tell them where I found you, if you won't tell them I was wandering around down there. . . . Come on, boy, it's only a cat!"—this when he jumped at a sound too close to them—". . . I think Katherine will be just as happy if I stay in Riverside after all. . . . This is the Bridge, Theron, we're nearly home. . . . Pull yourself together, boy; you're going in the front door with me."

Then there was the familiar smell of his own hall, and light in his eyes, and his companion saying, "Do forgive me. I asked him to sneak out and meet me down by the docks before I put in my official appearance—childish, I know."

And Sophia's hands and voice were turned, not to him, but to the other; her voice was hushed with tears and she said, "Oh, my dear—you have your father's eyes, his very eyes as I remember them so well—the little lines right there—and there. Jessica, welcome home."

chapter III

WHEN LORD NICHOLAS GALING WENT TO CALL
on Lord Theron Campion, he dressed as though for
courting, in amethyst-colored wool cut very close to
his figure, a waistcoat embroidered with water lilies, and a car-
nelian nestled in the discreet ruffles at his throat. Aping the severe academic style, he'd slicked his dark curls away from his face
with gold clips and worn a gownlike cloak in place of his usual
coat. He slipped two of Ysaud's drawings into a flat leather case,
found a chair, and paid the chairmen the exorbitant sum they required to carry him across the Bridge to Riverside House.

He felt pleasantly excited, like a hound with the quarry in
sight. He'd play Lord Theron, show him Ysaud's pictures if neces-
sary, bring into clear focus the hazy pattern that surrounded him.
No great scandal: just two men in a room, getting things straight.
The boy was clever, but not subtle. To a man used to dealing with
Arlen, it would be as simple as a game of checkers.

The first obstacle to Galing's admirable plan was Lady
Campion's butler, who told him Lord Theron was not receiving
visitors at present.

"Is he out?" Nicholas asked pleasantly. "Perhaps I might wait, then."

"Oh, he's here, all right. He just ain't receiving."

"Perhaps you might ask him? I am Lord Nicholas Galing."

The butler squinted at him. Since the great scar scrawled across his face from temple to chin traveled through his left eyelid, his squint was a fearsome sight indeed, but Nicholas did not quail. This steadfastness seemed to impress the butler, who said, "Well, I don't know. Come along of me to her ladyship, and we'll see what she has to say about it."

Nicholas laid his cloak across a chair, tucked the leather case under his arm, and followed the butler through a series of corridors spanning a variety of architectural and decorative styles. He'd never set foot in Riverside House before, although he'd heard the stories. Seeing the place now, it was hard to believe in the legendary masked balls, the orgiastic gaming parties and wild frolics of the old duke's times. These rooms looked respectable and comfortable, even cozy, with their rich, dark carpets and flowered tapestries, their deep sofas and tables crowded with beautiful things. Nicholas wondered whether the duchess had redecorated.

"You was noticing me face," the butler remarked as he led the way up a steep staircase to a narrow landing with a door at each end.

Nicholas made an apologetic murmur.

"It's worth noticing. Her ladyship does pretty work. Beau Dartwell nearly had the eye out my head, but she sewed it back, like a button on a shirt, good as new. *And* she took me on as butler when old Leverre went out to pasture. I'd do anything for her ladyship, and that's a fact." He gave Nicholas a warning glare, then tapped on one of the doors, opened it, and said, "Lord Somebody or Other, my lady, come to see Lord Theron. I'll just keep myself handy in case you want him thrown out."

Galing stepped over the threshold with his best social smile pinned to his lips in time to hear a woman's voice saying, "Davy, I'm insulted. Don't you think I'm up to protecting Lady Sophia from some city boy?"

The voice belonged to one of the two women in the pleasant, sun-lit room—the one who was lounging on the sofa, looking as out of place as a parrot in an herb garden. Her hair was hennaed a blazing red, her face was bony and sunbrowned, her clothes were purple and scarlet and turquoise, of no recognizable style or fashion. She was smiling at Galing with frank curiosity.

Conscious that he'd been staring himself, Galing nodded curtly and turned to Lady Sophia, who was sitting in the bay window at a large, cluttered desk. She said, "Wicked girl," with affectionate composure, and introduced the colorful woman as Lady Jessica Campion. "And you, sir, are?"

Galing bowed low. "Lord Nicholas Galing, and your most obedient servant, Lady Sophia, Lady Jessica."

The colorful woman gave a snort of laughter. "Very nice," she said. "I can't wait to hear what he says next."

Behind his smile, Nicholas was consigning the whole of this unconventional household to the bottom of the Seventh Hell, thugs, half-women, and all.

Lady Sophia seemed aware of his discomfort. "Hush, Jessie dear; you're embarrassing our visitor. Davy, you may go. I'll ring if I need you."

The scarred butler shrugged massive shoulders. "It's your funeral, my lady," he said ominously, and pulled the door to behind him with an ostentatious snap.

"Now, Lord Nicholas, come in and sit down and tell me what business brings you to see my son."

Nicholas was not accustomed to such plain speaking, especially from a woman. He took a moment to find a chair, glanced briefly at Lady Jessica, and said, "It is a private matter, meant for his ears only."

"Because," said Lady Sophia as if he'd not spoken, "if it is a matter of business, or money he owes you, you must apply to me, or to Marcus Ffoliot. My son is not yet of age."

"It is not business. I had the pleasure of meeting Lord Theron at the Randalls' at the time of his betrothal. We found we had interests in common. In fact, he was to attend the theatre in my party. But I hear he has been ill." Nicholas held out the leather case. "I brought him some offerings I thought might divert him."

"Oh, really?" Lady Jessica reached out one arm from the couch. "Art? I am something of an expert. Let's see."

Nicholas clutched the case tightly. "With your permission—I doubt a lady would find them diverting."

"Oh, dear," Sophia sighed.

"Smut," said Jessica. "Well, why not? Though I doubt you and he have quite as much in common as you'd think. What play, by the way?"

"*The Empress.* Do you know it?"

"I should. My mother created the role."

"My land," said Nicholas, inelegantly. "The Black Rose."

And this was her daughter: bastard off-shoot of the old duke and his actress mistress. "Lady" Jessica by courtesy only. The men at Lord Filisand's would be fascinated to learn she was in town.

"Just so," said Jessica, amused. "I'm surprised you've heard of her."

Nicholas smiled. "She was the greatest actress of her age, with a heart as great as her genius."

"A nice recovery," said Jessica. "But you did not come here to speak of my mother."

Nicholas regretted that it was no longer considered acceptable to call challenge on a woman. The quirk of Jessica's long mouth suggested that she knew just what he was thinking. He summoned his own smile back to his lips and aimed it at his hostess. "Have I your permission to see Lord Theron? For a moment only, of course: I do not wish to tire him."

Lady Sophia did not answer immediately, but studied Nicholas. It was not unlike Lord Arlen's attempts to fluster him, except for being oddly impersonal, as if Nicholas were a problem to be solved. He bore her scrutiny patiently, taking the opportunity to study Theron Campion's mother in return. She was handsome in a dark, foreign way, her black dress plain but well-cut, her thick hair braided artlessly around her head. Her only jewel was the massive ruby covering the first joint of her left forefinger like a glowing coal. Her black eyes were calm and direct.

"Very well," she said at last. "He might enjoy the company. But he is overtired. You understand?"

Nicholas nodded. "I will not keep him long. Your care for him does you credit."

"Poh," she said, and grinned suddenly. It made her look very like her son. "I am his mother, and a physician, and I am told I fuss too much. But not so much as Sly Davy, who thinks we must be protected from the world." She raised her voice. "Davy! You may come in now." The door opened with suspicious promptness. "Davy, please take this gentleman to a parlor and bring Lord Theron to him. And please don't listen at the door. I do not mind, but Lord Theron deserves his privacy."

Lady Jessica unfolded herself from the sofa and shook her costume straight. She was wearing a gauzy vest over a long shirt and loose trousers—Nicholas had never seen the like before, on man or woman.

"Nice, isn't it?" she said cheerfully. "My own design. I'll take temptation out of Davy's way, and fetch Theron for you myself." She grinned at the butler. "Put his lordship in the False Cabinet, will you, Davy? And then go give Helen a cuddle. I saw the butcher wink at her this morning." When Davy growled, she laughed and strode out the door.

Nicholas rose and bent punctiliously over his hostess' hand. It was strong and square and rough—a farm-wife's hand, except for the ruby. He realized that he liked her. *This house is full of surprises,* Nicholas thought, and turned to follow Sly Davy.

It was an easy house to get lost in. On any other occasion, Nicholas would have been fascinated by its intricacies, but this morning, he was just impatient to get on with what promised to be an interesting interview. At last Davy showed him into a small room and kindly recommended him to make himself at home, since there was no telling where his lordship might have got himself to.

Lord Nicholas nodded and went to help himself to an apple from a large bowl of fruit. When it turned out to be wax, he tried to take a book from the shelves next to the hearth. The books were false spines, hiding a cabinet, he presumed, with a concealed latch. Intrigued, he poked and prodded, but soon lost patience. A bunch of violets was made of enamel, as was the porcelain teacup holding it. The malachite box on the mantelpiece was painted wood and the leopard's pelt thrown over the back of a chair was unshorn figured velvet. He had just pulled back curtains printed to look like watered silk to reveal a

window-sized painting of a garden in high summer when the door
opened and Lord Theron Campion entered the room.

He looked nervous. As well he might, Nicholas thought
as he bowed and mouthed the standard opening platitudes.
Campion did not take his part in the verbal pavane, simply nodding jerkily in acknowledgment. Neither did he come fully into
the room, but clung to the door-handle, poised to bolt.

"Such an unusual room," Galing said after an awkward pause.
"Nothing in it is what it seems to be."

Campion's face relaxed. "No. It isn't, is it? I can come in,
then." He released the handle. "My sister tells me I have been
rude." He smiled charmingly. "Again. I forgot your theatre party.
Forgive me."

Galing gestured toward the open door. "Perhaps we could
shut the door and discuss it?"

Alarm widened Campion's long eyes. "I don't think—"

A hennaed head appeared over the young nobleman's shoulder. "I'll send Davy with some wine or fruit if you'd like," Lady
Jessica said cheerfully. "Everything here's wax and marble."

Her voice startled Campion, who leapt away from her and
stood clutching a chair-back, wild-eyed. Galing, who would have
given much for a glass of wine, remembered Sly Davy's habit of
listening at doors and said, "No. Thank you."

"Right," said Jessica. "Have fun, boys." And she departed,
pulling the door shut behind her. When he heard the latch fall,
Campion started nervously and put his hand out to open it again.

"Leave it closed," said Galing sharply.

Campion spun around, his eyes wide, his mouth ajar, clearly
panic-stricken. Overtired, indeed, Galing thought. Half mad was
closer to the mark. With guilt, perhaps?

"I have brought you something." Galing used a slow, calm
voice, a voice suitable for soothing horses. "A gift. But you may
not like it. It is of a very personal nature."

"I am betrothed," Theron said breathlessly. "I am not in a position to accept that sort of gift."

"You mistake me, Lord Theron. It is—how shall I say? An offering. To your youth, your beauty—and your indiscretion."

"My—"

The young man's head was up, his nostrils sniffing the air, the very picture of the man with the deer's head in Ysaud's pictures. The image was so strong that Galing said aloud, despite himself, "Ah, now I see! You did give them to her after all."

"What?" Campion asked frantically. "What did I give, to whom? The necklace will be paid for. I've done nothing—"

It was the opening Nicholas had been angling for, though a little early in the game. Still, he seized the moment and moved in. "Ah, but you have, sir. You have done much this winter, with who knows what more to come."

Theron was backed up to the wall. He tried for a haughty look, succeeded only in looking wild-eyed. "You mistake me, sir, or else yourself."

"Do I? Hear me out, my lord, and tell me how much I mistake." It was potent, the young man's fear; he could smell it on the air, and he knew that he had stumbled upon something critical, something hidden, a secret Campion held that no one else must know. His terror at discovery was manifest; perhaps, like most criminals, he would be relieved to be rid of it.

"I know much already," Nicholas said reasonably. "Since MidWinter, there has been a series of incidents in the city: a hunt, a scandal, a challenge. And I think you are at the heart of them all."

At the word "hunt," Campion threw back his head and went very still.

"I know of the Companions of the King. I know of your lover at University. I know of his incautious lectures, and the odd enthusiasms of those who fall under his spell. Is that your excuse, my lord? That you were led astray by insidious teachings?"

The boy's eyes narrowed. "Get out. Leave this house."

"Oh, I don't think so; not yet. Not until I've given you my little gift."

Galing untied the laces of the flat leather case and brought out two of Ysaud's drawings. One showed Campion lying on his back with one arm curled up over his head and the other crossing the vine etched into his chest, echoing the relaxed curve of his legs and his sex. In the other, he was seated, rampant and hungry, reaching out toward the beholder as if in supplication.

Campion stared transfixed at these living images of his obsession with Ysaud, the blood flooding his gaunt cheeks. "I don't remember this. I did not pose for these."

"But effectively you did, my lord—for months, as I understand. The lady has a very quick eye."

"These are private. Studies for the paintings."

"Yes, the deer series. Magnificent work. I admired them deeply. I hear she's getting ready to show them, soon," he added for effect.

"She promised no one would know who they were."

"And indeed, no one will—unless they've seen the sketches."

Quick as thought, Campion snatched them from Nicholas's hand, tore them across, and flung them into the fire.

But the fire wasn't real either. Campion's hips and yearning face lay obscenely disjointed on the brightly painted embers.

"It wouldn't have helped," Galing said. "I have more."

Campion's mouth opened in a soundless *No*.

"I see the fact discomfits you. As well it might. What, after all, is to stop me from offering some to Lady Genevieve as a betrothal gift?"

Campion fixed his bright, strained gaze on Nicholas's face. "Why?" he whispered.

"Why?" Nicholas shrugged. "I'd do it to prevent the alliance of a noblewoman with a traitor who seeks to overthrow all we hold dear."

"I'm not a traitor."

"Then what are you? A brawler and a whore? A man who always manages to be just where a nest of traitors is talking of kings and ancient rights? And if they triumph, who will then be king, my lord? A Northern farmer's son, a scrawny scribe with blue fingers and inkstains? Or a descendant of the last of the kings, the noble heir to Tremontaine?"

Galing wiped his brow. It was the speech he still dreamed of making to Arlen, the true vision he had of how the pieces fit together. It was a blessed relief to have someone to say it to, someone who knew the truth as he did.

"You're mad," Campion said.

"That," said Galing, "is very rich, coming from you. You are shaking so hard you can barely stand. Tell me what you know."

Ostentatiously, he sat himself down in a chair that looked like stone, gesturing Campion toward its mate. Instead, Campion went to the false book shelves and pulled on a spine titled *Wines of the South*. The shelves sprung open on an array of bottles. He poured himself a whiskey, not offering Nicholas any. But neither, Nicholas noted, did he drink it himself.

"Look," said Galing soothingly, "you're young. Youth will have its pleasures. And its enthusiasms. I don't want to ruin your marriage. Or your future. Indeed, I seek to promote a happy resolution of them both. If you will confess the plot to me, I will see to it that your name is never linked to it. My word on it."

"There is no plot."

"There is. I know it. If you were a common man, I'd have you thrown into the Chop and tortured until you confessed. As it is . . ." Nicholas tapped his portfolio. "I will surely draw your fangs and leave you toothless, brideless, and a mockery to all the city. You may seek your kingship then wherever you can find someone who will not laugh himself into stitches over your horns and your hooves and your rather extensive personal decorations."

Campion pushed back his hair with both hands, rubbed his temples as though they hurt him, and swung his head low, from side to side. The effect was disturbing. "What must I do? How shall I prove myself to you?"

"Write it down," Galing said. "I will have it all from you— your dealings with the King's Companions, your relations with St Cloud, who your allies are and what they hope from you. Give me a clear account, with all your part in it. When that is in my hands, you shall have the sketches in yours. Not before."

"Ysaud," the boy said miserably. "Did she give them to you?"

Galing almost felt sorry for him. He was such a pathetic creature after all, for a rebellion to pin its hopes upon. "Only upon compulsion," he said contemptuously. "She will not play the same trick twice, never fear. I am the only one who knows; and, if you are a good friend to the city, I will remain the only one. You will marry your sweetheart, and inherit your duchy. You will even sit in Council and enjoy the social rounds and summer on your country estates. Most people would not object to such a fate."

"Please go," the boy said. "I cannot bear the smell of you."

"Thank you," said Galing. "It has been a pleasure."

JUST FOR DIVERSION, JESSICA CAMPION WAS PRICING the tapestries in her father's room. She had not been in it since she'd attended his deathbed, and she wanted to see if they were as good as she remembered, or if the occasion had caused her to overvalue them.

She remembered staring at the woven pictures as she and the old duke played chess; sometimes he'd fall asleep, and she would sit patiently, silently making inventory, testing her fledgling knowledge of the world's goods: the paintings and fine fabrics, the carvings and silver that furnished the room. Yes, indeed—she inspected the back—the tapestries were Ardish work, from one of the great studios. She had a client who would surely want them, if Sophia were inclined to sell. Jessica snorted. Fat chance. The room was a shrine to the dead duke. Sophia would probably sell her last gown and wear the tapestries before she'd part with a single one of them.

Riverside House made Jessica jumpy—not because her father had died there, but because she had grown up in it. Of course, the duke had not been living in it then. He'd decamped shortly after her birth, gone off to the island of Kyros with one of his famous lovers. She remembered them both together, in the white house above the blue sea, the summer she had been sent to visit. She was eight. He wanted to see his daughter. The Duchess Katherine had bundled her off with her nurse, who had gotten very friendly with the sailors. Jessica had climbed a rigging, and they said she was a natural. She'd decided then and there she'd have her own ship someday. She told Marcus so when she got back, and she reminded him of it when she turned sixteen and dowries were discussed.

"I don't want a husband," she said, "and I never will. Katherine hasn't got one; why should I?"

Characteristically blunt, Katherine answered, "Because the city isn't going to put up with you running through its daughters until you're fifty. We're offering to get you settled now, before you create so much scandal that even money won't buy you into a decent family."

Jessica did not like to remember exactly what she'd said then; it had been coarse, without finesse. She'd learned a lot since then about getting people to do what she wanted. But the upshot was that she left the city on someone else's ship, with stake in the cargo and a few trinkets to sell abroad—trinkets she hoped Katherine had never missed. She'd always thought she'd stop someday at Kyros, see how the old man was getting on. But she'd never managed to route herself that way. There wasn't really much on the island but honey and ruins and goats and olives.

She found her father again back home in Riverside, anyway, lying in this room, transparent with illness, easily bored, still with a tongue on him, though, the terror of his physicians. She was twenty years old, Theron's age now, almost. She wondered what the old duke would have made of his son. Strange that they'd never even seen each other. But that was men for you—men, and death, she reflected, to be fair.

There was the ivory swordsman she had brought her father, still on the chest by the bed. She picked it up, and Theron walked in.

Well, not walked, exactly. Burst. Stormed. "What are you doing here?" he demanded.

She only looked at him. That usually worked.

"I've been searching the house for you! Davy said you'd not gone out."

"Nor had I. Or does this room somehow count as out?"

With one of his peculiar lightning shifts, he looked at the ivory in her hand and said brightly, "Ah! Adding to your hoard?"

She said, "Theron, sit down. Or at least stop pacing. You are welcome to count the silver when I leave, but please wait until then, all right?"

He stopped still, saying blankly, "What?"

She couldn't figure him out. Sophia said it was wedding nerves, and that he was high-strung. Sophia, of course, did not know about the incident with the knives in the tanner's yard. Jessica was saving it in case it should prove useful later. Knowing Theron, there was probably more where that came from. He was a Campion, after all.

"Never mind," she said. "Just tell me what you— Oh!" She thought it through. The pattern began to emerge. "It was that man, wasn't it? Stupid of me. The one who just left—Galing, right? He said something to you, did something to set you off— the pictures, right? The dirty ones? He showed you— No, wait, you wouldn't need me for that. So they must have been— Oh, no. Oh, Theron, no."

"No, what?"

"No, tell me you didn't pose for some dirty pictures which Galing now has his hands on and is trying to blackmail you with."

Eyes wide as a child's, he nodded. "But not—not exactly. I mean, it wasn't exactly like that." He told her about Ysaud. Halfway through, she began to laugh. Furious, he ripped open his collar, showed her the leaves etched into his skin. Here in this room, it sobered her up. "You should not have let someone mark you like that," she said. "Not you, Theron."

"Don't you find it beautiful?" he asked defiantly. "She is a great artist."

"Slaves are marked like that," his sister said grimly. "In places where I've been, slaves are marked with patterns cut in their skin, as other people's property." He raised his head, shook it as if shaking off some binding. "All right," she said, "it's the stupidity of youth; thank heaven none of mine left visible marks. I understand about the artist. Now, what does Galing want?"

Theron pulled his jacket tight about himself. "He wants me to confess to treason."

Jessica sighed. "You *have* been busy. And you were such a nice little boy."

"But I didn't!" the nice little boy cried. "He came here with some mad tale of conspiracy, University, the kingship— Oh, Jess." For the first time since he'd come into the room, he looked at her clear-eyed, direct, as if he finally recognized her. "I don't know what to do."

"Treason sounds serious, Theron. Tell Katherine."

"No!" He shook his head violently and actually pawed the ground with his foot. "No, she mustn't know. She'd probably believe him, not me. She's already turned me with a haying fork from this field to next. . . . It's all her fault, really. I *had* to get married, to get her off my back! I don't think she cares who I marry, as long as it makes me look harmless and gets me out of the city for a while. That's how bad it is with her."

His half-sister nodded in complete sympathy. "Well, then, let's think. This Galing—what's his interest? Will he take money?"

"I don't think so. He didn't ask for money. He wants a full confession—a *report*, he called it."

"Why don't you just make something up?"

Again, the violent headshake. "I cannot—there are others. People at University he wants me to accuse."

"Charming man. And when you fail to deliver, he sends your sketches to the Randalls?"

"So he said."

"Let him."

"*What?*"

"Let him. Who cares?"

"But the disgrace! And I'm not a traitor, Jess. Those men he wants me to accuse, they've done nothing. I cannot have this creature triumph over me!" Theron blew air out through his flared nostrils, shaking his head again in that disquieting way. "To think he holds me in his hands—to think of him—oh, God— *looking* at me, those pictures—"

"Ahhh." She studied her half-brother, the heir to Tremontaine. He revealed more of his heart than he knew; he always had. But, then, there always had been someone standing by to wrap it in warm blankets at the least sign of a chill. Even now that he'd been betrayed by his mistress and by a fellow nobleman, he didn't seem to recognize betrayal as the human condition. He probably wasn't as innocent as he claimed, either. He'd done *something* to get both Katherine and Galing roused. If she helped him, she'd be helping to perpetuate his illusion: that mistakes could be rectified; that people were kind; that he would always be loved.

And he would be in her debt. Well, let it be his problem. For herself, Jessica was beginning to see a very neat, very amusing, maybe even profitable piece of business. She said, "What do you want me to do?"

"Get the sketches back from Galing, of course."

"But you said he wouldn't take money."

He looked confused, as she'd intended. Delicately, he persisted: "You have a certain renown for finding and acquiring works of art—by your own stratagems."

"Steal them? From Lord whosis Galing?" She played out the outrage, then relented: "Come on, Theron. He'd only get more from Ysaud."

"They must all be found—found and burned."

"Oh, hardly. Hardly that. I acquire art, I don't destroy it. I've got a much, much better idea." But she wouldn't say what it was, only, "It'll be fun. And it will get everyone what they want—except Galing, of course. And . . . maybe, the Randalls. I can't guarantee you the Randalls."

When he said nothing, she took his chin in her hand and turned his face to hers. "Theron. You understand what I'm saying? You've asked for my help, and I will give it. But I may be giving you help you don't know you need." She looked at him for a long time. Her eyes were the same green as his own, as their father's in the portrait. "Say yes, Theron. Say that you understand and accept my help—or things will go very ill between us."

"I understand," he whispered. "But do not disgrace me, sister."

"You worry too much," she said, "about disgrace. This is an old, old city, and ours is an old, old family. It's like a splash of blood on the sea, your disgrace—quickly absorbed and forgotten. But I will not disgrace you, if you try not to disgrace yourself."

⁓

J ESSICA DRESSED HERSELF CAREFULLY, IN RICH COLORS that showed off her tawny skin. She braided a strand of tigereye through the coils of her blazing hair and lined her eyes with kohl and put gold in her ears. Then she hired a chair to take her to the home of the artist, Ysaud.

"Lady Jessica Campion of Tremontaine," she announced herself to the servant who answered the door, and Ysaud did not keep her waiting long.

The artist was small and perfect, with regular features and pale, dark-lashed eyes. Jessica's mouth watered.

"There are so many Tremontaines," Ysaud said. "Which hole did you crawl out of?"

"A very special one." Jessica smiled. "As you will see. I hear that you have pictures of my brother Theron."

The artist had to tilt her head up to view Jessica's face. "You look like him. A little. Come into the light. You are very much older. Are you sure you're not his mother?"

Jessica smiled wickedly. "Quite, quite sure." Their two faces were almost touching. Ysaud's eyes marked every fine line the sun had etched in Jessica's skin, even the down on her upper lip. She said, "I would draw your face as a landscape, I think, all peaks and soft valleys and unexpected ridges."

"I've seen that place, somewhere out past the Ardish Straits. There was a wicked wind, but it's a land well worth visiting."

"Is it? I am much occupied here."

"Drawing people. I know. Let me see your hands," Jessica said, and Ysaud gave her one. "Just as I thought. You don't take care of them properly." She smoothed the fingers, one by one, from base to tip, gently, with her own. "I knew a woman once, a sculptor . . . she never did anything but work, in clay and dust and marble . . . and her skin, it dried right up, and cracked—right there. . . ." Her tongue marked the spot. "She could barely hold her chisel." She traced the route to the wrist. "It was very sad."

Ysaud's free hand caressed the strand of tiger-eye, following it through the coils of Jessica's hair. "Clearly, you should have warned her sooner."

"It is an error I endeavor to correct." Jessica took the hand she held, and moved it to the high neck of her silk chemise, laced with a bronze ribbon. "Pull," she said.

"What will I get out of it?"

"Nothing much. There are still all the buttons."

Ysaud laughed, and pulled—and pulled some more, bringing

the thin, mocking lips to her own and kissing them crimson, biting them a rich vermilion.

"Take me to your studio," Jessica urged.

"Why?" the artist asked, amused; "you want to see my pictures?"

"Not a bit," Jessica murmured. "I want to see you naked, where you work."

"I want to see you naked, in my bed."

"We can have that, too. Why not? There's a whole night ahead of us. Maybe a nice kitchen table, too. . . ."

J ESSICA CAME AWAKE IN ROSE SATIN SHEETS, TO THE smell of burning wax. Candles were all around the bed. Ysaud was tracing their shadows on her skin with one fingertip, which Jessica bit.

Ysaud said, "You want the Theron pictures, don't you?"

"Sight unseen?" Jessica mocked. "I know you're good, but it's a big investment."

"Don't you?" the artist insisted.

"Of course. But only for one night."

"You don't have much staying power, then."

"Oh, do I not?"

And when the conversation resumed, Jessica said in a dreamy voice, "Theron never mentioned me, did he? Of course not. You didn't know he had a sister. You must understand who I am. The actress's bastard. Tremontaine hates me. The duchess was forced to take me in when I was a baby, to avoid a scandal. When I got to be too much trouble as a young woman, she shipped me off abroad, where I have fended for myself as best I could. In twenty years, I haven't done badly."

"Why are you here now, then?"

"The wedding." Jessica smiled thinly. "It's their great triumph, you see. Their beloved Theron, married to a great noble's daughter, father of a whole new crop of legitimate heirs. They want me to witness it."

"And you came? How—tame of you."

"The wedding," said Jessica, fingering Ysaud's navel, "is not for some months."

"Leaving you plenty of time to celebrate your brother's future happiness—no, don't stop."

"Leaving me plenty of time to ensure my own. And while this"—she kissed a rosy nipple—"is making me very happy, indeed, the long-term prospect takes a little more effort."

"*And* my pictures."

"Among other things."

"You are planning to expose Lord Theron and destroy his marriage."

"Among other things."

"For revenge?"

"Among other things."

Ysaud chuckled, then gasped at the sensations shooting through her, then chuckled again. "The pictures," she said, "are not immediately recognizable as Lord Theron. Not, at any rate, with his clothes on."

"Then I will have to contrive to have him pose naked next to your favorite one, won't I?"

Ysaud shuddered deliciously again. "Not necessary. I have sketches for the paintings which are unmistakable."

"Now, those I would like to buy. I have clients abroad who are collectors."

"Of smut?"

"Lady, of your work. Have I not told you how deeply I admire it, how honored I am to be received into your . . . presence?"

"In fact, you have not."

"I am deeply . . . so very deeply. . . ."

⌒

THE GRAY LIGHT OF DAWN WAS FILTERING THROUGH all the nine high windows of Ysaud's studio. "They are magnificent," Jessica said, staring at the canvases. "I could sell these easily in Tabor or in Elysia . . ."

"I wish you would." Ysaud flipped back another cover cloth. "I can't sell them here; they're too incendiary. I've already had one visit from a spy of the Council. He got all excited; I had to buy him off with a few of these." She flipped the sheaf of sketches. "I tell you what, Jessica: give me seventy-five royals for the lot, paintings and all, and you can do whatever you want with them."

"Make it fifty."

Ysaud looked at her. "I need the money. You'll easily double it. No, you take them, sell them abroad, make a nice profit, and I'll be washed clean of the whole episode, with money in my purse. Enchanting as you Campions are, you're also damnably distracting."

"I take it that's my dismissal for the day?"

"Oh, for the year, I think. You're a bit rich for my blood. And you've gotten what you came for."

"I've enjoyed it," said Jessica Campion.

She went whistling out into the street—a deplorable habit, to be sure—and took herself down to a Riverside tavern, the only place where the old Duke Tremontaine's daughter could be sure of getting a really solid breakfast and not be disturbed, while sporting a string of tiger-eyes around her waist.

⌐

J ESSICA WAS STILL AFRAID OF KATHERINE, THOUGH. And so she deemed it politic to send her a letter:

Dear Cousin,

You asked me once to turn all my gifts to serving the family, and I refused you. I have been happy with my choice. And grateful to you for giving me the means to set up in life. I'm go-ing to express my gratitude in the next few weeks by causing a scandal of no mean proportions, which will embarrass you greatly. But it will come out all right in the end. I am telling you this now only because I don't want you to suffer or to think that I would really do anything to harm you or Sophia or Theron. It will, however, look as if I am, and so if I were you I'd go to the

country and not come back til it's over. And by the way I need
a lot of money, 150 royals or so for now. If you were a client
I'd ask for much more, but I am serving the family and will not
see immediate profit; it's all for expenses.

She chewed on the end of her pen, and finally wrote, *Your loving*
daughter, and crossed it out—Katherine had been as a mother to
her for all of one day before turning her over to a series of
nurses— *Your devoted cousin, Jessica.*

chapter IV

TWO DAYS AFTER HIS VISIT TO LORD THERON Campion in Riverside found Lord Nicholas Galing a prey to doubt. After an unprofitable morning spent pacing the floor of this study and replaying in his mind what he had said to Lord Theron and what Lord Theron had said to him, Nicholas put on a coat of leaf-green and went to Lord Filisand's.

Despite the bright and beckoning weather, Lord Filisand's stuffy rooms were not thin of company. Spring in the city brought not only unfurling leaves and flowers in the gardens of the Hill, but also the Spring Sessions and the joint meeting of the Council of Nobles and the City Magistrates. As Nicholas threaded his way through the little knots of men in the greater salon, he overheard snippets of discussions on taxes, on the leather monopoly, on the rivermen's objections to the new storage tariffs—dull topics to one who had been sailing the deep waters of treason and intrigue.

"There you are, Galing." It was Lord Condell, sleek and graceful as a cat, with sapphire clips in his soft, fair hair. He tapped Nicholas on the wrist with his fan. "Have you heard the latest? The Tremontaine bastard's back in town—Jessica, the lady pirate."

Nicholas would have liked to astonish him by announcing that he had just been speaking to the lady, but discretion prevailed. "No!" he exclaimed, all polite incredulity. "Where is she living? She's not at Tremontaine House, I suppose."

"That's the thing," said Condell. "She's rented a house—a considerable house—on Albans Street on the Lower Hill."

"Not Lady Caroline's Folly?"

"The same. Ballroom, conservatory, stables and all. What do you think of that, eh?"

Nicholas beckoned to a footman carrying a tray, chose a leafy green roll and bit into it. Something was up. Two days ago, Jessica had looked very much at home at Riverside. Had she quarreled with Lady Sophia?

"Everyone knows there's no love lost between her and Duchess Katherine," Condell was saying. "Depend on it, this is some scheme to bedevil the poor woman."

Nicholas swallowed. "Or else she's simply decided to come home and settle down," he said in a bored drawl. "Surely pirating, if that's what she does, is a young man's—er, woman's—game."

Condell snapped open his fan. "Are those any good?"

"What? Oh, the lettuce rolls." Nicholas took another and held it out to the older man. "Very tender and fresh—an embodiment of Spring, in fact. Do try one."

Condell peered doubtfully at the crisp green roll. "I like my food cooked," he said. "She deals in art—figurines from Elysia and tapestries from Ardith—that sort of thing. She has a ship, sails everywhere, with a crew of women, it's said. A real virago. I can't see her settling down."

"Well," said Nicholas, sick to death of Campions, "time will tell. In the meantime, what do you make of Filisand's new protégé? Think he's grooming him for the Crescent's staff?"

Later that week, Lord Nicholas Galing returned home from his tailor's to find a large square envelope, addressed to him in an ornate secretarial hand, lying in creamy splendor on his hall table. Opening it, he found an invitation from Lady Jessica Campion, begging the pleasure of his company at a soiree the following evening. The occasion was a suite of paintings by the artist Ysaud, which Lady Jessica wished to display in her native city before packing them off to grace the court of an (unnamed) foreign monarch.

Nicholas turned the invitation over. On the back were scrawled the following words: *I invite you at my brother's urging. He says to tell you that he has something to give you. J.C.*

Waiting for a Little King to reach his moment of trial is among the greatest trials a wizard must himself face. In a way, it is the wizard's test as much as the Little King's, testing his skill in reading the demands of the time, the ability of his candidate, the needs of the Land. For in the end, the Land chooses the king it needs to serve it.

Basil St Cloud spent this time of waiting as his predecessors had passed it before him: in study. He was, he feared, a weak wizard, and most woefully unprepared. He'd had no magister to teach him, no colleagues with whom to dispute and discuss the theory of transformations, the signs of omen, the mysteries of grove and pool. All he had was the voices of the past, the voices of the dead speaking to him through the documents, the legends and the histories he'd been living amongst these past weeks. These, and his dreams, gave him an inkling of what he must do to bring the Land alive again.

Among all his questions, certain facts stood clear. The Fall had cleansed the Land of false kings, of false magic. Basil's dreams were of an older time: of the grove and the knife, the bearskin and the cup, the deer and the hunt. The Book spoke to him more and more clearly, telling him what to do. He was heir to what the Land had lost. If Theron was mad, it was as it should be. All the true kings were mad. If only Basil studied well, he might yet gain the final knowledge to master this Little King. Together, they would complete the circle and renew the ancient promise.

Meanwhile, he had a book to write, a debate to hold, a challenge to maintain. He did not fear Roger Crabbe; Crabbe was like the false mages of his own imagining: ruthless, ambitious, and utterly without truth. Crabbe was a charlatan. Basil had all the proof of real magic he needed, in his own power and the Book of the King's Wizard. But the Book was too precious to be paraded before a crowd of gawking skeptics. He would hide what he had become from his fellows as long as he could; he would clothe the truth in language they could understand, the language of logic and scholarship. When they heaped him with praises, bestowed honors upon him . . . then he could sit secure and work what he knew into the fabric of reality. They might not even know he was doing it. But he would know, and the Land would know. And Theron, his false true lover, Theron would surely know.

So he sat in the Archives late into the night, long after the librarian, who was old and trusting, had left him with instructions to lock up after himself when he was done and leave the key above the door. The Book lay open before him. He had brought it for a purpose, and he opened for a second time to *A Spelle to Un-Cover Hidden Trothes*. Speaking it, Basil felt how weak and halting had been his first attempt. He still did not understand the words, but as he uttered them, they sang along his bones and echoed in his heart, an intimate and well-loved part of him.

When he'd finished, he stood and walked along one of the narrow lanes dividing the long banks of shelves. He reached up his hand and found a plain wooden box, tied up with black tape and very grimy. Within the box were yellowed documents, bundled and tied. They were from the time of the last king, letters to a University librarian, one Carrington. Most of them concerned matters of great interest to a scholar of the history of the University in the last years of the monarchy, but no use to Basil. Except one.

He knew it as soon as he laid his hand on it, before he'd unfolded its crackling yellow pages and squinted at the spiky, archaic hand. He glanced at the signature, then read it through, his heart beating faster as his eyes scanned the glorious, damning text. This was the proof he needed. All he had to do was go up before the Governors and the Doctors, the Fellows and Scholars of the University and show them this letter and Crabbe would be effectively and efficiently silenced before he could open his mouth.

Basil St Cloud sighed and folded the letter up again. Doing that would win the debate straight off, but it would do very little to demonstrate the superiority of St Cloud's methods over Crabbe's. There was that to think of, too: he wasn't only a fledgling wizard, he was a Doctor of the University, whose skills should be enough on their own. He longed to test the edifice of scholarship he had built over the past weeks against the academic rocks Crabbe was preparing to fling against it. He wanted to win; but he wanted to win by his own skills of persuasion and argument.

Briskly, he tucked the letter into the sleeve of his gown and laid the other papers carefully back into their wooden coffer. A debate that ends before it begins is no debate at all. He'd present his argument as he'd constructed it. If Crabbe found a way to refute it, he'd trump him with this letter and take the debate and the Horn Chair in a single definitive move.

When Basil reached up to tuck the library key above the door, the Book, heavy in his sleeve, bumped against his chest. What did the Horn Chair matter anyway? Or the debate, except as a prelude to the binding of the king and the waking of the Land? But Basil had been a scholar before he was a wizard, and to the scholar in him, the debate did matter. He was right, he had always been right, and he owed it to the men who followed him, the men who looked to him to lead them down new paths in the careful quest for truth, to prove to them that he was right. The Book did not change that. And then the Land would wake to a world of men who saw things clearly, who trusted their own intelligence, their skills of reasoning and observation. It would be a new world.

G ALING WAS NOT THE FIRST OF LADY JESSICA'S guests to arrive. Even those with little interest in the Campion family or in modern art were curious to see what she had made of Lady Caroline's Folly in three days.

She certainly had not furnished it, which would have taken a warehouse full of massive tables and cabinets. She'd contented herself with a few necessary pieces: a very fine carpet in the entrance hall and a comfortable sofa and a long mirror in the small side room where the ladies left their cloaks. She'd scattered lighted tapers lavishly through the cavernous rooms, where they coaxed the best from the frescoes and inlays with which Lady Caroline had decorated her walls. The effect was kind to cracking paint and buckling wood. It was generally agreed among the older guests that the place hadn't looked so impressive since it was new.

The hostess herself stood at the head of the stairs, greeting people as they entered her hall. She, too, was impressive. Her purple gown should have clashed with the bright russet of her hennaed hair, but instead they seemed to lend one another fire.

Her underskirt was of turquoise silk, woven in a curious foreign pattern; her lace trim was of gold, and gold hung from her ears and about her neck. "Showy," Lady Nevilleson murmured, and "Magnificent," breathed her husband.

Inside the salon, her guests' palates were teased with pickled cherries and roasted goose livers and purple wine that tasted of foreign sunlight. As Cecily Halliday later said to her husband, whatever one thought of it as a whole, it was an evening whose component parts one would be very sorry to have missed.

Those present could not help but remark on who had and had not been invited. No city merchants, bankers, not even other art collectors; only the nobility, it seemed, and of them, almost exclusively men who sat on the Council of Lords and their wives. It was early enough in the evening that they were all on their way to other engagements, to the first balls of the spring season, or to theatre and supper parties. The artist Ysaud was not in evidence, nor were any other members of the Tremontaine clan: not the Duchess Katherine, the Dowager Duchess Sophia, nor her son, Lord Theron—not even the various Talbert nephews and cousins.

"Perhaps they've been given a private showing," Lord Condell muttered to Davy Tyrone. "I do hope Ysaud turns up at this charming fair, she's better than a juggler with knives."

"I think," his friend said, "you'll find Lady Jessica entertainment enough. One hears she robbed the Marquis of Carabas of his grandfather's diamond ring, and sold it as a love charm to the Emperor of Tierce—a *love* charm, mind you!"

"Oh, dear. I had best look to my purse," Condell said. "Are those candied *quinces?* Pray get me some. Look, there's Galing—I know he likes them, too."

⌒

Lady Caroline's Folly came complete with a paneled library, and it was there that Theron sat among the scattered volumes, awaiting what was to come. Jessica had said, "You've nothing to do but stay right here; don't come out until I tell you to, no matter what. If Galing wants to see you, I'll send him in."

He stared at the bowl of fruit on the table: hothouse grapes, and some apples. They had neglected to leave him a knife; or perhaps she did not want him to have one. There was also a carafe of watered wine.

He could hear music, and voices. They were gathering, his people, in the house. His sister had summoned them. But they did not know of his hiding place. The hunter could not find him, could not smell him, could not see him where he rested amongst the leaves of all the books.

He curled into the cushioned chair by the library table, and fell into an uneasy doze. There the bear-man found Theron, whose hair was braided in two-and-twenty braids, tied off with jewels and bits of polished bone.

"My lord." The bear-man did not touch him, but Theron could feel his breath, hot as sun on earth. "Why do you hide from your people? Come out, and let them do you proper homage."

Theron shook his horn-branched head. "They will not do homage to this."

"Truly. You have run in this form for far too long. One wonders if you are king at all. The proper rites have not been observed. You led the hunt in your own shape, and now you cannot rule yourself in this one. I fear the time of trial is at an end." From the fur of his cloak, he drew forth a knife, dully gleaming stone, with an edge like an animal's tooth. "Rise, Little King, and kneel to me; bare your throat, and give your power back to the Land."

"No!" Theron tried to fling up his hands, but he stood trembling in deer form; his hands were hooves, planted on the ground beneath him.

The bear narrowed yellow eyes. "Then will you run?"

"I have run," Theron said. "I have been hunter and hunted. I have a deer's horns and a man's heart. And I have the Blood of Kings."

"Yes," the bear growled. "That is a beginning."

"Where, then, shall I run?"

"Why, to the grove," the wizard said, handing him the knife of stone. It was cold as death in his hand. "Run to the sacred grove, where oak and holly ring the pool—where you may know whether you shall live to take up kingship, or die to feed the Land." He struck the deer a blow on the haunch: "Run!"

Theron awoke with his heart pounding, his breath coming in quick, tight gasps. The room was squeezing the life out of him. He dashed to the window, flung open the casement and breathed in the sharp, cold air. Above, the stars pricked glittering patterns in the sky. The rooftops of the city gleamed in their light. There was no footing for him on the slate of the rooftops—no escape for him other than through the forbidden door.

T HEY ALL CALLED HER "LADY" JESSICA BECAUSE THAT was how she had styled herself on the invitation; those who would refuse her the courtesy title would also have scorned the invitation. But the older ones there remembered Jessica Campion as a girl. The women, particularly, recalled visits to Tremontaine House, and a fox-faced child who could be coaxed to sit on their laps with offers of sweets.

The ancient and delectable Lady Godwin kissed both her cheeks. "Jessica, my dear. You quite put me in mind of your mother, standing there. You have her stature, the way she dominated the stage. Do you ever engage in theatricals, my dear?"

"As often as I can, dear Lady Godwin. How good of you to come."

Lord Philip Montague bowed deeply over her hand. "Congratulations, Lady Jessica." He was a collector, and had canceled another engagement to come to this viewing. "A year of Ysaud's work, one hears, and not yet seen by any of us. Generous of you to share it with us before it all goes off to—where did you say it was going?"

Jessica looked him in the eye. "To a foreign monarch, my lord."

"Just so. I didn't know you dealt in canvas; I thought bibelots and jewels were more your line."

"They're easier to transport, certainly. But I hate to disappoint my clients."

"Oh, indeed. And we do appreciate it, as you know. That jade carving you sent me has pride of place in my summer home. Ysaud's work, though, is a particular favorite of mine. Should I see any paintings tonight that I really cannot live without, I hope that your monarch will not be disappointed if his cache is a few pounds lighter?"

"I really cannot answer for him, sir."

"I am prepared to be generous." He cocked his fair head, birdlike, waiting confidently for her answer.

"Of course you are," she said affably. "Well, go on and see them, then. Don't be distracted by the food, though; just walk past it through the double doors to the octagonal ballroom." She turned to the next guest. "Can it be Lady Herriot? This is not fancy dress, yet I could swear you are masquerading as your own daughter!"

Having gorged himself on quinces to his heart's delight, Lord Condell had attached himself and Tyrone to Lord Nicholas Galing. "And where, dear Nicholas, are you off to after this?" Condell asked.

"Well, if you must know, and I suppose you must," Galing drawled, "for there is no keeping secrets from you, Condell; as well try to hide a bit of candied quince that's got stuck between one's front teeth!" and he had the pleasure of watching his friend surreptitiously try to find out if he did. "I have a little *assignation* this evening, not far from here."

"That," Tyrone said, "explains the beribboned package you carry?"

Galing gave the flat parcel under his arm a little hug. "Precisely. I would not want it to go astray. So you'll understand if I survey the artwork and vanish."

"Perfectly," Condell smirked. "Then let us proceed into the room where it hangs. Historical paintings, are they not? Very educational, no doubt. I myself always believe— Good god!"

At his side, Tyrone murmured, "Who would have guessed that history could be so exciting?"

They were staring at powerful images of a naked man, his body washed blue in the moonlight, dappled by midday leaf and shade, or licked by the light of flames.

It was the underside of all the fusty images you found in old carvings and stained glass panels: the kneeling deer, the horned king, the deer-headed man; they had all seen the formal

406 ～ Ellen Kushner & Delia Sherman

representations a hundred times. Ysaud's paintings were a dream of those things, raw and vivid as a nightmare, or a scene remembered out of childhood.

The images were everywhere, up and down the walls of the salon, on canvases large as the walls themselves and small as the pages of a book.

When they had stared for some time, Tyrone observed, "It's all the same man."

"Is it?" asked Condell, entranced.

"Certainly. Observe the arms, the turn of the leg. And the neck—when it's not covered in fur. What's that on his chest?"

"Leaves, I think." Condell leaned in closer. "No, they're painted—meant to be marked directly on the skin, I mean; see the way they crease here, and the shadow? What a pretty pattern. Perhaps I should have it done myself."

"Perhaps you should." Tyrone stepped back. "This is a year's work, this is. She painted someone for a year—"

"Indeed she did," Condell drawled, "and not so long ago. And I know who. What do you think, Galing?"

"I think," said Galing, "that if I were that man, I would be very displeased by this night's work. Was Lady Randall invited, do you know?"

"I don't. But I do think someone should tell her about it. Are you her particular friend, Galing?"

"Not yet," said Nicholas.

They heard a curious sound behind them: a sort of collective sigh from the group of people who had just entered, all struck dumb, all gazing at the vision that surrounded them.

"One hears," Condell murmured, "that our hostess has quarreled with her family. That is old news—now fully reconstituted, like a slice of dried apple soaked in very potent wine. I would now raise that 'quarrel' to a declaration of war."

Around them, the room was erupting into a frantic buzz. Condell added, "I am so glad we decided to come."

JESSICA WAITED UNTIL THE NOISE WAS LOUD ENOUGH TO signify that speculation was in full cry. Then she signaled to a footman to call for silence. She stood just inside the doors. Purple and turquoise and crimson and gold, she was a work of art in her own right, and those with a taste for history might have remembered the ancient Southern queens who led armies in royal chariots draped with silk.

"My lords, my ladies." She pitched her voice to carry melodiously into the eight corners of the room. "Noble friends. You all honor me with your presence this evening. I have been absent from my native city for many years. In that time, you have maintained the well-being of our land. You have nourished it with your sons and your daughters, your tears and your laughter, your toil and your watchful care. My thanks I offer, most inadequately, in the display of these pictures, this complete work of genius that renders the ancient soul of our country for all to see. After tonight, they will be gone, so I beg you to look your fill, and to accept the offering in the spirit of thanks with which it is meant."

There was a smattering of applause. Jessica smiled. "A moment ago, I called you 'friends.' And it is as friends that I make bold to speak to you now. The work you see around you celebrates our country's past with the handiwork of the present, and I believe it will resound to our honor long into the future." Murmurs, now, of approbation. "The past," she went on, "can be a source of glory. And it can be a source of shame, but only if we let it be. For what are we, friends, if we cannot rewrite the past by creating a present glory that eclipses it and shines forth the way to an even nobler future?"

"Right!" someone shouted. It was not Galing. He was watching with mute fascination as Jessica held out her hand and took from a servant a heavy piece of folded paper, marked with a seal that could be Tremontaine's. Lord Theron was not here. The woman was clearly poisonous, bent on bringing her half-brother down, or at least on humiliating him. Was this paper his report, his confession of treachery? And was she going to read it aloud, here, now, to the assembled nobles of the city, in the presence of the paintings that exposed him to gossip and ridicule? Galing closed his eyes a moment. She was not, as far as he knew, working for the Serpent Chancellor. But then, he knew so little of Arlen's plots and games.

Jessica spoke again. "What is the past? For me, it has been a thing of shame. You know of my father, David Alexander Tielman Campion, Duke Tremontaine. You know how I was born of his dalliance with an actress revered in the theatres of this city as the Black Rose. This is the past, this is my shame, though you are kind enough to overlook it, and to treat it as none." There were sympathetic murmurs from a few women.

"I wonder," Jessica said, "how you will feel when I show you this?"

She lifted up the paper, and held it high. She really did look like a queen in a play.

"I hope that you will welcome it and me among you as warmly as you always have."

Galing's eyes were riveted, waiting for her signal to him that it was time to come forth. She knew he was here; she'd greeted him cordially, and whispered to him not to leave until they had taken care of business. By which he'd thought she meant until she had produced Theron. Now, he thought he understood that she meant him to produce the sketches and finish her night's work.

"We cannot change the past," Jessica went on, "but we can reinvent it. Rediscover it, give new meaning to old actions, and uncover hidden truths. And thereby forge a new future, free of shame. And so with pride and joy I tell you, my friends, lords and ladies of this noble realm: I hold in my hand the secret marriage vows made between my father, the Duke Tremontaine, and his love, the Black Rose—sealed with his own seal, and dated six months before my own birth."

Pandemonium.

Nicholas found that he was crushing the edge of the port-folio. The treacherous bitch. He didn't for a minute think the "marriage lines" were real, but it didn't matter, did it? She could have Tremontaine tied up in the courts for years on this one, if she pursued it and the family denied it. What use would the Randalls have for their bridegroom now? His inheritance insecure, his last lover—no, make that his last lover but one—a res-urrected scandal . . . And so what power did Galing have left over the mad, treasonous, scheming, lecherous young noble?

"My lord." Galing did not look up. There were so many lords here. But the servant gently touched his sleeve. "My lord of Galing. Please come with me."

Jessica was in the middle of a crowd of well-wishers. "I'm sorry," Galing said. "I have another engagement. But if you would give her ladyship these—" He tried to push the packet of sketches into the servant's hands, but the man said, "If you please, sir. My lady said you were to follow me."

Galing followed, thinking furiously.

⌒

THERON STARED AT THE DOOR, THE SOLID WOOD bound with metal. It felt as dangerous to him as the forest at night once had. But now it was the barrier he must cross, the boundary between himself and the sacred grove where he would face his trial. He could hear, faintly, the cries of the hunt on the other side: people crying out, and laughing, making a music with their voices that rang with danger for him.

The door opened. Lord Nicholas Galing stood there, dressed in crimson. He was holding out a flat, brown package.

"Lord Theron," he said, "I give you these. I have no further use for them." He bowed. "Good night."

He was gone before Theron could move. The packet lay on the table. Slowly, Theron approached it, as if it were a beast that could spring and pounce. He sniffed at the ribbons before he untied them; they smelt faintly of mildew and sandalwood.

The sketches, though, smelled of Ysaud: her chalks, her pencils, her hands. Theron buried his face in the paper. He felt a chill along the vine etched into his flesh, a fierce pricking tingle like the ghost of the blade that had made it. He peeled off his jacket and his waistcoat, then his shirt, to expose it to the air. He turned the leaf of paper over and saw his own face, eyes closed in sleep. He was looking at a young man he did not really know, with a sweet mouth and winglike brows, captured in just a few lines; a

face washed free of all sorrows by the aftermath of pleasure—
drawn by the hand that had given him that pleasure.

"Ysaud," Theron whispered. He had loved the way she
looked at him—as if everything in him delighted her and she
could never have her fill. Basil looked at him that way, too.
Theron's hand was nearly steady as he turned up another sketch.
It was for one of Ysaud's paintings; he remembered the pose, the
way his back had ached from leaning over the silver mirror she'd
laid on the floor for him to peer into, half-kneeling, half-rising,
his arms braced against the floor. She had tormented him with
the placing of candles, moving them here and then there to get
just the right reflection. The sketch, though, showed none of
that—just his back, his haunches straining to flee and his body
riveted by what the pool disclosed: the shadow of horns upon his
brow.

Again, the door opened. Warm scented air rushed into the
room, and the breeze from the open window rustled the sketches
on the table.

"Ah," said Jessica, "good, you've got them. My guests are
gone. Do you want to see the paintings?"

N AKED TO THE WAIST, THERON CAMPION STEPPED
into the room that held the year of his life that he had
given to Ysaud so he could love her and she could paint him in
numinous, glowing scenes from their nation's golden history and
its dark legend.

The canvases lined the walls of the octagonal salon. They
were all light and shadow: acid yellow firelight hit the dull rose of
illuminated flesh half-obscured by a green-black tree trunk or a
star-dappled boulder. Blue stars danced in black water. Under a
noonday sun, sharp green holly leaves pricked out the gently cor-
uscated grays and umbers of an ancient oak. A still, silver pool
was tarnished with the shadow of horns.

Theron paced to the center of the grove. Around him oak
and holly rustled. He stood under sun and moon and stars. The
water of the sacred pool glittered, half-blinding him. He bowed

and, kneeling before it, looked into the water. His face was reflected in the pool. He recognized the liquid eyes and soft muzzle
of the stag. It was the hunted stag, the king stag, the deer that he
must slay.

He was full of power, devoid of speech. And yet he knew
himself. If he could speak, he would have spoken his own name.

Instead, he took the stone knife from his belt, the knife the
wizard had given him, and raised it on high.

He smelled the man's approach, smelled his skin and his
sweat and his fear. He saw the same fear in his own eyes, and the
same pride. One of them must die. Kill the deer and rule as king;
let the deer run free, and the man in him would soon be gone.

He thought then of the woods, of the sweetness of new grass
and the wild joy of autumn rutting, the quick fighting and
the slow dreaming without loss. And he thought of the stony
labyrinth of city streets, of running wild in the smoky dark, the
strain of sinew and the triumph of blood. He might now cast
away the knife in that human hand, and run on four legs to where
the hunt would never find him!

No one would ever find him. He would give up all the promises he had made, the duties his blood bound him to. He would be
free of his past. Free of the burden of his speaking, and the burden
of his dreams—and free of love and kindness, as well. Forget
them all. . . .

But he would not. Looking deep into his own eyes, he recognized that he had been born for this moment, trained to it all his
life. In the last year, he had imbibed love and power and knowledge and magic. Remembering that, he could not cast away his
name, his face, his humanity. He raised the knife. The stag
opened his mouth and cried out for the loss of his sure hooves
and branching horns, his leaping haunches and keenness of
smell, and the green stirring of a spring morning as he felt the
knife in his heart.

Then he lay still, a half-naked man on a marble floor, surrounded by art, with a painted ceiling above him depicting the
constellations in their seasons.

Theron felt the world fall away from him. Then he was hearing a voice, someone's voice, saying, "Theron. Theron." There

were hands on him, urging him to speak, and to look. Surely they must be Basil's, those kind and steady hands invading the darkness; Basil, come to the woods for him at last, to love him and reward him for having stood the trial, to bring him back to himself.

But when he opened his eyes, it was Jessica, his sister, gorgeously dressed and kneeling beside him, holding a cup of watered wine and saying, "Theron. Will you drink?"

He drank deep and came to himself enough to realize where he was—in Jessica's salon, surrounded by Ysaud's paintings. He started to shiver. She said, "For a moment, I thought you were dead. You were ungodly pale." She unhooked her overskirt and wrapped him in it. "You should go to bed," she said.

"No. Not now. This—" He gestured at the forest of canvas around him "—this is amazing. *You* are amazing—even more than I thought, I mean. Tell me all about it."

"At least get up off the floor."

That he could do, with her help. She settled him by the library fire, in a chair with blankets. Then she sent for wine and food for them both. Theron found that he wanted to eat everything on the tray: cheese and fruit and smoked goose and fish and meat. As he ate and drank, he seemed to feel his whole self becoming more solid. His hands were his hands, not something in a painting, not something like a dream on a forest path. The meat smelled good to him. The blankets were comfortably scratchy and warm. He gnawed on a cold joint, and Jessica drank red wine and answered his questions.

"How on earth did you get the paintings?"

"Worship me," she commanded around a mouthful of bread and cheese. "God, I'm starving. I didn't dare eat until it was over. And I was stone cold sober the entire time. Drink some wine, it'll settle your nerves. If I'd known they would affect you that way, I'd have kept you away from those pictures."

"No," he said, "it's all right. Really, it is. I feel fine—better than I have in days."

"I was wondering if you'd even ever seen them before. If not, the shock could kill you. I should have thought of that. I mean— she did show you them, didn't she? That woman is capable of anything."

She sounded simultaneously smug and appalled. Theron looked closely at her, and decided not to ask. "What did your guests think of them?"

"They were impressed."

"By the sight of my naked ass?"

"Now, now." She wiggled a drumstick at him. "They don't *know* it's your naked ass."

"Don't be naïve, of course they know."

"Nah." She took a deep swig of wine. "They may *suppose* it is. They may even be right in that supposition. But the only way for them to *know*, is to get a look at the sketches—which we now possess. Gossip is like ginger nuts: delicious, ten to the copper, and worthless cold. As I am leaving in a week or so to sell these abroad, it will all be forgotten in a fortnight, and your—body remains your private property, to dispose of as you will."

Theron irritably shrugged off one of the blankets. "Unless Galing chooses to tell someone."

"But he will not. For the same reason you're not getting married."

"Which is what?"

"I am contesting your claim to Tremontaine."

He stood up. He was quite warm now. "Jess! Are you serious?"

"Only temporarily. My mother was an actress, remember? I've got about a week left to be very serious about it, then I can leave and you can forget the whole thing."

He said, "My mother is a surgeon, but I'm not always trying to cut people open. How are you contesting my claim?"

"By pretending to be legitimate. I got one of my old friends to forge me some documents: it's not hard to do Alec's signature, and Rose could barely write."

He heard a brittle sorrow behind her words. "Jess," he said gently. "You know if you really wanted the duchy—"

It was her turn to jump up, waving her wine goblet like a banner: "No! I *don't* want the duchy! Even if I *were* legitimate. I've spent my whole life avoiding the duchy and what it means— can't you get that through your head? It's all a diversion—to convince the Randalls that you're a bad bargain after all."

"The Randalls! Were they here?"

"I'm not crude. They'll hear what they have to. But the paintings are not the point. If you think they didn't already know about you and Ysaud, you underestimate your soon-to-be-former future in-laws. What's a bit of talk about a man they already know can't keep his breeches closed, when the end of it is their daughter being installed as Duchess Tremontaine? No, my dear; what will scare off the Randalls is the notion that the girl might be stuck with you, without the title."

He said admiringly, "Katherine will never speak to you again."

"Yes, she will. I warned her, and I got her to finance my down-payment to Ysaud. Best investment she'll ever make. She'll thank me. They all will. No one liked this marriage but you, Theron. Katherine liked the idea of you being married, but the Randalls are no great catch. You can do better. As for Sophia, not to mention Marcus and Susan . . . I think they'll forgive my methods." There was a pause while she refilled her goblet. "By the way, you've missed something."

"What?" The wine and meat sat warm in his belly. He felt comfortable, unburdened, soft as warm wax.

"Galing! This also took care of Galing for you. He very nearly gave the sketches directly to me, since he thinks I'm trying to unseat you, something he's theoretically in favor of. But he's cautious, and he's a political creature. I could easily lose, and if I do, he doesn't want to risk being on Katherine's bad side. Never underestimate the advantage of powerful relatives."

"That's what Katherine's always telling me." Jessica grimaced at him. "I have just one last question," he said, rolling crumbs on the tabletop.

"Yes?"

"How did you know I didn't really want to get married?"

"Oh . . . lots of ways. You never talked about the girl, for one." She forbore to mention the fight near the Apricot. "When Galing threatened you with the sketches, you didn't even worry about how your betrothed would feel. That was pretty telling. But most of all . . . Most of all—you said Katherine talked you into it. I knew that was a bad idea."

Theron grinned at his half-sister. "How well you know us all." He leaned back in his chair. "You know, it's not that they're not both splendid people, Katherine and Marcus. But don't you find that their vision is a little narrow?"

Jessica idly sliced a grape into tiny pieces with her knife. "Council and taxes, you mean?"

"Taxes and Tremontaine. Tremontaine and the City. They don't really have a feel for the Land," he said with newfound certainty. "The whole land, I mean. It's all there, if you are looking for it. Metaphorically, of course: nobody can see it all with their eyes open. But if you close them, thus . . . I can see corn growing in Morpeth, and the worm gnawing at the root. The fish in the river—salmon racing past Buckhaven, and the way the rain falls to make the waters rise.

"What's Tremontaine to all that?" Theron asked.

⁓

Dear Sophia,

Theron and I are having such a good time catching up with one another that I've asked him to stay here with me for a few more days. You and Katherine will be hearing shortly from the Randalls, I make no doubt, and a few other people as well. Pretend to be annoyed with me, and if anyone asks, please tell them Theron is shut up with you there in the Riverside House, sulking and plotting revenge. He sends his love, as do I—

Jessica

chapter VI

LORD NICHOLAS GALING HAD PLAYED HIS HIGHEST cards and the pirate queen had trumped them all. He found he could not take his loss philosophically. His conviction that Campion was a threat to the city's peace was not yet dead, though his reason insisted that Lady Jessica's action had neatly gutted it. What could the boy do, exposed before all his peers as an artist's model and plaything? No one would remember how beautiful the pictures were, how fine the compositions, how vivid and living the tints. All the nobles would remember was Campion's shame. Were he proclaimed king twenty times over, all they'd do was laugh.

Immediately upon returning the sketches to Campion, Nicholas had left Lady Caroline's Folly and strode off into the night, ignoring the chair-men and linkboys clamoring for his custom. By the time he had turned into his own street, his feet were sore from walking so far and so briskly in thin slippers, and his heart was sore with his failure to bring Campion to heel. It was all very well for the city to be saved, but Galing was too honest, at least with himself, not to acknowledge that he wanted to be the one who'd saved it—not some showy bastard with dyed hair and gaudy, foreign clothes. Waiting for his manservant to let him in, he decided to burn all the paper cluttering his study: Edward's notes, Arlen's ambiguous messages, the transcripts of the examinations of Finn and Lindley at MidWinter. All Henry Fremont's letters. Then he'd drink a glass or two of brandy, go to bed, and put the whole disaster out of his mind. It was what Arlen had told him to do, after all.

But when Nicholas took off his velvet coat and picked up a handful of paper with the intention of casting it into the flames of his study fire, his eye fell on the words written at the top: "From the first days of the Union, the nobles hated the wizards, and plotted to weaken them."

Basil St Cloud's words, transcribed by Henry Fremont just as he'd spoken them. They were incautious words by any measure. Seditious words, if heard and taken to heart by men who hated the nobles. Dangerous words, if uttered by a man who believed that magic was real. And hadn't the magister offered to defend that very proposition before the whole University this spring?

Did Basil St Cloud honestly believe in magic? How could he, when the wizards had been debunked by every major historian of the past two hundred years, beginning with Vespas in *The Book of Kings*, and proceeding through Fleming and Trevor and White to old Doctor Tortua in *Hubris and the Fall of the Kings*? Why, the man's lectures were peppered with quotes from them all; how could he be planning to debunk the debunkers? Nicholas ground his teeth. Maybe there was something in Henry's lecture notes he'd overlooked.

Impatiently, Nicholas began to rummage through the mess of papers. His manservant came in with the brandy and a face like a priest at MidWinter, asking if he'd like something to eat. Nicholas rejected the brandy with loathing. If he was going to make sense of all this and prove that Arlen was wrong, for once, he was going to have to work all night. And if he was going to work all night, he needed chocolate, not brandy.

He ordered the chocolate and returned to the papers. He'd

allowed them to get out of order, piling this on that without regard to chronology or subject. Well, he'd just have to arrange them and see what turned up.

It was a tedious process. He needed to read at least a little of each paper before assigning it a pile, and many of Fremont's reports touched on several subjects at once: the Northerners, the enmity between St Cloud and Doctor Roger Crabbe, St Cloud's lectures on ancient history. He kept at it doggedly.

Chocolate appeared. He drank it, and ate the cold meat that appeared with it. Afterward, his head was clearer, and the work went faster. Midnight came and went, and still Lord Nicholas read and sorted with increasing excitement. The pattern he had outlined to Arlen was clearer than ever, but now he saw that the figure standing in the center, the figure to whom all paths led, was not Theron Campion, but Campion's lover, Basil St Cloud. Basil St Cloud, who believed the wizards' power to be not only true magic but a benevolent gift to the land and its people.

There it was, in plain view, for anyone who bothered to look for it, transcribed from St Cloud's lectures: "*The ancient wizards were first, servants of the Land, and second, servants of the Truth. When they came South with King Alcuin the Diplomat, they learned to serve political expedience as well. It weakened their magic and weakened their minds.*" And there: "*The nobles mistrusted the wizards from the beginning and passed law after law limiting their influence and the practice of magic.*"

Basil St Cloud was a careful man, meticulous and scholarly. Surely he would never have posed the challenge if he wasn't very sure he had the proof to win it.

It was the only thing that made sense of it all. Galing could not imagine what St Cloud had found, but it would have to be something spectacular, something incontestable. It would, he realized reluctantly, have to be something that genuinely demonstrated magic's potency. Not a letter, not a document. The real thing: a talisman, perhaps, or a wizard's manual. Whatever it was, he'd use it to win the debate on the Great Hall steps. And then what? Take up the Horn Chair and go tamely back to lecturing and writing? Nicholas laughed at the thought. No. The Horn Chair couldn't possibly be the point of this ridiculous challenge.

If Basil St Cloud had found something to waken a sleeping magic from the past, waken it to life and to his service, what would he—what would any man—do with it but use it to take everything? Say St Cloud had found the means to transform himself into a latter-day wizard. Surely his ambition was to rule the land as the wizards had ruled it in ancient times.

Galing had read Henry's lecture notes. By St Cloud's own evidence, a wizard needed a king to help him realize his full power, a king who was his lover. How fortunate for the good doctor that he had just such a lover ready to hand!

Nicholas turned over a page headed "*Notes on the Spring Festival*," and read, "*Northern kings were consecrated to the Land every year at the Festival of Sowing. For a new king, the consecration served as his formal induction as Servant of the Land—his coronation, as it were; although the Northern kings wore no crowns.*"

As far as Nicholas could tell, Theron Campion was likely to be made king at the debate whether he'd plotted for it or not.

Having reached this point in his cogitations, Nicholas rang for his manservant. He had to ring three times, and when the man turned up at last, his nightshirt showed under his unbuttoned livery.

"What time is it?" Galing demanded.

"Five, sir, or thereabouts. Not quite dawn."

"Damn." Galing rubbed his eyes. "Go get me something to eat, will you? I'm ravenous."

When the manservant returned with toast and jam, his master had fallen asleep in his chair, his curly head cocked back at an uncomfortable angle and his legs stretched out before him. The manservant contemplated his sleeping master for a moment, then spread a rug over him, laid another log on the fire, extinguished the lamp, and left him to it.

～

THE DISSOLUTION OF THE BETROTHAL CONTRACT BEtween Alexander Theron Campion of Tremontaine and Genevieve Beatrice Halliday Randall was quickly and easily achieved. The young lady, her mother said, had given certain indications that she was not yet ready for the solemn duties of marriage. Since it would be rude for Theron's family to seem not to mind, Tremontaine's lawyers put up a token fuss, which allowed the Randall lawyers to point out an irregularity in the contract's provision for the return of dowry in case of death without issue, which they had somehow previously overlooked. This, the Tremontaine side said, was unfortunately a point not open to discussion. And so, to the satisfaction of all parties, the contract was declared null and void. Corollary papers were signed, including the old-fashioned statutory agreement that all had been settled with honor, and thus no swordsmen were to be employed. Theron's necklace, however, was not returned; clearly the Randalls considered it just recompense for all the trouble and embarrassment he had subjected them to.

His family considered the necklace a small price to pay. Sophia in particular was nothing if not relieved. And it freed the Duchess Katherine to turn her attention to the fuss everyone was now making about Jessica's announcement. The duchess had written to Sophia:

> In typical fashion, Jessica has managed to turn this whole affair into a masquerade ball. As people are watching all of us to see which way the wind blows, it follows that you must be seen visiting me at Tremontaine House, to show that I continue to support Theron's claim to Tremontaine. I shall not, however, be allowed to go and see what J. has made of Lady Caroline's Folly—although the friends of mine who were there tell me it is quite something. And, of course, Jessica cannot be seen to be speaking to either of us; which means, in this case, that she will visit me in disguise, probably this afternoon.
>
> Theron is in hiding at the Folly (how appropriate!); probably the best place for him. I hope you will not mind too much, but there with his sister is the last place anyone will look for him. Of course I think it would be best for him to go to the country until it has all blown over, but in view of his recent illness, Jessica says we should wait before he makes the journey. I do think it advisable, however, that he go soon. People will be talking for a while, and you know how he suffered over the Ysaud gossip the

first time around. This will be much worse. It will die down
when J. leaves and the Randall girl finds another fiancé. But we
have all been worried about his health. The summer heat is
bound to be bad. Will you go with him? I thought to
Highcombe, which did him so much good when he was a child.
And everyone there loves him. Perhaps you can leave soon after
this absurd debate, which both Arlen and the University
Governors assure me I must attend. I suppose you will be there,
too, looking official in your robes.

Sophia was used to allowing Katherine to judge what was best for
public displays of Tremontaine policy. But the physician could
wish that she had gotten a letter from her son herself.

Theron had in fact written to Sophia, but his sister had not
sent the letter. She did not think it would reassure his mother to
be invited to witness the ceremony of his union with his wizard
and lover, on the steps of the Great Hall, at the Festival of the
Spring Sowing.

⌐

HAVING DECIDED THAT HE MUST, AT ALL COSTS, PRE-
vent Theron Campion and Basil St Cloud from coming
together on the steps of the Great Hall, Nicholas Galing was not
as pleased as he might be to hear that Theron had been bundled
off to the country by his cousin. Perhaps it was because the rumor
was only one of the half-dozen or so speculations concerning the
Tremontaine scandal making the rounds of Hill gatherings.

"Wasn't it delicious, my dear?" inquired Lord Condell, re-
splendent in rose brocade and opals at Lady Horn's musical
evening. "One suspected that she was painting him all that time,
but one didn't actually *know*. And the poses! I hardly knew where
to look." His fan, his wickedly sparkling eyes, said he'd known
very well where to look, and how much he'd enjoyed the view.
"I've been at the point of challenge with Tyrone, whether those
leaves were actually painted on young Campion's body or a
charming invention of the artist's imagination. What do you
think, my dear?"

"That I prefer leaves on trees, Condell, and a human head on my lover's shoulders. It's no wonder he's slunk off to the country."

"Oh, no, my dear," Condell said. "He's not in the country at all. I'm sure of it. The redoubtable dowager would certainly have accompanied him to the country, and she's very much in evidence, I hear, doing good as usual. No, they've got him locked up somewhere he won't do any harm."

The Duke of Karleigh wandered up, wanting to know if anyone could find something else to talk about other than the Tremontaine affair.

"What else is there to talk about?" Lord Condell asked rhetorically. "The Great Wizard Debate at the University?"

"I don't know what the world is coming to," said Karleigh. "Not that the Tremontaines ever were any good. Bad blood, is what I think. And bringing a foreigner into it didn't help. Perhaps we're better off with the bastard chit after all—at least she's pure native blood on both sides."

"Pure?" Lord Condell was amused. "The Black Rose was an actress, Karleigh."

"From Riverside. Not from some island no one's ever heard of. No reason the bastard chit shouldn't inherit, if she's legitimate after all."

"Now, Karleigh, you don't believe in those marriage lines, do you?" asked Condell. "You couldn't. She was amusing herself at our expense, the minx. Just look at what she was wearing!"

That conversation, or the gist of it, echoed through the salons and dinners and card parties. Theron Campion was ill; he was mad. He was in the country; he was locked up in Riverside; he was confined to Tremontaine House for trying to murder Ysaud. Jessica Campion was a legitimate contender for heir of Tremontaine; she was an upstart, or even a foreigner who had killed the real Jessica on board her ship and was trying to claim her inheritance. The Duchess Katherine would recognize her claim and step down; she would call blood challenge on her and fight the challenge herself. Unless Lord Theron did so. He was, after all, known to have run as a boy with killers in Riverside, in one of those gangs that required three dead bodies as an entrance fee. Also, it was entirely possible that Jessica was the legitimate heir in more ways than one; there had been talk of the young Katherine Talbert being with child when she first came into the duchy, either by a family servant or by her uncle himself. Why else would the old duke have left everything to an underage girl, unless it was to make it up to her? Stories of the Mad Duke's habits and proclivities were brought out of storage and aired anew.

Nicholas Galing listened to it all, exclaiming, wondering, doubting volubly that there was anything in it, whatever it was. He'd have given his sapphire neck-pin for hard information on Theron's whereabouts and state of mind, but the troublesome young noble seemed to have stepped from his half-sister's house into oblivion. There was nothing for it, Galing decided, but to turn up at the debate and see what came up. If nothing else, he told himself, he'd be able to follow the arguments.

JESSICA APPEARED IN KATHERINE'S STUDY DISGUISED AS a gardener, her straw hat pulled low over her face. When her cousin greeted her she took off the hat and shook out her hair and gratefully accepted a drink. Handing her a glass of wine, the duchess said, "Aren't you going to check to see if it's poisoned?"

"Alas," said Jessica, "I left my Authentic Guaranteed Unicorn's Horn back on the ship. Along with my fortified Blood Stone. I'll just have to trust you."

"It's mutual," said the duchess. "For, God help me, Jessica, if you are using my money and family to pull off the greatest scam of your career, you'd better hope that horn is authentic."

Jessica flicked an imaginary bug from the rim of her glass. "Don't be melodramatic. Haven't I worked miracles in barely a week for Theron and Sophia?"

"Sophia!" Katherine exclaimed. "Sophia hasn't heard what they're saying out there. I have. It's every piece of scandal we've worked to bury for the past twenty years, trotted out for an airing. It's her worst nightmare. All she cares about is Theron—"

"And sick people. And poor people."

Katherine looked impatient. "Yes, I know, but she'd do all that anyway."

"Because she cares about people," Jessica said doggedly. "Admit it, Katherine—just because your whole life is Tremontaine doesn't mean that hers is."

Katherine breathed deeply through her narrowed nostrils. She hated the way Jessica could make her lose her temper. She was not going to do it this time. She said evenly, "Sophia gave up a lot to come here."

"That is the myth, isn't it?" Jess said coolly. "But you know what? I've been to Kyros. It's nothing, Katherine. It's an island with some goats and some rocks and some honey bees. Sophia was a village healer, a midwife. Here she's a duchess, a trained surgeon. Just what is it she's supposed to have given up?"

Katherine looked steadily at her flamboyant kinswoman. "You don't care even about Sophia? I thought she was the one of us you loved."

It was Jessica's turn to look impatient. "Stop trying to get at my feelings, Duchess. That's not how I do business. You want to pull on levers labeled *Love* and *Loyalty* and get me to do what you want—but I'm not fitted with them. All I want to do is tell you the truth, but you'd rather not hear it. Well, now I'm going to tell you an important truth, and you'd better listen." She leaned across Katherine's desk, her scarred hands spread on the bright wood. "You're going to have to start looking for another heir. Because Theron is mad."

Katherine's voice shook with fury. "What have you done?"

"What have *I* done?" Jessica threw back her head and laughed. "That's rich! I'm the only one who *hasn't* done! He's been stark staring bonkers since I got here, and probably before, and not a single blessed one of you has noticed a thing. Not you, not Marcus, not even Sophia. He's been fighting knife duels down by the docks. He's been having visions. He doesn't know where he is half the time. And now he thinks his University lover is going to make him king."

"*What?*" Appalled, Katherine remembered Arlen's visits. "That's not madness, that's treason."

"Now I have your attention. Treason touches Tremontaine."

"*Stop it!*" Katherine shouted, temper irrevocably lost. "You want me to leave your heart out of it? Then you leave mine, Jessica, and stop goading me. You have your ship, your people—I assume you care well for them, or you wouldn't have them still. I have the duchy. If you're not going to help me care for it, then get out of my house."

"I've got Theron," Jessica said softly.

"So you have," Katherine snapped. "But if he's mad, I don't want him."

Jessica watched her for a long minute. "You're bluffing."

Katherine nodded slowly. "I am. How perceptive of you. I do want him. Now: are you bargaining or threatening?"

Jessica Campion removed her hands from the desk and went to the window. "Neither." She spoke to the view outside, the long green lawns of her childhood. "I'm telling you he's safe with me at the Folly. He's locked up, and he's angry, but he's not going anywhere. If I can keep him from the debate this week, he might calm down. If he does, then maybe he can go home. If he doesn't, he's all yours." Her back still to her cousin, she asked. "Do you understand what I'm saying?"

"I think so," said the duchess. There was a long and uncomfortable pause. "Will you let me send a physician?"

Jessica turned from the window, all business. "Only if there is someone you trust not to tell the city and not to tell Sophia."

"Marcus, then?"

"I'd rather not. It's hard to know how Theron will react to things. How's this: I'll ask Theron to write you a letter, and let you judge for yourself. If you genuinely think he's better off locked up in the attic of Tremontaine House, like his great-grandfather, Marcus can come get him, and I wash my hands of the lot of you."

Katherine regarded her problematic relative thoughtfully. "Very well," she said at last. "I believe you're trying to help. But I'll want to see that letter. There's a lot at stake here you don't entirely understand."

Jessica picked up the disreputable hat and bundled her hair into it. "I won't argue with that," she said agreeably, and left the duchess to her thoughts.

THE COMPANIONS OF THE KING MET IN A BACK ROOM of the Green Man over cider and venison stew. There were six men in the little room, all sporting braids and carved wooden oak leaves: the First Five of the King's Companions, plus another, more junior one. They were all tall men save for the youngest of them, a small, bird-boned youth with bright copper-colored hair. They were silent, just now, with that gravid silence that falls over a group of men who have temporarily argued themselves to a standstill.

"Look," said Lindley. "We don't have to understand all the details. It's a mystery. We just have to have faith and be ready for whatever happens."

The tallest and grimmest of the Northerners held Lindley's gaze for a long moment. His name was Robert Coppice, and before the arrest of Greenleaf and Smith, he'd been Third Companion. Now he was First Companion, Master of the Hunt and Keeper of the Mysteries, and he felt his responsibilities weigh heavy on his shoulders. After the MidWinter Hunt, Greenleaf and Smith had spoken of a new king who would appear to lead them. The Companions were to hold themselves in readiness for his advent, after which everything would become clear.

These prophecies troubled Coppice. In the manner of all prophecies, they raised more questions than they answered. And Greenleaf, who kept the Mysteries very close, had taken them with him to the Chop, putting Coppice in the awkward and irritating position of being dependent on the Southron scholar Lindley for some of his knowledge of the lore and rituals of the ancient North.

The arrest of Greenleaf and Smith was a thorn under Coppice's nail for many reasons, not the least of which was his fear that they had revealed everything they knew to the Serpent Chancellor's torturers. Even after all these weeks, Coppice walked abroad with his shoulders itching, waiting for a Guard's heavy hand to grab him and a Guard's Southern voice to announce that he was under arrest for treason. There was something to be said for the fact that he and his Companions were still walking free.

"It is a mystery," he said heavily. "We are agreed on that, at any rate."

The Third Companion Farwell laid a comforting hand on his friend's arm. "We're agreed on more than that."

"We are?" said Coppice wearily. "All Greenleaf told us was that the new king is to be consecrated in the spring, and that we must be witnesses. We still don't know exactly where or when the consecration is to take place, nor who is to perform it."

"A wizard," said Farwell, in the tone of one stating the obvious.

The strong-necked natural scientist Hob sneered. "All the wizards are dead, Farwell, unless you happen to be hiding one under your bed."

"Guidry," said Lindley patiently. "I keep telling you. Guidry will come again and bind the new king to the Land. It says so in Martindale." He closed his eyes and recited: "*So Guidry retired to the Grove Within to rest him there and tarry in a place beyond the ken of man until that time when the Land's great need should call him forth to bind and dedicate a new king to its service.*"

"And what in the Seven Hells is that supposed to mean?" Hob burst out. "It didn't make sense to me the first twelve times you recited it, and it doesn't make sense now. How are we supposed to know that this debate is the right time?"

Coppice's long hands bunched themselves into fists. "Greenleaf said it was, remember? And there are the other signs."

Lindley obligingly quoted them. "*A trembling in the earth; a star that trails bright hair across the heavens; a famine.*"

Hob shook his head. "Foolishness. The earth trembles often in the North, and famine is a more or less constant fact these days. These things are natural science, not a message from the Living Land."

This opinion inspired Farwell, as it always did, to demand whether Hob even believed in the Living Land, and if he didn't, why he was a King's Companion. And that inspired Hob, as always did, to declare that he believed in the North and the power of the North, and that was what he'd always thought being a

King's Companion was about. The debate went on, treading ground already trodden to bare rock. Lindley quoted extensively from Martindale, his lecture notes, and heroic poetry; points were brought up and argued. Obscure ritual phrases were parsed and analyzed.

"*From the seed of kings comes the fall of kings and their rising again,*" Lindley repeated. "It's Campion. Who else could it be?"

"Any noble at all," said Hob truculently. "They all have royal blood, if you go back far enough. For that matter, so do we. And why now?"

"The star trailing bright hair," Lindley said patiently.

"It was up there, right at the start of Harvest term," Coppice reminded them.

"And we know that Greenleaf saw the horns on Campion at Last Night and drank magic from his lips," said Farwell. "I saw them too. He's the king, Hob, Southron or not. The Land has chosen, and it is not our place to question its choice."

There was a rather depressed silence, and then Burl, the Second Companion, asked, "What about the wizard? It's all very well to say that Guidry will come again, but where, and how? Did Greenleaf know?"

Coppice shrugged. "If he did, he didn't tell me. Lindley's got an idea that his magister, Doctor St Cloud, will summon him out of wherever he is—"

"The Grove Within, beyond the ken of man," Lindley interrupted eagerly.

"—the Grove Within, at some point during the debate he's challenged Crabbe to. No, Hob, before you ask, we don't know how he'll do it. This is magic, man, not a chemical demonstration."

"Well," said Hob with some satisfaction, "your precious magister is going to have to conjure up a king as well as a wizard. No one has seen hide nor hair of Campion for days. There's some scandal with those nobles—rumor has it he's been bundled off to the country and locked up until it all blows over."

Lindley smiled a fox's smile at him. "If you hate it all so much, Hob—me, Campion, magic, Guidry—then don't come to the debate. Stay home and study whatever it is natural scientists

study, and leave your fellows to support their king in the first moments of his triumph. You'll miss it all, of course, but you won't
mind that."

Hob stood up, knocking over his stool with a clatter. "You're
right there, city boy. I won't mind never seeing your carrot top
again, or hearing your damned Southron voice braying about
magic and wizards. The mysteries of the wood are one thing," he
said, appealing to Coppice. "They are the strength of the North
and the bond of our brotherhood. But I'll be damned if I'm going
to wait for a wizard out of the mists of time to appear on the steps
of the Great Hall on the word of a Southern boy who has never
run the Northern Hills or drunk deer's blood in the winter twilight."

When he was gone, Coppice took a deep breath and said,
"Right. Does anyone else feel as Hob does?"

"We all do," said Burl forthrightly. "But we're mindful of our
oaths. And some of us have known things in the mountains and
in the rites that make us less sure than Hob is that magic has fled
the Land."

"You'll go to the debate, then?" asked Lindley.

"We'll go," said Burl. "And we'll entreat the other Companions
to come with us. But if it so falls out that this debate comes and goes
and nothing comes of it but one Southron Doctor of History being
preferred over another, you'll have us to answer to, Lindley, and
you, too, Coppice."

Coppice glanced anxiously at Lindley, looking for some sign
of reassurance. But the young redhead's eyes were on the candle
flame and his hand was on the oak leaf around his neck, and the
expression on his face was that of a man who has heard all he
needs to hear.

chapter VII

FTER A WEEK OF UNSETTLED RAIN AND WIND, THE first day of Spring Festival dawned warm and clear. The breeze could not have breathed more sweetly, the sky shone more blue, the sun smiled more benignly upon the warming earth. It was a day for dancing on the grass and lying with your lover on soft moss—or at the very least, walking out by the river beyond the city walls.

Officially, it was a day for attending services in honor of the Green God of growth and plenty. In these secular days, the only celebrants in the Cathedral were gentleman farmers hedging their bets, the Crescent Chancellor and his staff, and a few old men and women raised to honor the gods. Those who ignored the Cathedral bells pursued other traditional activities: settling bets, announcing betrothals, digging gardens, fighting challenges.

As the University bell tolled six, Master Leonard Rugg stood in Minchin Street, beating a brisk tattoo on the door to Basil's lodgings. He was attended by Benedict Vandeleur, Peter Godwin, and Henry Fremont, all of them clean as soap and water could make them, and dressed in their festive best. Of St Cloud's inner circle of followers, two were absent: Anthony Lindley, off with his Northern friends, and Justis Blake, presumably lost in love.

The scruffy boy let them in with a yawn and the news that he hadn't seen hide nor hair of Doctor St Cloud in days. Vandeleur and Godwin exchanged worried glances; Fremont felt his heart sink to the patched soles of his scarlet boots.

"Don't worry," Rugg told them. "He was well enough two days ago to tell me to go soak my head and leave him alone. He wouldn't even let me in, but I heard him just fine through the door."

They mounted the stairs. Remembering his visit to St Cloud with Justis Blake, how strange the magister had been, how gaunt and haunted, Henry wondered what they'd find waiting for them.

"St Cloud?" Rugg banged on the door. "It's Rugg and your students. Let us in. We've come to take you Crabbe-hunting."

A perfectly sane voice bade them enter. Maybe it was going to be all right after all. And, at first, it looked as if it might be. The curtains were pulled back to let in the sun; the casement was open to let in the air. The room smelled of candle wax and ink. The man by the mantelpiece was dressed respectably in brown, with white linen showing at the wrists and neck. It took Henry a moment to realize that St Cloud's stubble had been allowed to grow into a full beard. And he'd hacked his hair short to his ears, where it curled vigorously.

"My god, Basil, you look like a carter!" Rugg sounded more angry than distressed. "They'll laugh you out of the University before you even open your mouth. Are you mad?"

It was a real question, delivered with some force. Doctor St Cloud gave it a moment's consideration before smiling and saying, "No, Leonard. Only preoccupied. It's been so long since I shaved, I simply forgot." He ran a hand over his beard, thick and glossy as an animal's pelt. "I've gotten used to it."

"Well, you can just get unused to it again," Doctor Rugg snapped. "What's your excuse for your hair?"

St Cloud shrugged. "It kept getting in the way, and one night I couldn't find so much as a piece of string to tie it with. So I cut it off." He smiled ruefully into Rugg's worried eyes. "It was a daft thing to do, Leonard, and I regretted it at once. But I'm not the only magister in the University to decide that long hair is an af-fection he can just as well do without."

"Quite. The hair's a minor point," said Rugg, "but the beard has to go. I was going to treat you to breakfast at Bet's, but we'll go to the baths instead, get you decently barbered. Got every-thing? Where's your gown?"

St Cloud collected his black gown from the back of a chair and put it on. The long, green sleeves swung heavily, weighted with his purse, perhaps, or books. He noticed his students, stand-ing in an uncomfortable knot by the door. "Vandeleur, Fremont, Godwin, I thank you for coming. You have all paid dearly for my pride, and I am grateful for your patience and loyalty. When this is over, I'll repay you with all the attention and knowledge at my disposal."

It was the old St Cloud who spoke, charming and self-assured and reasonable. But Henry could not help whispering to Vandeleur, as they followed their magister out into Minchin Street, "What does he remind you of?"

"A man who's worked himself into a state of exhaustion," snapped Vandeleur. "What should he remind me of?"

"The window in the Great Hall," said Henry. "The bearded man. The wizard."

Peter Godwin, overhearing this last, stopped dead on the landing and stared up at Fremont. "So he does!" he exclaimed. "I'll be hanged. I wonder if he realizes?"

"So do I," said Henry grimly. "And that's not the only thing I wonder."

"Debate's today," Rugg announced from below. "Not next week."

"Coming!" Vandeleur shouted, and grabbed Henry's arm. "I swear, Fremont, if I hear another word out of you about wizards, it's the last word you'll utter in this life. Am I clear?"

⌒

N ICHOLAS GALING DRESSED FOR THE HISTORIANS' debate with all of his usual care. He wore green, for spring, with a waistcoat embroidered with jonquils. In deference to the gravity of the occasion, the green was dark, and he wore no lace. He put on the jet signet his father had given him when he came of age and a jet pin in his neckcloth, then picked up, after some hesitation, the dagger he carried when he made his occasional excursions to the docks.

He stopped at the Gilded Cockatrice and downed a meat roll and a tankard of ale by way of fortification for the trials of the day, then set off for the Great Court. The narrow streets were crowded with Scholars, Fellows, and Doctors, chattering excitedly, hailing their friends, chewing a last mouthful of breakfast, buying steamed buns and slices of tomato pie from stalls the provident hosts had set up in the windows of their taverns.

As Nicholas got closer to the Great Court, the press grew until he could hardly push his way along. Long experience in negotiating crowded Hill parties came to his aid; he slid and darted among the shifting clumps, and finally found a side street that let him out at the corner of the Great Court, right at the foot of the Hall steps.

The steps ran the full length of the building, and were wide and shallow in proportion, creating a kind of natural stage above the Court. Just now, they were packed with Doctors and Governors and minor officials of the University, their bright sleeves waving like flags as they jostled for places.

"You here, Galing?" It was Lord Halliday, who made a hobby of philosophy, and never missed a public lecture on an interesting subject. He was standing on the bottom step as if he'd taken root there, arm in arm with Lord Edmond Godwin. "Some fellow in a red dressing-gown told us to stand here, and we're holding our position against all comers. Care to join us?"

Nicholas did, and made himself absentmindedly charming while the mess around them settled slowly into an orderly pattern. He studied it and positioned himself carefully, one step below the bottom-most row of Governors, at the inner edge of the little cluster of nobles. Besides Lord Halliday, there were few interested enough in University matters to abandon their holiday amusements to listen to a historical debate. Lord Edmond

Godwin was there because he was concerned about his youngest son, Peter. Others were present in their capacity as University Governors—the Duchess Tremontaine, for example.

Galing stole a glance at the duchess, who stood two steps above him, talking to her neighbor. She was small, round-faced, all but overwhelmed by the scarlet glory of her Governor's robe. He thought she looked strained. She caught him watching her and stared forthrightly back, clearly wondering whether she knew him. Boldly, Nicholas Galing gave her a smile and a bow. Still puzzled, she nodded back.

He turned to look out over the Great Court, which was stuffed as full of bodies as it could hold—a sea of black academic robes, broken here and there by small, bright shoals of civilians. Galing's eye fell on a familiar face not far from the steps: Henry Fremont, looking sullen as a donkey. And those men around him must be St Cloud's students.

Edmond Godwin said, "Oh, there's my boy! There's Peter!" and waved. The young boy beside Fremont cracked an embarrassed smile and waved back. Galing saw Fremont glance toward him, start, and blanch. Galing nodded to his erstwhile spy in a friendly manner, then watched him flush and shrug as the stalwart lad behind him questioned him.

Whatever else happened, this was going to be fun.

⁓

I N THE YEARS BEFORE DAVID, DUKE TREMONTAINE, killed Gerard the Last King, the Spring Festival had been the gaudiest and most licentious of the four seasonal celebrations. A great stag woven of rushes and fluttering with green ribbons was borne through the streets to the music of pipe and tabor. Crowds of women surrounded it, leaping and grabbing at the ribbons. She who succeeded in detaching one and holding on to it was assured of a man or a child—whichever she lacked—by year's end. Young girls tied their ribbons around their necks, or laced their dresses with them as a signal to the young men. Young wives tied theirs in a more private place, to show their husbands where their duty lay. Long ago, the court had camped in the fields beyond the city walls, and the king and his companions lay with every woman who pleased them, naked on the new-ploughed earth like foxes.

Over the course of the generations, the Great Stag had shattered into a dozen lesser deer—horned heads on poles, antlered dancers, a comic hobby-deer with a huge, stuffed pizzle under its scut—and the green ribbons were tossed to the crowd or given, with a kiss, to the girls who ducked, squealing, under the hobby's wide skirt. Anyone wore a ribbon who could come by one—granddams, schoolboys, toothless, grinning infants. Justis Blake wore one around his tail of sandy hair, tied in a jaunty bow. So did the fair Marianne, who'd insisted on seeing the debate that had put her Justy in such a swivet.

There weren't many green ribbons to be seen in the Great Court; hobbies and horned men didn't come into the University. There was plenty of greenery, though. The two statues of Reason and Imagination flanking the steps were rakishly garlanded with ivy. A clump of men gathered on and below Imagination's pedestal carried new-budded branches. Justis automatically registered the branches as oak, since oak leafs out later than most other trees, and then noticed that the men were Northerners, braided, gowned, and grim as death. The crowd shifted, and Justis caught sight of Lindley's hair flaming out among them, then disappearing again.

So he wasn't the only one to have deserted St Cloud's flock. It wasn't a real desertion, he reminded himself: he still agreed in principle with his magister's philosophy and scholarly method. It was just that St Cloud's irresponsible attitude had distressed him, and Marianne needed him, and it was nice to be making a little money and not always having to defend every word he said with examples and quotations. Still, he should have gone with the others this morning to lend a hand getting St Cloud to the Master Governor's house on time.

Marianne squeezed his hand. "Why so down-in-the mouth, love?"

"This is a serious moment. You won't see many smiles until this is all over." Justis looked down at her pretty, soft face. "I shouldn't have brought you. It'll take hours. You'll be bored silly."

"I'll be with you," Marianne said. "You'll tell me what's happening, and I won't be bored a bit. Oh, look there, on the steps! That's never a woman!"

Justis squinted. The sides of the steps were packed with dignitaries, a divided sea of scarlet and black. On the deep top step he saw that wooden seats had been set out for the older or more important officials. The outgoing Horn chair, old Tortua, was tottering toward one of them, supported by a tall, graceful figure crowned with a coronet of dark hair.

"That's Lady Sophia Campion," Justis said. "She holds a Chair of Surgery. I've seen her once before. She's a fair piece of work, as my mother would say."

"She'd have to be, to get around all those old men. Handsome, too, considering she'll not see forty again. When's the party start, then?"

Over the ocean-swell noise of the crowd, Justis heard a faint, melodic blaring and the measured pulse of a drum. "Soon," he said. "Listen. That's them now."

"Where?" asked Marianne, tiptoeing vainly. "I can't see a thing."

A MONG ALL THOSE PRESENT FOR THE DEBATE, JESSICA Campion had arguably the best view of the proceedings. She stood all alone at an excellent vantage point on the carved stone gallery that ran along the exterior of the Great Hall above the frieze of the kings, right below the glass window of the wizard and the deer. She wasn't afraid of heights and she disliked being jostled. It had been surprisingly easy to slip into the hall and up the winding steps to the gallery. Now she leaned in the shadow of an arch with her elbows on the balustrade and watched the crowd below shift and settle like a kaleidoscope.

Jessica enjoyed ceremonial display, and the procession currently winding its slow way through the Great Court was as fine of its kind as one of the Prince of Cham's Public Breakfasts. The University may not have had much recent experience with academic challenges, but it was at great pains to let everyone know that this was a solemn and important occasion.

First into the square marched two trumpeters and a drummer, their long hair clubbed, their black sleeves edged in the green denoting Fellows of the Humane Sciences. Four flags followed— one for each of the four colleges of the University: Humane Sciences, Natural Sciences, Law, and Physic—borne by the College Bursars, robed each in the appropriate color. Behind them came the two disputing Historians, accompanied by their seconds, carrying staves decorated with flowers and ribbons. Even at University, it was Spring Festival.

Jessica enjoyed the show. Theron had been telling her quite a lot about the University and its denizens over the past week; she couldn't wait to get a look at the famous Basil St Cloud. It was a pity Theron wasn't there to see it, but there was no question of letting him out before the debate. After it was over, Jessica expected he would either be cured of his delusions or turned over to Sophia for good. He had been making Jessica some very interesting promises, to be sure, but she doubted he could deliver.

T HE SPRING FESTIVAL WAS A GOOD TIME FOR EVEN the most carefully brought up young people to slip loose from the constraints of everyday life. Tutors and governesses were given a holiday, and parents went off to enjoy themselves. Thus it was that, on the Hill, two young girls were lurking on a street they had no business being on, in the shadow of a house they were not supposed to know about.

"Frannie! Come on!"

Looking up at the crumbling wall surrounding Lady Caroline's Folly, Lady Francesca knew a moment of panic. She wondered if it was too late to go home and slip back into the drawing room where she and Lady Agatha Perry were supposed to be weaving ribbons into festival crowns. But, she reminded herself sternly, people in books are never frightened by adventure; it is only afterward, when they discover the blood running down their backs, or the chunk of their shirt that has been torn away by dogs, that they feel the aftershock of fear. She did not hear any dogs on the other side of the wall. So she followed her friend and climbed it, and tumbled down next to her.

Both girls huddled together on the grass with the wall at their back, staring at the battlements and towers rising beyond the ragged lawn before them, gripping each other's hands. Their palms were clammy with excitement and gritty from the dirt of the wall they had just climbed.

"See?" whispered Agatha. "Nobody lives here. Not for years. They're all afraid of *her*."

"Her?" Frannie shivered. This was possibly the most exciting thing that had ever happened to her.

"Lady Caroline. She built the house. And then she died here. In the upstairs room. That one."

Frannie swallowed a scream. She'd seen a curtain move, right where her friend had pointed. "Aggie," she said, willing the words past the tightness in her throat, "let's go. What if someone lives here after all? Look, see, the gravel's been raked."

"The gardeners," Aggie said sepulchrally. "But they won't stay here after dark. Because of the ghosts. Just like in your story, only real. And we're going to see one. Unless you really want to go home now, of course."

"No." Francesca swallowed mightily. Her cousin was the only friend she'd made in the city so far. "I'm game."

They edged along to the stables, where Aggie found an ancient ladder. They half dragged, half carried it over the grass, trying to avoid splinters and discovery—although, of course, no one was there. Aggie laid her hand on the side of the house; the stone was cracked with frost and lichen. "I feel a deathly chill."

"Naturally." Now that they were there, it was do or die. They positioned the ladder under the window of Lady Caroline's room. It reached to the sill, settling into the stone in a comforting way.

"Hold the ladder," said Aggie; "I'm going up. If I see a ghost, I'll hoot like an owl."

"No you won't, you'll scream. I want to go first."

"If you see a ghost, you'll faint."

Frannie said with dignity, "I do not ever, ever faint."

Now was not the time to mention she was afraid of heights. Just think of it as a tower, she told herself, a tower with a princess at the top who needs rescuing. She put her feet on the first rung. It felt reassuringly firm. She reached for the next step. Her skirt was tucked into a pair of canvas gardener's trousers that Aggie had cached with great foresight for their adventure. She could be a cabin boy climbing a ship's rigging. There were no ghosts, not during the day. The curtain had not moved.

There was the window above her, the stone sill within reach of her hands. She stood tiptoe on the ladder, and looked in.

At first she thought he was a statue, leaning back against the elaborate bedpost, pale and beautiful, with ivy twined around his chest. But statues do not have long dark hair that caresses their naked shoulders, nor yet more dark hair springing in a place whose details are usually hidden by drapery. Frannie stared. It occurred to her that this statue looked familiar. He had, in fact, once given her half a cheese tart, and a very fine ghost story of his own.

She tapped softly on the glass. He turned then, his hair whipping behind him, and saw her. He dashed to the window and flung it open and pulled her inside with him.

"Softly!" he said. "We have little time."

"Oh, yes!" she breathed, caught in the story, whatever it was. "I know. How can I help you? What happened to your clothes?"

"My sister took them," he said. "She locked me up in here, and I need to get out."

"My sister did that to me once. She'll get it when your mama finds out."

"I don't think so. But never mind. Give me your breeches."

She scrambled out of the canvas trousers. They came only down to his calves and rested low on his hips, so that the ivy disappeared around his back and down into them behind.

"Wait!" She ran to the window, in time to see Agatha, clutching a stout stick, on her way up to rescue her. "Aggie, back down! It's a friend, he needs to escape. Hold the ladder below!"

He put his hands on Frannie's shoulders and looked down

into her face. "You are a true friend of the Land," he said. "As you have helped me to my kingship, you shall be first among my Companions. My sister has lost that right."

He was out the window before she could ask him what he meant. He really did look like art, especially his chest.

───

A S THE PROCESSION PASSED THROUGH THE COURT, the crowd moved to fill in behind it. Justis shuffled into a spot behind a short man, and put his arm around Marianne. "Which one's yours?" she asked as the Historians followed their seconds up the steps. "I do hope it's not the squidgy one."

Whatever his feelings about Roger Crabbe, Justis did not like outsiders making judgments. "Doctor Crabbe is the smaller man," he said austerely.

Marianne snorted. "He ought to take a leaf from your man's book and cut his hair short. There's nothing more pitiful than a man with his twelve long hairs bound back in a tail that's thinner than the string."

Justis had been thinking that St Cloud looked different, but hadn't quite known how until Marianne spoke. The familiar sheaf of thick, black hair was gone. With his hair curling at his ears, he looked broader in the jaw, older.

"He's a looker, whatever else he may be," said Marianne.

"Pity the Governors aren't all as susceptible as you," said Justis. "He's going to need all the good will he can get." Even at this distance, he could see that the Master Governor's formal greeting was distinctly warmer for Crabbe than for St Cloud, and that several of the Doctors frowned when St Cloud made his bow to them.

The Master Governor climbed to the speaker's platform and held up his arms. The horns gave one final admonitory blast, and fell silent.

"Fellow scholars and lovers of truth," the Master Governor began. "I welcome you here as witnesses to this debate between two men of learning."

While the Master Governor droned on about the procedure

and the nature of the debate, Justis contemplated history and ethics and how the study of the former had demonstrated the complexity of the latter as the most brilliant lecturer could not. Was it wrong to break a law when the law enforced belief in a lie? What did it matter whether a wizard, dead two hundred years, was a charlatan or the misguided priest of a dying religion? Finally, what did it matter whether magic had been real or not?

He came to himself at a tug on his sleeve. Marianne was growing restless. "Don't he love the sound of his voice, though?" she said scornfully. "Too bad he's the only one that does."

At last the Master Governor entered his peroration, made an end, and stepped down. Doctor St Cloud mounted the platform with no more ceremony than if he'd been mounting the dais in his drafty lecture hall, folded his hands before him, and spoke in a clear, carrying voice, "I call challenge upon Doctor Roger Crabbe. I challenge him on his facts, his reasoning, and his conclusions. The wizards were true wizards, and their power was true magic."

AFTER HIS ORIGINAL SHOCKING STATEMENT, ST CLOUD spoke moderately and well. Nicholas Galing listened with an interest informed by months of Henry's lecture notes while he took his audience back five hundred years and more, to the ancient Kingdom of the North. Everyone there knew of it, of course—the land it comprised was a third of their own country. But few of them knew anything of its history: a mountain kingdom, isolated and rich, protected by warrior kings and ruled by wizards.

"It was not a society in which the written word carried much weight," St Cloud explained. "There are no formal histories, saving Martindale, who is very late, and not even much written poetry or other literature survives from those ancient days. What does survive is lists: of the kings and their battles, of the wizards and their acts, of the villages visited by the kings on their progress, of the children of royal blood. The documents, when studied in conjunction with certain legends, are very suggestive of the role the wizards played in the government of the North."

One by one, St Cloud picked up the strands of his evidence: he cited folk tale, legend, balladry, the chronicle of a foreign prince who had fallen in love with King Martin Swordsmaster and run afoul of his wizard. He added in harder evidence—the lists, passages from Martindale's *Chronicle of the Wizards and their Deeds*—and wove them together into a tightly argued tapestry that pictured, in colors bright as life, a tableau of wizards who had the power to command both storms and men. He spoke of barren women growing fertile, of rivers no foreign soldier could cross, of hunts through forest and mountain in quest of deer who spoke in the tongues of men. He spoke of kings honored for their potency, and nobles vying for the honor of letting their daughters serve them.

"You may wonder," he said at last, "why I am insisting so strongly upon ancient history when the facts under dispute are so much more recent. My answer to you is this. Our realm, our little world of city, of university, of river, of farmland and upland, of mountain and ravine, did not appear all at once, perfect and whole as we see it today. It grew, as an apple grows, from a seed to a sapling whose branches, cut and grafted onto a sturdier stock, blow blossoms and bear fruit in their season. Our realm is of the Southern Kingdom, which was ruled equally by a monarch and a Council of Nobles. But it is of the Northern Kingdom as well. And, as I have demonstrated, the Northern Kingdom was shaped by magic."

Uneasy murmuring rolled down the banked rows of Doctors and Governors and out into the crowd. Nicholas, who had been listening to St Cloud's argument with growing excitement, felt his blood bubble with joy. Everything up to this point had been so much scholarly flourishing, like the formal moves with which a swordsman begins an exhibition bout. Now the fight was joined in earnest.

"I suggest," Doctor St Cloud went on, calm and steady as before, "that it is illogical to believe that the wizards left their magic behind them when they came South. In fact, there is ample evidence that they continued to cast spells after the Union. The nobility often called on the wizards to clear their wells and bless their fields, even as they petitioned the kings to curtail their political power. For generations, an uneasy truce prevailed, and under it the Kingdom climbed toward a pinnacle of brilliance it was never to know again: the reign of King Anselm, called the Wise.

"Anselm was an innovator, a patron of the arts. And he was a reformer. Influenced by his queen and the Duke of Hartsholt, he divided the wizards from the rest of the court, severely curtailing their political power. He encouraged them to bring their knowledge and skills to this University—and limited their role in the training and upbringing of the royal children. After Anselm, the wizards' magic seems to have weakened, although they retained enough power to protect their increasingly erratic and unpopular monarchs until David, Duke Tremontaine, found a way to bind them before he killed the last king.

"The form of the binding is instructive: 'He bound them, Duke David of Tremontaine, behind an oaken door chained three times three: locks of iron, of gold, of lead thrice worked, with three great words upon them.' The words are from a popular account, quoted by Vespas in his *Book of Kings*. Master Vespas presents the passage as a quaint metaphor of thoroughness, as a farmer might say he'd harnessed his ox with wood and leather, with collar and nose ring."

He waited for his laugh and got it, but Galing noticed that it was a nervous one—they weren't sure they liked where this was heading. "I present you," St Cloud went on, "with another reading. I believe that David, Duke Tremontaine, bound the wizards into that hall with a spell he may have learned at this very University, where it was once possible to attend lectures in the Arts Magical."

First blood, Nicholas thought. The group of braid-bedecked Northerners gathered at the pedestal of Imagination raised a cheer and their leafy branches. An opposing group booed and catcalled until the Master Governor rose ponderously to his feet and raised his hand for silence. It was a while in coming, but St Cloud, undaunted, lifted his voice above the noise.

"Doctor Crabbe teaches that the wizards after the Union held power through chicanery and corruption alone. Furthermore, he assumes in every lecture he gives that their Northern forebears were charlatans likewise. By ignoring the evidence of the historical record, he paints a false picture of our antecedents, and misprizes the wit and courage of David, Duke Tremontaine, who alone was able to free our land from the tyranny of Gerard the Last King. By this reasoning, I submit to you, my lords, learned Governors, admired doctors of this University, that Doctor Crabbe's scholarship is no such thing."

St Cloud took his seat amid mingled applause and booing, and Nicholas reflected that an academic challenge is not a swordfight, where the give and take of blows occurs faster than an eye can follow. Now that St Cloud was no longer speaking, Nicholas could see that he had brought scarcely a single acknowledged authority to bear upon his subject. If this was all he had to go on, then Nicholas could relax. There was no danger of anyone believing him. And there was still no sign of Theron Campion.

D OWN IN THE GREAT COURT, JUSTIS BECAME AWARE of Marianne clinging to his arm, and looked down. Her cheeks were bright, her eyes were opened to their widest extent, and her plump lips were curved in a delighted smile. Feeling her lover's gaze on her, she tilted her head coquettishly. "Why did you say I'd be bored," she demanded. "It's as good as a play. The things he does say! I'd no notion history was so exciting. And those eyes! They burn right into you."

She'd hit it precisely, Justis thought. St Cloud was in his element, lecturing to a class of hundreds. And he was telling the truth at last—triumphantly, defiantly, completely, without hold or stay.

"I collect it's the little one's turn now," Marianne went on. "Don't he look smug—like a cat at a mousehole. He thinks the booing meant they didn't like our man, but he's wrong, isn't he, Justy? It just meant they're scared of him. He'll see."

Watching Crabbe take his place upon the speaker's platform, Justis wondered at the little magister's confidence. Hadn't he been listening? Didn't he know, even if his blindly faithful supporters did not, that he was already beaten? Was it ambition or simple prejudice that allowed him to stand up in front of them all with his narrow chest thrown out, smiling like a man who knows that the dice are loaded?

"You have been told," Crabbe began, "that my scholarship is nothing, that it is founded on faulty evidence—on lies, in fact. Now, it is easy for one man to call another a liar, and no harder for the second man to throw the lie back in the teeth of the first. Schoolyards are full of children whose idea of argument rises no higher than this. But I am not a child. I am a Doctor of History, approved and licensed to teach the history of our noble realm by the illustrious Governors of this ancient University. That alone should shield me from such a challenge to my scholarship and my honor."

It soon became apparent that Crabbe had decided to take the position that St Cloud's challenge was not really worth responding to. He began by rehearsing the death of Gerard and the binding of the wizards as it was recorded by Vespas, who had witnessed it, and Trevor, and "our own august Master Tortua, the current Horn Chair," who had collated all the available sources and commented on them in *Hubris*.

"Shorn of the elaborate figurative language that was such a prominent feature of Late Monarchical prose, the story is a simple one. Twenty-five nobles of the Council of Lords called challenge on Gerard. They fought his Companions, who tried to protect him, and David, Duke Tremontaine, won through to deal the fatal blow. The wizards were not present, Duke David having invited them that night to a great banquet in a pavilion near the oak grove to celebrate the coming of the spring solstice.

"Now," said Crabbe, sweetly reasonable, "you must keep in mind that this was a time of great superstition and general fear. Gerard was quite mad, and his madness manifested in particularly violent and bloody ways. Any man who displeased him in the smallest way might find himself losing his fingers one by one to the axe of the First Companion. If Gerard were more seriously displeased, it would be his toes, his nose, his genitals, oh, and his lands and goods as well. Five years before the Fall, seven nobles had conspired to put a stop to his tyranny, and had come to a nasty end. The uprising failed, leaving disappointingly little evidence behind it. Our only source for it is Vespas, who rather poetically tells us, 'The wizards did reap them as corn is reaped at harvest, and thereafter no blade of grass did grow on their lands for a twelvemonth and a day.' The exact interpretation of this sentence has been the subject of much controversy among later scholars. Trevor had it that . . ."

Marianne tugged at her lover's sleeve. "Justy?"

"Hmm?"

"Why should scholars argue over the meaning of something that's as plain as the nose on your face?"

Justis, familiar, by this time, with all the arguments Crabbe was citing, drew breath to explain about obscure texts, about interpretation and documentation, and stopped short. He considered what St Cloud had said, what Crabbe was saying, all the books he himself had read over the winter and the disputes he'd had over their contents, and then he said, "I'm not sure, sweetheart."

"I thought it might be to hear themselves talk, but there must be a better reason than that," she insisted.

"There must be," he agreed. "I'll have to think about it."

And think about it he did, while Crabbe went on with his scholarly digression. When he started listening again, the little magister had returned to David and the wizards.

"Duke David was clever enough to know that the other nobles would never rebel without some assurance that the wizards wouldn't interfere. So he built the famous Spring Pavilion, and invited the wizards to a banquet to consecrate it. When they were all inside, he locked them up, very thoroughly indeed, and set fire to the place. Then he met his fellow conspirators in the Great Court, where you are all standing, and led them into the Great Hall, where they killed the king as I have related. There was nothing more mystical to it than that.

"As for the strength and power of Gerard's wizards, well, that is as much a fairy tale as the legends of talking beasts and living waters Doctor St Cloud was entertaining us with earlier." Crabbe went on to cite the case of the wizard Noris, thrown from the clock tower early in the reign of Gerard Last King, and the wizard Durant, stabbed to death in an alley two years later. "And Doctor St Cloud asks us to believe that men like these, who had proved incompetent even to save their own lives, were masters of a power that could uncover the thoughts of men's hearts and cause grain to sprout in barren land. Before you know it, Doctor St Cloud will be asking us to believe that the wizards meant well, and then, that the kings weren't so bad after all. And if that is so, why were they ever deposed? This line of argument, followed to its logical conclusion, must bring us, and Doctor St Cloud, inevitably to treason."

Pandemonium. Justis found himself shouting, "No! No! Down with Crabbe!" with all the considerable force of his lungs, while behind him a group of men chanted "Crabbe! Crabbe! Crabbe!" in a frenzy of enthusiasm. Marianne was laughing wildly and clapping to the rhythmic roaring around her.

The Master Governor called once more for order, which was even longer in coming than it had been before. Trumpets sounded, people shouted. Crabbe stood unmoved in the middle of it all, smiling very lightly with his head tipped to one side, the picture of smug triumph.

"There is no question, naturally, of calling Doctor St Cloud a traitor," he said when he'd a hope of being heard. "His colleagues are all aware of his unworldly and unpolitical nature. I do not doubt that he is searching, in his own way, for truth; I only wish to point out that his search has led him into dark and dangerous places. Our esteemed Governors"—he turned to his right and nodded—"have, in their infinite wisdom, decreed what courses of study students shall follow to hone their minds and train them in the skills of scholarship. They have also decreed what texts shall be set, and how they should be studied. My greatest quarrel with Doctor St Cloud in this affair is not that he should impugn my learning and methods, but that in so doing, he should impugn the methods of study laid down by tradition and experience as the best—the only—way of getting at the truth, and to offer in their place old wives' tales and ballads."

"Well, isn't he pleased with himself?" Marianne exclaimed as the little magister stepped down and St Cloud took his place. "Condemning poor Doctor St Cloud with every word he says, all the while swearing he don't mean a thing by it. If he told me I was pretty, I'd watch my purse."

Justis smiled at her gratefully, but his smile was worried. It was going to be difficult for St Cloud to find a defense to Crabbe's words that would cut any ice with the Governors.

F ROM HIS VANTAGE POINT RIGHT NEXT TO THOSE Governors, Nicholas Galing was thinking much the same thing. During Crabbe's speech, he'd heard many approving murmurs. Crabbe was telling them what they wanted to hear, making them feel comfortable and justified and pleased with themselves. St Cloud had set them off-balance, questioned the foundations on which their decisions and their University were built, and they resented him for it. The man might as well forfeit his challenge right here and now and slink off into the ignoble exile that was his only possible future.

It was a bit of a surprise to see St Cloud stepping onto the platform looking as calm and assured as if Crabbe had not just knocked his entire argument into flinders.

"I had hoped," he said, "to be able to make my case by reference to my own period of study alone, without presuming so much on my colleague's territory as to teach him his own subject. I could not believe that he would so fail in his duty as a scholar and a teacher as to present Vespas as his ultimate authority for the events leading up to the Purging of the Wizards and the death of the Tyrant. Vespas did not personally witness those events, but derived his account, at the Council's behest, from a document written by the Crescent Chancellor, the ancestor of the current Lord Condell, who did not witness them either."

Crabbe stood up. "This is ridiculous," he shouted. "Condell interviewed Tremontaine, Perry, and Wellingbrook, all of whom were indisputably there. I hope you're not trying to say that Condell falsified his facts, or that the Liberators were lying to him?"

Basil turned to him with restrained dignity. "Doctor Crabbe. You may challenge me all you like on my facts, my scholarship, and my reasoning—that is, after all, the purpose of this debate— but please wait your turn, as I did mine."

Nicholas, who had a tolerably clear view of Crabbe, saw his second pull insistently on his sleeve. The little magister glared down at his friend with narrowed eyes, then flung up his hands and sat down with an air of utter disgust.

"Thank you," said St Cloud tranquilly. "Doctor Crabbe is correct. Lord Condell's account of the death of Gerard was indeed compiled with the help of the king's surviving executioners. However, I am in a position to prove that document does not represent the most authentic account of those events. In the Archives of this very University, there exists a letter from Duke David himself, addressed to the University Librarian, one Carrington." Calmly, he pulled a yellowed paper from a small portfolio, and handed it to Leonard Rugg. "Perhaps the esteemed Governers would care to examine it to ascertain its authenticity?" Rugg opened it, and stared; without comment he handed it to the row behind him. "I will describe the contents, for those who can't see it," Basil went on. "In it, the Liberator thanks Carrington for searching out the *Spell for Binding a Renegado*, and for discovering the circumstances under which it might be executed."

St Cloud paused to let the implications of this sink in. When the murmuring started, he spoke over it, quoting the salient points of Duke David's letter, including a paragraph in which the duke warned his friend that he would find the official version of the Purging of the Wizards a little different from what he might expect. "*The Northern magics proving a wild and unchancy force,*" the duke wrote, "*we have determined to purge them as well as their unhappy acolytes from this our fair land, so that no wizard may rise to practice upon us again.*"

Crabbe was on his feet before the end of the sentence. "Doctor St Cloud, what kind of mockery are you trying to make of this debate?"

St Cloud turned to face his rival. "Why, Doctor Crabbe, I am but putting forth evidence and authority, as you wished."

"Evidence?" Crabbe shrilled. "Authority? I'll need a lot more proof, Doctor St Cloud, before I accept the authority of such a convenient and unconvincing document. Furthermore, I do not see that this letter, even if it is indeed what you say it is, changes the facts of the case in any way. There is nothing in Duke David's words to support the interpretation you have put on them."

St Cloud made as if to answer, but Crabbe shouted him down. "This debate was your challenge, St Cloud, not mine—but I challenge you anew: I call you a liar, with no more respect for history than a penny balladeer!"

"Do you say so?" St Cloud answered quietly.

"You know you are," Crabbe hissed. "Everything you've laid out before us is so much rubbish dug from the refuse heap of the past, a rotting pile of used papers and moldy documents you wish to dignify with the title of History. Perhaps you also want everyone to study the Condell laundry lists from the last hundred years? Or letters from some king to his whore? You claim, because these things exist, are even in some way *true*, you dare to claim that such trivia, such garbage, makes up our sacred History! A very pretty magic, indeed, St Cloud, to turn the dross of a disturbed mind into the gold of true scholarship."

St Cloud had been listening to this diatribe with his hands tucked into the long green sleeves of his gown. From the crowd, he probably looked as serene as he had throughout the debate, but Nicholas could see the tremors shaking the heavy folds that fell from his shoulders. The Master Governor was on his feet, sputtering that Crabbe was out of order, that decorum must be maintained, but no one was paying him any attention. For a moment, the two men stood confronted, Crabbe panting and slit-eyed with passion, St Cloud furiously restrained. And then St Cloud drew forth from his sleeve a small, fat, dark book. He opened it, turned over two or three pages, ran his finger down the text, found his place, and raised his voice once more.

"If it is history you demand, Roger Crabbe, then I will give you history, pure and unmediated by commentary or the passage of years. This book is the Book of the King's Wizard. And I will show you true magic now: *A Spelle to call upp the Beeste in a Man, Eche According to Hys Nature.* Listen, Crabbe, and learn."

He's mad, Nicholas thought reflexively, and then, with a rush of elation: *I knew it!* And then he thought nothing at all, pinned in place by the strange words, ponderous and loud as thunder, that rolled from St Cloud's lips. Like a rising tide, they flowed on and outward, gathering force and substance, pouring over Crabbe and his second, over the Doctors and Governors and over Nicholas himself, out over the crowd, the Northerners, the Scholars, the Fellows, and all the tradesmen and servants whose world was the University.

Crabbe began to growl and snarl. The voice rolled on; Crabbe crouched down and launched himself at St Cloud. Contemptuously, St Cloud kicked him aside, and he yipped and retreated to a safe distance, from where he barked defiance. The Master Governor swung his head heavily from side to side and let forth a long, unhappy bellow.

Nicholas stood bewildered by the scents that suddenly assailed his nose: the scent of prey—of poultry, of dogs and horses and small, frightened rabbits and mice and somewhere, far off and coming closer, a royal stag. Water sprang to his mouth, but the presence of other predators constrained and confused him. Their stench was rank in his nostrils: hawks and hunting cats and swift-footed foxes. A brown mare stood behind him, watching him gravely from wise, dark eyes. And then he knew that the brown mare was Katherine, Duchess Tremontaine, and that he was not a wolf at all, but Lord Nicholas Galing, who, whatever else he might be, had a wolf's heart and a wolf's hunger.

OUT IN THE COURT, JUSTIS PLANTED HIMSELF STUR-dily at his mate's side and growled low in his throat. It was puzzling that his mate should smell like a robin, but she was his to guard, and guard her he would until his last breath. The weasel near him recoiled, then turned into a Fellow with yellow bands on his sleeves and blank fear on his face. Justis shook his head, half-expecting to feel the pull and swing of dewlaps against a sturdy muzzle, then rubbed his face.

Small, trembling fingers plucked at his sleeve. "Justy?" piped a little voice, "What was that, Justy?"

He put his arms around her, his little robin, his sweet girl, and felt her shudder with the force of her heartbeats. "I'm not sure, love," he said. "But it may very well have been magic."

⌒

Henry Fremont shuddered convulsively from head to toe and examined his hands. Had they indeed been hooves only a moment ago, and had he really been ready to kick in the brains of the high-bred hunting dog shivering and whining beside him? He worked his fingers and snuck a look at Godwin, who whimpered as if the fit were still upon him.

Vandeleur's voice sounded in his ear, shaky and hoarse. "I thought . . . Never mind what I thought. Are you well, Fremont?"

"No," said Henry frankly. "But I'm better than Godwin here."

"See to him, will you?" said Vandeleur. "You're closest. Land, I miss Justis."

⌒

Jessica Campion shivered with the notion that she could fly, fly with a hawk's grace and sureness out over the square below her, riding on the currents of the peoples' awe and fury as they eddied up to her. Her knuckles gripped the railing. She had been within an inch of casting herself from the gallery of the Great Hall. But from there with her hawk's eyes, she saw what no one else could see: a single man entering the plaza, a man naked to the waist, his chest bound with oak and ivy, his hair flowing free around him. She did not jump, but hastened down the conventional way.

⌒

From his place on the steps, Galing, too, had a good view of the square. He saw the crowds parting, parting like grass in the wind to let the man pass through them. Some people jeered and laughed; others shouted warnings. A few people were ignoring the man altogether, holding on to themselves as if they were afraid they'd shiver into pieces, their faces shocked or streaked with tears. By this, Nicholas knew that what he had just felt, others had felt as well.

The man, of course, was Theron Campion. Not off in the country after all. Just where he was, he did not seem aware himself. He strode through the crowd now as if it really were a field of grass, wearing nothing but a pair of rough breeches, his decorated chest bared for the world to see. Nicholas smiled with grim fascination.

Lord Theron's chest flashed in and out; he had been running. But now he approached the steps with a gliding, measured pace, his head held high, his eyes fixed on his lover, Basil St Cloud.

A year ago, Nicholas would have been anticipating a scene out of a bad melodrama: a lover's quarrel grown into a public scandal, with one or both of the participants driven mad by love. But Nicholas had lost the comfortable certainty that he knew how the world worked. A moment ago, St Cloud had produced a wizard's book and read from it, and something had happened. Nicholas hadn't known about the book. But the rest of it—that St Cloud fancied himself a wizard and Theron his sacred king— he had deduced from the evidence he'd collected for Arlen. Arlen, who was not present at the debate. Lord Arlen, the Serpent Chancellor. Other Council posts passed from man to man, but the Serpent was always Arlen.

Over by the statue of Imagination, the Northerners had set up some kind of chant. He couldn't catch the words, but he would bet anything it had to do with kings. Crabbe's followers were shouting, "Foul!"; a fight had broken out in a corner of the plaza. He heard a woman's voice cry, "Theron!" and saw the ranks of Doctors shift as Lady Sophia struggled through them toward her son.

Ignoring it all, Theron saw the man who waited for him on the steps. His lover was the man in his dreams, the man in the wood, the man with the knife and the pelt of a bear. His lover was his teacher and his magister, who had filled him all winter with his magic, and waited for him now to achieve his trial and take up his new responsibility. Theron climbed the steps and knelt before him and looked up into his face.

Basil smiled, intimate and loving, as if they two were alone in the world. "It is well that you kneel, my king. For it is the time of Sowing. The time of testing is done, and now the Land may rejoice in you."

From inside his robe he drew forth a chain, the gold chain that Theron had given him in love. He lifted the chain in both hands so that the sun ran like fire through its heavy links. "And now," he said, "be bound to the Land: blood and bone, beast and man, until the day of your death and ever afterward."

The tableau held for a moment, still and bright as the painted glass window in the Great Hall above them, gesture for gesture and pose for pose: the black-robed wizard holding aloft the blinding gold chain, the young king kneeling before him to receive its weight.

The picture was not lost on the crowd in the plaza. "Look!" Nicholas heard the cries from the crowd, and saw what he had feared: a legend being brought out of the shadows and into the world.

He had no more time, now. This is what he had been sent for. Arlen's last words to him rang clearly and precisely in his head: "Have you come across anything in your investigation to convince you that magic exists?"

Arlen had not said, "I do not believe in magic." He had asked a question, and Nicholas had answered it with a diplomatic lie. Now was the moment for him to return a true answer. If he was wrong, he would face disgrace, banishment, death. But if he was right, he would be as great a liberator as the great Duke David—even if only one man ever knew the truth.

His knife in his hand, Nicholas Galing leapt forward to kill the king.

⌒

H E'D HAD TRAINING WITH A KNIFE, OF COURSE— anyone who carried a knife without knowing how to use it was a danger chiefly to himself. But he'd never really used it on a man before. Galing had time to be amazed at how easy he found it to stab into living flesh again and again before he was caught and held fast by two horrified magisters. His hands were sticky with blood, his face and coatsleeves spattered with it. He was sweating and panting as if he'd been running. He heard people sobbing and wailing, and shouting for order or for help. Roger Crabbe was yelling, "What is it? What happened? We must finish the debate! Where is St Cloud?"

Basil St Cloud could not answer him. He lay on the steps un-hearing, surrounded by Doctors of Physic. But even the immense bounty of their knowledge was helpless against the wounds he had taken. It had happened too quickly. There was no breath left in him now, no thought, no life. His heart and mind had stopped together.

And Theron Campion lay bloody across his mother's lap. She was muttering, very softly and quickly, a stream of words in a language no one understood, and twisting the cloth of her robes and petticoats around the gashes in his body, as the blood kept welling through. Nicholas Galing had managed to do a lot of damage with his dagger between the time that Basil had flung himself in front of Theron and the nearest scholars had realized what was happening and pulled him off them both.

"Sophia."

She did not look up. "Jessica. More bandages."

Jessica leaned down, handed her a sash. "Sophia. They are taking Galing away. Say the word, and I'll do for him now."

Sophia shook her head, twisting the sash. "Put your hand here—right here, and press hard."

Jessica was used to blood. "I know."

Leonard Rugg stood by Basil's body, spinning like a top, look-ing for something, someone who could do something. He didn't know who, and he didn't know what, but there must be some-thing. Cassius and Elton were holding his shoulders, saying his name and Basil's, and then he saw what he was looking for: the men, the young men, the flowers of scholarship, the fruit of Basil's garden, they were here, fighting toward him through the swirling crowd, and he called to them, "Men! Men! Don't let this be for nothing!"

Lord Edmond Godwin saw his son, Peter, all childhood gone from his face. He seized the boy's arm, saying, "We must go; this is going to get worse."

But Peter shook his head. "You go," he said through tear-swollen lips. "Tell them what happened here. You saw. Tell them, Father. Tell them."

Lord Edmond looked out over the square. "The Guard is coming, not a moment too soon. Peter—"

And then he shouted, because one of Peter's friends, a scrawny scarecrow of a fellow, had hurled himself in the direction of Lord Nicholas Galing. "You fools!" Lord Edmond bellowed to Galing's captors. "Get him out of here *now!* Can't you see what will happen? *Now,* I say!"

A big student wrestled down the scrawny one with Peter's help, and all Edmond's attention fell to clearing a path and giving commands to move and secure Galing inside the Great Hall, where they could wait while order was restored to the riot brewing outside.

But save for the main participants in the drama, the witnesses to the debate had little stomach for riot. As the City Guard marched into the square, the people dispersed, leaving a clear path to the steps. And the Guard themselves parted to admit a sweating horseman in Council livery, who delivered his message to Lord Edmond as the man in charge: Lord Nicholas Galing was to be transported directly to Arlen House, there to answer to the Serpent himself.

The great Doctor Tortua, Horn Chair Doctor of History, author of *Hubris and the Fall of the Kings,* looked down on the milling, muttering Doctors and Governors, on the Guards and nobles, students and shopkeepers, the dead man and the dying. Of all of them there, only he had come close to knowing what Basil St Cloud had known. He no longer remembered who St Cloud was, but he recognized what he had just witnessed as a page of his beloved ancient history, torn from the Archives and enacted on the bright courtyard steps like some schoolboy pageant.

He waited a long time, until he realized that there was to be no more ceremony, no more speeches, no more challenge or sacrifice, and that the beautiful lady who had held his arm was not coming back either. Doctor Tortua turned away in dismay.

"They got it wrong," the old scholar said, disappointed. "They got it all wrong."

chapter VIII

THE GREEN MAN WAS TOO PUBLIC, COPPICE'S room too small, so the Northerners went to earth in the oak grove. Tamed and threatened by the city though it was, the grove still felt more like home than any other place in this uncaring South. They might rage there, and huddle among the roots of ancient trees and mourn the death of all their hopes.

Lindley was with them, weeping convulsively in the arms of a man whose name he did not know. Basil St Cloud was dead, and Lindley had seen him die, watched him leap into the path of the assassin's knife and receive it in his breast, his neck. He'd seen the blood and the pain in his magister's face, and it hadn't been beautiful or noble or romantic. It had been horrible. And now it was over—Basil St Cloud was over—and Anthony Lindley was feeling such pain as he had never felt before, not when Finn had died, not even in the Chop.

"Steady, steady," the man murmured. "Remember you're a warrior, a King's Companion. The battle goes on, though the king is dead."

Lindley sat up at that, wet-faced. "I don't care about

Campion," he gasped. "He never understood any of it. Kings come and go, or they would if there were any. It's wizards that are important, and the last one is dead, and I loved him."

The Northerner shrugged himself away from Lindley and got up. "Suit yourself, Southron," he said.

Forlorn, Lindley hugged his knees and watched as the Northerners drifted in ones and twos to the center of the clearing. This was where he'd found Finn, and where they'd built the fire and danced at MidWinter. He had understood then, or thought he did. His blood had certainly understood, igniting his flesh so that he had felt himself a lantern, a torch flaming with wisdom and joy and love. It was what Lindley had loved in Alaric, the burning intensity of his belief in the old ways; in possessing him, Lindley possessed the secrets, the history, the magic of the ancient North, his true heritage.

The Northmen had linked arms, and were circling slowly, heads bowed so that their braids fell down over their faces. After a time, they stopped, and drew the knives from their belts. Coppice stepped inward and held the edge of his knife over his outstretched arm.

"It is the time of Sowing," he said formally. "If we are to have a merry Harvest, the Land must have its mede of blood to quicken it. Lacking a king, the ritual has fallen on the Companions as it has for these many years. This Spring, we had hoped for a true king to lead us, but he was killed before we might even greet him.

"Perhaps this is not an age for kings. But as long as there are Companions to perform the ritual, we will perform it, and the Land will prosper."

He brought the edge of the knife down on his forearm and sliced open a shallow cut that bled freely.

"We give our life's blood to you," he said. "Drink well. Bear well. Love us as we love you."

One by one, the Northerners cut their arms and spoke their prayers and let their blood fall on the bright new grass. At some point, Lindley went to the circle and drew his knife and touched the shoulder of Burl, who was Second Companion and had the right to refuse or accept him. Burl hesitated a long moment, then moved aside to give Lindley a place. And when the time came, Lindley cut his arm and said the ritual in a steady voice, and lay with Burl afterward, as the custom was, and kissed each man on the mouth. For all the magic that was left in the Southland was here, and he wanted to be a part of it, as it had become a part of him.

But when the ritual was done and the Northerners began to talk of practical matters—whether the guard would arrest Coppice and his second, what to do about Greenleaf and Smith—Anthony Lindley left the grove and returned to the city and university that were his home.

T HREE WOMEN STOOD WATCH OVER THERON CAMPION as his fragile flesh swung his soul between the worlds of life and death. His breathing was shallow but even, punctuated by little moans of pain he did not know that he was making. His mother sat beside him, taking his pulse and feeling his brow, feeding him liquid when he would take it. If there was infection, she might not save him, but she had cleaned the wounds and bandaged him with fresh linen.

"The knife was clean," Jessica said again. "What else would Galing use it for? Opening letters? He was no swordsman. Anyway, I have it. With his crest. He'll hang. Katherine, you'll see to that, I hope?"

"I don't know." The duchess was barely aware of what she said; she was watching the boy on the bed. "I'll need to know more. Arlen will find out."

Theron was so pale—so different, Sophia thought, from the color he'd been born, all fiercely red and blue. She took his hand and sang a song about a little boy and a goat on a sunny hillside. While he still breathed, it would not make her weep.

"Kyros," Jessica said, hearing her voice. "I remember. I visited my father and Richard there, and the cook sang me that song." She knelt by the bed. "Sophia. Shall I take you home?"

Sophia shook her head, kept singing. His eyes behind the thin lids were moving. "Come back," she sang, the song of the boy to his goats. "Come back and we'll have honey cakes." Come back, my son, from the land that has possessed you, the land that drank your blood. Come back from whatever you are looking for, whatever you are running from. Come back to those who truly love you, and we will kiss you and let you go where you will.

"He should go to Kyros," Katherine said.

Sophia shook her head again. "I want him to lie by his father."

"Not yet," said the duchess; "it isn't time for that yet. I mean when he is better. When Jessica leaves. You go with her. I'll take care of things here."

Jessica chuckled. "Lovely. A ship full of mythic paintings, plus the genuine article."

"Kyros." Sophia trilled the "r" like a bird. "We begot him there, on a festival night. My husband didn't want a child, but I called him forth because I knew it was time."

"He should go back," Katherine said again. "Not forever, but for a little while. I hear the climate's nice." She smiled. "And people will forget, here."

"Will they?" asked Sophia, doubtful. "Perhaps we go into exile, as his father did after the disgrace."

Katherine came behind and leaned her cheek on Sophia's hair. "I was a girl then," she said. "I didn't know what else to do. I've learned a few things since then. Take him and heal him if you can, and let me do the rest."

"Kyros," Sophia trilled softly and in her own tongue she said, "Theron. Come home with me."

Jessica had been pacing the room; it was hard for her to be still in the fog of pain and love. She went out into the hall, nodding her head for Katherine to follow her.

"Well?" said the duchess. "I know it may not be on your way . . ."

"Ask me." Jessica stood still, but she twisted her fingers together. "Just ask me."

Katherine drew a deep breath. "Is Kyros on your way?"

"Not really."

"Will you take them there?"

"Maybe."

"Jessica."

"This once, just ask me for something I can actually give you."

"Will you take them both? Please."

"Yes." Jessica turned away to hide the fact that she was weeping. "Good God," she said brightly, and cleared her throat. "What's this?"

It was a package, tall and square, wrapped in cloth and twine. All too familiar.

"It came this morning," the duchess said. "I forgot all about it. Someone's left it here in the hall. They shouldn't have. I'll have it cleared away—"

"The devil," Jessica muttered, and cut the twine with her knife and pulled away the wrappings.

Theron looked out from the canvas, splendid in peacock blue. He was sitting at a table piled with fruit and books; one hand rested on an open page, the other touched his throat, where a jewel gleamed among the folds of white under his beautifully articulated fingers. Behind him, an open window showed the lawns of Tremontaine House.

"Damn her cheek." Katherine stared. "It's the portrait I commissioned."

"Well," said Jessica. "I hope you didn't pay her in advance."

ONCE AGAIN LORD NICHOLAS GALING FOUND HIMself in Arlen House in the salon overlooking the river in which he had waited for Lord Arlen more than once since autumn. This time, he was accompanied by a pair of City Guards, and his hands were bound behind him. Nobody had very much to say, least of all Galing himself. He was half-sick on the dregs of violent action and the knowledge that he had gambled everything on a single, daring cast and could not tell how the dice had fallen.

The same soft-footed servant who had waited on Galing in palmier days slid into the room and said, "Lord Arlen will see Lord Nicholas now. No need for you gentlemen to wait. Lord Arlen's men can see to him from here."

The same shadowy halls, the same paneled library, softly awash in the clear light of a perfect spring afternoon. The servant piloted Galing to a chair and helped him sit, conscious of a bound man's difficulty keeping his balance. He did not offer to remove Galing's bonds, nor did he offer refreshment. Galing found his heart pounding with the beginnings of panic.

"Lord Nicholas," a familiar voice purred. "How nice to see you. Montjoy, you may leave us. Is my swordsman at the door? Good. I'll call if I need him."

Lord Arlen came around his desk and stood in front of the chair Galing sat in, so close that Nicholas was forced to tilt his head uncomfortably to meet those amused gray eyes.

"I understand you've given me a gift, Lord Nicholas: Basil St Cloud's heart on a platter."

It was hard to see his face from this angle, harder to read his drawling voice. The words were ironic, but then Arlen was always ironic. Everything was a test. Nicholas felt very tired.

"I did it for you," he said flatly. "It was the answer to the question you asked me."

"Ah," said Arlen. "I see. You unmasked the last wizard, and you killed him. And you did it for me. I'm flattered."

The smooth voice had deepened, grown rougher. Warmth? Anger? Galing couldn't tell. Arlen reached out a well-tended hand and brushed at his cheek. "There's blood on your face, did you know? On the whole, you've done very well. You didn't allow predjudice to stand in the way of the facts, and you recognized the truth when you saw it."

"Thank you," said Nicholas stiffly. "Are you going to untie me?"

"Dear Montjoy. Such a cautious man." Arlen collected a knife from his desk—a slender, jeweled toy—and bent over the young noble to cut his ropes. Galing felt his breath warm on the nape of his neck and his fingers cool against his wrists, and then Arlen was across the room, pouring out a glass of wine while Galing rubbed at his bruises and got his breathing under control.

"Drink this," Arlen said, "and tell me what happened. I've only got the most garbled accounts."

So Nicholas delivered his report and sipped at his wine, and began to entertain hopes that the dice had fallen well after all. When he'd made an end, he felt in his pocket and drew out a heavy golden chain.

"St Cloud dropped it when I stabbed him, and I caught it without thinking. You should have it." Belatedly, he noticed that its links were dark and sticky with blood. "It's a bit of a mess, I'm afraid."

"Disgusting," Arlen agreed, but his expression was not disgusted. He looked up from the chain dangling from Galing's stained hand and his eyes were heavy and approving. "Why don't we go clean it up, and I can thank you properly."

LORD ARLEN'S THANKS WERE ALL NICHOLAS GALING had dreamed they would be. There were moments during that long and magnificent night when Nicholas thought he might die of pleasure. When at last he lay sated, with Arlen's corded arm thrown across his chest, he knew he'd won the throw.

"Lovely Nicholas," Arlen said. "You will always serve me, will you not?"

"To my last breath," Nicholas declared, meaning it absolutely.

"Good. I shall hold you to that." Arlen sat up among the pillows and stretched. "There's going to be some unpleasantness ahead for you, and I'd hate for you to think it was for nothing."

The warm, heavy stupor of sexual satisfaction receded a little. Nicholas turned over to face the Serpent Chancellor. "Unpleasantness?"

"Your trial for the murder of Basil St Cloud, and possibly of Lord Theron Campion, if he succumbs to his wounds. You didn't really think, did you, that you could get away with striking down two men in front of the entire University without anyone's taking notice?"

Nicholas sat up in a surge of bedclothes. "The man was talking treason—hell, he was performing treason. They both were. Everyone there saw it, but no one did anything about it but me. Damn it, I'm a hero!"

"So you are, my dear. So you are. I know that and you know that. But no one else had the information to thoroughly understand what was going on. They saw a noble run amok, attacking two harmless members of an august institution without so much as the courtesy of a formal challenge. For you to be a hero, the Council of Nobles must explain why your action was heroic. You're a clever man. You understand why we cannot do that."

Nicholas understood perfectly.

T HE DAY AFTER THE HISTORIANS' DEBATE, THE TAT-
tered remnants of St Cloud's class came slinking one by one into the Blackbird's Nest. There were more of them than one might have expected, gathered around their usual tables, talking quietly. They toasted the magister's memory in ale, and stole respectful glances at Historians' Corner, where the inner circle, or what was left of it, sat in grim contemplation of their shattered lives.

"Where's Justis?" Peter Godwin asked for the tenth time. "Justis ought to be here."

"It's that damned girl," Henry began fretfully, but Vandeleur stopped him.

"Screw the girl," he said. "Screw Justis. He made his choice when he scuttled off without even staying to see whether the magister was alive or dead. He didn't come home last night, and I hope he has the sense to stay as far away as possible for as long as possible, because I swear if I see him, I'll break his clod-hopper's neck for him."

"I'll help you," Henry offered, but his heart wasn't in it.

They subsided into a depressed silence, broken by Godwin. "What are we going to do now?"

"The magister's scarcely cold," Vandeleur said brutally. "I don't much feel like doing anything."

"I don't either, but that's not the point," Godwin said. "He was right, don't you see? Even before what happened happened, everybody knew he was right. But now he's dead, they'll try to hush it up and lie about it, like Duke David and Condell. We can't just sit here drinking and moaning and let that happen."

"Well said, Godwin," someone agreed; the three friends jumped, then frowned when they saw that the newcomer was Anthony Lindley. He still wore his hair in Northern braids, but he'd lost the strained, glittering intensity that had made him so difficult these past weeks.

"Get stuffed, Lindley," said Henry, who was not of a forgiving nature.

Lindley was unmoved. "I understand you're angry with me. I don't blame you. But we have to stay together. The truth is important—Doctor St Cloud taught us that—and it's going to take all of us to see to it that it doesn't disappear."

Vandeleur eyed him with small favor. "Does this mean you're giving up your Northern friends? No more oak leaves? No more hunts in the wood?"

"No, Vandeleur, it doesn't. The Northerners are my friends. Furthermore, I believe, as they do, in the divinity of the Land. You have no right to ask me to abandon them, any more than they have a right to ask me to abandon you. I don't see why being a Companion of the King should keep me from being a historian. Quite the contrary."

There was a pregnant pause while everyone thought about this, and then Godwin moved over on the bench and Lindley sat down beside him. Vandeleur called for another tankard, and the conversation resumed, with more spirit than before.

"I suppose we're going to have to try and reproduce his scholarship," Vandeleur said doubtfully.

"We can't," Henry objected. "You have to have permission to get into the Archives, and you can be sure after yesterday, the Governors are going to start making all sorts of rules the point of which is to keep out any historians whose politics are not guaranteed to be respectable. Which isn't any of us."

"There's plenty we can find without ever going in the Archives," Godwin said.

"But we can't teach unless we're Doctors," Henry went on, "and we can't become Doctors without a sponsor, and who's going to sponsor us? Crabbe?"

Vandeleur ground his teeth audibly. "Why don't you go ask

him, Fremont? Then he'll hand you over to the authorities and we won't have to put up with your whining anymore."

"I'm just trying to inject a note of common sense into the discussion," Henry protested.

"You're just trying to make us feel worse than we do already," said Godwin. "Why don't you go away, if you think it's all so hopeless?"

Henry looked around him at the stern faces of his three closest friends and his throat closed with grief, or perhaps it was fury, so that he must weep or beat the disgust from their faces. He had half risen from his seat, undecided whether to launch himself at Vandeleur, who was nearest, or make a dignified exit, when a large and familiar hand took him by the shoulder and a deep and familiar voice said, "Shut up, Henry, and sit down. We've got a lot to talk about."

~

JUSTIS BLAKE HAD HAD A DIFFICULT TWENTY-FOUR hours. He had not slept since St Cloud was killed, and he looked as though he'd been climbing walls and hiding in cellars, which was, in fact, exactly what he'd been doing.

"The first thing I thought of was his books and papers," he explained to the four friends. "Sooner or later, the Governors or someone would have come and taken them away and probably burned them, and I couldn't bear for that to happen. It would have been like killing him twice."

He stopped and blinked away the tears that had been surprising him at intervals all night. He'd found himself weeping in a back alley where he'd hidden to avoid the Guard, and again standing in St Cloud's room, seeing the inkwell still half-full, the hairs still in the comb, the notes on the pages left on the table: *Look up? Compare R's version?* It was not so much embarrassing as inconvenient, distracting him from the task at hand. Which, just now, was to persuade four skeptical and grief-stricken men that, despite appearances, he was really on their side.

"As if you cared two pins about St Cloud," Henry Fremont

sneered. "You haven't been around for weeks—couldn't even be bothered to come with us yesterday morning, or stand with us, or—"

"Yes, I know," Justis interrupted impatiently. "I was confused. But it's not important now. What's important is that it all not be for nothing—Doctor St Cloud's work and the debate and all. Now, I have all his books and his papers . . ."

They all exclaimed at that, incredulous, jealous that they hadn't thought of it themselves, excited at the possibilities, nervous of the consequences. Vandeleur wanted to hear how he'd done it; Godwin wanted to know where he'd stashed them; Fremont hoped the girl hadn't had anything to do with it: women could never keep secrets. Lindley swept the room with a suspicious eye and said they'd better not talk of it in such a public place.

"No," Justis said. "A public place is just where we must speak of it. There have been enough secrets and mysteries. The more people who know about all this, the better. This is the Blackbird's Nest, man. It's full of historians and metaphysicians. It's in their interest to support us, not turn us in."

"Us," said Henry. "Who is us? I thought you were sick of scholars and University and anything that didn't put food on the table."

"I thought I was, too," Justis said. "I was wrong. I'm going to take my degree in history, using St Cloud's methods, and I'm going to become a Fellow and then a Doctor, and I'm going to teach ancient history the way Doctor St Cloud taught it, without lies."

There was a stunned silence. "Right," Godwin said. "And I'm going to be Dragon Chancellor."

"No," Lindley said slowly, "he could do it. With the sources he'd found and his notes—you did get all the notes, didn't you?— and if Godwin here can persuade his father to talk some of the Governors around . . ."

"We still need a sponsor," Fremont pointed out.

Vandeleur and Godwin answered as one: "Rugg."

"He's always held that History and Metaphysics were closely allied," Vandeleur explained.

"And he called on us for revenge," Godwin said. "You remember, Vandeleur, on the steps, when, when . . ."

They did, indeed, remember, although they had temporarily lost sight of it in the excitement of Justis Blake's revelations. The horror of Basil St Cloud's death fell on them afresh at Godwin's words, and they sat in silence, fighting or surrendering to their grief according to their several natures. Justis knew he had not loved St Cloud as the rest had. In his eight months as a historian, he had been dazzled, charmed, inspired, and deeply disappointed by the young magister's romantic devotion to the past. But the flame St Cloud had carried was a true flame, and its light should not pass from the world.

Justis wiped his eyes and beckoned to the potboy. "I know you've got good wine here," he said. "You keep it for the magisters. You'd give it to Doctor St Cloud, if he asked for it. We'd like a bottle to drink to his memory."

The boy looked doubtful. "Can you pay for it?"

Justis reached for his purse to check, but Godwin said thickly, "Yes. Just get it. The best you have."

When the boy was gone, Henry said, "What about the papers? Did you take them to your rooms?"

"No. I didn't think Vandeleur would let me in, and I didn't feel like arguing."

Vandeleur slugged him on the arm. "Clodpole," he said affectionately. "I'd have killed you first, and argued later."

"Just so, hot-head. And I wanted them out of University, in case there was a search."

"The Book," Lindley asked eagerly, "the spellbook—it wasn't there, was it?"

"How do you imagine it would have gotten there, dolt?" asked Henry. "Magic?"

There was an uncomfortable silence while everyone remembered that magic was no longer a joke, and then Justis said, "There were some notebooks, a lot of loose papers—nothing like the book Henry and I saw him with a couple of weeks ago."

Godwin looked indignant. "You went to see him? When he'd specifically asked us to leave him alone? Without telling us? Why?"

Justis caught Henry's darting glance and held it steadily. "I'd overheard something I thought he should know. It doesn't matter now." He turned deliberately to Godwin. "He had a book in his hands—fat and dark, the same book he read from on the steps."

"It's probably ashes by now," Henry said. "And good riddance to it."

"So," persisted Godwin, "where'd you take them?"

Justis glanced around the tavern, growing noisy now as conversations began to wander from the debate onto other subjects. No one was paying Historians' Corner the least bit of attention. He leaned forward. "Marianne's hiding them in her shop, at the bottom of a box of ribbons."

The students were speechless. Finally, Vandeleur found his voice. "You hid Doctor St Cloud's papers and notes in a box of *ribbons?*"

"The ribbons are of unfashionable colors," Justis reassured them. "No one's likely to disturb them, and they'll be safe until the dust has settled."

He glared at Henry, daring him to say something about women or milliners, but Henry, mindful of the wisdom of being civil, said, "I'm sure Mistress Marianne will guard them well. What does she think, by the way, of this plan of yours to take the scholarly world by storm?"

"She's for it," Justis said. "We talked about it last night. We're going to get married and set her up in a shop of her own with my wedding portion and she can support us until I start getting students."

"How nice for her," Henry said, rather sourly. The congratulations of the others weren't much more effusive. It was all too much to take in and respond to. It would take weeks and months before they could think of St Cloud, or even of Ancient History, without being dogged by a shadow of horror and grief.

Max himself arrived with a bottle of wine and six glasses on a tray. It was a Deerfield red, very fine indeed. As Godwin fumbled at his purse strings, Max said, "It's on the house. The Doctor brought in good custom and always paid his tab. He'll be missed."

When Max had poured the wine, with a glass for himself, the five Ancient Historians lifted their glasses, self-conscious, sad, aware that this moment marked a change in their lives whose repercussions they could not imagine. Expectant, they looked at Vandeleur.

"Blake," Vandeleur said. "Will you offer the toast?"

Justis allowed himself a moment of astonished dismay at his sudden change of status. This is what it was going to be like from now on, and he'd brought it on himself. He stood and raised his glass to the table and his voice to be heard over the tavern noise. "Gentlemen," he said, and paused while the conversations around him ebbed. "Doctor Basil St Cloud was great of mind and great of heart, an adventurer in the forest of Truth. He perished on the journey, but left a path for us to follow—not historians alone, but all of us, humane scientists, natural scientists, every scholar and fellow of this University. Our most fitting memorial to him is to walk the path he blazed. Gentlemen, I give you Basil St Cloud, first Doctor of Empirical Studies."

He lifted the scarlet liquid to his lips and took a respectful swallow—even a country boy knows that you don't toss back a Deerfield red like water—and the rest of the room followed suit. They all sat for a moment with their heads bowed over their glasses, cups, and tankards.

As Justis sat down, he thought he heard Lindley add, low-voiced, ". . . and last Wizard of the Land."

T HE KING AWOKE WITH THE KNOWLEDGE THAT SOME-thing terrible had happened. Over and over he had dreamed it, that his heart was being pulled out of his body, the muscle stretched like a cord that must ultimately break. He cried out and woke—this time, not to more dreams of grief with men in long robes performing sad rituals in a strange tongue, but to a bright, clean room that smelt of salt and beeswax.

His body ached all over, with sharper pangs in his arms and at his ribs. He was terribly thirsty and the taste of something sweet was in his mouth. The ceiling flickered with a restless, rippling pattern of light, like the river reflections in a Riverside tavern. The room was rocking gently. Was he on a barge?

When he struggled upright, he discovered how weak he was—his muscles like water, his head swimming dizzily with each movement. But his heart was pulling him to the window, the pain of his desire more poignant than his bandaged wounds. Grimly, he pushed back the coverlet, swung his feet to the floor, and hauled himself, sweating, two steps to the tiny window and looked out.

They heard his cry up on the main deck.

The Land! The Land was nowhere in sight.

He was shouting now, holding on to the window like a prisoner in a cell. Sophia appeared and pulled him away from it, held him to her on the cabin floor while he wept and ground his knuckles into the wool of her skirt. "Theron, hush, it's all right. It will be all right. . . ."

"I'm bound to the Land," he cried. "You're killing me; take me back!"

She had wanted him to wake and to be strong, but this was closer to the madness of fever. "Theron, please, my darling, my child . . . look at me. Please. You are hurting yourself, my love, you must stop. . . ."

It was her voice that soothed him, more than her words. He breathed deeply, as she told him to, and the pain receded to where he could bear it. He let her feed him a syrup that sent him back to sleep. When he woke again, he was less frightened, but sadder. His mother gave him honey to eat. "We are going back to Kyros," she smiled, "where you will find the honey is even sweeter than this. You will be well there, my son."

The ship sang in its ropes and sails the song the wind taught it. He heard men's voices, and women's, too, shouting orders and cursing and telling jokes and singing. His sister Jessica came in, sunbrowned and trousered. He clutched her callused hand. "Take me back, Jess. I need to go back."

"No, you don't," she said curtly. "Be still and listen, and I'll tell you why."

"You don't know—"

"I know more than you think. Much more, in fact. You told me things in the Folly, and you've said things when you're asleep. And I've been doing a little reading. So listen to me."

He lay back in the pillows. She sat on a stool beside the bunk and fixed him with her bright eyes.

"You need to be away," she told him. "You need to be washed clean. Some of what has happened to you will stay with you, and that's the good part, the true part, the part that should stay. Some of it will not stay: you'll forget, and it's just as well; that part's no good to you. You gave up a lot of your blood. You left it behind on the steps of the University; it's gone into the Land. What is new in you, you make yourself. That new blood is yours, to do what you want with, for now and always."

Her words quieted the panicked clamoring in his head. He had forgotten that his sister was famous for having sold ice to the frozen kingdom of Arkenvelt. But that was her gift.

"There are some things you need to think about," she went on. "Sophia will take care of you as long as you need her to. But if I were you, I'd try to be useful. I'd try to gain strength and mastery. Take your time," she went on in a steady, soothing tone. "In a day or two, I'll have you carried up on deck. Can you still tie a half-hitch knot? I'll teach you others. And I'll teach you to navigate by the stars, and when you're feeling stronger, we'll make a sailor of you."

He was very nearly asleep, lulled by the promise of something new to learn. He did like knowing new things.

Softly, Jessica closed the cabin door. She took a small brown leather book out of her pocket, grinned at it, tucked it under her arm. Its gold leaf bore a bloody thumbprint, and it wasn't the first.

Dear Katherine, Jessica wrote that evening. *The voyage is well begun.*

NOTES AND ACKNOWLEDGMENTS

THE EVENTS OF THIS NOVEL TAKE PLACE SOME SIXTY YEARS after those of Ellen's first novel, *Swordspoint*. Some of the intervening years are touched on in her short stories "The Swordsman Whose Name Was Not Death" and "The Death of the Duke" (in Datlow & Windling's *The Year's Best Fantasy and Horror* for 1991 and 1998).

Ellen can't thank Delia enough for agreeing to play in her sandbox, and for increasing the population and breadth of the city. Delia's story of the love of King Alexander for Fair Rosamund, "The Tragedy of King Alexander the Stag," was published in Colleen Doran's *A Distant Soil* #29 (Image Comics). Ellen is planning another novel set fifteen years after *Swordspoint*.

The Fall of the Kings is based on a novella of the same name, our first collaboration, published by Nicola Griffith and Stephen Pagel in their landmark anthology, *Bending the Landscape: Fantasy*. We thank them for their encouragement.

Both authors also thank the Somerville Genrettes—Laurie J. Marks, Rosemary Kirstein, and Didi Stewart—and all the other patient and creative souls who have read parts and versions of this work in manuscript over the years: Mimi Panitch, Patrick J. O'Connor, Sarah Smith, Kelly Link, Justine Larbalestier, Terri Windling, Anne Hudson, Paula Kate Marmor, Eve Sweetser, Alex Madonik, Shweta Narayan, Elizabeth Wein, and Deborah

Manning. This book took a long time to write, so if we've lost some people's names along the march, we hope they'll forgive us and still accept our thanks. We do not forget our editor, Anne Lesley Groell, and our good agent and friend, Christopher Schelling.

In addition, Ellen is grateful to her *Sound & Spirit* colleagues at WGBH Radio—Jon Solins, Helen Barrington, Stephen Snyder, Jeff Nelson, Gary Mott, Titilayo Ngwenya, and Joellen Easton—for all their support and good work even when the host of the show was off in Riverside looking for action.

Delia thanks the staff and denizens of the Diesel Café in Davis Square, Somerville, for office space, salads, coffee, and occasionally, inspiration.

For those who, like us, grew up in the Land of Books and still claim citizenship in that country, the influence of other authors is abundant and bountiful. Here we would particularly like to acknowledge the work of the late Dorothy Dunnett, a great historical novelist who leaves her mark on a whole generation of writers, and Ronald Millar, whose play *Abelard and Heloise* each of us turns out to have gone with our mothers to see in London in the summer of 1970.

Ellen Kushner & Delia Sherman
Boston & NYC
March 2002

ABOUT THE AUTHORS

Ellen Kushner's first novel was *Swordspoint, a Melodrama of Manners*. Her second novel, *Thomas the Rhymer*, won the Mythopoeic and the World Fantasy Awards. She has edited two fantasy anthologies, and her short fiction has appeared in *The Year's Best Fantasy and Horror*. In 1987 she left an editorial career in New York City to become a producer/announcer at WGBH Radio in Boston, where she created an eclectic variety of local and national programming. Since 1996 she has entertained and enlightened audiences across the country as the host and writer of PRI's award-winning national public radio program *Sound & Spirit* (www.wgbh.org/pri/spirit).

Kushner's performance pieces for stage and radio include *Esther: the Feast of Masks* and *The Golden Dreydl: a Klezmer 'Nutcracker'* (winner of the 2001 Gracie Allen award), which she performs with Shirim Klezmer Orchestra live and on CD. With *Sound & Spirit* she created the CD *Welcoming Children Into the World* (Rykodisc). She is a popular speaker at a variety of venues from synagogue pulpits to science fiction conventions.

In her spare time, she complains about not having any spare time. She is a good cook and a terrible housekeeper. She likes to sing.

Delia Sherman has spent much of her life at one end of a classroom or another, at Brown University where she earned a Ph.D. in Renaissance Studies and at Boston University and Northeastern, where she taught Freshman Composition. Her first novel, *Through a Brazen Mirror*, was published as one of the prestigious Ace Fantasy Specials. *Publishers Weekly* called her second novel, *The Porcelain Dove*, "fantastic in every sense of the word." Her short fiction has appeared in *The Magazine of Fantasy and Science Fiction* and the anthologies *Xanadu II*, *The Armless Maiden*, and *Ruby Slippers, Golden Tears*, and the children's anthologies *A Wolf at the Door* and *The Green Man* as well as numerous volumes of *The Year's Best Fantasy and Horror*. She was nominated for the Campbell Award for Best New SF Writer of 1990, and won the Mythopoetic Award for Fantasy Fiction for *The Porcelain Dove*. She has twice served as a judge for the Crawford Award for Best First Fantasy Novel and is a member of the Motherboard of the James Tiptree Jr Award.

In 1995, Sherman exchanged academia for publishing, becoming a contributing editor for Tor Books and co-editing the fantasy anthology *The Horns of Elfland* (Roc) with Ellen Kushner and Don Keller, along with the latest of the *Bordertown* punk-elf anthologies with Terri Windling frorm Tor. She is working on an anthology of Interstitial Fiction with Heinz Insu Fenkl.

She loves gardening and researching in libraries, and prefers cafes to home for writing (they bring you things to eat and the phone's never for you) and traveling to staying put.

Delia Sherman and Ellen Kushner share homes in Boston, New York, Paris and Tucson. They are currently working on a musical theatre piece with New York composer Ben Moore, and on novels written by only one person. They have no cats, and enjoy travel. They are both active members of the Endicott Studio of Mythic Arts (*http://www.endicott-studio.com*). They have taught at the Clarion Writers' Workshop, the Odyssey Workshop, Cape Cod Writers' Center, and are founding members of the Interstitial Studies Institute at SUNY New Paltz.